Smiling at him again, she wal[...] the next aisle.

Laughing, Ronald slapped Nicholas on the back. "You don't even have to ask. I'll be happy to be your best man."

Nick lifted a heavy brow. "Very funny. Let's go to the bakery and get a chess pie for dessert."

Still chuckling, Ronald fell into step beside Nicholas. Neither noticed the excited chatter of Nicholas's coworkers as they hurried to check out.

Nicholas pushed open the double glass doors of Memorial Hospital at a quarter to nine the next morning. He felt as if he could conquer the world. After the overcooked steak and undercooked fish last night, he and Ronald had decided against trying to prepare another meal. Instead they'd gotten up early and gone out to breakfast and stuffed themselves. Afterward Ronald had left in his rental car for the airport in Austin. His last comment had been a teasing remark that he was going to start looking for a tuxedo because he wanted to look good as Nicholas's best man.

"Hello, Mr. Darling."

"Morning, Mr. Darling."

"Good morning," Nicholas returned to the two smiling nurses who had greeted him, then hastened his steps to catch the elevator.

"Morning, Mr. Darling," an attractive woman in a stylish red suit said as he got on. "You didn't have to rush. I would have held the door for you."

"Thank you," Nicholas said, stepping aside to make room for three other passengers, all women.

"I don't think we've had a chance to meet," another woman in a white uniform said, extending her hand. "My name is Gwen Stradford. I'm the charge nurse on the west wing of the med-surg floor from seven till three."

No sooner had the woman finished speaking than all the other women on the elevator introduced themselves. Puzzled, Nicholas shook their hands, almost glad when the door opened on the second floor and he could get out.

Wishes for a good day followed him down the hall, but he also heard the distinct sounds of giggles. Shaking his head, he kept walking.

"Morning, Mr. Darling."

"Good morning," Nicholas replied to a tall woman in green scrubs who looked at him as if he were the last piece of birthday cake and she intended to have it. His pace quickened. He didn't relax completely until he opened the outer door to his secretary's office.

"Good morning, Mr. Darling." Michelle Rhodes, his secretary, glanced up at him from digging in the file cabinet.

"Morning." Continuing to his connecting office, Nicholas covertly watched her pull out a file and flip through it. She hadn't acted any differently toward him. With each decisive step across the room, the uneasiness he'd felt faded more and more.

In his office he saw the stack of files he'd left on his desk when Ronald arrived unexpected Monday afternoon. Loosening his tie, Nicholas promptly forgot about the women and set to work.

By eleven he'd made a decent dent in the records for the last quarter. Stretching, he tightened the tie he'd loosened earlier and then pulled on the navy blue double-breasted jacket to his suit. He was meeting with the head of radiology in five minutes. She wanted a new MRI machine. They cost upward of a million and a half dollars, but if it would help with early detection or diagnosis he'd certainly see if there was a way for the hospital's overtaxed budget to obtain one.

He was barely in the hallway before it started again.

"Hello, Mr. Darling. Have you eaten lunch yet?"

"We're going out; do want us to get you anything?"

"It'll be our treat."

"They have fantastic stuffed baked potatoes."

Nicholas looked from one smiling woman to the other. They worked in the administrative offices on his floor. Until now they'd been cordial, but not overly so. Now they were acting as if he and they were old friends. Something wasn't right. "Hello. Thanks for the offer, but I'll pick up a bite later."

"If you change your mind, I'm two doors down from your office. I'm Carolyn Johnson."

"Alice Wilson."

"Sylvia Atkins."

"Gloria Quigley."

"Thank you," Nicholas said, and hurried away. He stopped and turned when he heard what sounded suspiciously like giggling again. Yet when he turned, the women were simply staring innocently at him. Rubbing the back of his neck, he continued to the elevator. Perhaps he was working too hard.

Nicholas kept the thought until he stepped off the elevator on the ground floor where radiology was located. Every step he made, women were saying hello, introducing themselves. It was so bad, he was late for his meeting with Dr. Bradford and two of her staff members. Nicholas relaxed on seeing they were men. Thirty minutes later, when he was the first to leave her office, he paused briefly, hand on the doorknob. Then, feeling foolish, he opened the door and strode down the hall.

He made it ten feet before it began again. Women were everywhere. He couldn't seem to get away from them. Any men he saw just shook their heads as if they felt sorry for him.

Opening the door to Michelle's office, he strode across the room to her desk and planted both hands on top. "What is going on? Why is there a woman smiling at me everywhere I go?"

Her hands left the computer keyboard and she swirled in her chair toward him, tucking her long braided hair behind her ear. "Don't you know?"

"If I knew I wouldn't be asking," he said tightly. He sighed and made an effort to relax. This wasn't her fault. Michelle was hard-working and ran his office efficiently. And, as his predecessor had informed Nicholas, she was privy to all the latest gossip in the hospital. Until now, he hadn't availed himself of that particular talent of hers. "Please, tell me."

She sighed dreamily. "You've been granted a wish."

"A wish." Nicholas straightened, a strange foreboding sweeping through him.

"Yes," she said. "Mrs. Augusta granted you your wish to be married. Isn't it wonderful?"

Nicholas's jaw dropped. "Mrs. Augusta . . . ? You mean that little old lady in the grocery store who was hard of hearing? She got it all wrong. I did not wish to be married."

"You didn't?" Michelle's large eyes rounded in uncertainty.

"I most definitely did not," Nicholas said, beginning to pace in front of her desk. "I was teasing Ronald, and that woman . . . Mrs. Augusta or whoever she is . . . well, she simply misunderstood what I said. You know how elderly people get things mixed up."

Michelle shook her head. "Despite being up in age, Mrs. Augusta is still as sharp as they come."

Nicholas spun and pinned his secretary with his fierce gaze. "If you mean an elderly black lady wearing gloves and a hat in a grocery store at five in the afternoon, I think the way she dresses says otherwise."

"She always dresses that way. She's a real Southern lady," Michelle said as if that explained everything.

"She's a kook." Nicholas started pacing again. "Spouting off about my wish being granted and that I'd be married soon. I should have walked away from her instead of thanking her."

"Oh, Mr. Darling."

Nicholas spun around and saw the distress in Michelle's face. "What?"

"You thanked her."

"I was being polite."

Michelle shook her head again. "In thanking her you accepted the gift of your wish being granted. I told you, Mrs. Augusta is a real lady. She wouldn't bestow a gift on someone who didn't want it."

Nicholas rolled his eyes. "Look, I don't know how you know her and why you believe any of this nonsense, but the simple truth is, I did not wish for a wife."

Michelle brightened. "That's what makes Mrs. Augusta so unique and magical. She has this uncanny ability to grant unspoken wishes. Did you ever wish for a wife?"

Nicholas opened his mouth to emphatically tell his secretary that he hadn't, then recalled his wish as a young boy, a wish he had thought about only moments before Mrs. Augusta had appeared. He scoffed at the absurdity of it all. "Maybe when I was a kid and believed in fairy tales and happily ever after," he admitted reluctantly, then quickly added, "but after watching so many marriages go bust, I've come to realize that lasting happiness seldom happens in marriages these days."

"Simon and I are very happy and we plan to remain that way," Michelle told him, her face glowing.

Not wanting to point out that a year was hardly enough time to test a marriage, Nicholas said, "I'm glad you and Simon are the exception." He took a calming breath. "I can't believe I'm getting worked up about this. By tomorrow, it will all be forgotten." He waited for his secretary to confirm his words, and when she didn't he plopped down in the chair in front of her desk. "Drop the other shoe."

She twisted uneasily in her seat. "Mrs. Augusta's predictions and wishes have always come true. Since she's a Christian lady and the wishes are welcome, people usually want her to grant them a wish."

"No one can grant wishes," Nicholas scoffed.

"Five years ago, after church, Mary Kennedy wished that she wouldn't die an old maid. She wished that she'd find a good man to marry and have a big family to love. Mrs. Augusta heard and right there in front of everybody granted her wish. Before a year had passed, Mary was married and had a baby girl."

Nicholas waved a dismissive hand. "Sheer coincidence."

"Before Mary dated John, her husband, she'd been on one date. They now have five children and are as happy as can be. There have been several others whose wishes were granted, including the mayor's unspoken wish for his son to stop drinking and settle down with a loving, Christian woman."

Nicholas continued to look dubious.

"And if that's not enough, Mrs. Augusta saved the lives of hundreds of schoolchildren when she called the sheriff's department to tell them to evacuate the elementary school. There wasn't a cloud in the sky. The tornado hit less than two minutes after the last kid got out. The building was flattened. Me and my sister and three cousins were at school that day." Michelle folded her arms. "At the beginning of the school year, the principal, Yolanda Thompson, had wished that all the school children have a safe year. You'll never convince me Mrs. Augusta made a mistake."

Seeing the surety on Michelle's face, Nicholas realized what he was up against. Augusta had had one lucky guess, albeit a miraculous one, and the townspeople took her word as gospel. The rest of her "wishes" were all coincidental. "This time she's made a mistake."

"Mrs. Augusta never makes mistakes." Michelle turned to her computer. "If I were you, Mr. Darling, I'd accept the wish and start thinking about who you planned to invite to the wedding."

"This is ridiculous."

The door behind them opened and three women surged in. Nicholas barely kept from grinding his teeth. Just what he needed. More women!

"Mr. Darling, I just had to tell you the good news," Delores McKinnie, the hospital's director of human resources, said, her smile growing as she crossed the room. "You won't believe how many tickets we've sold." She glanced between the two women on either side of her. "Eula and Rachel just gave me the good news."

"We're on our way to post the tabulations of the most wished for items on the bulletin board of the cafeteria," Eula said.

"We thought you'd like to be the first to know," Rachel

added, staring at him with undisguised interest. "I bought twenty tickets myself."

Delores hugged the notebook to her chest. "It looks like this year will be the biggest in the ten-year history of the wish list. You're new to this, but half the money raised goes to one lucky winner to make their wish come true and the other half goes to charity. Since news started circulating this morning, sales have tripled for the wish list for Christmas, and we have you to thank for it."

Nicholas went very still. She couldn't possibly mean what he thought she meant. She just couldn't.

"I wanted to tell you personally," Delores said, grinning. "You're at the top of the wish list."

Chapter 2

Andrea Strickland sat cross-legged in the window seat of the family room, her upper torso bent with an unconscious grace over the sketch pad in her lap, her slim hand making quick, decisive strokes as she brought the young prince to life once again. This was the last scene in the children's book she'd been hired to illustrate and the most important. The handsome prince had just professed his unending love to the beautiful but poor young woman in a tattered dress before him.

The story had been told hundreds of times in varying ways, but it had never lost its appeal. What young girl, poor or rich, hadn't yearned at one time or another to marry a handsome prince? Andrea would settle for a simple man who was honest, kind, and intelligent.

Her mouth curved ruefully as she outlined the prince's muscular thigh. All right, she wouldn't mind if he had a body like an Adonis, a voice that made her shiver, and a face to make an angel weep with regret. His large hands would be slow, inventive, and clever.

"Andrea, stop daydreaming and answer the front door."

Andrea jumped. Her startled gaze flew to her diminutive aunt in the doorway. Heat flushed Andrea's amber cheeks as if Aunt Augusta could read her thoughts. "Ma'am?"

"The door," Aunt Augusta repeated with unending patience and love. "The timer is about to go off for the tea cakes."

At that second a bell sounded on the gas stove that was almost as old as Andrea. "The door," Aunt Augusta repeated with a smile. She left the room and went down the hall toward the kitchen in the back of the house.

Placing the sketch pad on the window seat, Andrea stood, then stretched her slim arms over her head to loosen the stiff muscles in her back and shoulders. When she worked she often forgot time. Lowering her arms, she headed for the front door, her thoughts returning to the man she'd envisioned.

Melissa Manning, the heroine of the romance novel Andrea was writing on speculation, would have such a man in Braxton Savage. Tall, dark, and brooding, Braxton, an ex–army ranger, was a cynic who didn't believe in love . . . until he met warmhearted Melissa, who was nobody's pushover. She'd proven that when she escaped from the two men sent to kill her. Melissa intrigued Braxton as much as she aggravated him. For the first time in his lonely life, he had found someone he could love, someone he couldn't walk away from.

Andrea readily admitted living vicariously through her heroine, since she didn't have a man of her own. She'd had fun with Melissa and Braxton's verbal sparring while the sexual tension crackled around them like a downed electrical wire. The chemistry between them was explosive, the loving hot and intense.

Aunt Augusta would probably be shocked if she knew what her niece had written. On second thought, perhaps not. Her aunt was definitely a woman of the twentieth century, even if her gift dated back centuries.

Augusta Venora Evans was a modern-day fairy godmother. She had no idea why she was the conduit to tell people their wish had been granted. She simply accepted her unusual gift, since the wish always led to happiness.

That ability alone should have alleviated Andrea's worry about being called home by Aunt Augusta a month ago.

When she had called Andrea in New York, insisting she come home immediately, she'd come, afraid her aunt had had a premonition that something bad was going to happen to her.

Since Andrea's return her aunt remained as spry as the day nine-year-old Andrea had come to live with her eighteen years ago after Andrea's parents had died in an automobile accident. Dr. Jones, Aunt Augusta's doctor, had assured Andrea her aunt was in excellent health for a seventy-three-year-old woman.

However, Aunt Augusta still became agitated if Andrea mentioned returning to New York. Thank goodness as an illustrator for a children's book publisher she could work anyplace. Although she'd been hoping not to spend another Christmas holiday dateless, Jubilee had slim pickin's when it came to eligible bachelors.

Her mouth twitched. If Aunt Augusta could grant Andrea a wish, she knew exactly what it would be: the man she'd envisioned earlier. What a wonderful Christmas present he would make. Her aunt wouldn't even have to put a bow on him. Laughing, Andrea reached to open the front door.

Nicholas, tired and irritated after another day of being ogled by women, was in a foul mood. After he'd rung the bell several times and there was no answer, he was strongly considering pounding on the door when it opened. "I'd—" His thoughts scattered as he stared at the woman in the doorway.

Small, delicate, vibrant—his breath caught at the sheer joy she radiated. The fading sound of her silken laughter shimmered down his spine. Thick black lashes shaded deep chocolate eyes in a stunning almond-hued face. Her lush mouth was painted a rich raspberry color that he instinctively knew would taste sweeter than any fruit.

The laughter died on Andrea's lips as she stared at the man in the doorway. He was absolutely gorgeous, with a strong jaw, piercing black eyes, a beautifully shaped mouth. His shoulders were broad beneath the tailored wool sports coat, his chest wide, his legs long in gray charcoal slacks. He was six fabulous feet of toned, mouth-watering muscle.

At five-foot-two, she usually didn't like big men, but she irrationally felt this man would protect her with his life if need be. His skin was the color of honey poured though sunshine. The thought made her want to touch the tip of her tongue to his skin to see if he tasted as good.

"Andrea, where are your manners?" Augusta said from down the hallway. "Invite the gentleman in."

Andrea flushed, hoping the man hadn't been offended by her staring. But considering what a handsome specimen of manhood he was, he probably had been stared at before. "I'm sorry. Won't you come in?"

"Thank you," Nicholas said, stepping inside the foyer, trying not to stare at her or notice that she had on shorts that revealed legs that demanded a second look or that the long-sleeved knit shirt clung enticingly to her high breasts. He cleared his throat. "I'd like to see Mrs. Augusta Evans, please."

"Auntie?" Andrea frowned, hoping he wasn't a salesman who preyed on the unsuspecting elderly. "I'm her niece. What's this about?"

"I want her to take back her wish or do whatever she has to do so my life can get back to normal," he said, annoyance creeping into his deep voice.

"She granted you a wish?" Andrea asked.

"No one can grant a wish," he stated emphatically. "However, the women at the hospital seem to think she can."

Andrea glanced behind her to see her aunt come out of the living room. Her quickness never ceased to amaze Andrea. "He's here to see you, Auntie."

"Good afternoon, Mr. Darling," Augusta said as she came toward them. Hardwood gleamed beneath her feet. "This is my niece, Andrea Strickland. Andrea, Mr. Nicholas Darling."

Andrea nodded and thought how aptly named he was. "Mr. Darling."

"Andrea," he said, then switched his attention to her aunt. "You know my name?"

Aunt Augusta smiled. "Of course. You don't think I'd go around talking to strange men, do you?"

"I'm not sure," he said slowly. He wasn't committing or agreeing to anything Augusta Evans said.

"Auntie, Mr. Darling wants to talk about his wish," Andrea said, wondering what the wish had been.

"I expected as much." Augusta extended her small hand toward the first door on the left. "I already have refreshments set up in the living room."

Nicholas shook his dark head. "Thank you, but I just want you to take back your wish and then I'll be leaving."

"We can just as well talk while we eat." She affectionately patted his stiff arm. "I have iced tea cakes. I'm sure you're hungry."

His unhappy stomach rumbled in agreement. He hadn't had a good meal since breakfast with Ronald two days ago. Since then, Nicholas hadn't dared to venture out of his office or go to a restaurant for fear of women throwing themselves in his path.

"We had fried chicken and macaroni salad for lunch, if you'd care for some," Andrea said. The poor man looked as if he were at his wits' end. "It won't take me but a minute to fix a plate."

Nicholas thought of telling her not to bother, then caught himself watching the alluring sway of her hips as she hurried down the hall.

"Mr. Darling."

Nicholas jumped and jerked his head around, half-afraid Mrs. Evans had picked up on his lustful thoughts. He didn't believe she had any special powers, but she had eyes. "Yes, ma'am."

"Why don't you follow Andrea to the kitchen? You'll be more comfortable eating at the table. I'll get the tea tray."

"I'll get it for you," he said.

She gifted him with another smile. "I knew you'd be a gentleman."

Nicholas said nothing, just followed her to the living room filled with antique furniture. He picked up the heavy silver tea set from the claw-foot coffee table and took it to the kitchen. He licked his lips as he stared down at the golden palm-sized cookies glistening with butter cream icing on a white dolly.

Entering the bright yellow-and-white kitchen, he saw Andrea spooning macaroni salad on a stoneware plate laden with crispy-looking fried chicken, black-eyed peas, rice, and two corn muffins.

She threw him a glance over her shoulder. "I nuked it already." She placed the plate on the scarred round oak kitchen table that seated four. "There's also iced tea, coffee, fruit juice, and soft drinks."

Nicholas placed the tray on the spotless Formica counter, his eyes on the plate of food. His mouth watered. "Coffee. Black."

"Please sit down and eat," Andrea instructed, and went to pour him a cup of coffee. She didn't like the stuff, but Aunt Augusta couldn't start the day without it. "Here you are."

"Andrea," Aunt Augusta said, "I need to make a phone call. Keep Mr. Darling company." When Nicholas looked as if he'd object, she said, "By the time you finish I'll be back." Then she was gone.

"Don't worry, Mr. Darling. I'm sure everything will work out."

Nicholas turned to Andrea and felt his body stir. "Call me Nicholas and have a seat." Hearing her say "Darling" conjured up a fantasy he wasn't ready to deal with.

She shook her head of short auburn curls and smiled impishly. "If I hurry, I can grab my sketch pad and be back before Auntie returns. You probably can't eat with me staring at you."

Nicholas picked up his fork. For some odd reason, he didn't object to her being near him, unlike the other women he'd had to deal with over the last two days. "I don't mind if you sit with me."

Her face dimpled into a pleased smile. "I'll be back in a minute."

Nicholas stared after her, then dug into the macaroni salad. One bite and he closed his eyes and sighed. He hadn't had food this good in weeks.

By the time Andrea returned and slid into a seat beside him, he had finished off a chicken thigh. Giving him a shy smile, she propped a pad on her knees. Her brows bunched in concentration as she sketched. His food was forgotten as Nicholas watched the quick, graceful movements of her small, delicate hand and her beautiful profile as she worked.

Afraid she'd catch him staring and see the desire in his eyes, he looked down at his plate and began to eat again. He enjoyed the food, but he was very much aware of the woman sitting near him.

Finished, he pushed his plate aside. "That was the best meal I've had in a long time. Thank you."

"Would you like your tea cakes with ice cream?" Andrea asked.

"I think I've stuffed enough." Nicholas picked up his coffee cup.

"Then I'll put some in a tin for you to take home." Placing the sketch pad on the table, she went to the cabinet, then bent to open the bottom door.

Her shorts lovingly cupped her rounded hips, and Nicholas looked away, disgusted with himself. He'd never been this lustful over a woman in his life. Needing a distraction, he drew her sketch pad toward him. "Do you mind?"

Straightening, she glanced around and shook her head. "Help yourself."

Flipping though page after page of pencil drawings, he was captured by the fine detail of the sketches. "These are wonderful."

"Thank you," she said, pleased as she finished putting cookies in the round red canister lined with wax paper.

"Let's hope the author of the book and her editor think so."

"You're a book illustrator?" he asked with genuine interest.

"Yes." Placing the canister beside him, she retook her seat. "After I graduated from art school, I headed to New York. I got lucky when I was sketching on the train and an author of children's books sat beside me. He introduced me to his editor and, as they say, the rest is history."

"That's amazing," Nicholas said, not sure if he meant her success or the allure beckoning in her deep brown eyes.

She nodded. "People in Jubilee thought Auntie was crazy to let me go to New York on my own without a job. She told me to follow my dream. She never doubted."

Something about Andrea's statement caused uneasiness to run through Nicholas. "How long were you in New York before you found a job?"

She wrinkled her nose and laughed. "Three days. I know I'm blessed, and I never take my good fortune for granted."

"Did you wish for a job?" he asked, unable to keep the skepticism out of his voice.

If she heard it, she didn't appear offended. "No, but it wouldn't have mattered."

"Why is that?"

She smiled sadly. "Auntie has never been able to grant anyone in the family a wish."

He was outraged. What kind of sense did it make to grant a wish to him that he didn't want and keep one from a person as vibrant and beautiful as Andrea?

"Sorry to have kept you waiting, Mr. Darling," Augusta said as she entered the room. She waved Nicholas back into his seat and took the cane-backed chair beside him. "How can I help you?"

"By taking back your wish. I don't want it," he promptly told her.

She folded her hands in her lap. "Are you sure?"

"Positive." Nicholas placed his arms on the table and leaned toward her. "I was joking with my brother. Marriage is the furthest thing from my mind."

"Your wish was to get married?" Andrea asked softly.

"I wished my brother was married," he stated emphatically.

"But you accepted the gift," Augusta reminded him.

Nicholas straightened, then shoved his hand over his head in frustration. "I only did that because people were watching and I didn't want to embarrass you by telling you you had made a mistake."

"That was very kind of you, Nicholas," Andrea said. "Thank you."

He looked over at her and became ensnared in Andrea's dark gaze and soothing voice for a long moment before wrenching free. "I have to be honest and admit that knowing the consequences as I do now, I'm not sure if I would have acted the same way."

"What consequences?" Andrea asked.

"Women," he answered tightly. "Everywhere I go, they're there. Introducing themselves. Asking me out. Offering lunch. It has got to stop. I can't run a hospital like this. Take the wish back."

"Once accepted, it cannot be given back." Augusta patted his arm, then rose. "A wish has never brought anything but happiness. You'll see."

"Mrs. Augusta, I beg you to help me," Nicholas said, pleading for the first time in his life and uncaring.

"By Christmas, you'll be happily engaged. Andrea will see you to the door. Please come back anytime."

With stunned disbelief, Nicholas watched Augusta Evans leave the room. He'd been so sure when he obtained the address from his secretary that he would be able to get Augusta to publicly announce that she'd been wrong. He oversaw the operation of millions of dollars. When he talked, people listened. But Augusta Evans had fed him, patted him on the arm, then politely dismissed him. His visit had been futile. Standing, Nicholas pushed back his chair, then walked to the front door.

"This cannot be happening to me," he mumbled, his hands clamped around the top railing of the porch.

"If there was any way to help you, I would."

He spun toward Andrea. Hope glittered in his eyes. "If you mean that, then get your aunt to take back the wish."

"I'd never interfere with Aunt Augusta."

"Then wish my wish away." Nicholas knew his words were ridiculous, but he was desperate.

Slowly Andrea shook her head. "As I've told you, Auntie's abilities have never extended to the family. No family member has ever been involved with anyone who was granted a wish or benefited in any way from a granted wish. My wish doesn't count." At the doubting expression on his face, she continued, her voice barely above a whisper. "I remember my first wish when I was nine."

Thinking she was going to say she had wished for a doll, Nicholas was ready to dismiss it as being frivolous.

"I wished my parents were alive." Her words were like a sharp punch to his gut. "That there had been some horrible mistake and that they hadn't been killed in an automobile accident."

"Andrea, I'm sorry," he said, wanting to take away the pain and shadows that had appeared in her eyes. His situation was nothing in comparison to that of a young child who had lost both parents at once. "I'm so sorry."

"My mother was Auntie's only sister, her only sibling. Auntie held me and we both cried." Andrea swallowed. "I've never wished for anything again. Not that I don't believe in Auntie's power and am not happy for others she's granted wishes to, but I see how it hurts her when she can't help her family."

Nicholas stared at Andrea and hadn't a shred of doubt that she was telling the truth. He'd seldom seen that kind of selfless love and devotion. Without thought his fingers brushed across her cheek in wordless comfort. He watched her eyes widen in surprise, felt the warmth of her skin, the silky softness, and experienced the need to keep on touching.

His hand fisted. "I should be going. Thanks again for the meal."

Andrea remained on the porch as Nicholas backed his big black Mercedes out of the driveway. Almost immediately a late-model sedan pulled up in its place and two middle-aged women piled out. They kept looking over their shoulders at the disappearing Mercedes as they hurried along the flagstone walk, then up the three wooden steps.

"Good evening, Mrs. Freeman, Mrs. Kimbrew," Andrea greeted both women, members of the church she and her aunt attended.

They returned the greeting, but it was obvious their minds were on the man in the Mercedes. "Wasn't that Nicholas Darling?"

"Yes," Andrea answered. Both women had single daughters. It didn't take much to guess why they had dropped by.

"Wonderful," Mrs. Freeman said. "Perhaps now Mrs. Augusta can tell us who the lucky woman is."

"I hope it's my Annie."

Cheryl Freeman shot her best friend, Evelyn Kimbrew, a proprietary look. "My Jackie would be better for him."

"Why don't we ask Mrs. Augusta?" Mrs. Kimbrew sniped.

Without waiting for Andrea to invite them in, they surged inside, each trying to get through the door first. Instead of following them, Andrea propped her shoulder against the square white post on the porch, her hand lifting to her cheek. She could almost feel the warmth and tenderness of Nicholas's powerful hand.

Strong, sensitive, and caring, he was the kind of man women dreamed of finding, of loving. But that woman could never be her. She'd told Nicholas the truth. For some unknown reason, her aunt's gift didn't extend to family members. Andrea would never find out how it felt to be held against his hard body, if his mouth was hot and greedy, if his hands were slow and thorough. Blushing at her uncharacteristic thoughts, she went inside and closed the door.

Chapter 3

Nicholas's bad day on Tuesday was turning into a bad week. It was Friday afternoon and the number of women who somehow managed to ambush him increased hourly. It had gotten to the point where he was afraid to leave his house.

Women seemed to materialize out of thin air. He'd try to avoid one and end up facing three more. He hadn't known women traveled in groups or giggled so much. And he could have happily gone to his grave ignorant of those two facts. His orderly, well-organized life had been turned upside down by a mite of a woman.

Nicholas pulled into the driveway of Augusta Evans's house and parked. He wasn't sure why he'd come. He didn't hold out any hope that she would change her mind. Besides being stubborn, she believed she had right on her side. Sighing, he draped his arm over the steering wheel and studied the house in front of him.

Neat and inviting, the pale yellow house had a second floor with gabled dormers. The trim around the arched windows, the railing, and the four posts on the long porch were white. The shutters and roof were slate blue. White wicker furniture with colorful cushions was tucked in a corner of the porch. At the end of the meandering flagstone walkway stood a mailbox, an exact replica of the house.

Despite it being the middle of November, blooming

flowers were everywhere. They trailed from baskets on the porch and sprouted from the well-tended beds. The house had an air of grace and serenity that reminded him of Andrea. It sat on a huge lot at the end of a two-lane graveled road. The nearest house was a half a mile away.

On the green lawn was a five-foot burlap scarecrow. Straw protruded from the stuffed sleeves of the denim shirt and the legs of the overalls. Beneath one extended arm, pumpkins overflowed from a wheelbarrow. Several clay pots of yellow and rust-colored chrysanthemums sat nearby. In his mind's eye he could almost picture Andrea laughing with delight as she created the scene.

It was quiet and peaceful here with only the wind sailing through the branches of the maple trees, causing the leaves to shimmer like quicksilver. Colorful beds of snapdragons and pansies circled the trees. Monkey grass marched up the sides of the driveway of the detached garage off to the left. In one of the double bays he could see the back of an older-model blue Pontiac.

When he had visited yesterday there had been a much older model Pontiac there as well. The missing car most likely belonged to Augusta.

Picking up the empty red canister on the seat beside him, he got out, went up the steps, and rang the doorbell. When there was no answer, he knocked, then knocked again. Reasoning told him they could be out together, but that didn't stop him from stepping off the porch and going around the side of the house. In the back he saw more trees, and underneath one, a yellow legal pad in her lap, was Andrea.

He was unaware of the tension leaving his body. Today, in deference to the twenty-five-degree drop in temperature, she wore faded jeans, a bulky red sweater, and sneakers. A bright purple wool scarf lay beside her. Wind playfully tossed her hair. She looked serene and breathtakingly beautiful.

He was almost to her when she glanced up. Surprise widened her eyes; then she scrambled to her feet.

"Nicholas."

"Andrea." Now that he had found her, he had no idea what he wanted to say. He finally admitted to himself he'd been searching for her. Why, he wasn't sure. He handed her the tin. "I ate every crumb." Bending, he picked up the discarded scarf and looped it around her neck. "It's chilly today."

She stared into his warm eyes, inhaled his spicy cologne, and wanted to go in search of the elusive fragrance just as Melissa had done with Braxton in her novel. She moistened her dry lips. "I guess I was busy and didn't notice."

He frowned. "You're so delicate. You have to be careful that you don't get sick."

She grinned. She had a black belt in karate. Another thing she and Melissa shared. "I'm tougher than I look. Country girls have to be."

"I suppose." Finally releasing the scarf, he glanced around the well-tended yard. "My mother would love it here. Dad's due to retire from the accounting firm he works for in a few years, and when he does she wants to move out of Philadelphia to a little town where the pace is slower, but close enough to visit me and my brother and her future grandchildren," he finished with a derisive twist of his mouth.

"Is that where you're from?" she asked. He'd have beautiful children.

"No. I was born in Flint, Michigan, and lived all over the country while Dad climbed the corporate ladder. He transferred to Philadelphia from Akron when I was a freshman in high school." He chuckled. "Mom told him point-blank once we were settled that if he moved again before he retired, he'd go without us."

"Four generations of Radfords have lived here. My great-great-grandfather was the town's blacksmith and built the original house," Andrea said with pride. "Each generation has worked to improve the place without changing its personality." She laughed. "I still have the claw-foot tub in my bathroom my grandmother ordered from the Sears and Roebuck catalog."

Nicholas's black eyes narrowed; then his gaze traveled leisurely over her body. "I'd like to see that."

Andrea's body went hot. She wasn't sure if he meant the tub or her in it. Self-consciously she drew the tin and the tablet closer. "I'm sure you wouldn't be interested."

"You'd be surprised in what interests me lately," he said cryptically, then nodded toward the tablet. "Another drawing?"

"No. I'm working on an entirely different project." She wasn't ready to tell him about her book. Most people laughed themselves silly when she mentioned wanting to write a romance novel.

His finger traced the top of the tablet, coming precariously close to the rounded curve of her breast. "Can I take a peek?"

Her heart thudded. There it was again. The double meaning. "No," she said, her voice a wobbly squeak.

"Perhaps some other time." His hand fell, but his eyes watched her with the intensity of a large cat studying his next meal.

Andrea gulped. "You just get off work?"

The seductive laziness vanished. In its place was the same frustration she'd seen when he'd visited yesterday. "Yes."

"Things haven't been going well, have they?"

"It doesn't seem to matter that it's illogical for women to think they can win the wish pot and get me like I'm some toy in a box of Cracker Jacks." He snorted. "I'm running five to one ahead of everything else on the wish list. I can't go anyplace without women looking at me as if I'm the cherry on top of an ice-cream sundae."

Andrea caught herself before she licked her lips hungrily. Then she shook herself; Nicholas had felt safe coming here. "Auntie's gone to visit a friend, and I was just about to go in and make biscuits for supper. Would you like to join us?"

"I don't want to be any trouble," he told her.

Andrea smiled at the grudging wistfulness in his deep

voice. "You won't be. I love to cook and so does Auntie. Come on in." She crossed the backyard and went into the house.

Inside the kitchen she placed the pad on the counter and washed her hands. "Have a seat or, if you want, you can go to the living room and watch TV." She dried her hands on paper towels and turned on the oven. "It's a black-and-white, I'm afraid. Neither of us watches much television."

Folding his arms, Nicholas leaned against the counter next to her. "How do you spend your spare time?"

"We both like to read. At night, Auntie knits and I do the less meticulous sketch work." Taking a bowl from beneath the counter, she mixed the ingredients for the bread.

"What do you read?" he asked, watching her quick, easy motions.

She cut him a sharp glance, transferred the dough to a lightly floured surface, then picked up a rolling pin. "Fiction."

"What kind of fiction?" he asked when she didn't elaborate.

Picking up the round pan of biscuits, she put them in the oven and faced him. "Romance."

Nicholas came out of his slouched position. He almost took a running step toward the door until he remembered the little girl who hadn't made a wish since she was nine and why. Girls dreamed and wished for their Prince Charming just like the young woman he'd seen in Andrea's sketches. What must it be like for her to see other women's wishes come true, but not her own?

"If I could give you my wish, I would. I'd wish that you'd find a man to love you as much as you'd love him. As much as you deserved to be loved." The words just slipped out. No one could have been more surprised than Nicholas. After the fiasco with his last wish, he thought he'd completely removed that word from his vocabulary.

His hand swept down over his face. Maybe he should give more thought to ordering the MRI machine. He could be the first to have his brain scanned.

Andrea's face softened. "Thank you."

"For what? I don't believe in your aunt's power."

"I know. That's why I thanked you, because you wished from your heart."

The way she was looking at him did strange things to his body. Mercy, she was gorgeous. Delicate and beautifully proportioned. He'd have to be careful of her when they made love for the first time.

His mouth dropped open.

"Nicholas, what's the matter?"

Clamping his mouth shut, he swallowed. His hand scoured his face again. He was definitely losing it. The one woman in town who wasn't coming on to him, and he wanted her more than he'd ever thought possible to want a woman. "I-I just remembered I have an appointment. I'd better go."

"Wait!" she called as he started toward the door. "I'll fix you a plate."

He was already shaking his head. "That's not necessary."

Andrea wasn't listening. She quickly put smothered steak and rice into a microwavable container. "Here."

Nicholas's unsteady hands clamped around the container. She was treating him like his mother did, and he wanted to pull her into his arms and make love to her until he had just enough energy to breathe . . . maybe not even then.

He swallowed again. "Thank you."

"You're welcome. Once you finish with your appointment, you can stop back by for biscuits."

Nodding, Nicholas tore his gaze away from her mouth and hurried to the door. If he came back, it wouldn't be for biscuits.

Tuesday evening the women in the Beauty Boutique cheered and applauded Augusta as she entered the salon with Andrea. A week had passed since Augusta had granted Nicholas Darling his wish. Women whistled, stomped their feet, and waved their hands. Augusta took it all in her stride, nodding to the women as she made her way to a padded green chair in the small reception area.

Andrea glanced around at the cheering women and felt sorry all over again for Nicholas. Perhaps if he wasn't handsome enough to make a woman lick her lips, he wouldn't have half the single women in town after him.

"Mrs. Augusta, you sure have livened things up," Glenda Hobbs, the owner of the shop, said. She removed the cape from around the neck of a customer she'd just given a finger wave and gave it a brisk snap of her wrist. "I'm ready for you."

"Thank you, Glenda." Her black patent-leather purse dangling from its strap in the crook of her arm, Augusta took her seat in the stylist's chair. She placed her purse in her lap as the cape whipped around her neck with a flourish.

"Yeah, Mrs. Augusta," Hazel, the beautician at the next station, said. "I saw him yesterday at the post office. He's one fine-looking man."

"I wouldn't mind finding him under my tree Christmas morning wearing a big red bow," Rebecca, getting her waist-length braids redone, commented with a wide grin.

"Why waste the bow, since you'd rip it off?" joked Glenda. "I know I would."

The women howled with laughter. Glenda, robust, with dyed blond hair, had been married three times and made it no secret she was looking for number four.

Andrea smiled, remembering she'd had a similar thought about a man for Christmas and wondered if she'd be bold enough to rip the bow off. If the man was Nicholas, it would be gone in seconds. The smile faded. Nicholas was not for her. Why did she keep forgetting?

"Come on, Mrs. Augusta. Let's go to the shampoo bowl," Glenda said as she helped Augusta to the floor. "I don't suppose you know who the woman is?"

Hair dryers clicked off; scissors and curlers halted. Breaths were held. Ears strained to listen. Eyes locked on Augusta.

Augusta kept them waiting until her head was over the shampoo bowl. "She's one of our own."

An excited buzz raced through the shop.

"I think the hospital should open the wish list to the whole town," Glenda suggested, squirting shampoo into her hand. "Give some of the rest of us a chance to win that pot. I can think of ten ways to use that money right off the bat to get his attention and him."

This time the excitement rose higher as women listed ways they'd use the money to entice and lure Nicholas. *Poor Nicholas*, Andrea thought. It would be all over the town by tonight. Gossip from the beauty shop traveled faster than the speed of light. "Auntie, I have an errand to run. I'll be back in an hour."

Eyes closed as Glenda worked up a lather in her thick gray hair, Augusta answered, "I'll be fine. Take your time."

Andrea headed for the door. By the time she reached her car, she had her keys out. Six minutes later she was parked at Memorial Hospital. Another three and she stood in front of Michelle's desk. They'd gone to elementary and high school together. "Hi, Michelle. Is Nicholas in?"

"Hi, Andrea," Michelle greeted her, then frowned and glanced toward the closed door behind her. "He's in, but he asked that he not be disturbed. I guess you know why."

Andrea's fingers tightened on her bag. *And it's about to get worse.* "This is important. Please ask him if I can have a few minutes of his time."

"Well, since you're Mrs. Augusta's niece, he probably won't mind." Leaning over, Michelle pressed the intercom. "Nicholas, Andrea Strickland is here to see you. She says it's important."

"Send her in."

Swallowing nervously, Andrea opened the door. Nicholas was already striding across his office toward her. The sight of him caused her heart to pound, her pulse to leap. She'd almost forgotten how handsome he was.

He frowned. "What is it? What happened?"

Andrea moistened her dry lips. "I don't know how to

tell you this except to just say it. Auntie just told the women in the beauty shop that the wish woman is one of the town's own. In a couple of hours it will be all over town. While it will stop the women from surrounding towns who may have heard about the wish by working in the hospital or through gossip, those from Jubilee will be even more enthusiastic about the wish."

For a long moment he simply stared at her. "Do you know how difficult these last days have been for me?"

Andrea heard the underlying frustration in his voice and reached out to touch his arm. A little jolt raced from the tips of her fingers back up her arm. She quickly withdrew her hand, but not before she felt the muscled hardness beneath the fine wool suit coat. "It's difficult now, but it will work out."

"In the meantime, what am I supposed to do?" he asked, gesturing toward his desk. "I can't get a thing done. The hospital board hired me to get Memorial out of the red, to make it profitable and efficient. I can't do that now with these women showing up every place I go."

She'd already guessed he was conscientious. He took his responsibility to the hospital seriously. He didn't like not being able to do the job he'd been hired for . . . or being on display. Everywhere she'd gone for the past few days, his name had been mentioned. Successful, intelligent, and handsome—what woman wouldn't want him? "I'm sorry, Nicholas."

Nicholas saw the distress in her eyes, and his irritation evaporated. She had such a capacity for empathy. Her eyes were clear of guile and deceit. She'd want him for himself, not because of some wish. The thought brought him up short. He stepped back.

"Is there a problem?"

His pager vibrated, saving him. Pulling it from his belt, he threw it a sharp glance, scowled, then deleted the number. "I've changed numbers twice and they continue to find me."

A knock sounded on the door; then Michelle stuck her

head inside, a worried frown on her face. "I think you'd better take this call. It's Kay Smith, a reporter from the local newspaper."

"What does she want?" Nicholas asked.

Michelle glanced from Andrea to Nicholas. "She's heard about the wish and she wants to do a story."

He scowled. "Tell her I'm not in."

"I'll tell her, but it won't stop Kay." The door closed.

Nicholas shoved both hands over his hair. "This has got to stop."

"It will. Unfortunately, the women have tied the wish pot and your wish together. But once . . . once you find her, the other women will realize they don't have a chance and they'll leave you alone," Andrea said, experiencing a pang of remorse that it wouldn't be her.

"What?" His hands lowered.

Happy that she could finally help, Andrea continued. "Everyone knows it's just a matter of time before you find the woman you wished for. Once you find her, the other women will bow out."

"You mean a woman got me into this mess and a woman can get me out?" he asked.

She shifted uncomfortably. "I wouldn't have put it that way, but essentially what you said is true."

A wide grin split his face. "If that's all it takes, I've already found her."

Misery swept through her. "Who is she?"

"You."

Chapter 4

"What!"

"You said you'd help me. This is your chance," Nicholas rushed to say. "If people believe you're the woman I wished for, they'll leave me alone and I can get back to running the hospital."

Andrea looked at the excitement on his face and wanted to kick him on the shin for making her foolishly hope he felt anything for her, and at the same time wanting to join him in his happiness. "This wasn't exactly what I had in mind, Nicholas."

He stepped closer. "Please. You have to help me. You're the only woman I can turn to."

Andrea gazed into his dark eyes and gorgeous face and felt herself weakening. "I don't like the idea of fooling people."

"Please," he repeated, an engaging smile on his face. "You're my only hope."

She shook her head. Nicholas wasn't for her. "Family members have always been excluded from Auntie's wishes."

His hands gently circled her upper arms. "The townspeople don't know that, do they?"

"I-I don't think so." It should be against the law for a man to touch a woman and fry every circuit in her brain. Why wasn't she telling him no?

"Then, this will work." He grinned liked a little boy on Christmas morning who'd had every wish granted.

"What about the woman you wished for?" she asked weakly.

He tsked. "If there is such a woman and we're fated to be together, it won't matter what you and I do. This wish woman and I will see each other and no power on earth will be able to keep us apart."

Andrea's spirit sank. Nicholas was joking, but that's exactly how it would be. "I believe in my aunt's gift."

"Then prove it," he challenged. "Go out with me."

"Out?"

"If, as you say, this wish woman and I are destined to be together, you and I going out won't matter, and it would get all these women out of my face," he said, obviously warming to his plan. "You aren't seeing anyone, are you?"

"It would certainly put a cramp in your plan, wouldn't it?" she evaded. It wasn't fair that he could turn her into mush when he'd never be hers.

His dark eyes narrowed, the look in them hard. "Are you?"

She allowed herself all of two seconds to think that was possessiveness she saw in Nicholas's eyes and not simply irritation because a man in her life would interfere with his plans. "No. I'm not seeing anyone."

His fingers flexed. "Good." Releasing her, he stepped back and slipped his hands into the pockets of his dress slacks. "What are you doing tonight?"

"I thought I'd work on my special project," she said slowly. How ironic; she had reached the part in her book where Melissa had to rescue Braxton.

"Could you spare a couple of hours? The president of the hospital board is having a small get-together at his house. I'd like to take you."

"You certainly aren't wasting any time putting your plan into action, are you?" she asked, the hurt she'd tried to keep from feeling surfacing.

His hands whipped out of his pockets. "I don't use people, Andrea."

"But you're not above using a situation to your advantage."

"No, I'm not. But if this is going to make us enemies, let's forget it." He strode behind his desk and picked up a folder.

His cavalier dismissal infuriated her. "I suppose now you'll find another woman to take my place." She tried to be blasé, but her hands shook.

Slowly his head lifted until their gazes locked. "I don't think that's possible."

The deep timbre of his voice caused her insides to shiver. Her problem, not his. She had promised to help. It wasn't his fault that he was the first man who'd interested her in a very long time. "What shall I wear and when should I expect you?"

He arched a dark brow. "Just like that?"

She shrugged carelessly. "I did say I'd help."

"And we'll still be friends?"

"And we'll still be friends," she repeated. Friendship was better than nothing, and she'd get over whatever this was in fifty or sixty years.

Pulling out the leather chair, he finally took his seat. "Dressy, and I'll pick you up at seven-thirty."

"I'll be ready. See you then." Hefting the strap of her bag over her shoulder, she went to the door.

"Andrea?"

She glanced around. "Yes?"

"There's something you should be aware of."

"What?" *Please don't tell me you have a woman in Philadelphia.*

"If I did believe in wishes, you would be the woman I would have wished for."

Andrea felt the heat and desire in his gaze, felt the softening of her own body in response, felt her regret. "She's out there, Nicholas."

"There is no wish woman," he said stubbornly.

Arguing would settle nothing. Time would prove him wrong. "I'll see you tonight." Opening the door, she said good-bye to Michelle and went to her car.

Andrea had no intention of keeping her date with Nicholas a secret from her aunt. They had always been honest with each other. The instant they returned home from the beauty shop Andrea told her aunt that she was going out with Nicholas and why.

Augusta's fragile hands palmed her niece's cheeks. "What will be will be."

"He doesn't think so," Andrea said.

"He will. In the meantime we'd better find you a dress to wear." Augusta took her niece's arm and steered her into her bedroom. "It's not ladylike to keep a gentleman waiting too long."

"It's not like it's a real date," Andrea said, sorrow creeping into her voice.

Augusta paused in front of the door to Andrea's closet. "It's always important to look your best." Reaching inside, she pulled out an indigo light wool sheath with long sleeves. "You always look lovely in this."

"You aren't going to let me mope and worry about this, are you?" Andrea said, taking the dress from her aunt.

"Each breath we take puts us that much closer to our reckoning day. Wasting life is stupid. You've never been stupid."

Practical and straightforward, Augusta Venora Evans never minced words. Andrea hugged her aunt, who was two inches shorter and fifteen pounds lighter. "I love you."

"Enjoy life. Don't take a backseat." Patting her niece's arm, Augusta left the room.

Holding the dress to her, Andrea gazed into the mirror. "Auntie's right. You aren't stupid. So why can't you stop thinking about Nicholas?" There was no answer, only the slow beating of her heart.

*   *   *

Nicholas had had his first date at the precocious age of eleven. His parents had taken him and his girlfriend to a Saturday movie matinee, then picked them up and taken her home. Nicholas remembered handling the entire affair like a pro. Tonight, as he walked onto Andrea's porch and rang the bell, he was caught between anticipation and annoyance.

He hadn't been able to get out of his mind what he'd said to her about her being the woman he would have wished for. While he'd spoken the truth, the reason behind why he'd said it bothered him.

He simply had been unable to let her leave his office thinking he was callous or that she didn't matter. This tendency to want to protect a woman from the slightest hurt was a new experience for him. Ever since he'd made that idiotic wish, he'd lost control of his life. But after tonight he'd have it under control again.

The door opened, and he realized he was wrong.

Andrea stood in the doorway, the light from the chandelier in the hallway framing her. She was exquisite. The dress skimmed over her to reveal the sensuous curves of her body. He wanted to grab her and gobble her up. He wanted to savor her inch by luscious inch.

"Good evening, Nicholas. Come in. I'll get my shawl."

"Good evening, Andrea," he managed, stepping inside, then following her into the living room. Augusta sat in an old-fashioned rocking chair knitting a red scarf. A colorful basket of yarn sat by her feet. Gold-framed eyeglasses were perched on her nose. "Good evening, Mrs. Augusta."

"Good evening, Mr. Darling." Metal clicked as she continued to rock and knit.

"Please call me Nicholas," he said, wondering when his annoyance at her had left.

She sent him a smile. "I'd be honored."

Picking up her black cashmere shawl, Andrea leaned down and kissed Augusta's thin cheek. "We shouldn't be too late."

"I'll be fine," Augusta said. "Drive carefully, Nicholas."

"Yes, ma'am." Taking the shawl from Andrea's hands,

he draped the soft material around her shoulders. "The temperature's dropped again."

"Thank you." She smiled up at him over her shoulder, her warm breath caressing his lips.

Every nerve in Nicholas's body went on full alert. He hoped Augusta was paying close attention to her knitting and not to him. He cleared his throat and placed a white card near the telephone on the end table. "The name and phone number of where we're going is on the back of my business card, if you should need to contact Andrea."

The needles and chair stopped. "Thank you, Nicholas. That's very thoughtful of you."

For some reason he felt like shuffling his feet. "I should have her back by eleven."

Augusta set the chair in motion once again. "I won't worry, since she's with you."

It occurred to Nicholas as he escorted Andrea to his car that Augusta trusted him with Andrea because she, like Andrea, was under the misguided belief that his "wish woman" was out there and that he was a gentleman. That was a gross miscalculation on both their parts. He went after what he wanted. Always had. Always would.

Try as he might to control it, he wanted Andrea, not some mythical woman. And the need grew stronger each time he saw her.

Cars were lined up on both sides of the street where Bob Hawkins and his wife, Beverly, lived. The stately neighborhood of two-story homes had long been the enclave of the wealthy and elite of the city. Bob Hawkins, as president of the largest of the three banks in Jubilee, was both. His appointment as president of Memorial Hospital's board only served to elevate his stature.

Nicholas helped Andrea out of his car, his mouth tight. "I've been in Texas four months and I know size is relative, but it's stretching it to call this a small gathering."

"Thanksgiving is only a couple of days away; maybe there's another party," Andrea said hopefully.

"Somehow, I doubt it."

When the maid let them inside the entryway, with its twenty-five-foot ceiling and double crystal chandelier, Andrea saw that Nicholas was right. The "small" get-together of the six other board members, their spouses, and a few others had expanded to over thirty people. Most of them were women.

Their eagle eyes centered on Nicholas the instant they entered the spacious den, then jerked to Andrea. Clearly they were trying to determine if she might be an obstacle in their path to Nicholas.

Unconsciously she stepped closer to Nicholas. Almost simultaneously he moved closer to her.

The dual stimulus of warmth and the hardness of his body aligned with hers drew her gaze to his face. His black eyes burned into her as much as his possessive hand on her waist. Time stood still. The other people in the room vanished. His eyes drifted to her lips. Her stomach muscles tightened. She had the overpowering impression that he wanted to kiss her. Her lips parted.

"Hello, Nicholas, Andrea," Beverly Hawkins greeted them, holding out her hand and breaking the spell that had held them. Diamonds and sapphires glittered. "There're going to be some very disappointed women when this gets out."

Bob Hawkins, likable and robust, sent his wife of thirty years a stern look. "I told you not to let all those women talk you into letting them come over. Perhaps now you'll listen when I tell you not to interfere."

"That will be the day," she said with a laugh, then hooked her arms through Nicholas's and Andrea's. "Let me introduce you to the other people you may not know. Andrea, be thankful you're Mrs. Augusta's niece or you'd have to watch your back. If Dianna wasn't engaged, I might be a little upset myself."

"Beverly!" Bob hissed, then shook his balding head. "But I must admit that I'm glad it's over and you can concentrate on Memorial. We want Memorial financially sound."

"It will be, Bob. Count on it," Nicholas said, not a trace of doubt in his voice.

"Excellent. Business comes first." Nodding, Bob walked off.

Beverly harrumphed. "Good thing Dianna takes after me, or she'd be snuggled up to a calculator for the rest of her life instead of a man."

Andrea smiled. She was used to Beverly's frankness. "Your daughter is a beautiful, intelligent young woman. You must be so excited that she's graduating from Cornell next year."

"Yes, we are." Beverly beamed with pride. "I'll never be able to thank you enough for helping her when she first went to college in New York. She was so homesick."

"It was my pleasure," Andrea said, fondly remembering the shy young woman who was nothing like her gregarious mother. "I met her fiancé when I was in New York. I like him very much."

"Me, too," Beverly said, her eyes twinkling. "They haven't set a date yet, but we're already looking at wedding gowns. If you'd like the names of the shops, I'd be happy to give you a list."

Andrea didn't have to see Nicholas's face to know he probably wore a stunned expression. "Thank you. I'll let you know."

"Please do," Beverly said, then proceeded to introduce Nicholas and Andrea around the room.

Andrea already knew some of the other guests, or they knew of her through her aunt. She'd never had any difficulty meeting people, and she didn't tonight. She wouldn't have lasted a week in New York if she had. Beverly's daughter almost hadn't made it. But with all her timidness, she had managed to find a man to love, a man who would love her back.

Andrea was still looking.

With Nicholas by her side and Beverly's obvious approval, most of the guests responded warmly to Andrea. If the single women were less than enthusiastic to see her she readily understood. She wasn't quite sure how she'd respond when the woman Nicholas was fated to marry showed up.

For only the second time in her life Andrea toyed with the idea of making a wish, a wish to hold back time. But she realized that the wish would be as futile as that first wish she'd asked for when she was nine.

She'd lost then, and she'd lose this time.

As the evening progressed, Nicholas could see that the plan was working. Andrea had been right. Once women thought he had the woman he'd wished for, they left him alone. In the hour and a half since their arrival, the number of women had thinned out to about ten.

You could actually move around the lavishly decorated gold-and-white living room or sit on one of the overstuffed white sofas, if you were so inclined. For himself, he leaned against the side of the black baby grand nursing a glass of chardonnay and watched Andrea.

He'd been doing that a lot tonight. He couldn't help himself. Something about her drew his gaze, again and again. And each time it did, he discovered something he hadn't noticed before. How delicate her hands looked holding the stem of a wineglass, how her soft auburn hair shone in the artificial light, how kissable the smooth column of her neck looked when she laughed.

Desire stirred. He wanted her in his bed. She protected him from other women, but who would protect her from him?

"You lucky dog, I don't blame you for staring. Wish I had seen her first."

Nicholas turned to see Samuel Ferrell, a surgical resident who worked part-time at the hospital. Nicholas didn't even try to suppress the spurt of jealousy. "Not if you want to use your hands to operate again."

Samuel chuckled, then tipped his glass. "Message received and understood, but if this wish thing doesn't work out, surely you won't begrudge me asking her out."

"What makes you think she'd go out with you?" *Arrogant twerp.*

"Women like doctors' bedside manners, if you catch my drift," he said, and strolled off to the buffet table.

Nicholas felt like going after him and pushing his big head in the punch bowl. If he so much as touched Andrea, he'd draw back a nub.

"Nicholas, why are you frowning?"

He looked down at Andrea, saw the concern in her face, tried to relax, and couldn't. "If you're ready, we can leave."

"Of course." She allowed him to lead her through the house to find their host and hostess. After thanking them, they said their good-byes to the other guests and left.

In Nicholas's car, Andrea kept sneaking secretive glances at him as he drove her home. He was angry. She didn't understand why. She'd thought he'd been pleased with the way things had gone. They hadn't had to say a word. People had just assumed they were a couple, that she was the woman he had wished for. They'd soon find out how wrong they were. Her hands clutched her shawl and drew it tighter around her shoulders.

"You're cold? You want me to turn the heat up?"

She shook her head. "No." *That* wasn't what she needed, wanted. She glanced out the window as he turned onto the narrow two-lane road leading to her house. Darkness surrounded them. She'd traveled this road thousands of times, but she'd never felt so alone or so lost.

Nicholas pulled into her driveway and parked. The twin porch lights on either side of the front door gave off a muted glow. Through the curtain in the living room another light shone. Opening his door, he went around the car and helped her out.

Silently they walked up the porch steps. "Give me your key."

"I can do it," she said, trying and failing to insert the key the first time. Her hand shook so badly, it took three tries before the key slipped in. Twisting the key, she unlocked the door and stepped over the threshold.

When she turned, her gaze went no higher than the middle of his broad white-shirted chest. "Good night and thank you."

"Aren't you going to look at me?"

It hurt too much. "I'm really tired."

"Regretting your decision already?"

Before Nicholas, she'd never been afraid to face the truth. Her chin jutted. Inch by inch her gaze climbed higher until their eyes met. The light cast his face in shadows. "Perhaps you're the one regretting your decision."

"Never." He brushed his knuckles down her cheek. Andrea was unable to control the tremor that raced though her. "You're cold. Go inside."

She shook her head. "Why were you angry?"

"We can talk about this later."

"I want to talk now."

A deep sigh drifted between them. Removing his jacket, he placed it around her shoulders. It enveloped her just as he wanted to. "You're going to be stubborn, I see."

She said nothing, just continued to stare up at him. He almost smiled. He hadn't noticed the stubborn streak before. But he wasn't about to admit the entire truth. "I'm not sure what's the matter. Maybe it's the holiday blues. I may be thirty-three, but this is the first time I won't spend Thanksgiving with my family. Since Mom and Dad are the oldest children and both their parents are gone, their sisters and brothers all come to our house. Mom and her two sisters are fabulous cooks. We stuff ourselves; then the men settle in for some serious football watching on TV."

"And the women clean up the kitchen, watch the children, admire the new babies, and catch up."

This time he did smile. In his too-large jacket, she looked like a little girl playing dress-up. "Sounds as if you've been to a few family gatherings yourself."

"When I was younger. It's just the two of us now," she said.

Disquieted, he pulled the lapels of the coat closer together. "That's rough. I come from a big extended family."

"Auntie and I both have a lot of friends here," she told him. "In fact, many of them will probably drop by on Thanksgiving. Why don't you come for breakfast and stay for dinner?"

"I don't want to impose."

"You won't," she told him. "Please come. I'll fix your favorite dessert. What is it?"

You, whipped cream, and cherries. Nicholas blinked. He couldn't believe the thought had just popped into his head like that. He was definitely losing it. "Ah, whatever is fine. You'd better get inside. Good night."

"Wait." Slipping off his jacket, she handed it to him.

"Thanks." Firmly he pushed her inside, then closed the door.

Andrea stared at the door. She just didn't understand Nicholas. Sometimes he looked at her as if he'd like to gobble her up, then other times, like now, as if he couldn't get rid of her fast enough.

Men.

Chapter 5

The hospital's grapevine was alive and well.

By eleven the next morning Nicholas was able to move about the hospital without a woman in his path. There was a briskness to his walk that had been lacking. He was finally getting back on schedule and getting some work done. He didn't even hesitate to get on the elevator when he saw three female staff members already inside.

"Hello, Mr. Darling," said a curvy young woman in an abstract-print smock. "I think it's wonderful about you and Andrea. I had a chemistry class with her in high school. Tell her Nancy Logan said hello."

"Good morning. I'll tell her," Nicholas said, mulling over the fact that Nancy was the fifth woman to ask him to tell Andrea hello. He had no idea that many people in the hospital knew her.

"She was three years behind me," commented a lanky orderly, his hand wrapped around an IV pole. "I remember she was cute and kind of scrawny. Saw her the other day. She's filled out some since then."

"That's an understatement. She's gorgeous."

Nicholas turned to see who had spoken. Samuel Ferrell grinned back at him. *Impertinent twerp.* "A wise man doesn't need to be told the same thing twice."

The grin slid from Ferrell's thin face. The silence was so thick in the elevator, you could slice it. The doors slid open and no one moved as the two men stared at each other.

"I believe this is your floor, Mr. Darling," Nancy said, holding the door open for him.

"Thank you." This time Nicholas didn't have to worry about giggles as he exited, but there wasn't a shred of doubt in his mind that the story of his confrontation with Ferrell would be all over the hospital by the end of the day.

It took less than an hour.

Women thought it was romantic. Men thought it was manly. Nicholas just thought why hadn't he kept his big mouth shut? Especially when he received a call from Beverly Hawkins, who told him point-blank not to worry about Ferrell. Andrea, in Beverly's opinion, was too intelligent to fall for Ferrell when she had Nicholas. She was just as down-to-earth and charming as the day she had left for New York six years ago.

Nicholas was trying to think of a polite way to end the conversation when Beverly dropped a bomb. "I guess now she'll forget about going back to New York and stay here."

"Andrea can work anywhere," he said, repeating what she'd told him and fighting the sudden unease he felt.

"Isn't that just like a man, to think his career is more important than a woman's?" Beverly scolded. "In New York she could make more contacts. In this day and age, women can have both a career and a marriage."

The word *marriage* was like a bucket of cold water over him. But if he corrected her, the madness would start all over again.

"Well, I have to run. I'll see you at the hospital party on the twenty-fourth. Guess your ranking on the wish list has dropped since Andrea has grabbed you." Soft laughter echoed over the phone. "A parting word of advice on Andrea's engagement ring: Nothing warms a woman's heart like diamonds. Big ones."

With Beverly's last words ringing in his ears, Nicholas hung up the phone. He hadn't thought past getting women off his case. They expected him and Andrea to become engaged. When that didn't happen, where would that leave

Andrea? An unpleasant picture of Samuel Ferrell popped into his mind.

Coming to his feet, Nicholas left his office. "I'm going out for lunch."

"You have an appointment in thirty minutes with Mrs. Ratcliffe, the head of food services," Michelle told him.

"Let her know I may be late and see if she wants to wait or reschedule," he said, never breaking his stride.

"But you're booked up through the end of the day," she protested.

"Then tell them all the same thing." Opening the door, he left.

It took Nicholas exactly nine minutes to reach Andrea's house. His frame of mind worsened with each second that ticked by. Seeing both cars in the garage, he took a chance that Andrea might be in back and went around the side of the house. His gaze immediately found her.

Sitting beneath the same giant maple tree she'd been under last week, she was bent over a legal pad. Today her bulky sweater matched the purple wool scarf beside her. He'd bet anything Augusta had knitted both.

This time Andrea saw him well before he reached her. Her eyes widened. She placed the pad on the grass beside her.

He crouched in front of her, their knees almost touching. "Half the people in the hospital know you. Several asked me to tell you hello."

Not sure if it was an accusation or a statement, Andrea said nothing.

"What's going to happen when there's no wedding?"

That she did have an answer for. "There'll be a wedding; it simply won't be mine."

His eyes narrowed to slits. He obviously hadn't liked that answer. "Do you know a doctor by the name of Samuel Ferrell?"

Andrea frowned, trying to follow Nicholas's train of thought and failing. "Wasn't he at the party last night?"

Nicholas's expression turned cold. "He wants to take you out if we break up."

Since they weren't officially in a relationship they could hardly break up, but with the fierce way Nicholas was watching her, Andrea didn't think it prudent to remind him of that fact. "What he wants is immaterial to me."

Nicholas wanted to haul her into his arms, taste her mouth, stake his claim. "You might as well know I warned him away from you." He'd never been possessive or jealous or irrational about a woman in his life. "Last night, then this morning in a hospital elevator. It'll probably be all over the town by tonight. It's already spread through the hospital."

She tried not to let it matter that it was all part of his plan. "My hero."

Fierce anger shot through him. "I'm not a hero. I don't want this to hurt you. I know you believe in your aunt, but I don't."

Her eyes filled with unbearable sadness. "You will."

He didn't want to pick a fight with her; he wanted to lay her down in the grass and love her until she cried out in sweet ecstasy. "I'd better get back and let you work on your sketches." He picked up the pad and noticed there was writing, not drawing, on the pages. "What's this?"

Grabbing it out of his hand, she flipped the pages closed. "My special project."

He recalled her mentioning a special project in his office. "What kind of project?"

"I'm writing a novel. A romance novel," she qualified, her chin jutting out defiantly.

He sat there absorbing the information, thinking of the woman who believed wishes weren't granted to her but didn't begrudge those to whom wishes were granted; a woman who sketched happiness for others but not for herself. A woman who dreamed.

His hand grazed her chin. "What's the hero like?"

Her mouth curved upward. "Braxton is an ex-operative. He's intelligent, masterful, and a loner. Fiercely private, he's fighting tooth and nail not to fall in love with Melissa, but he's a goner."

"Can I read it?" He was intensely interested in Andrea's take on love and romance. She deserved so much of both.

Her arms tightened. "Perhaps one day."

He reached out to stroke her hair. He couldn't help himself. If she was within reach, he wanted to touch her. "Does that mean you're sticking around and not going back to New York?"

She didn't bother asking him how he knew. In a small town, gossip was the main source of entertainment. "I'll go back eventually, but I'm not sure when. Perhaps after the holidays."

The fierce look came back in his eyes. "Why can't you stay here and work?"

"In my business, contacts count. Auntie is on a fixed income. I'm the only one she has to depend on. I have to help," Andrea explained. "I mailed the illustrations Friday for the last book I had a contract for. Publishing houses slow down this time of year, but after the New Year things will pick up and I have to be there."

It made sense, but he didn't have to like it. He wanted her here . . . with him. "What if you sold your book?"

"I could stay here, but editors receive hundreds of submissions," she told him. "It might not sell."

"Do you believe in Braxton and Melissa?" he asked.

"Yes," she answered immediately.

"Then the book will sell." He pushed to his feet. "Don't doubt yourself, Andrea."

"I don't usually."

"Good. Get back to work. I'll see you tomorrow morning."

"Wear clothes you don't mind getting dirty. After dinner we're going in the woods to get the Christmas tree."

"Another tradition?"

"Yes."

He nodded, liking being included. Whistling, hands in his pockets, he strode off.

Andrea leaned back against the tree trunk and watched Nicholas round the corner of the house. She'd have to be careful and not get caught up in the pretense of caring for him. Nicholas could steal a woman's heart.

Flipping the pad open, she began to write. Melissa had just dared Braxton to come skinny-dipping.

Thanksgiving morning Nicholas drove into Andrea's driveway and a red haze of jealousy came over him. A giant of a man he'd never seen before was swinging Andrea around in his arms. Nicholas came out of his car like a shot. Andrea's squeals of delight propelled him across the yard.

"Put her down!"

The man, three inches taller and forty pounds heavier, stopped and stared down at him. Andrea gazed at him with wide, uncertain eyes. "Nicholas."

"I'm not going to say it again."

Pushing against the man's wide chest, Andrea scrambled out of his arms. "He wasn't hurting me, Nicholas. Travis is a friend of mine. I'm sorry if my silly cries gave you the wrong impression."

The man, who was built like a linebacker, smiled. "I don't think that's the problem."

"Of course it is," Andrea said, staring up at Nicholas.

Nicholas jerked his gaze to Andrea, then shoved his hand over his hair. What was wrong with him? He didn't want any man holding her for any reason. First thing Monday he was putting in the request for the MRI machine.

"Travis Gabriel," the man said, extending his hand. "Andrea and I go back to the third grade. I already know who you are."

The handshake was firm even if the man's lips were twitching. "Hello."

Andrea moistened her lips. "Breakfast is ready. Come on in."

Nicholas took Andrea's arm and started toward the house. He wasn't being possessive. He was being a gentleman.

They were barely on the porch before a black Lexus SUV pulled up and parked behind his car. With a shout of joy, Andrea ran to meet the two men and one woman scrambling out. Travis was two steps ahead of her. They laughed and hugged and jumped up and down like children.

Nicholas wasn't prepared when they all turned to look at him. Only Andrea smiled. He could tell when he was being sized up. He could handle it. There wasn't anything about him that Andrea would have to be ashamed of.

He stepped off the porch and met them on the sidewalk with a friendly smile. Andrea made the introductions of the rest of the Fab 5 of Jubilee High School, as she laughingly called them, who now lived all over the country but got together every Thanksgiving as they had since high school. Their parents, who still lived in Jubilee, had come to expect it and, in fact, would drop by themselves later on.

In the kitchen, Andrea's friends greeted Augusta with the same enthusiasm. The oak table had been extended to seat eight. Nicholas made sure he sat next to Andrea. Travis, a college history professor in Atlanta, might be all right; the jury was still out on John Williams, a photojournalist in D.C., and Clint Mack, a headhunter for a large corporation in Miami. The other woman, Elaine Bennett, a vivacious brunette, was a magazine fashion editor in San Francisco.

As soon as they'd finished breakfast and cleaned up the kitchen, they all set out to find a Christmas tree. Once again, Nicholas positioned himself by Andrea's side.

"It's just not right."

"Too skinny."

"Too lopsided."

Andrea's reasons varied as she ruled out tree after tree and tried to find the "perfect" Christmas tree in the acreage behind her house. The other men groaned, Elaine teased her, but if Andrea wanted the perfect tree, then that was exactly what Nicholas would see that she got. "We'll keep searching," he always said.

Each time, she smiled at him as if he was all that she

could hope for in a man. Inexplicably, he wanted to stick out his chest. An hour and a half into their search, they finally found the tree.

"That's it!" Andrea said, staring at the plump seven-foot fir shaped like an inverted cone.

"Give me the ax, Travis." Holding out his hand, Nicholas turned to the man standing next to him.

Travis's grip tightened on the wooden handle. "Perhaps you should let me do it."

"Maybe you should," Andrea suggested, worry in her face. "He's done it before."

Nicholas's hand remained extended. "I may not have chopped down a tree, but I've chopped plenty of wood."

Travis handed him the ax and a pair of gloves. After a couple of swings, Nicholas's body remembered the motion; his mind, the technique. Several minutes later the tree toppled, to the delighted laughter of Andrea and the good-natured jibes from Travis that he could have done it faster.

Nicholas didn't care; all he cared about was the pride in Andrea's face. Putting the ax on his shoulder, he caught her hand, leaving the other men to load the tree on the rolling cart they'd brought.

Andrea couldn't get her heart to settle down. Every time Nicholas looked at her it would go crazy. She tried to tell herself he was just playing a part, but her body wasn't listening. This morning he'd been ready to fight Travis to protect her. He'd cut down the Christmas tree for her. He'd chosen her first for his team when they played tag football. It had been her idea to download the digital pictures John took to Nicholas's parents, but he had asked that a picture of *her* be sent to his computer.

It was too romantic. Even if it was pretend, she felt giddy with delight. He was the perfect prince.

"Since Mrs. Augusta has gone to bed, are you going to jump Nick on the couch or by the Christmas tree?" Elaine asked, a wide grin on her beautiful face.

Andrea laughed, but her heart went crazy again. She'd walked her friends to the door. Nicholas waited in the living room where they'd put the Christmas tree. "Ladies do not jump men."

Elaine sent Travis a speculative look. "There's always an exception to the rule."

Travis grinned. "A man would count himself lucky if he were that exception."

Andrea didn't know if Travis and Elaine were finally going to act upon the attraction that had always been between them or keep on dancing around it. She loved them both and wanted the best for them.

"Maybe it'll be me," John chimed up.

"Or me," Clint said.

"Or none of you," Elaine said with her usual style. She hugged Andrea. "My plane leaves tomorrow afternoon. I'll call when I get back."

"I thought you'd stay over the weekend," Travis said with a frown.

"Work," she said succinctly. "Good night, Andrea. Get back in there, and for what it's worth, I think you hit pay dirt."

"Thank you." She trusted her friends, but she'd decided not to tell them she and Nicholas were just pretending. She didn't want them to think ill of him.

"I think Nick's a little stiff," John said, then clicked the camera around his neck when Andrea's expression turned mutinous.

She laughed. "If you show that picture to anyone, I'll have your head."

"It would rattle, because nothing is in it." Clint laughed.

"Come on, children," Elaine said, grabbing both men and going down the steps to her parents' car.

Travis stared longingly after her before turning to Andrea. "Be happy, Andrea, and if you ever need a big brother, you know you have three."

Andrea hugged him. "If you ever need someone to talk to about you-know-what, call." She now knew what it was like to care for someone and not be sure how he felt.

"Maybe one day." After another brief hug, he went to his car parked on the other side of Nicholas's and drove off.

Going inside, Andrea cut off the porch lights, took a deep breath, and slowly walked to the living room. At first she didn't see him. The only light came from the hundreds of twinkling star-shaped lights decorating the tree. Her mother had bought them the year before Andrea was born. "Nicholas?"

He emerged out of the deep shadows near the couch. Andrea felt a chill race through her. For some reason he reminded her again of a large cat stalking his prey. He walked unhurried, his body loose yet poised to act if his intended prey tried to escape. She shivered again. Would she flee or remain?

He didn't stop until only a wisp of air separated them. She sensed his intention, the need pulsing through him. His hand lifted. Her breath caught, held. Then, his fingers traced her lower lip.

Her knees wobbled. "N-Nicholas?"

She swallowed. She couldn't gather her thoughts. His hand moved to her cheek, the curve of her ear.

"I like it." His hand trailed down to the hollow of her throat. "I've wondered what my name would sound like on your lips when need rushes and burns through your blood like sweet fire."

His hand continued down to the rounded curve of her breast. "Tonight I intend to find out. I've thought of little else all afternoon. If you have any objections, you have three seconds to voice them."

Voice. What voice? Her mind was numb, her body trembling with want of him.

"Time's up." His head lowered.

Chapter 6

The first brush of his lips shattered her; the second buckled her knees. Automatically her arms lifted, her hands clutching fistfuls of his shirt. His mouth was tender one moment, his tongue boldly erotic the next. He wasn't asking permission now; he was taking what he wanted.

Andrea pressed her body against his, heard him groan. Fierce pleasure swept through her that she could affect him this way.

Then as if part of him recognized that she wasn't going to flee, that she burned with the same wild desire that possessed him, his hold gentled; his mouth, sipped, teased, tantalized, rewarded.

"Nicholas."

Her ragged whimper sank into him. This was what he wanted. He wanted to fill her thoughts as much as he wanted to fill her body. Her small hands now clung around his neck; her body eagerly, if inexpertly, tried to match the erotic rhythm of his hips.

Her eagerness, her inexperience, her trust in him did what he hadn't expected. Tearing his mouth away, he held her fiercely against him. He couldn't take from her with no thought of the consequences. He held her until their breathing settled.

Sensing she wasn't going to be the first to speak, he

tipped her face up. "I want you more than I've ever wanted any other woman."

She bit her lip. "I-I shouldn't have let you kiss me."

Nicholas didn't bother answering such an idiotic statement; he just took her mouth again, letting the truth sink in that her body hungered for his as much as his hungered for hers. A vague memory of his wishing something like that for her stirred on the fringes of his mind, but the sweet lure of her mouth was too strong.

A long time later, he ended the kiss and pulled her securely against him. The top of her head barely came to the middle of his chest. He felt both protective and powerful with her in his arms. "How about a movie tomorrow night?"

"I'm not sure it's wise to keep seeing each other."

He could argue, but he'd always found reasoning worked better with intelligent people. "There's no reason we can't continue to see each other. We haven't done anything to be ashamed of. People do more on first dates."

"I don't."

He'd already figured as much. "Everyone will be suspicious if we aren't affectionate. We're just getting used to each other."

She was silent so long, he began to worry. His father always said if a woman was silent a man was in trouble. He thought fast. "How's the writing coming with Braxton and Melissa?"

Her head lifted, surprise shining in her dark eyes. "You remembered their names?"

He started to kiss her nose, then thought better of it. "Of course I did," he said, then went on to tell her exactly what she'd told him about the hero and heroine of the book she was writing.

"They're at an impasse. Melissa had to put herself in danger to rescue him, and Braxton didn't like it. They're out of immediate danger, but they aren't speaking to each other."

Nicholas was determined that he not end up like Braxton. "He's only angry because she put herself in danger for his sake."

"She knows that, but she doesn't like his macho double standard. If the situations had been reversed, he would have rescued her."

"That's the way it's supposed to be," Nicholas said emphatically.

"Men," Andrea said, and it wasn't a compliment.

Laughing, he stepped back before he kissed her again. "Now I'll have to read the book to see how he gets back in her good graces. In the meantime, I'd better go." He picked up his jacket from the arm of the green velvet sofa, then went to the front door and opened it. "What time should I pick you up for the movie?"

She glanced away. "Maybe I should stay home and work on my book."

"It'll be fun, and I promise to be on my best behavior," he cajoled. She was not getting away. There was no wish woman. He raised the ante. "You did promise to help."

Her head lifted, but she crossed her arms defensively over her chest. "I'll check the newspaper and call you."

"I'll expect to hear from you, then. Good night." He gave her a brotherly peck on the cheek, then strolled to his car, whistling.

Andrea was trapped between wanting to keep her word and wanting a man who would never be hers. More than once she'd caught Aunt Augusta looking at her strangely. She didn't blame her aunt. Andrea had left out the soda in the biscuits, broken a glass doing the breakfast dishes, turned on the washing machine without adding detergent.

"You troubled, child?" her aunt finally asked when they were making the grocery list.

Andrea's hand clenched on the yellow ceramic top of the mushroom canister containing sugar. "A little, I guess."

Out of the corner of her eye, she saw Aunt Augusta nod her gray head. "You were always sweet and caring. Worried about everyone before yourself. That's why you attract people. When you were in high school this house was always full of your friends. They sense you're for real."

Not daring to face her aunt, Andrea checked the next canister and scribbled "flour" on the growing list. "You always see and think the best in me."

"And I'm right," Augusta said. "I think you forget that you deserve happiness just as much as the next person."

Finally, Andrea turned, her expression filled with anguish. "But suppose what I want affects another person's happiness?"

Augusta's gaze was steady. "What will be will be. Neither you nor I can change that no matter how much we might want to. To worry about it is useless. So stop worrying and live life like I've always taught you." She opened the refrigerator. "Add eggs, milk, butter, sour cream, whipped cream. We're outta so much, and the stores are probably picked bare from Thanksgiving. You want to go shopping this afternoon or wait until in the morning?"

"In the morning. Nicholas and I are going to the movies this afternoon. The feature starts at five-thirty," she said, trying to keep her voice light.

"Mighty early to go to a movie," Augusta said, rummaging in the refrigerator.

"I want to get back and work on *A Risk Worth Taking*." And it would be light enough when they returned so Nicholas wouldn't attempt to kiss her good night.

Augusta closed the refrigerator door. "Always liked that title. Says a lot about life and those two in your book. They're lucky that they've found someone worth risking their hearts for. Some people go through life and never do. My prayer is that you'll be brave enough to risk it all, that you'll dare to grab your dream."

"It may not be possible," Andrea whispered.

"You'll never know until you try."

All through the romantic comedy at the only movie theater in Jubilee, her aunt's words kept running through Andrea's head. Her aunt loved her. She wouldn't want her to fall in love with a man who could never be hers, but that was exactly what Andrea was doing, tumbling and falling deeper with every second that ticked by.

There was no stopping her fall, just as there was no way to alter what was to be. Could she be as brave as Melissa, to risk it all for love? But whereas Melissa would have a lifetime with Braxton, Andrea would have a few brief weeks, if that.

She couldn't very well depend on Nicholas to stop trying to entice her. Clearly he was a man who went after what he wanted, and since he didn't believe in her aunt's prophecy, he felt no compunction in tempting Andrea every time the opportunity presented itself. It was up to her to keep their relationship platonic. But how could she do that when she wanted to gobble him up like a chocolate bar?

"Hungry?"

Startled, Andrea turned to Nicholas in the seat beside her. He wore a lazy grin that made her want to lick her lips, then lick him. "W-what?"

"I know the plot is predictable, the actors wooden, but you're not even looking at the screen, so I thought you might want to leave and go get something to eat," Nicholas explained.

"You'd have to be looking at me to know that," she told him.

He grinned. "Guilty."

She couldn't help the smile that formed on her face. "You're incorrigible."

"My mother would call you a smart woman."

Her smile never wavered. She'd never meet his mother. "Did they like the pictures John sent?"

"*Shhhh.*"

"Sorry," they both whispered. The holiday season combined with all the schools' being out meant the theater was crowded.

"Let's get out of here," he whispered. Her hand in his, they went into the lobby, then burst into laughter.

A man who made her laugh couldn't be that bad for her.

And she'd never been a coward. Suddenly she was ravenous. "I'd like a box of popcorn, a hot dog, and a Pepsi, please."

He steered her to the counter. "I thought I'd get out of this with just the movie."

"Not a chance." She bit into the hot dog as soon as she squirted it with mustard and sweet relish. "Delicious. Want some?"

His eyes on her, he bit into the wiener and bun. "You're right. Delicious."

She remembered him tasting her, her tasting him. Her hands trembled a bit, her insides were full of butterflies, but she wasn't afraid any longer. As her aunt had always said, what will be will be. "There's a park nearby, if you want to walk there."

"It's cold. We'll drive." Pushing open the glass door of the theater for her, he followed.

"Hot dogs can be messy," she said.

Opening the passenger door of his car, he helped her in, then handed her the box of popcorn he was holding. "So can a head cold."

"Ha. Ha. Very funny."

"I thought so." He closed the door.

By the time he'd gotten inside and started the motor, she'd propped the popcorn between her arm and the seat and placed the Pepsi in the drink holder. "You didn't want anything to eat?"

"I thought we'd share."

The idea pleased her. "The park is two blocks away on the left."

When they arrived at the park, Nicholas insisted they stay in the car. Twisting toward him in the seat, she offered the box of popcorn. "You never answered me about the pictures."

"Mom loved them." He grabbed a handful of the buttered popcorn. "My brother teased me about cutting down the tree for you. He thought I was trying to show off."

Andrea sipped the cola. "Were you?"

He grinned. "What do you think?"

She grinned back. "The tree is beautiful."

"Mom asked about my tree. I told her I hadn't had time to get one." He finished off the hot dog. "I probably won't have one this year."

The straw stopped midway to her mouth. Her eyes rounded. "You have to have a tree."

He shrugged, digging into the popcorn and trying to keep a straight face. Her compassionate heart was leading her exactly where he wanted her: alone with him. "Maybe if I find the time."

"Do you want to look for one on our property or get one from the tree lot?"

There was no reason to be coy. "Tree lot is fine."

She reached for her seat belt. "We'd better go or all the good ones will be taken."

"Now?"

"Now."

Nicholas soon found out that Andrea was as particular about his tree as she had been about hers. After three tree lots he was willing to try a fourth until she started making noises about going in search of a tree by herself the next day. He chose the next tree he came to.

"Nicholas, you can't be serious!" Andrea cried. "It's barely three feet and it's lopsided."

"It'll do," he said, picking up the scrawny tree by the crown and carrying it to the cashier. "A few decorations will make all the difference."

"You want it flocked?" the young attendant asked, popping his gum and nodding his head to the uptempo beat of "White Christmas." "We got pink, blue, or white."

Andrea shuddered. "It looks pitiful enough."

"We'll pass." Grasping Andrea by the arm, Nicholas went to his car and put the tree in the trunk. Straightening, he saw Andrea, her arms folded. "What?"

"I've been thinking."

The only thing worse than a silent woman, Nicholas's

father had said, was a thinking woman. "You have?"

"Your quick decision to buy that tree wouldn't have anything to do with my offering to cut you a tree tomorrow, would it?" she asked silkily.

Nicholas read the writing on the wall. "How long was Braxton in the doghouse for acting macho?"

"Two days."

"Care to tell me how he got out?"

Her composure faltered. Her arms fell to her sides. "Ah, Melissa got tired of his sulkiness and took matters into her own hands."

"What did she do?"

"You'll have to read the book," she said primly.

Nicholas opened the door and she slipped inside. "Just tell me one thing. Did he get over his sulks?"

Andrea smiled impishly. "Oh, yes."

It was close to 10:00 P.M. when Nicholas pulled up in her driveway. "Would you like to come in?" she asked after she'd opened the front door.

"I'd better get the tree home and out of the trunk."

She made a face. "I doubt anything will make it look better, but we have plenty of tree decorations in the attic. You're welcome to come over tomorrow and go through them."

"Thanks, but some of the staff are decorating the children's wing of the hospital and I volunteered," he told her.

Her expressive face saddened. "How terrible for a child to be in the hospital for Christmas."

"Yeah. We've set up a little store for them to purchase gifts for their parents with their smiles, so hopefully that will help."

"What a unique idea. Who thought of it?"

He shuffled his feet. "I guess I did."

She smiled up at him. "The first time I saw you, I knew you were a wonderful man."

His knuckles grazed her cheek. "The first time I saw you, my mind went totally blank."

Her heart drummed in her chest. "It—it did?"

"I thought you were the most stunning woman I'd ever seen. I still do." His hand continued the mesmerizing, body-stirring motion.

"Th-thank you."

His knuckles rimmed her chin. "If you're not busy to-morrow afternoon, we could use all the volunteers we could get."

Andrea tried to gather her thoughts. "I'll be there."

"Maybe you could go through the decorations for me; then afterward we could decorate the tree together." He'd traded the tips of his fingers for his knuckles.

"A-all right."

"Great. Good night."

"Good night, Nicholas."

He bounded off the porch and climbed inside his car. Going inside, she closed the door. He hadn't kissed her. He'd been a perfect gentleman, and if he did the same thing tomorrow, she might be tempted to jump him as Elaine had suggested. Laughing at her own temerity, she checked on her aunt, then went to bed, and dreamed of Nicholas.

Chapter 7

The pediatric wing of Memorial Hospital was filled with the happy laughter of children. Every child who could possibly participate in decorating did so. The hallways were turned into varied scenes of the North Pole, from the elves making toys to Santa hitching up his reindeer.

In the atrium stood a twelve-foot Douglas fir. Scattered over the branches were colorful metallic glass ball ornaments, each personalized with the name of a hospitalized child. And to ensure that Santa Claus received their requests on time, a special delivery mailbox, wrapped in red and white satin ribbon, sat nearby for the nightly run to the North Pole.

The adults took as much pleasure in the transformation as the children. Many of the parents had come to visit and stayed to help. It wasn't long before the person—Nicholas Darling—who had initiated the project was singled out and thanked repeatedly. Each time, he'd say it was only his idea, and he couldn't have made it a reality without the generous donations of so many of the volunteers. Andrea watched the scene over and over again and felt her heart swell with pride. Nicholas was a caring, thoughtful man.

"You think he'll give you a ring Christmas Eve or Christmas morning?"

Andrea turned to see Priscilla Campos, a friend from high school who now was a charge nurse on a surgical floor of the hospital. Three other female employees of the hospital were with her. All waited anxiously for an answer.

Andrea's happiness vanished. There'd be no ring on Christmas Eve or any other day. "I try not to think about it," she answered truthfully.

Priscilla, a leggy brunette, sighed dramatically. "If he were mine, that's all I'd think about."

"That's not all I'd think about," said Voncile Hale, a nurse with the sleek curves of a cover girl. They all howled with laughter.

"You ready to go, Andrea?"

The women's attention centered on Nicholas. He didn't seem to notice. His entire focus was on Andrea. She felt the melting softness, the tingling of her body. Whether it was real or he was pretending, he affected her as no other man ever had. "If you are."

"I'm ready." His hand closed possessively around her waist. Only then did he turn to the other women. "Ladies, thanks again for coming. You made the children very happy."

"We were glad to help," Priscilla said. "This is much better than the usual crummy decorations at the nurses' station. I guess the children were wishing, too."

Nicholas's expression didn't change at the mention of the word *wishing*. "Perhaps. Good night."

"Good-bye," they chorused, their expression speaking volumes to Andrea.

Blushing, Andrea said good-bye, then walked with Nicholas to the elevator. He hit the down button.

"You want to grab a bite to eat or tackle the tree first?"

"The tree." Weak as she was, she wanted to know as soon as possible if this time he'd kiss her.

Her palms were damp when she pulled up behind Nicholas's car in his driveway. For the first time they'd be completely alone. Her aunt had a meeting with the women's auxiliary of the church, then afterward they were having potluck at Auntie's house, so Andrea didn't have to worry about her aunt driving at night or being alone. She'd just have to worry about her feelings for Nicholas. She wanted to be with him, touching, laughing, sharing. She wanted to do all the things people in love did.

While she was still trying to calm her nerves, he got out of his car, then came back and opened her door. "This is it," he said, indicating the ranch-style home in a quiet residential neighborhood. "Are those the decorations in the backseat?"

She wiped her damp palms on her gray wool slacks. "Yes."

He handed her a ring of keys and picked up the box. "I usually go through the garage. You open the back door and I'll follow."

Gripping the keys, Andrea went through the tidy two-car garage and opened the door, then held it open for Nicholas. He brushed by her. She closed the door with a hand that wasn't quite steady. When she turned, he was watching her.

"You don't have to be afraid I'll jump you."

She wanted to say something urbane and sophisticated to let him know she was worried that he wouldn't, but the words wouldn't come. "I trust you."

He scowled. "Well, don't. Didn't you learn anything in New York? You're too gorgeous to trust any man."

He'd said it again. He thought she was gorgeous. Her insides went as gooey as cotton candy on a warm summer day.

"If you don't stop looking at me like that, the tree won't get decorated for a long time, if at all," he said, his voice husky.

A delicious little tingle raced over her. "Auntie will probably ask me how it went."

"Thought so." Turning, he went through the kitchen. In the living room, he knelt with the box in front of him, then reached out a hand to Andrea. "Come on and tell me the story behind what you've brought."

Placing her trembling hand in his, she felt the strength

and the zip of awareness that leaped from his fingertips to hers. Swallowing, she knelt down beside him and reached inside the box. Many of these Christmas decorations dated back over seventy years. Whether store-bought or hand-made, each carried a special story.

Unwrapping the thick tissue paper, she picked up the crystal icicle ornament. A rainbow of colors glinted in her hand. "Grandpa Radford walked five miles through a sudden ice storm to reach his wife. He had a feeling she needed him and he was right. She was in labor with their first child. He delivered the baby boy himself. It was a week before Christmas. He gave his wife the ornament to signify that he'd always be there for her and their children. Each Christmas he added another ornament."

"What about this?" Nicholas asked, unwrapping several miniature figures.

"My Great-grandpa Will carved those for his five children because they were too poor to buy real ones."

"I thought he was the town's blacksmith?" Nicholas asked, marveling at the details of the three horses and two dolls. The dolls wore gingham dresses and their feet had been painted black to appear as though they wore boots.

"He was, but the town was poor. They paid with produce or other goods." She picked up the foot-high doll and ran her finger over the face. "The story goes the children loved these. They could carry their gift wherever they went."

Nicholas couldn't imagine a child today accepting a carving for the real thing. His cousin's children wanted the real thing and lots of it. Each Christmas there was a hot new toy. His thumb grazed over the horse's mane. "Did the children ever get their real horse and dolls?"

Andrea smiled warmly. "They did."

"Good." He picked up the next carefully wrapped bundle. Inside were strands of star-shaped lights. He was momentarily speechless. "These belonged to your mother. She bought them after she and your father wished upon a shooting star for a child. You were that child." He'd never forget the sparkle of tears in Andrea's eyes when she'd unwrapped the lights at her house on Thanksgiving. Travis had whispered the story to him.

There were no tears now, just a sadness about her that tore at his heart. "Mama bought all the store had. She wanted to make sure there would still be lights when I had a child of my own."

A knot formed in his throat. "Honey." Setting the lights out of harm's way, he pulled her to him. "She sounds like a beautiful, caring woman."

"She was. So was Daddy," Andrea said softly. "The first Christmas without them was so painful. I went up into the attic and got the lights. I wished so hard that it was all a mistake. That it was a dream and I'd wake up. Auntie found me there."

His arms tightened around her. "You were so young to have so much taken from you."

She rubbed her cheek against his shirted chest. "But I have wonderful memories no one can ever take away, and I had Auntie and Uncle Richard. He's gone, too, but Auntie and I still laugh about the fish yarns he used to tell us about the one that got away." She laughed. "He once claimed he had to throw a catfish out of his fishing boat because it was so big the boat started sinking."

Nicholas laughed himself. "Sounds like my dad when he's talking about his golf game."

"Your family sounds nice."

"They'd adore you," he said.

Shadows came over her face again. Pushing away from him, she picked up the lights. "It's getting late; we'd better get the tree finished."

Helpless, Nicholas watched her kneel, then carefully wind the lights around the scrawny branches of the tree. He wanted so much for her to be happy. She deserved no less. It wasn't right that she wasn't. "You're sure you want me to have the lights?"

"They're meant to be enjoyed and to remind you that wishes do come true," she said softly.

He wanted to argue with her that there was no wish

woman out there waiting for him to fall in love with, but Andrea seemed so sad, so vulnerable. She'd had so much taken from her and yet she still went out of her way to help others. It angered him all over again to think that her wishes didn't count. That he didn't believe in wishes didn't seem to matter. Andrea did. "I hope you gave Melissa some of your qualities."

Her hands paused on reaching for the next set of lights. "She is a bit stubborn."

Nicholas shook his head, then began stringing the lights himself. "You're a pushover." He talked over her sputtering. "But you're loving, generous, compassionate, intelligent."

She picked up an icicle. "That's a backhanded compliment if I ever heard one, but Melissa is all that and more."

Nodding briskly, Nicholas spread the red felt skirt that had been a cousin's poodle skirt in the sixties. "You're sure Braxton is the man for her?"

"Unknowingly Melissa witnessed a hit. Bad guys are coming out of the woodwork, trying to kill her," she told him as she hung icicles. "Braxton is the only man tough enough, smart enough, to ensure that she sees another sunrise. They're both strong and independent. Each can give to the other what they've secretly longed for all their lives."

About to place the last wooden carving beneath the tree, Nicholas glanced up. "What's that?"

"Unconditional love that'll last a lifetime and beyond."

Nicholas studied the assurance in Andrea's face, the absolute conviction, for a long time. Then he placed the wooden doll beside the other carvings. Two weeks ago he would have laughed at such a statement, but somehow he couldn't with Andrea. "My parents have that kind of love, and so apparently did yours. I'm not sure that it exists anymore. My brother, Ronald, falls in love every other week."

"Perhaps because he hasn't met the right woman or, if he has, he isn't ready to take the next step. Loving a person makes you vulnerable." She began gathering up the tissue paper. "In *A Risk Worth Taking* the dangers are emotional as well as physical."

"My point exactly. Falling in love is dangerous."

"Living with no hope of love is one of the saddest things I can imagine." She picked up the box and stood before he could help her. "The tree is finished. I have to go. Good night, Nicholas."

Shocked, he scrambled to his feet. "I thought we were going out to dinner?"

"Perhaps some other time." She started from the room.

He caught her arms and saw the pain in her dark eyes and cursed himself. He'd caused that. "You can't leave until you see how the tree looks. Won't Mrs. Augusta ask?"

"All right." Her fingers gripping the corner of the box, she faced the tree.

"Let me take the box and if the lights need any adjustment, you'd do a better job than I could." He breathed easier as he took the box from her, then set it by the light switch and cut off the light.

He didn't even glance toward the tree. His entire concentration was on Andrea standing in the soft glow of lights that her mother had bought while thinking of her. He went to stand just behind her. "I have a confession to make."

"What?" she said, a whispered strain of sound.

"I got you over here under false pretenses. I fully planned to buy a tree and decorate it. I played on your goodness, but if I'd known it would make you so sad I wouldn't have done it." His hand rested lightly on her shoulder; he felt the shudder that swept though her. "Please believe me when I tell you that it never entered my mind that you'd bring your mother's lights. Forgive me."

Andrea momentarily closed her eyes, absorbing the heat seeping through her sweater from Nicholas's strong hand, from his powerful body next to hers. "That's not the reason."

He stepped in front of her. "Then what is?"

How could she explain her jumbled feelings when she was still trying to understand them herself? She wanted him to find love, to be happy, but she wanted that woman to be her. But he didn't even believe in love or happily ever after.

"Andrea?" He lifted her chin. "Tell me how I can help."

For the moment there was only one way. "Kiss me."

He took her in his arms, his mouth brushing across hers, letting the heat, the anticipation, the hunger build. When his mouth finally took possession of hers, both were trembling. With a whimper of pure, unadulterated need, Andrea joined in the kiss, experiencing once again the passion that burned fiercely within her for this man.

It was a long time before he ended the kiss and pulled her to him. Their fractured breathing sounded loud in the room. "You'll never know how much I wanted to do that." His mouth brushed against the top of her head. "I wasn't sure how much longer I could keep my hands off you."

She refused to listen to the little voice that warned he'd never be hers. In his arms she could only think of him; out of his arms she only longed to be there once again. "But did you have to choose such a pitiful tree in order to get me over here?"

He gave her another quick kiss, then turned so they both faced the little tree in the bay window. "I kind of like it."

After a moment she said, "Me, too."

He palmed her forehead. "You don't feel like you have a fever," he joked.

She laughed. "I just remembered a cartoon I watched as a child, about misfit toys and how nobody wanted them. It made me feel so sad. If you hadn't bought the tree, it might have stayed in the lot. Now, it's almost beautiful with the star-shaped lights sparkling off the glass icicles." And she liked the idea of them sharing the decorations. It made her feel connected to him.

"Will wonders never cease? A woman who admits when she's wrong," Nicholas teased.

"That's because it so seldom happens," she said with a lift of her brow.

He chuckled, hugging her to him. "It's going to be very interesting getting to know you better."

"You can count on it," Andrea said, hugging him back. What will be will be. "What should we do next?"

Make love to each other until we're too weak to move.

Before the thought had completely formed, he knew he wouldn't follow through with the rest of his reason for getting her to his house. Not with them standing in the glow of years of family tradition where intimacy meant love and lifelong commitment. Not with Andrea staring up at him with such complete trust.

An idiot could see she longed for the same thing in her own life. He wasn't ready for that type of commitment. He wasn't sure if he'd ever be. She'd been denied too much for him to carelessly take more. He wasn't taking her dream. "Why don't we go outside and see how the tree looks through the window, then go out to dinner?"

"I'd like that."

Chapter 8

In the past Nicholas never had any difficulty remaining focused. Like his father, he was very detail-oriented. At least he had been until he'd met Andrea. In the three weeks since Thanksgiving, they'd seen each other almost every day. He'd catch himself thinking about her instead of working. *Like now.*

Twisting in his seat in his office, Nicholas leaned closer to the computer monitor as if that would help his concentration. He'd been working on a report for three hours, a report that usually took one hour to do. But it was difficult to think about operating costs when he'd much rather be thinking about Andrea or, better yet, be with her. But that was creating its own problem.

He scrubbed his face. He wanted her so badly, he ached. He couldn't hide his need from her, and although he knew she wasn't experienced and still thought there was another woman out there for him, she never pulled back. That kind of trust and caring made his body ache and his spirit smile.

He lifted his face to the ceiling. "Spirit smile," he muttered. What kind of thing was that for a man to say? His phone rang and he pounced on it, ready for any distraction. "Yes?"

"Mr. Darling, you're needed on Pedi South," Michelle told him.

Nicholas frowned. "I don't have a meeting, do I?"

"No, but I think you should go up there."

Nicholas transferred the phone to his left hand and began hitting keys with his right. "Michelle, I'm in the middle of the report—"

"Andrea is up there."

He shot up from his chair before he realized that if she'd been hurt, she wouldn't be on the pediatric floor. "Why? What's going on?"

"I guess you won't find out, since you're so busy with the report. Sorry to disturb you."

Nicholas held a dead phone. In a matter of seconds he was standing before Michelle, his hands planted firmly on her desk. "Talk."

"You'll understand when you get there." Michelle placed the calendar she kept for him by his hands. "Your next appointment isn't for another hour."

How much he wanted to go didn't surprise him. But if he saw Andrea, he'd experience the same churning need that kept him awake at night. Andrea or her aunt might be fooled, but not the hospital staff. "I really need to finish that report," he said, with little conviction in his voice.

"Wouldn't you rather see Andrea?" Michelle asked.

He started to ask how she knew Andrea was in the hospital, then recalled that Michelle had an open pipeline to all the gossip in the hospital. Women no longer bothered him, but many of them were acquainted with Andrea. "I'll be on Pedi South, if you need me."

All the way to the floor, he kept telling himself that he was simply going to say hello. It would appear strange if he didn't. She was probably reading one of the books she'd illustrated to the children.

With that thought in mind he wasn't surprised when, without asking, he was directed by several staff members to the atrium at the end of the hall. Entering the sunshine-filled room, he immediately spotted Andrea. She didn't have a book; she had a sketch pad.

Sitting in front of the lit Christmas tree was a little girl of about five in a wheelchair. She was precious, with huge

chocolate eyes and a smile that was as bright as the sparkling lights behind her. One arm was wrapped securely
around a bedraggled doll; the other was connected to an
IV. As Andrea's hand moved swiftly across the page she
chatted with the child.

"She came to read, but when one of the nurses mentioned that Andrea drew the pictures in the books, the children wanted their pictures drawn," said Nurse Cipriano
from beside Nicholas. "She's been at it for almost three
hours. I called Michelle. I thought Andrea should take a
break."

"What's wrong with the little girl?"

"Juvenile diabetes," Nurse Cipriano said. "Barnarda is
one of the lucky ones. She'll be home for Christmas. But
for those who can't leave even on a pass, you've helped.
So has Andrea. The children want the sketches to give to
their parents."

He watched Andrea leave her chair with the pad, then
kneel beside the child to show her the drawing. The child's
eyes rounded. With a squeal of delight, she wrapped her
free arm around Andrea's neck. Andrea gently hugged her
back.

The nurse sniffed. "You've got a good woman there, Mr.
Darling."

"I know." He walked over and hunkered down. "Hello,
Barnarda, Andrea."

Andrea looked at Nicholas, inches from her, and accepted that he'd always make her heart ache a little bit.
"Hello, Nicholas. Barnarda, meet Mr. Darling; he helps run
the hospital."

"You want to see my picture?" the little girl asked, already turning it around. "Andrea drew it, just like I asked."

Nicholas looked at the picture of smiling Barnarda in a
tree swing, her doll in her lap. "It's beautiful."

The little girl nodded, then turned to Andrea, a frown
stealing over her plump face. "You won't forget, will you?"

"No, sweetheart." Andrea brushed her hand over the

child's curly hair. "I'll have it framed and get it back to you."

"Time to go, Barnarda." Nurse Cipriano came up and grasped the handles of the wheelchair.

"Bye, Andrea." The child's face scrunched up as she looked at Nicholas; then she smiled. "Good-bye, Mr. Man."

Nicholas smiled. "Good-bye." He helped Andrea to her feet as the nurse rolled the child away. "You've made a lot of sick children happy. Thank you."

"Christmas is a time for children, a time for dreams and wishes to come true," she said without thought. Then she went still, expecting to see irritation replace his smile as it always did when the word *wish* was mentioned.

His expression didn't change, but his eyes did. They narrowed and burned with an intensity that caused her to shiver.

He stepped closer until they touched from chest to knees. His other hand caught her arm. "Guess what I dream about?"

She didn't have to guess. Too many mornings she'd awakened restless and aching. Her lips parted.

"There you are!"

The irritating voice broke the spell. Andrea jumped. Nicholas cursed, then wanted to curse again when he saw Ferrell. Despite the interested eyes of the two staff members who'd just brought a group of children to the atrium, Nicholas slid his arm around Andrea, anchoring her to his side.

"Yes," Nicholas said in a clipped voice.

The other man's eyes stayed on Andrea. "I wanted to ask if you needed any more volunteers."

"No."

"Perhaps I could help you, Andrea," Ferrell said with a winning smile. "I've heard you plan to have all the pictures framed. I'd be happy to help you financially and with anything else you might need."

"I—"

"She won't need your help, Ferrell," Nicholas said. "Now, if you'll excuse us, we're about to go to lunch."

Ferrell's face hardened. "Why don't you let Andrea decide if she needs my help or not?"

Nicholas had the urge to punch Ferrell in the nose for even daring to say Andrea's name. "Tell him."

Andrea was caught between being flattered and wanting to hit Nicholas over the head with her sketch pad for acting like a Neanderthal. "If I don't, are you going to drag me off by the hair?"

Ferrell hooted. "She told you."

Nicholas's body stiffened. His arm fell from around her waist. "My mistake."

"We can discuss everything over lunch, then dinner tonight," Ferrell suggested smoothly.

She would have to be stupid to think that's all he had in mind. "Thank you for your offer of a financial contribution, Dr. Ferrell. Since Nicholas is the unofficial chairman, you can give him the check. If I need any additional help, I'm sure Nicholas will be there to assist me." She slid her arm through his rigid one. "Please excuse us. As Nicholas said, we were about to go to lunch."

She could have been walking beside a mannequin. Nicholas was stiff and unsmiling as they went down the hall, then boarded the elevator. She punched 1 for the parking lot. He punched 2. Hospital employees in the enclosure took one look at Nicholas's face, then busied themselves elsewhere.

The elevator doors slid open on 2. She didn't even think of disregarding the firm pressure of his hand urging her off. At Michelle's questioning look, Andrea sent a wan smile. He didn't stop until he was inside his office.

She took consolation that he hadn't slammed the door and was preparing to state her case when his mouth crashed down on hers. The kiss was hot and greedy, flaring to life the second their lips touched. There was also need and desperation.

Andrea dived into the kiss, giving, reassuring. Whatever it was he needed from her she'd gladly give. Eagerly she leaned into him, heard his hoarse groan of pleasure. Boldly his hands cupped her hips against his hard arousal. Her tongue stroked his as he stroked her.

The world tilted. By the time she realized he'd picked her up, she was flat on her back on the leather sofa in his office, his hard body above her. Uncertainty swept though her. "Nicholas?"

His head came up, his eyes dark and intense for a long moment; then he shut his eyes and sat up, his face in his hands. Andrea didn't move for a long time, then tentatively touched his tense shoulder. He flinched.

She drew her hand back. She wanted to comfort him but didn't know how. "Nicholas?"

"I'm sorry. I don't know what came over me." He glanced over his shoulder at her propped up on one elbow, her hair mussed, her lips swollen from his kisses, and wanted to drag her back in his arms. He surged to his feet. "I have no excuse."

"Since I was eagerly participating, I don't expect any." She slid her legs over the leather cushion and sat upright.

His hands clenched and unclenched by his sides. "You have every right to see whoever you want."

"Not if your plan is going to work." Coming to her feet, she went to stand in front of him. "I spoke up for myself, so there won't be any doubt."

Her answer didn't appease him. What would happen once the need for the charade was over? His gut twisted.

Not wanting to think about it, he bent to pick her sketch pad up from the floor, then handed it to her. "Getting these framed will cost a lot of money. Why don't you ask the hospital auxiliary to help you?"

"I've already spoken with Mrs. Ricks, the president, and she's agreed to help." Andrea tucked the tablet beneath her arm. "You ready to feed me so I can go back upstairs and finish?"

Frowning, he rezipped her sweater-coat, then fingered her hair. She looked like a woman who'd been thoroughly kissed and enjoyed herself immensely. While it gratified him and he didn't care what people said about him, he didn't want her to be the topic of hospital gossip. "Maybe you should go into the bathroom and freshen up."

She handed him the pad, then went into the room he'd indicated to apply lipstick and comb her hair. "How do I look?" she asked when she came out.

"Tempting." He grabbed her arm. "Let's get out of here before I have to apologize all over again."

Nicholas barely touched his meat loaf. If one person came over to their table in the hospital cafeteria to say hello to Andrea or mention the sketches, fifteen came. She never seemed to mind that her hamburger was getting cold, her strawberry malt getting warm. She was heaped with praise and hugs. Almost every person who stopped by asked her to give their regards to her aunt. Clearly, both women were loved and respected in Jubilee.

That irrefutable fact caused Nicholas a bit of uneasiness. How would the townspeople react when there wasn't an engagement? Christmas was a little over a week away. Not even his impetuous brother would become engaged to a woman he'd never met before in such a short time.

Hours later Nicholas was still mulling over the situation when he knocked on Andrea's door. He didn't have an answer, but he was going to make darn sure people knew he thought she was special.

"Nicholas, come in," Andrea said as she opened the door. Her eyes and face lit up at the sight of him.

"Get your coat and come outside," he said. Andrea started out of the door, but he blocked her path. "Coat and gloves first. Your scarf, too."

"Andrea, do as your guest says," Aunt Augusta told her. "Good evening, Nicholas. You want to come inside?"

"No, thank you. I'll just wait here for Andrea."

"I'll be back in a minute." She rushed down the hall.

Nicholas shifted restlessly. He liked Augusta, but lately he got the feeling she saw right through him. Considering what he'd done with Andrea and what he'd like to do *to* her, he guessed Augusta had a right to make him nervous. "Nice weather we're having."

"Very nice," she replied.

"Think we'll have a white Christmas?"

"A little snow Christmas Eve, but it won't stick or stop a man in love from doing what has to be done."

Nicholas blinked and snapped his attention back to her. "What?"

Augusta simply smiled, then stepped back for Andrea, who was putting on her gloves as she raced down the hall. "Have fun and tell Larry to drive carefully."

Nicholas's mouth literally dropped open, but then Andrea was there and he couldn't ask her aunt how she'd known who was outside.

"I'm ready. What's up?"

Mentally shaking himself, Nicholas led her onto the porch. "I'd thought we'd view the Christmas lights around town the old-fashioned way."

Andrea followed the direction of his gaze and squealed with delight. Grabbing his hand, she raced toward the horse-drawn open carriage that Larry Adair rented out for weddings and other special occasions.

Helping Andrea inside, Nicholas climbed up and sat beside her, still puzzled until he saw what he'd forgotten. From the living room you could see the road. Obviously Augusta had been looking out the window and had seen them pull up. Chiding himself for his overactive imagination, Nicholas tucked the blanket around Andrea's knees. "Let's go, Larry, and Mrs. Augusta said to tell you to drive carefully."

"Sure enough, Mr. Darling. Mrs. Augusta might do good with her gift, but that might change if a man harms Miss Andrea."

Laughing softly, Andrea shook her head. "Mr. Adair, shame on you. You know Auntie has never harmed a soul."

"That don't mean she won't," Larry said with an emphatic nod of his black top hat.

The disquiet Nicholas had experienced earlier returned.

Frowning, he glanced toward the living room window. Then Andrea snuggled closer and laid her head on his shoulder. Curving his arms around her shoulders, he forgot everything but how good it felt for her to be in his arms again.

Barely three days later he regretted that lapse.

Five days before Christmas, Nicholas knocked on Andrea's door and received no answer. He'd seen her earlier when she and a couple of volunteers had delivered the children's framed and wrapped portraits. The staff on the floor, Andrea, and the two women volunteers had all cried.

He knocked again. Since both cars were in the garage, he had a pretty good idea of where he'd find Andrea. He came off the porch.

Rounding the corner of the house, he saw her beneath the huge maple tree, but she was neither writing nor sketching. She was crying. His heart in his throat, he raced to her. "What's the matter? What is it?"

Andrea sniffed. "I just finished *A Risk Worth Taking*. Braxton finally learned that no risk is too great to keep the woman he loves by his side. They made it, Nicholas."

He bent to kiss the tears away from her eyes, her cheeks, the corner of her mouth, then her mouth. They ended up stretched out on the grass. He had just enough presence of mind to keep his hand from wandering. "Congratulations."

"Thank you."

"What are you two celebrating?" Augusta said from less than five feet away.

Nicholas shot to his feet, dragging Andrea with him. He opened his mouth to apologize, then noticed Augusta was smiling. It was the same smile he'd seen when she granted him his wish. He began to tremble.

"No," he whispered. "It can't be."

"Your wish has come true, Nicholas," Augusta told him.

A whimper of pain came from Andrea. She closed her eyes. She'd lost him.

Nicholas grabbed both of Andrea's arms. Black eyes blazed. "Did you know?" he shouted.

"Know what?" she questioned, frowning.

His mouth tightened into a thin line before he said, "That you're my wish woman."

Chapter 9

"I can't be," Andrea said, regret in her voice. She looked at her aunt. "Tell him."

"Perhaps we should go inside and discuss this," Augusta said calmly.

"We'll discuss it now." Nicholas stepped away from Andrea. "All I want to know is were you in on this? Did you know?"

Andrea glanced from her aunt to Nicholas, the enormity of what was going on finally sinking in. She was to be Nicholas's. She swayed. Nicholas reached out to steady her, but when she reached toward him, he stepped back. His cold gaze sliced through her.

"I didn't know." She spoke to her aunt: "Is . . . is it true?"

Augusta smiled. "Didn't I tell you what will be will be?"

Andrea shook her head. "I . . . I thought you meant his wish."

Her aunt laid her hand gently on Andrea's arm. "And your unspoken wish. When the dream came to me of you and Nicholas together, I wept with happiness. After all these years of having the gift, I'd finally be able to bring happiness to a member of my own family."

The women hugged each other. "Oh, Auntie! I can't believe it." Smiling, Andrea turned to Nicholas. His face remained cold. Then she remembered he didn't believe in love, didn't want it. Tears sparkled in her eyes.

"Ma'am, you really pulled one over on me," he said tightly. "I was a fool not to realize that you'd never condone Andrea going out with me if you thought there was another woman out there for me. But your little plan failed."

Augusta silently studied him for a long moment. "You mean you don't care about my niece? That you wouldn't do anything to keep her from the slightest harm? That you wouldn't put her needs before your own?"

Nicholas's eyes widened. Her words were too close to things he'd thought and felt. "You keep forgetting. I wished for my brother, not me."

"Then," she said with a nod. "But how about when you were growing up? When you were a little boy in Akron? Before your friends started having marital problems?" she asked.

He ignored the chill that raced over him, refusing to believe. Andrea had told Augusta he was from Akron. She just had a lucky guess about the rest. "I'm leaving."

Augusta wasn't finished with him. "Once a wish is granted, I'm not allowed to interfere. But I should tell you that if you keep on running from the truth and refusing to believe, it may be taken away from you."

Andrea gasped. Nicholas's knees almost buckled. "Nothing will happen to Andrea."

Augusta shook her head. "Andrea will find happiness. If not with you, then with another. Is that what you want?"

For Nicholas, even the wind stopped blowing. It was as if nature and time stood still, listening, waiting for him to speak. He wanted to scoff at Augusta's words but couldn't. Neither could he look at Andrea. Just the thought of any man touching her enraged him, but there was no such thing as a person being able to grant wishes or see the future. Turning, he walked away.

Behind him, Andrea wept in her aunt's arms. "Auntie, what am I going to do? I love him so."

"I'm afraid there's nothing you can do. Nicholas has to decide."

Brushing away tears, Andrea lifted her head. "What if he can't?"

"He'll lose and so, my precious darling, will you."

The hospital's grapevine was running true to form. Less than two days after Nicholas stopped seeing Andrea, his name was back on the wish list. But women weren't chasing after him as they had before. In fact, people in general left him alone. That was fine with him. He needed to get things in shape before he went to Philadelphia for the holidays. There was nothing to keep him in Jubilee. He was flying out early Christmas morning. But first he had to attend the Christmas Eve party at the hospital.

Straightening his tie, he jerked his jacket from the bed and headed out the door, reminding himself that he needed to ask the housekeeper to take down the tree. It wasn't cowardly not to do it himself; he simply didn't have time.

"Are you just going to give up?" Elaine asked, sitting beside Andrea in the middle of her living room floor.

"If he's what you want, go after him. Or I could beat him up for you," Travis offered.

"I'll help," said Clint.

"Me, too," agreed John.

Andrea blinked away the tears that were never far since Nicholas had walked out of her life. "I told you, he has to make the decision on his own."

"Pleeazze." Elaine waved her slender manicured hand. "Since when has a man been able to come to a decision without the help of a woman?"

Her comment garnered the expected howls of disagreement from the men. Travis was the loudest. "Since when has a woman been able to come to a decision, period?"

He and Elaine went nose to nose, then lip to lip. Elaine slipped her arm around his neck and deepened the kiss.

Andrea sniffed. She couldn't be happier for her friends.
Tears rolled down her cheek.

"Stop that! You're making Andrea cry," Clint said,
snatching a tissue from the box on the coffee table.

"I'm sorry," Andrea said. "Don't mind me."

"You want us to go and beat him up?" John asked.

"I don't think that would help, fellas." Elaine sat down
beside her again. "You really love him, don't you?"

"More than I ever thought possible."

"Then why are you sitting here?" Coming to her feet,
Elaine pulled Andrea up. "When we get through with you,
Nick will be drooling."

"But will he accept his wish?"

"There's a sure way to find out."

The Bluebonnet Ballroom of the hotel was jumping. People
in the medical profession worked hard and partied harder.
They, better than most, knew how fragile life could be. The
only person not having a good time was Nicholas. Arms
folded, he sat in the back of the festive room in gold and
white. Unlike the many people on the parquet dance floor
doing the Electric Slide, the live music of the band didn't
move him at all.

He'd planned on putting in an obligatory appearance,
then leaving. Beverly Hawkins had insisted he stay. He was
fully prepared to ignore her request until her husband and
the other board members started talking about it being good
for morale. He'd give it another five minutes; then he
was—

His arms unfolded. He was unaware of coming to his
feet.

Andrea stared hungrily at Nicholas, but when she started
toward him he sat back down. Her hands clenched inside
the deep burgundy velvet cloak that matched her long dress.
He looked as miserable as she felt. "I never wanted him to
be unhappy."

None of her friends said anything, just stepped closer,
giving her moral and emotional support. Andrea didn't no-

tice them or that she and Nicholas had become the center of attention. If his caring for her made him that unhappy, she didn't want it for him.

She went to the table where Delores, Eula, and Rachel were selling wish tickets. "May I buy one?"

"I'm sorry, Andrea, but it's for hospital employees only," Delores said, her regret obvious.

"Can't an exception be made?" Elaine asked. "This is important to her."

Beverly Hawkins strolled up to the table, bringing her husband with her. "I'd like to purchase some tickets. How many do you think I'll need, Andrea?"

"I have to buy them myself," she said.

"Sell her the tickets," Bob Hawkins said. "After what she did for the children, I can't see anyone objecting. But if they do, send them to me."

"Yes, sir. How many?" Delores picked up the pad of printed tickets.

"All of them," Andrea said. "I intend to win."

Nicholas had tried to act as if he didn't care that Andrea was there, but he couldn't take his eyes off her. When she'd stopped at the table where the women were selling the wish registration tickets, he couldn't quite believe it. Andrea hadn't made a wish since her parents died.

He knew that with bone-chilling certainty. Then what was she wishing for? *Me.* He came out of his chair to cross the room. People parted. All except her friends. "Move out of the way."

"It's all right." Andrea turned the pad she'd been writing on over.

Nicholas glanced at the back of the pad, then at her. "It won't do you any good. Even if they pull my name, I don't believe in wishes."

"I know, but you'll be free." Getting up, she went to the table and gave Delores the tickets. She didn't even glance at him as she went to the other side of the room. Her friends gathered around her.

Nicholas heard the drumroll, then a call for silence. He stared at Andrea and felt unease scuttle down his spine. Out of nowhere he heard Mrs. Augusta's voice: *If you keep on running from the truth, refusing to believe, it may be taken away from you.*

That was nonsense. A person couldn't grant wishes.

"This is the moment we've all waited for." Delores spun the metal drum. "The winning ticket will receive half of the money made through sales to make their wish come true, and the remaining half will go to charity. Good luck." She stopped the tumble of papers. "Mr. Hawkins will draw."

Bob Hawkins reached inside. Nicholas watched tears roll down Andrea's cheek, saw her mouth, *Good-bye.* It clicked all at once. She hadn't tried to trap him. Her wish had been to set him free.

Even as Nicholas shook his head in denial, he heard Bob Hawkins speak: "Well, I'll be. The winning ticket belongs to Nicholas Darling."

The more she swiped, the more tears fell. Nicholas was lost to her forever. Curled up on the sofa, she didn't move when she heard an impatient knock on the front door. "Please tell them I just want to be alone." As soon as Elaine had stopped her parents' car, Andrea had gotten out and forbidden them to follow. It had started to snow and she didn't want them on the roads.

"Andrea."

Her head came up. Nicholas stood in the doorway, snowflakes sprinkled over his black topcoat. "Don't cry. Please don't cry. It took me a long time, but I love you. I love you."

She leaped from the couch. He caught her, lifting her against his wide chest. "I love you. I love you," he repeated over and over.

"But what did you wish for?" she asked.

He drew the winning ticket out of his pocket and handed it to her. "That you'd be able to stay in Jubilee, and that you'd find a man who'd love you through all time."

Her eyes misted again, this time with happiness. "Nicholas."

He drew her into his arms again. "I bought the ticket on impulse after we started going out. I admired you so and wanted you to be happy, even if I wasn't that man."

She grinned up at him. "Did you really?"

"Yes . . . after I broke him into little pieces."

She kissed him. "My hero."

"Finally. Like Braxton, I learned no risk is too great to keep the woman you love by your side. We'll have our happily ever after. Will you marry me?"

"Yes, oh, yes."

In the hallway, Augusta smiled, remembering the dream she'd had the night before. Nicholas and Andrea were decorating their Christmas tree in this very house with the added tradition of snowflake ornaments while their four happy children helped.

On the coffee table were several published books by Andrea. Among them was a hardcover copy of *A Risk Worth Taking*. Nicholas and Andrea had taken a risk and had been rewarded with a lifetime of happiness.

And it had all started with a wish.

Homecoming
BY BEVERLY JENKINS

Chapter 1

Detroit, Michigan
December 1883

The December afternoon was so cold and windy that by the time Lydia Cooper made it up the steps to the boardinghouse where she planned to spend the night, she was freezing inside her thick wool cloak. The train ride from Chicago to Detroit had been exhausting. Due to the snowy weather, all of the scheduled stops had been late. To make matters worse, she and the rest of the passengers had ridden the long stretch from Kalamazoo to the Detroit depot being tortured by the ear-piercing screams of a howling infant. Setting aside her personal woes for now, Lydia gave the hack driver a tip for bringing her trunks to the boardinghouse's porch. He departed with a smile and a touch of his hat.

In answer to Lydia's knock upon the door, a tiny elderly woman appeared. The warm smile on her aged brown face made Lydia feel instantly welcomed.

"Good afternoon," Lydia said. "The driver said you let rooms?"

"I do, miss." The woman stepped back and beckoned. "Come in out of that wind. You look like you've come a long way."

Lydia brought in her trunks, and the woman closed the door. The shivering Lydia glanced around the front room with its well-worn furniture and replied, "I have. From Chicago."

"That is a piece," the woman remarked. "How long you staying?"

"Just the night. I'm going on to Sumpter in the morning."

"Is that home?"

Lydia took off her gloves, then nodded. "Yes, ma'am."

"Well, my name's Shirley Harrison."

"Pleased to meet you, Mrs. Harrison. I'm Lydia Cooper."

"Pleased to have you."

Mrs. Harrison led Lydia up a short flight of stairs, then down a short hallway. Lydia wondered if the two rooms they passed held other boarders, but her curiosity fled when Mrs. Harrison ushered her into the room on the end. Inside, Mrs. Harrison opened the plain brown drapes on the lone window. The last pale light of the late December afternoon filtered in. The room was sparsely furnished but clean. The space held a bed with a flowered quilt. Beneath the window were a chair and a slightly lopsided writing desk. A large armoire made up the last of the furnishings.

Mrs. Harrison asked, "Will this do you?"

Lydia could already feel herself starting to relax. "Yes, it will. How much?"

"Thirty cents if you want dinner tonight, too."

"I do." Lydia fished around in her handbag for her coin purse, then handed over what she owed.

Mrs. Harrison walked to the door. "Dinner's at seven. Bathing room's down the hall. You want me to heat you some water for a bath?"

"That would be a blessing."

Mrs. Harrison nodded, pleased. "I'll let you know when it's ready." Then she was gone, closing the door behind her.

Lydia dropped tiredly onto the bed. It had been a long, long day. Had she the strength, she would have just gone on to her small hometown of Sumpter, but she couldn't see traveling another thirty miles, not tonight. Tomorrow would be soon enough. Christmas was in a little over a week, and for the first time in four years she'd be spending the holy time with her mother, Miriam. Lydia was the headmistress of a private school for young women of color, and she was usually obliged to spend the holidays at school in order to chaperon the two or three young women without families or to cheer up the girls with parents who were traveling or too busy to include them in their lives. This year, however, she had made arrangements far in advance for a few of the local families to take in the girls needing sheltering. Miriam had recently broken her ankle. Her letters assured Lydia that it was nothing serious, but Lydia needed to see that with her own eyes. She and her mother had been through a lot over the years, and Lydia wanted Miriam to remain a force in her life for as long as the Good Lord was willing. Lydia had also come home to lick her wounds. Her engagement to Burton Shaw had ended abruptly six months ago and she hoped this short visit home would revive her lagging spirits.

Lydia undid the ribbon tie at the throat of her cloak and set the damp garment over the back of the lone chair. Her first order of business would be to start a fire in the grate. The December chill had invaded the room. Blowing on her cold hands, Lydia grabbed two logs from the box beside the fireplace and set them inside. A few strikes of the matches started a small blaze. It began to lick its way over the wood, and soon the flames grew in strength. Satisfied, she went to her trunks to unpack some clean clothes for dinner.

Once Lydia had her bath, her world seemed brighter. She donned a fresh high-collared brown dress, brushed her hair and redid her bun, then went downstairs to see about the meal. She had no idea if there were other boarders about but assumed that if there were, they'd all be dining together, as was customary in such establishments.

She was just about to enter the small dining room when the sight of the tall dark-skinned man standing near the table talking with Mrs. Harrison froze Lydia in place. For a moment the shock of seeing Grayson Dane again after so many years was so overwhelming, her knees went weak.

What is he doing here?

Although she hadn't seen him in fifteen years, there was no mistaking him. The fabled good looks had aged like a statue—gracefully, majestically. He had a mustache now, something he hadn't had when she knew him before, and it added a dangerous edge to his chiseled features. The fit of the well-tailored dark suit showed him to be a bit thicker through the chest and shoulders than he'd been as a youth, but because of his height it made him appear even more commanding. Memories of her love for him rushed back with such sweet pain, she lost herself in its eddies for a moment. Lydia knew the wisest course would be to beat a hasty retreat back to her room before he noticed her, but the thought came too late; he'd turned her way.

Gray Dane stared at the woman in the brown dress standing in the doorway, and her familiar face caused his eyes to widen with shock. *Lydia?* His breath caught in his chest and his hands began to shake. *Lydia Cooper? My God! Where did she come from?*

A thousand questions shouted in his mind at once, but he was so stunned by the sight of her, he couldn't form words.

Mrs. Harrison beckoned Lydia into the room, then said to Gray, "Mr. Dane, this is the young woman I spoke to you about."

Still unable to believe what he was seeing, Gray said to Mrs. Harrison, "The lady and I are acquainted." *How could she be here?* Forcing himself to calm down, Gray managed to say evenly, "It's been a long time, Lydia. How are you?"

Lydia met his familiar dark eyes, and bittersweet memories rose from her heart. "I'm doing well, Gray. And yourself?"

For Gray, seeing her again was like finding water after a trek through the drought-stricken Texas badlands. "I'm well."

Lydia understood his surprise all too well; she, too, had been caught off guard by seeing him here. This was a decidedly awkward meeting, to say the least. Because of their shared past, she once again wanted to turn and hightail it back to her room; however, she reminded herself that she was no longer sixteen and in love with him. She could handle this.

Mrs. Harrison, unaware of the subtle currents flowing between her boarders, said cheerily, "Well, since the two of you are already acquainted, why don't you take a seat and catch up on old times? I'll bring out the food directly."

Lydia had no desire to catch up on old times, especially with Gray, but rather than decline and appear waspish, she said, "Thank you, Mrs. Harrison."

After the landlady's departure, Gray and Lydia were left alone. Their eyes met for a long moment. They were both aware of what stood between them, as well as what they'd once shared. Gray wanted to reach out and caress her cheek. He wanted to ease her into his arms, hold her close, and whisper to her how very sorry he was for what he'd done to her and to their love. However, such fantasies were the stuff of dime novels; reconciling with her wouldn't be easily accomplished, even if she was open to reconciliation—which he tended to doubt. In reality, Gray was just glad to see her. Keeping that in mind, he gestured her over to the table.

Lydia walked past him with a continued confidence in her ability to handle this evening. From the letters she'd received from her mother, Lydia knew Gray had moved back to the area a few years ago and that by coming home she stood a good chance of encountering him. And now she had. She told herself that the passage of time had dulled her heart to the love she once had for him and to the pain he'd caused her as well. She was over Gray.

When Lydia reached the table and took her seat, he politely helped her with her chair, but she was unprepared for the heat of his nearness. It had been a lifetime since he'd touched or kissed her, but the woman in her reacted as if it had been but yesterday. Blaming it on her fatigue and the shock of seeing him again, she set her unsettling reaction aside, all the while chastising herself for letting anything about him affect her.

Savoring the faint lingering scent of her perfume, Gray stepped away from her chair and sat in one of the chairs on the opposite side of the table. Honeysuckle. She met his gaze for a second, then slowly looked away. He wasn't offended. In truth, he'd earned her disdain, so he used the opportunity to observe her profile more fully. He still found it hard to fathom her being here. On a beautiful June day back in '68, Lydia Cooper had disappeared from his life as if she'd never been born, and tonight she'd walked back into it like a specter. Had she married? He saw no rings on her slim brown fingers, but he knew that to be no true indication. Many married women wore no ring. Had another man claimed her heart, the heart that had once been his own? That the answer might be yes did not sit well with Gray, even though he knew he'd tossed away the right to have any say in her life fifteen years ago.

Mrs. Harrison returned, bringing with her a roast chicken, vegetables, and corn bread. She set the tray of dishes down on the table, then with a departing smile withdrew to the kitchen once again.

Gray looked at the small bounty and his stomach reminded him that he hadn't eaten since leaving Chatham, Ontario, early this morning. He hoped the food tasted as good as it looked. "Shall I carve?" he asked the still-silent Lydia.

"Please."

Gray and Lydia had grown up together and over the years had shared many things, including chicken dinners at their small local church. "Pass me your plate."

She did.

Without thinking about the task, Gray cut her the part of the bird she'd always favored in the past: the wing, with a slice of the breast attached. Only after he'd placed the meat on the plate did they both realize the significance of his unconscious act. His remembering what pleased her spoke of a familiarity Lydia didn't want to acknowledge, but it affected her nonetheless. Shaken, she looked away from his vibrant eyes. She added vegetables and bread to her plate and hoped he didn't notice how her hands trembled.

Gray did notice, and it made him wonder if the trembling stemmed from nerves or anger. He was too much of a realist to think it might be because she was not as unmoved by his presence as she would have him believe. To believe that was nothing more than wishful thinking. After the way he'd treated her, if she chose to anoint his head with the contents of the gravy boat, it would only be what he deserved. That reality saddened him in many ways, because he'd never forgotten her.

Lydia began to eat. The food was excellently prepared, but she was unable to savor it the way she wanted because her appetite was being blunted by a disturbing truth: somewhere beneath the ashes that had once been her heart, an old ember still glowed. Once upon a time her love for Gray had burned day and night. Now the tiny ember was all that remained. Even though she told herself a snowball in hell stood a better chance, she could feel the ember struggling to glow bright again. After all, how does a woman forget the first boy to hold her hand or the one who on a moonlit night took her behind his parents' barn and taught her to waltz? Added to that was the fact that Grayson Dane was still an astoundingly handsome man. From the dark eyes, to the square jaw, to the full and, yes, sensual lips, he was the man of a woman's dreams. He was also a free man again. According to her mother's letters, he'd been free to remarry for many years now. Anna Mae Dexter had been the cause of the rift that now yawned like a canyon between Lydia and Gray. Fifteen years ago, Anna Mae's claim that Gray had fathered Anna Mae's unborn child hit Lydia in her heart like a cold bucket of water in the face.

But Anna Mae and Gray were no longer married. Were Lydia so inclined, it would be very easy to pick up where

she and Gray had left off and start again. Her protests to
the contrary, Lydia knew that the bonds that had linked
them in the past would remain with her to the grave, but
she had no plans to make herself or her feelings vulnerable
to him again. And on the heels of her disastrous engagement to Burton Shaw, she had widened the criteria to include any other man as well. She was tired of picking up
the shards that had once been her heart and soldiering on.
She'd come to the conclusion that the perils of love were
not for her. Her school and her students were all she needed
in life.

Gray found it hard to concentrate on eating as well. He
instead wanted to question Lydia about her past, the things
she'd done in her life since moving away, the people she'd
encountered, but he didn't ask. He'd given up that right as
well. Were he a drinking man, he'd be getting stinking
drunk right now so he wouldn't have to look into her face
and see the adolescent she'd once been or remember the
fun they'd had. He didn't want to see that she was still as
lovely as the last time he'd seen her, even more so if that
was possible, or that maturity had added a sultriness to her
honey-colored face that had only been hinted at in her
youth. Her tawny brown eyes were still sharp and intelligent and her mouth . . . lush as Michigan in springtime.
Drunk he might even forget how much he'd hurt her or the
fact that because of his betrayal Lydia Cooper would never
be a significant part of his life again.

Lydia set her cutlery aside. She'd eaten enough. She
asked him softly, "How is your mother?"

He smiled ruefully, the first he'd shown since the evening began. "Age is finally slowing her down, but she's
doing well. I'm sure she'd welcome a visit from you while
you're here." He wondered how long she might stay in
town.

"I'd like to see her as well. She was always kind to me."
Lydia remembered how upset Gray's mother had been
when the scandal surrounding Anna Mae surfaced. Lydia

had been so devastated by the news of Gray's betrayal and the subsequent wedding announcement that her mother had sent her to Chicago to live with her aunt, Queen-Esther, for a while. Mrs. Dane hadn't wanted Lydia to leave town, but she understood that Lydia's going away was in everyone's best interest. To this day, Lydia remembered the tears in Mrs. Dane's eyes when Lydia came over to say good-bye.

Gray could see the memories fanning across Lydia's face and the soft sadness in her eyes. Had he the power to go back and change things he would. Back then, he hadn't known that deceit could ripple across one's life like a stone skipping on a river or that that same small ripple could turn into a torrent, sweeping away love, lives, and the smile of the girl who'd been his entire world. Lydia had entrusted him with all of herself and he'd proven himself unworthy by trysting with Anna Mae. It had been the mistake of a lifetime, one he realized fully the day Lydia disappeared and his marriage to Anna Mae began. "How're you getting home?"

"Tomorrow morning's coach. It leaves at nine."

"My wagon is here. You're welcome to come along if you want to get to your mother's place faster."

Lydia considered the offer. She wanted to turn him down. One evening with him was enough, but his logic had merit. The coach might not pull into Sumpter until late tomorrow evening, depending on the number of passengers aboard and how many stops it had to make. "What time are you leaving?"

"Seven."

"Where shall I meet you?"

"Front door will be fine."

"Then I'll come along if you don't mind."

"I don't."

What Lydia saw reflected in his eyes reached out and touched her with such intensity, she had to look away from him or be lost. She stood then and said, "I will see you in the morning. Good night, Gray."

He nodded. "Good night, Lydia."

As she walked away and disappeared from Gray's view, he whispered softly, "Sweet dreams, my lady. Sweet dreams."

Chapter 2

True to his word, Gray was waiting when Lydia ventured downstairs early the next morning. He greeted her distantly. "Mornin'."

"Good morning."

"Mrs. Harrison has some breakfast waiting. We can load up your trunks afterward."

In a way, Lydia had hoped to awaken this morning and find last night's reunion had been a dream, but of course it hadn't. Gray was as real as her heartbeat. "I'm not very hungry, but I'll have some tea while you eat."

"Tea isn't going to keep you warm on a morning like this. It snowed again last night."

"I'm well acquainted with the weather, Gray. I was born here, remember?"

He'd forgotten how prickly she could be sometimes, and because of the past she had even more of a reason to be so. "You still need to eat."

"I'll be fine."

"Stubborn as ever."

"And you're as bossy as ever."

To which he replied softly, "Touché."

Lydia had to admit she still found him mesmerizing, but when she reminded herself of what all that mesmerizing had done to her soul, she had no trouble shaking it off and saying to him, "The sooner we eat, the sooner we can get under way."

"And the sooner we bury the past, the better off we'll both be."

"Don't pry open a box you can't close, Gray." That said, she turned away and walked into the dining room.

Gray knew he'd deserved that. He was trying to push her into a conversation she plainly didn't want to have. He had to respect that, but how could he confess to her the depths of his remorse if she wouldn't talk to him? He supposed had the shoe been on the other foot and he'd been the one wronged, heaven and earth would turn to dust before he opened up to her again, but that didn't solve his dilemma. If he couldn't talk to her, he couldn't tell her that for the past fifteen years he'd never stopped loving her.

They shared a silent breakfast, and because Lydia didn't want Gray fussing like a mother hen, she had a piece of toasted bread to accompany her tea. He, on the other hand, had a plate piled high with grits, eggs, sausage, and bread, all of which he washed down with hot cups of Mrs. Harrison's excellently brewed coffee. Lydia knew he was a full-grown man, but she couldn't believe how much he ate.

When he was finished, it was time to depart. Lydia pushed away from the table and went in search of Mrs. Harrison, who was in the kitchen cleaning up. After thanking the elderly landlady for her kindness and hospitality, Lydia paid her boarding bill, then left to meet up with Gray for the ride home to Sumpter.

He was already outside seated on the bench seat of the wagon. Lydia had taken a few moments to pull on a pair of wool men's trousers that were now hidden beneath her wool dress and cloak. Her legs were nice and warm as her boots crunched atop the snow.

He held out his hand and she stuck her gloved hand into his so he could help her up. She tossed her handbag onto the seat above, then, after hiking her skirts a short ways, climbed up aided by the strength of his grip.

"Thank you," she said to him as she adjusted her cloak

and the plush velvet bonnet covering her head and ears.

"You're welcome." He snapped the reins and the horses started forward.

Last night's snowfall had blanketed the trees and the surrounding countryside with a white brilliance that twinkled like diamonds under the pale sunshine. The temperature was cold enough to make a person seek shelter beneath layers of clothing, but since both Gray and Lydia were accustomed to the weather, they were dressed warmly enough.

Gray, guiding the team, looked over at Lydia sitting statuelike in her heavy cloak and hood. "It's not as cold as I thought," he said.

"No. It isn't too bad. The sunshine helps."

"We should be home in an hour or so."

Lydia nodded her understanding, then trained her attention on the rolling fields of white. Seeing the snow reminded her of her childhood days when times were simpler. On a day like this, she, Gray, and the rest of their friends would need their snowshoes to reach the small school they all attended. If there was no school, they'd rush to get their chores done, then meet at the old tree to go sledding or skating or play snow snake, the game taught them by their Pottawatomie friend, Patrick. She remembered many an early morning lying on her back in a fresh field of snow making snow angels. She wistfully realized she hadn't made snow angels in ages; being headmistress prevented such joys.

Gray wondered what she might be thinking, but he did not want to ask and risk raising the tension again, so instead he asked, "How long you planning on staying?"

She shrugged. "I'm not real certain, but until the New Year for sure."

He found the answer pleasing. "Then, back to Chicago?"

"Yes."

"Can I ask what your life is like there?"

She saw no harm in telling him the truth. "I run a school for girls."

He smiled his surprise. "You're a teacher?"

"Yes, I am."

"Do you enjoy it?"

"I do in some ways, but not in others."

He appeared puzzled by her answer, so she explained. "I enjoy the girls, and the teaching, but not the administrative responsibilities." Lydia almost added that she was considering closing the school and opening a smaller one here, closer to home so she could be with her mother, but she kept those thoughts to herself. Back when she and Gray were young, they'd often shared their dreams and plans, but the scandal and the passage of time had changed all that.

Gray knew he had no business asking, but he wanted to know: "Is there a man in your life?"

In response to the question, Burton Shaw's face shimmered across her mind's eye. "No."

Gray noted her hesitation before answering. He wondered about it but didn't ask her to explain.

Lydia felt turnaround fair play. "Is there a woman in your life?"

He didn't hesitate. "No. There's been no one since I sent Anna Mae packing."

Lydia heard that the marriage had ended badly. A few months after the wedding, Anna Mae allegedly lost the babe in a riding accident; rumor had it that she hadn't been carrying at all and that the whole tale had been hatched by Anna Mae and her nefarious kin so that Anna Mae could snag a wealthy husband.

Lydia glanced in his direction and took in the familiar way he held the reins, the way he sat, the confidence in his face. Once, she'd known practically everything about him: his likes and dislikes, that he preferred leather driving gloves to cotton, was allergic to blueberries, and had a small crescent-shaped scar on his back that he'd gotten during a fight they'd had when she was eleven years old. It was from a rock she'd thrown; she'd been aiming at his head. The only thing she hadn't known about was Anna Mae.

He asked, "When was your last visit home?"

"About five years ago, but it was only for a day or so."

"That would've been before I came back."

"Yes. Mother wrote me and said you'd only recently returned."

"Yes, It's been almost two years now."

"Where were you before?"

"Texas."

"So that accounts for the accent I hear."

"Still pretty thick, isn't it?" he asked, smiling over at her.

She shrugged lightly. "I suppose. You must have been there quite some time for it to have affected your speech so strongly."

"Eleven years."

"Doing what?"

"U.S. Cavalry."

Lydia found that surprising.

Gray met her gaze, then added, "Joined up after the divorce."

An awkward silence followed. Lydia turned back to the countryside. What happened to his dreams of attending college and becoming a doctor? she wondered. Had his parents blessed his enlistment into the military, or were they as taken aback by his decision as Lydia herself? She wanted to question him about why he'd made such a choice, but she no longer had the right to ask him anything so personal. Not anymore.

Gray had enlisted in the cavalry in order to get away from everyone and everything he knew. The marriage to Anna Mae had been disastrous. For the sake of the baby, Gray had tried to make a go of it at first, but the only thing Anna Mae seemed intent upon was spending him into the poorhouse. Her greediness was exceeded only by the greediness of her relatives. After she lost the baby, Gray had allowed her to recover, then instructed his barrister to draw

up the divorce papers. Two weeks after the decree from the
judge became official, Gray headed west. He drifted for a
while, taking odd jobs here and there to keep money in his
pockets, then enlisted with the Tenth Cavalry at Fort Davis,
Texas. When he first arrived at the isolated fort, the bleak
barren landscape and the cold faces of the mountains mirrored how he felt inside. The marriage had left him bitter,
angry. Over the years, the hard life of a pony soldier
molded him into the man he'd become, but he'd never forgotten Lydia.

Lydia and Gray were mainly silent for the remainder of
the journey. Mrs. Harrison had graciously filled a canteen
with steaming hot tea, and the sips Lydia and Gray shared
kept them warm.

As they finally turned off the main road and onto the
track that led into town, the familiar surroundings pulled at
Lydia's heart. She and Gray had climbed the trees here,
hunted frogs in the creeks, and caught fireflies. They'd
taken long silent walks during the rustling season of autumn, raced horses down to the Huron River, and fallen in
love with the richness of their lives and each other. Back
then, Gray's father had enough wealth to employ a cook
and a housekeeper. In the small clean cottage where Lydia
resided with her mother, Miriam, Lydia did those jobs.
Gray's parents were active, well-known Republicans;
Lydia's father was dead, and her mother did laundry and
any other domestic work she could find. There had been
no time for balls or political rallies at the Cooper house-
hold; Lydia and her mother were too busy putting food on
the table.

Lydia now gave Gray a sidelong glance from beneath
her lashes. Back then, he hadn't cared that the Coopers
were poor as church mice. Prominent young women from
all over the state had set their caps for him, but he'd chosen
her, Lydia, the daughter of a washerwoman. In reality,
Lydia had no idea if she would have become Gray's wife
had Anna Mae never come into their lives; maybe they
would have simply drifted apart as young sweethearts oft-

times do, but because of Gray's actions they would never know, and that was what hurt her the most.

When Gray pulled the team to a halt in front of the small cottage belonging to Lydia's mother, he didn't immediately move to go around and help her down. Instead he sat there a moment, thinking about the past, the present, and all the empty years in between. He said, finally, "Welcome home, Lydia."

His tone touched her. "Thanks, Gray. It's good to be here."

Gray searched her eyes and savored the face that had once been his whole world. *Why haven't I been able to forget you?* It seemed as if he'd spent his entire adult life trying to resurrect Lydia's radiance in every woman he encountered.

Lydia could feel the ties that had once bound them trying to reconnect themselves, and she fought to keep her barriers up. One betrayal was enough. She knew the incident had happened over a decade ago and that maybe she should have set it aside by now, but she couldn't; she'd loved him that much. By keeping her heart under lock and key, she'd never be vulnerable to Gray, Burton, or anyone else again. She was too old for heartbreak. "Thank you very much for the ride home."

"I'll get your trunks," Gray said, but instead of putting actions to words, he stayed seated. He found he didn't want to leave her, not yet, not after just finding her again. And in the silence that rose, their eyes met. Gray, moved by all she'd meant to him, reached out and stroked a fleeting finger down her soft, cold cheek.

The sweet jolt tore through Lydia with such force her eyes shuttered in response.

He whispered, "I've missed you, Lydie. . . ."

Lydie had been his name for her before they'd been forced to part. Hearing him address her that way after the passage of so much time filled her with such powerful memories she couldn't find her breath. *This wasn't supposed to happen!* She wasn't supposed to be this moved by him, not after all this time. Lord help her, she still loved him; in reality, she'd never stopped. Not sure where that admission might lead, Lydia drew back and said, her voice husky with emotion, "I have to go in. . . ."

He studied her for a moment more, noting that she refused to meet his eyes. "I'll come around and help you down."

Lydia nodded her agreement, hoping to regather herself in the interim, but when he appeared at her side, all she could think about was his fleeting caress, the softly whispered words, and how rattled she'd been by both.

Gray politely handled her down. When she moved to step away, he gently held onto her gloved fingers, making her stay. "We need to talk."

Lydia didn't want to for myriad reasons. Putting her heart at risk was the obvious one. The others had to do with the anger she knew was buried deep inside, an anger directed solely at him for treating their love so lightly.

"Can we talk?" he asked.

Lydia slowly disengaged her hand, then shook her head. "There's no reason, Gray. What's done is done."

Gray wanted to press her into agreeing to talk but didn't. His pride wouldn't permit him to beg, so his mask descended again.

Without a further word, he went around to the back of the wagon and took her two trunks out of the bed. Lydia headed up the snowy path that led to her mother's door.

Miriam Cooper's brown face lit up with joy when she saw Lydia on the other side of the door. "Oh my goodness!"

Mother and child embraced in a long rocking hug, and both had happy tears on their cheeks when they finally drew apart. It had been so long since they'd been together.

When Miriam saw Gray coming up, she asked, her tone curious, "What's he doing with you?"

"He was at the boardinghouse where I spent last night. I'll explain later."

Gray joined them and said distantly but politely, "Good morning, Mrs. Cooper."

"Morning, Gray." Miriam smiled softly. "Thanks for seeing Lydia home. Just set those trunks inside the door."

He did as instructed. He left again in order to retrieve Lydia's carpetbag and a hatbox. Once those items joined the trunks, he said to Mrs. Cooper, "I'll drop off that wagon wheel you wanted as soon as it arrives."

"Thanks, Gray."

Lydia noted the ease with which her mother and Gray dealt with each other, and it gave her pause.

Gray said, "I'll get going."

Lydia looked up into his face, and her heart began thumping all over again. "Thanks again." Then she and her mother turned and went inside the house.

Gray headed back to his wagon and drove away.

Lydia was so happy to see her mother that Gray was immediately put out of her mind. Miriam looked older and because of her ankle injury moved around a bit slower, but the dark eyes were still clear and intelligent. "How's the ankle?" Lydia asked.

"A bit stiff. The cast came off last Thursday, but it's getting stronger every day. You want some tea?"

"Oh, that would be lovely."

While her mother busied herself with the tea making, Lydia took a seat on one of the worn but comfortable overstuffed chairs and looked around. Memories rose. The place hadn't grown any larger, but it was home. The small bedroom she and her mother had shared was through the door there, and this outer space served as both the parlor and dining room. The tiny kitchen, built onto the back of the cottage when Lydia was ten, was accessed through an alcove and constituted the rest of the interior. No one would ever mistake the place for a mansion, but she had been happy here. Growing up, Lydia hadn't had much materially, but she'd never gone hungry and her secondhand clothes had always been clean. There had been cakes for her birthdays, cookies at Christmastime, and more love than her heart could hold.

Her reminiscing was interrupted by her mother's return. The hot, sweet brew warmed away the chill of the morning ride.

Lydia's mother said genuinely, "The money you've been sending me has been a blessing. The school must be doing well."

"It is, Mama. Much better than I ever dreamed. I've almost thirty girls taking studies with me."

"That's wonderful, but are you sure you can afford to keep sending me bank drafts every month?"

"Yes, I can, and even if I couldn't, I'd find the coin. I know how hard you worked raising me. Now, it's time for me to return the favor."

Her mother nodded her understanding. "OK. I'll take your word for it, but if your funds start running low, I want to know."

Lydia offered a dutiful daughterly, "Yes, ma'am," knowing all the while she had no intentions of telling her mother any such thing. Lydia would do whatever necessary to keep Miriam Cooper from ever again having to work from sunup to sundown.

Miriam asked then, "How was the train ride over?"

Lydia described the trip and they both laughed over her description of the howling infant.

Lydia's mother then asked, "How'd you and Gray get along?"

"We didn't fight or argue, if that's what you meant."

Miriam shook her head sadly. "What a mess that was. Broke my heart, because I loved him, too."

Their eyes met. Lydia placed a consoling hand atop her mother's. "I know, Mama, but what's done is done. It can't be changed and we can't go back."

"But you loved him very much. Everyone knew that."

"Yes, I did. Very much." She paused a moment to remember her sixteen-year-old self and how it felt to be in love. Lydia shook off the memory. "Well, he and I aren't in love anymore. I doubt I'll see him again while I'm here, anyway." Lydia added then, "What was that about a wagon wheel?"

"I needed a new one and Gray said he'd take care of getting me one. He stops over every now and again to see how I am."

"Oh, really?" Lydia asked.

"Yes, really. He's grown into a fine man, but enough about Gray. The holidays are for making merry, not dredging up sad acts of the past." Miriam then raised her cup to her daughter in salute. "Welcome home, child."

A smiling Lydia raised her own. "Thank you, Mama."

Chapter 3

Unlike the Coopers, Grayson Dane's family did not live in a small three-room cottage. Gray had grown up in a large Victorian home accented with turrets, gingerbread trim, and expensive glass windows. The Danes also owned the land for as far as one could see. The lumber and coal business Titus Dane had carved out during his son Gray's younger years had passed down to Gray upon Titus's death unattached by creditors and solidly structured. Because of the nature of the Dane business, the increasing rise of Jim Crow had not affected their operations as much as it had other businessmen of the race, because everyone needed coal and lumber and most suppliers didn't care who sold it to them as long as the price was fair and the product sound.

But profits and Jim Crow weren't on Gray's mind as he entered his mother's home; Lydia was. He found his mother having tea in the well-furnished parlor. From her perfectly coiffed graying hair to her expensive gowns, the fifty-five-year-old Elizabeth Dane was a study in good taste. Born free, she relished being a ruling member of the state's Black representative society and wielding the power that went with such a position. Her ivory face brightened upon seeing him. He'd been gone for three days. "You're back. Did the shipment get off all right?"

"Yes. Everything's fine. Bumped into someone at the boardinghouse, though."

"An old friend?"

"Yes. Lydia Cooper."

His mother's green eyes widened with delight. "Really? How is she? Is she well? Is—"

"Whoa, whoa," he said, laughing softly. "One question at a time. She's well, and is here to visit her mother for the holiday season. I happened upon her at Mrs. Harrison's boardinghouse."

Mrs. Dane sighed. "I do hope she will stop in and see me while she's here. I was in Philadelphia the last time she visited Miriam. Better yet, I will go and see her." Mrs. Dane thought for a moment. "You do think she will see me if I go?"

"You? Of course. Me? No."

His mother said to him, "Well, darling, what did you expect? You broke her heart, my heart, her mother's heart. Personally, I'd make you walk to the moon and back before even considering forgiving you."

Slightly amused, he shook his head. "The moon?"

"Maybe Mars. Which is farther?"

"Mars."

"Then Mars."

He took her ribbing good-naturedly. "Maybe going to Mars would have helped me forget her. Texas sure wasn't far enough." In his mind's eye, Gray could see Lydia sitting across the table from him last night, could remember the way her eyes had slid shut when he stroked her cheek, just now. "She's still beautiful."

His mother sighed. "I've missed her."

Gray had, too, but he had no idea how fiercely until she walked into Mrs. Harrison's dining room.

"So what are you going to do?" Elizabeth asked.

"I'd like to try and make amends, but she refuses to talk about it."

"Then you have a mountain to climb." Mrs. Dane added softly, "Gray, I love you with all of my heart, but fifteen years ago you made a randy, stupid mistake that cost you the most precious thing in your world, and a darkness has walked with you ever since."

Gray didn't disagree. His life had held little light.

Elizabeth asked quietly, "Has she married?"

"No."

A pleased smile slowly surfaced on her face. "Well," was all she said, and in a very pleased tone.

Gray read her mind. "We aren't going to pick up where we left off. It's plain she doesn't want that." He again remembered the way Lydia's eyes had closed when he touched her.

"It's the Christmas season, dear. Miracles happen."

He chuckled lightly, "My mother—ever the optimist."

"Someone around here has to be," she responded with a smile. She then asked him, "Do you wish to attend the ball with me, tomorrow night? We'll be raising money for relief."

"You know I'm not high on balls."

"Neither am I, but the hostess is Edwina Franklin and she's the ball organizer. Since I am on the committee, I must attend. I saw her yesterday at Bible study and she asked if you were coming."

"Why?"

"She said her daughter Blanche is so looking forward to seeing you again."

"Blanche is a twit."

"I agree, but come anyway. If you can't abide it you can duck out discreetly."

"I'll think about it. Tomorrow night?"

"Yes."

"I'll let you know in the morning. Is there anything to eat?"

His mother laughed. "Gray, you are thirty-three years old and still sniffing out food like an adolescent."

He had the decency to look embarrassed.

"There should be some of last night's leftovers in the cold box. Help yourself, but don't eat it all. The cook is off this evening and I'll want to eat later."

He smiled. "Yes, ma'am."

"What are your plans for the evening?" Elizabeth asked.

"Only to get some real sleep in my own bed."

His mother studied his face. "Well, come back over if you want company or wish to talk."

He nodded.

"And, Gray?"

"Yes?"

"Give Lydia time."

He didn't respond to that, but came over and kissed her on the cheek. "I'll see you later."

She cupped his strong jaw. "You go on home and get some rest."

Never one to disobey his mother, Gray did just that.

Much later that evening, Gray poured a jigger of cognac into a snifter, then sat before the fire roaring in the fireplace. He was supposed to be looking over the Dane business accounts, but he'd sat at his desk for over an hour unable to focus on the task because visions of Lydia Cooper kept rising to distract him. No matter where he set his mind she was there, shimmering, beckoning, tempting, so he'd pushed the ledgers aside and left his study. For fifteen years he'd wondered about her, worried about her, never stopped thinking about her, and now she'd returned, beautiful, polished, and encased in steel. Convincing her to talk with him was going to be tougher than fighting Rebs in Texas.

Gray took a small sip of the French spirit and let his mind drift back to the past. At the age of eighteen, he'd been the only son of a prominent family, well traveled, well educated, and well dressed. He'd had friends, status, and an underlying layer of arrogance that grew out of all that he was, but he had also been respectful, churchgoing, and honest; his parents would not have tolerated less. He wasn't entirely truthful, however, and that fault precipitated his downfall. Admittedly, society encouraged a young man to sow his oats, and when Anna Mae Dexter let him know she was willing to help him do that, Gray had taken the boon willingly. Looking back, Anna Mae hadn't been particularly good at it, although at the time he hadn't known that; neither had he for that matter, but when you're eighteen and a girl offers to show you the way. . . ?

Gray took another small sip. In his mind, he'd justified laying with Anna Mae as a way of showing his respect for Lydia. Lydia was a *good* girl. Although the two of them had engaged in some pretty serious kissing, he'd never touched her in any way that could be seen as compromising because one: Lydia wouldn't have allowed it, and two: if his parents had ever gotten wind of such carrying on, they would have killed him and turned his dead body over to Lydia's mother to burn and bury. So, he'd gone with Anna Mae.

In reality, his so-called justification didn't hold water then and held even less now that he had a lifetime's worth of experiences to call upon; he'd wanted to lie with Anna Mae because she'd been willing and able. Nothing more. He'd loved Lydia, heart and soul, but his young male body had had no such allegiance. When Anna Mae singled him out as the father of her unborn child, he'd expected some of the other men who'd slid between her thighs in the barn behind her father's house to confess that that they'd been with her, too, but of course they hadn't. Over the weeks that followed, his life descended into hell, and he'd been there ever since.

But now, after years of trying to live with the life he'd made for himself, Lydia was back, not knowing how he'd wished for her or that memories of her were what he'd turned to on those long lonely treks that were so much of a pony soldier's life. He'd never imagined he'd see her again or that in spite of all that stood between them, his touch would make her eyes slide shut. That tiny response gave him hope, because hope was all he had.

When Lydia was a youngster, it was common practice to poach on old man Dane's lumber and steal fruit from his vast orchards of apples, cherries, and peaches. Titus Dane always had more lumber than he'd ever sell and far more fruit than he'd ever harvest, so he didn't mind his neighbors' thievery as long as they didn't carry off a whole stand of trees or wagonloads of fruit. He also tended to look the other way if the poachers had children to feed. Lydia had liked Mr. Dane, and when Miriam wrote to her of his passing Lydia had offered up a prayer for his soul.

She thought of him now as she trudged through the snow in search of a Christmas tree. She wondered if he was churning in his grave knowing she'd returned home and was on the hunt for one of his trees or if he didn't mind at all. Not that it mattered. The bundled-up Lydia was out on this cold, sunny Saturday morning because she needed a tree, and she wanted to have it home by the time her mother returned from volunteering at the church later today.

It was nearly nine in the morning, and Lydia hadn't seen another soul since entering Dane property over an hour ago. Most of the trees in the acres-wide stand of evergreens she was now tramping through were sky-towering giants, too big to fell even if they would fit into her mother's tiny abode, so she trudged on.

A short while later, she spotted the perfect tree. It was standing alone in a clearing filled with freshly fallen snow. The sight of it filled her with delight. The field surrounding the short pine was as pristine as if the Good Lord had laid down a blanket, and there were no footprints left by man or beast to mar its quiet beauty. Lydia felt as if the clearing and its tree had been put there just for her.

She removed the small ax from the red flannel bag tied to her back, then went to investigate the size of the trunk. While she walked, the cold air and the crunch of the snow beneath her feet were so exhilarating, she felt like a child again. The feeling bubbled up and she found herself laughing and hooting like a snowy owl, her head thrown back as she turned round and round in the snow. Then she spread her arms wide and dropped backward onto the cushion of snow. The landing hurt a bit more than she remembered it doing as a child, but the shock of it passed as she lost herself in the making of snow angels. She reveled in the cold snowy spray sent up by the wild movements of her arms and legs.

"Having fun?"

Lydia's eyes popped open. A smiling Gray was looking down at her from atop a big chestnut stallion. Her eyes widened.

He added, "Could hear you hooting a mile away."

As Lydia rolled out of the angel and got to her feet, she was more than a bit embarrassed. She took a moment to brush away the snow caking her heavy coat and the wool men's trousers she was wearing to keep her legs warm beneath her wool skirt before looking up into his amused eyes.

He asked then, "Do your students know you like to make snow angels?"

She brushed at the snow on the scarf covering her hair. "No."

He looked her over. Was she thirty-one or thirteen? She appeared to be both. "What are you doing out here?"

Lydia saw no sense in lying. "I came to cut a Christmas tree for me and Mother."

"Ah, you're poaching."

The amused glint in his eyes was so reminiscent of the Gray of old, she prayed for a blindfold so he wouldn't affect her. "I suppose, but I will pay for the tree. How much?"

"Dinner."

That caught her off guard. She studied him silently. "Why not take coin instead?"

"Because I've plenty of that. I want something dearer."

Lydia debated how best to handle this situation. Although she wanted the pine very much, she didn't want to have to dine with him as payment for it. She sensed the attraction they'd once had for each other rising like a phoenix. In the wagon yesterday, the jolt of his touch let her know just how vulnerable she was to him; sparks had flown. Lydia didn't think it would take much for those sparks to flare into full-blown flames.

"Well?" he asked.

His voice brought her attention back. She said to him, "I don't wish to dine with you, Gray."

"I know, but that's the only way you're going to get that tree."

The boyish smile he gave her then was so sweetly familiar, she had to force herself not to smile in response. "Why not just be a good neighbor? It is the Christmas season."

"Then gift me with your presence at dinner."

Temptation licked at Lydia from all sides. A part of her dearly wanted to give in and say yes, but another part, the part that was wary of his intentions, was certain having dinner with him would be a bad idea.

Gray peered down into her face. "What are you thinking?"

She told him the truth. "That a part of me wants to say yes, while another part says no."

His horse fidgeted from the lack of movement and from the cold. Gray steadied the animal easily. "Then how about we cut down the tree? You can decide which part you want to listen to afterward."

Lydia was mildly surprised. "I can have the tree?"

His voice softened. "Have I ever been able to deny you anything?"

His voice and presence swirled around her like pungent smoke. She forgot the cold, her mother, the tree. Her entire being seemed focused on Gray.

He added, "I also won't deny that the man I've become would like to explore the woman you've become. . . ."

The provocative declaration made Lydia look away from the man he'd become, because the woman she'd become had no idea what else to do. "I'm a spinster headmistress now, Gray, and—"

"And what?" he quizzed softly. "Being a headmistress is supposed to make you less beautiful, less desirable?"

Lydia's knees weakened for a moment. Grabbing hold of herself, she told him, "We . . . should get the tree. I'm too old to be a rich man's holiday bauble."

"I'm not looking for a quick roll in the hay. That has proven to be a bad choice."

She noted the seriousness now claiming his face. "Then what do you want?"

"For you to have dinner with me tonight. That's all."

The offer tempted her again, but she didn't want her feelings for him to emerge any further; they would rise and bloom if she continued to keep company with him. Lydia preferred that her love for him remain sealed up like a bear hibernating in a cave. "I don't think it's wise."

"Then dine with me as an old friend. We were friends once, too, remember?"

She did. She studied him. The fine chesterfield he was wearing was a muted charcoal in color and sweeping enough in length to brush the tops of his gleaming black western-made boots. He wore a big Texan-looking brown hat and had a heavy woolen scarf around his throat. Its color matched the coat. *Why did he have to be so dazzling?* "Gray, I don't want to spend the evening arguing."

"Then we won't."

Caught between her feelings as a woman and what her mind knew to be sound judgment, Lydia spent another few moments mulling over his offer, then asked, "What time?" Every part of her being shouted warning, but she set the warnings aside. Maybe this one night would allow them to put the past behind for good.

Gray wanted to grin with glee when she accepted but kept his face void of emotion. "Seven?"

She nodded.

He slid from the horse's back to the ground. "Let's chop down your tree before we both freeze to death."

Although Lydia had intended to chop the tree down herself, she gladly handed him the ax. Her hands and feet were nearly numb from standing in the cold.

It took only a few minutes for him to fell the small pine.

"How'd you plan to get it home?" he asked, gesturing to the tree.

Lydia stamped her feet to try to get the circulation going in them again. "Drag it. That's one of the reasons I chose a small one."

"Well, let's tie it to the saddle and get going."

"I can get it home."

"I'm sure you can, but this way will be faster, don't you think?"

She did, and since it was too cold to argue further, she helped him drag the tree over to the horse. After Gray trailed the tree from a rope tied to the stallion's saddle, he mounted up, then stuck out his gloved hand for her to grab. She did so and climbed up behind him. Her arms circled his waist so she wouldn't fall off.

When her arms went around him, Gray had to close his eyes against the rising heady sensations that came from the feel of her snug against his back. Determined to be a gentleman, he gathered himself, then turned around and looked at her face framed by the snow-crusted scarf. "Ready?"

Lydia hadn't ridden with him this way in a long time. Although he was broader now than he'd been back then, the familiarity of their positioning made the memories of those other times rush back with dizzying speed. "Yes, I'm ready."

He turned back and set a slow pace for the horse through the snow.

Once they were under way, she asked, "What did you do in the army?"

"Cavalry. I was with the Tenth."

"You were a Buffalo Soldier?"

The awe in her voice pleased him. "Yep."

"I'm impressed."

"You know about the Tenth?"

"I do. The men of the Ninth and Tenth are highly thought of by my students."

Gray was pleased by that news as well.

Lydia said, "Wait until I tell them I've an old friend who served with the Tenth."

The members of the all-Black Tenth Cavalry were well decorated and well known for their bravery during the settlement of the West.

She asked him, "Where did you serve? Fort Davis?"

"I did, but we patrolled from the Canadian border to the Rio Grande. I got the chance to see a lot of the country."

"And you returned here with a Texas accent."

He chuckled. "My mother gave me a hard time about it when I came back to Michigan, said I spoke like I should be wearing spurs."

Lydia smiled. She liked the sound of his voice, but then, she always had.

They arrived at her mother's a short time later. Gray untied the tree and, per Lydia's instructions, left it leaning against the front of the house.

"I'll bring it in later. I need to see where Mama wants it set up."

"Okay."

"Thanks for your help," she told him genuinely.

"You're welcome."

Once again, silence rose, and as it lengthened and her awareness of him met his awareness of her, Lydia's heart pounded. A yearning had taken root in her that she couldn't quite control. "I'll see you later?"

He nodded and touched his hat. Walking back to his horse, he mounted up and rode away.

Lydia watched until he was out of sight.

Chapter 4

When Miriam returned home from church, she came rushing into the house excitedly. "Where on earth did you get the tree?"

Lydia enjoyed the happiness brightening her mother's face. "Dane land."

Having a tree during the Christmas season was a tradition made popular by America's German immigrants. Now every year more and more people were embracing the holiday practice.

Miriam removed her scarf and coat. "Did you pay Elizabeth for it?"

"No. Gray."

Her mother went still. "Gray? He didn't make you pay a lot for it, did he?"

"I'm not sure."

Studying her daughter's face, Miriam hung up her coat. "What does that mean?"

"I'm paying for the tree by having dinner with him."

Miriam responded cryptically, "I see. Do you think that's a good idea?"

Lydia shrugged, then added, "It was the only form of payment he was willing to accept."

"Is there water for tea? It's freezing out there."

"Yes. Would you like a cup?"

Miriam nodded, saying, "I would."

"Sit. I'll get it."

Once they were both seated with cups of tea, Miriam said, "Dinner with Gray."

"Yes," Lydia replied. "He says he wants to talk."

"About what?"

"Settling the past, I assume."

"Is that something you wish to talk about?"

"I tell myself yes, but inside . . . I don't know." Lydia's mind went back to her chance meeting with Gray this morning. When she climbed up behind him on the horse she didn't want to admit how good it felt to wrap her arms around him once again, but it had. "How am I supposed to act? Do I tell him how much he hurt me? How angry I was? Should I pretend it's all in the past and that it no longer matters?"

Miriam told her honestly, "Only you know the answer to that. All I know is I don't ever want you hurt that way again."

"Neither do I," Lydia replied truthfully. The idea of dining with Gray had her more than a bit concerned. She dearly wanted to maintain the distance the passage of time had set between them, but her feelings for him were re-awakening and she didn't know if she was capable of keeping them at bay.

Miriam poured herself more tea from the pot and said, "Well, let's set Gray aside for a moment. Tell me about you and Burton. What happened?"

Lydia sighed. She hadn't talked to anyone about it. "He wanted children, and I can't give him any."

Miriam looked stricken. "You never told me you couldn't have children. How do you know?"

"The doctors in Chicago told me. Remember when I first went to live with Aunt and I took ill?"

"Yes, she wrote to me."

"Well, I was much sicker than she let on, because she didn't want to worry you."

Her mother paused and stared, then asked, "So, you two

thought it would be better for me to worry now that fifteen years have passed?"

Lydia shook her head with amusement. "Mother—"

"Don't 'Mother' me, little girl. Wait until I see that sister of mine. I entrust her with my child, and she lets you get so sick she's afraid to tell me?"

Lydia said to herself, *Here we go.* "Mama, it wasn't like that. I was the one afraid, afraid you would make me come home if you knew."

"Well, you were probably right and I'm sorry I'm fussing, but you were wrong to keep the illness from me, Lydia. I feel terrible that I wasn't there."

"You shouldn't. Aunt took very good care of me, she really did, but the doctors said all the infections and fevers left me barren."

Miriam whispered softly, "Sweet lord. And that's why your fiancé cried off?"

"Yes."

Miriam shook her head. "If he's that shallow, you're better rid of him."

Lydia agreed. "I know."

Miriam then said, "I have something to tell you."

Lydia scanned her mother's still-beautiful face and saw a seriousness there that made Lydia wonder what Miriam was about to say. "What is it?"

"When your papa died, I swore I'd never love another man—I was determined to stay true to him."

Lydia's father, James, had died of pneumonia a few days shy of her third birthday. She knew that he and Miriam had loved each other very much, but Lydia had no memory of him. She wondered where this story was going. "Is there more?"

"Yes, so let me tell it in my own way, please."

A smiling Lydia dropped her eyes in embarrassment. "I'm sorry. Go on."

"Thank you. Now, where was I?" She then added with a mock reproach, "I had this speech all planned out and now you've thrown me off."

Lydia chuckled. "Sorry, again."

Her mother's eyes sparkled with humor. "Let's see. Oh, yes. I was talking about the vow I made to say true. Anyway, I stubbornly stuck to the past and turned down every man who came around."

Lydia was mildly surprised by the revelation. "You never told me anything about men coming around."

Her mother pointed out slyly, "Can't tell your children everything."

Lydia grinned. "Were any of these beaux men I'd know?"

Miriam nodded affirmatively. "Yes. Watson Miller for one."

Lydia was very surprised now. "Our Watson Miller? The doctor?!"

Miriam nodded proudly. "Yep, the doctor."

Lydia was past surprised. *Stunned* was a better word. "When was this?"

"A few years after you went away. He and I had crossed paths a few times and I always thought he was a fine man, but what would a doctor want with a washerwoman—besides having his wash done, of course."

Lydia could only stare.

Miriam smiled at the look on her daughter's face. "Then one day, he came calling. Had flowers and everything."

"What?!"

"Wanted me to have dinner with him."

"And you said—"

"No."

"Why?"

"Can you imagine what kind of talk that would have caused? He's very respected, Lydia. He didn't need to be gossiped about because of me."

"So, you turned him down."

"I did. Again, and again, and again."

Lydia was puzzled. "He kept coming back?"

"And back, and back, and back."

Lydia chuckled. "How long did this go on?"

"It's still going on."

Lydia's eyes widened. "What do you mean, it's still going on?"

"Just what I said. We started seeing each other about six years ago, and two years ago . . . we began courting."

Lydia's mouth dropped open. "You did not—"

Her mother smiled. "Yes, we did. No one knows, of course."

Lydia doubted that to be true. "Mama, this is a small town. Everyone knows."

"Well, no one has said anything."

Lydia grinned. "Well, now. That is news."

"He wants to marry me."

Lydia's eyes lit up. "Oh, Mama. Did you say yes?"

"Tentatively, yes."

"Why tentatively?"

"I wanted to talk with you first."

Lydia felt her heart swell with emotion. "You don't need my approval."

"Yes, I do. I love you more than anything in this world. Your opinion matters."

Lydia loved her mother more than anything in the world as well. "Then the good doctor has my blessings to make you an honest woman whenever the two of you decide."

"He wants to get married Christmas Day."

"So soon?"

"I know it's only a few days away. We just want to have a simple ceremony and be done. No one's invited but you."

Lydia found that surprising, too. "What about your friends at the church? Won't their feelings be hurt if they aren't invited?"

"They'd only make a fuss over everything. Watson and I don't want that. If the ladies decide to give us a reception later on, fine, but our wedding day will be the way we want it, and that won't include a lot of hoopla."

Lydia was still a bit staggered. "Well, OK, but what made you decide to say yes to him after saying no so many times?"

"He threatened to leave town and never come back."

Lydia studied her mother's now-serious face. "I see."

"Told me last Sunday either I marry him or when he moves to Boston after the first of the New Year he goes without me. I thought about how much he's come to mean to me and how much I enjoy his company, and I knew what I had to do. Lydia, I'm fifty years old. I may not have a lot of years left, but I know I don't want to spend them alone."

Lydia sensed the depth in her mother's words. "There's nothing wrong in that, Mama. Nothing at all."

Her mother smiled. "Thank you, daughter. I tried many times to put all this in a letter, but it never said what I wanted it to say, so when you wrote and said you were coming at Christmastime, I told Watson I'd talk to you about us then."

"I'm glad you did it this way. A letter would have probably brought me racing home to confront the masher taking advantage of my poor old mama. Instead, I can confront him in person. When is he coming to dinner, so I can put him on the rack?"

Her mother laughed. "Lydia!"

"I'm serious, Mother. Suppose he's only after the family fortune?"

Miriam grinned and said, "You are such a silly goose. He'll be at church and afterward plans to join us here for Sunday dinner. You can interrogate him then."

"Good."

Miriam chuckled.

Lydia walked over and hugged her mother fiercely, whispering, "I love you, and I wish you all the happiness in the world."

"Thank you. Now what are you going to do about Gray?"

"There's nothing to be done. We'll have dinner—then, he'll go his way, and I will go mine."

"Is that what you really want?"

Lydia searched her mother's face. "What do you mean?"

"You two were very much in love at one time."

"And? Are you suggesting I forgive and forget?"

"No, only you can make that decision. I'm suggesting you two talk. Who knows where it might lead?"

"Mother, aren't you the same one who wanted his head on a platter fifteen years ago?"

"I did, and for breaking your heart I still do in a way, but he's paid for his sins. You can see it in his eyes. Don't be like me, Lydia. Don't close yourself up in the past. I tried that road and it led nowhere. Were it not for Watson, I'd be just another lonely old woman. Talk to Gray so that the two of you can move on. Apart or together, it doesn't matter. Promise me you'll at least listen to whatever he has to say."

"What about what I have to say?"

"I've never known you to be shy, Lydia," her mother said with a wry smile. "I'm sure you'll get your turn. Just let him get in a word or two, OK?"

Lydia couldn't tell her mother no, so she said, "OK."

"Good. Wouldn't it be something if you and Gray fell in love all over again?"

Lydia was caught completely off guard. "What?!" She laughed with amazement.

"I said—"

"I heard what you said; I just don't believe it. That is not going to happen."

"Why not?"

"Because."

"Oh, that's a very sound argument. You must be a schoolteacher."

Lydia dropped her eyes in smiling embarrassment. "Stop it, Mama."

Miriam then asked, "What would be so wrong with finding out you two still love each other? You're both adults, now."

Before Lydia could react to that, Miriam added, "Do you know what would make Christmas Day even more special?"

Lydia was almost afraid to ask. "What?"

"If you and Gray were to get married, too."

Lydia snorted with disbelief. "Will you stop, please?! I am not marrying Gray Dane, Christmas Day or any other day. You're really grasping, Mama. Really grasping."

"Think about it for a moment, Lydia."

Lydia rolled her amused eyes. "How about we pop the corn for the tree instead? You obviously need something to do."

Miriam laughed, and her daughter did as well. They went to get the corn.

Lydia and Miriam spent the rest of the afternoon decorating the tree with strands of yarn strung with popcorn, nuts, and dried red berries, then to top it off added the traditional cookies that were shaped like angels, stars, bells. According to one of Lydia's immigrant neighbors, Christmas trees were originally decorated with apples and little white wafers to represent the blood and body of Christ. Over time, cookies replaced the wafers and more decorations like the new lightweight glass balls she'd seen recently in the shop windows were coming into vogue. Some of the more elaborate trees Lydia had seen in Chicago were so weighted down with fruit, glass balls, and lit candles, the trees had to be staked to keep them from falling over, but she thought the simple tree she and her mother were now stepping back to admire just right.

Later Lydia went into the bedroom to get ready for her evening with Gray. After washing up and donning fresh underwear, she was standing in front of the mirror trying to decide what to do with her hair when her mother knocked on the open door and said, "I have something for you."

Lydia saw the small tin box Miriam was holding, and the familiar sight of it froze her.

Miriam said softly, "I've kept it all this time."

Entranced, Lydia put down her hairbrush, then slowly walked over to where her mother stood and took the box from her mother's hand.

While Lydia stared at this token of her past, Miriam quietly backed out of the room, leaving Lydia alone.

Lydia sat on the bed and tried to quiet her racing heart. Gathering herself, she slowly opened the lid. Inside were small folded squares of vellum aged and faded by time. Lydia knew immediately what they were and began to shake with such emotion her hand rose to her lips. Reaching down slowly, she lifted one out and unfolded it. Gray's familiar scrawl leapt from the page. *"My dearest Lydia. How do I love thee? Let me count the ways. I love thee to the depth and breadth and height my soul can reach . . . I love thee with the breath, smiles, tears of all my life . . ."*

Lydia set it aside and pressed her hand against her wildly beating heart. The words of Elizabeth Barrett Browning's sonnet brought back such sharp memories. Their love had been so young then, tender as new shoots of grass, and Lydia had placed all the sonnets he'd penned for her in this small box, a box she'd deliberately left behind when she went off to Chicago.

Unsure about what other memories the box might hold, Lydia warily withdrew the five folded sheets of vellum and beneath them found the cameo. The sight of it moved her as well. Gray had purchased it from a shop in Boston on a visit there with his parents. He'd presented it to her upon his return, and the only time Lydia ever took it off was when she bathed; she'd even slept in it, but she'd removed it from her neck for good the day she found out Anna Mae and Gray were going to marry.

Lydia picked up the cameo and visually inspected it. She determined that the clasp still worked and, although the woman's brown face was a bit dusty and the ivory around it a bit faded, the piece had survived the passage of time well. It was as if it had been waiting for her to return and reclaim it. Lydia had warned Gray about the dangers of opening a box he couldn't close, and now she'd done the same. Inside the box lay proof of how deeply he'd cared for her, and that, coupled with her mother's advice about living in the past, gave Lydia food for thought as she put everything back inside, closed the lid, and went back to the mirror.

At half past six, Lydia was dressed and ready for her dinner with Gray, but she was pacing back and forth in front of the grate, debating with herself what she wanted to do about her situation with him.

Her mother, seated in a chair while reading a newspaper, drawled, "You're going to wear a trench in the floor with all that pacing. Please take a seat, dear. You're making me dizzy."

Lydia, still pacing, said, "I shouldn't have agreed to this."

"For somebody who claims the man doesn't move her anymore, you're awfully jittery, Miss Lydia Cooper."

"I never claimed that, Mother."

Miriam lowered the paper. "So, you do still have feelings for him?"

"I do." Lydia had never been able to lie to her mother. Ever.

Miriam nodded understandingly. "Then don't let anything get in the way of that, especially if he still has feelings for you as well. Life is so short, Lydia. So very short. Don't waste it on something that happened in the past. Yes, Gray's actions affected many people, but if you hadn't gone away, would you be this polished? Would you be headmistress of your own school? In a way, your leaving has turned out to be a blessing."

The words made Lydia pause. She thought about it for a moment, then confessed, "I never thought about it in those terms before. I suppose you are correct, though."

"Mothers are always right."

Lydia chuckled. A knock sounded on the wooden door.

Miriam put down her paper. "Well, let the man in."

Lydia took one last look down at her blue velvet gown. It was the best dress in her closet, the one she saved for very special events. Taking in a deep breath, she swallowed her nervousness, then went to the door.

Chapter 5

When she opened the door, the sight of him made her knees weaken. At seventeen, he'd been gorgeous. Now, at thirty-three, he was as handsome as a dark-skinned archangel. The sweeping black coat, the snow-white scarf about his neck— she had to keep reminding herself that he was real and that this was no dream.

Miriam's chuckling voice broke the spell. "Lydia, are you going to invite him in or not?"

Lydia shook herself. Fighting off her embarrassment, she stepped back so he could enter.

Gray nodded a greeting to Mrs. Cooper, but his attention was immediately captured by Lydia's loveliness. She'd drawn her hair back into a simple bun, leaving her face free for his eyes to feast upon. Jet bobs hung gracefully from her ears, and there was a touch of rouge coloring her lush mouth. The long-sleeved satin gown was a stunning midnight blue; fashionably draped and gathered up at the waist, it sported an even darker overskirt. The conservative heart-shaped décolletage offered only a glimpse of the satin tops of her breasts, but he nonetheless wondered if the skin would be as soft to the touch as it appeared. At the age of seventeen, it had never occurred to Gray that his skinny little Lydia would grow up to be such a stunning woman, but she had. Needing to calm himself a bit, he settled his attention on the fetching indigo ribbon she had tied around her throat. The small ivory cameo hanging from the ribbon made his heart stop. His startled eyes flew to hers.

Lydia acknowledged his surprise and then fingered the cameo nervously. She asked softly, "Then you remember?"

"I do." Overwhelmed, he searched her face. "I never thought you'd still have it." Gray was glad Miriam was in the room. Were she not, he would have already eased Lydia into his arms and kissed her the way he'd been wanting to do since first seeing her back at the boardinghouse. Unable to deal with what significance her wearing the cameo held, he asked of her, "Are you ready to depart?"

She nodded. "Just let me get my cloak."

The voluminous wool-lined velvet cloak represented six months' salary. The last time she'd worn the cape, she'd been on the arm of her former fiancé, Burton Shaw. Banishing the memory of him as quickly as it appeared, Lydia fastened the frogs at the neck and picked up her small beaded handbag.

Miriam's eyes beamed over Gray and Lydia. "You two were always such a striking pair. That hasn't changed."

Lydia cut her mother a loving look of warning. "We'll see you later, Mama."

Miriam simply smiled and said, "Have a good time."

Gray bowed politely to Miriam, then escorted Lydia out into the December night.

Accompanying Lydia to the sleigh, he damned himself for being nervous; he was shaking like an untried youth. He kept thinking about all that could go wrong, then decided to set the worrying aside and simply enjoy being with her again. If the evening blew up in his face, he would at least have the memory of his cameo hanging around her neck like a jewel.

When Lydia saw the sleigh, her eyes brightened with excitement. "Is this . . . our—I mean, the same sleigh you had when we were young?"

Gray heard the stumble. He and Lydia had taken many rides together in his father's sleigh. "No, this is a different one. Bought it this afternoon."

Lydia's face took on confusion. "Today?"

"Yep. Spent most of the day searching. Finally found one over in Whittaker. Got it pretty cheap—needs a new coat of paint, but it should do well for the rest of the winter."

Lydia ran a gloved hand over the polished top edge. She'd always loved sleighs. "How long had you been looking to buy one?"

"Since this morning."

Lydia wondered if all of his years riding under the hot Texas sun had addled his brain. He wasn't making a bit of sense. "This morning?"

He chuckled softly. "You're sounding like a parrot I once saw in Houston. Damned if that bird didn't repeat everything a man said."

Amused, she ignored that.

Instead of baiting her further or telling her that he'd purchased the sleigh specifically with her and this evening in mind, Gray asked, "So do you want to stand here and freeze, or take a ride in my sleigh?"

Lydia swore she saw mischief in his eyes. "Ride," she replied softly.

"Good."

He handed her in, and while she sat down on the bench he went around to the driver's side and took his seat. Once they were both comfortable, he picked up the reins and said, "There's a big blanket under the seat. Make yourself comfortable and we'll be on our way."

Lydia reached beneath the seat and almost fell over trying to extract the heavy covering from beneath the bench. "Good Lord," she complained good-naturedly. "What is this thing made of, iron?"

"No, buffalo hide. Here, let me get it for you."

Perfectly willing to let him play the gentleman, Lydia scooted over so he could retrieve it, but she was unprepared when he draped it over her so gently. He was close enough for her to see her cold breath mingling with his in the moonlight. Needing a way to distract herself from his captivating allure, she asked inanely, "Did this really come from a buffalo?" The texture was soft, and the skin was as warm as it was heavy.

"Yes," he replied, his eyes holding hers. They were only a kiss apart, and Lord knows, Gray wanted to, but if he did kiss her, he'd never let her go and they would freeze to death, right here in front of her mother's house. "How about we get moving?"

Lydia could feel the warmth of his nearness in spite of the cold temperature. "Where to?"

"To my house. If that's OK? It's about a mile and half from Mother's."

In response to his overwhelming presence, all she could do was nod.

The Danes and Coopers only lived a few miles apart, so the journey over the moonlit snow didn't take very long. However, because Lydia hadn't ridden in a sleigh in such a long time and loved traveling in this fashion so much, she admitted to being a bit disappointed when he drew the horses to a halt a short while later.

The darkness made it hard for Lydia to determine the color of Gray's home, but it was a small two-story farmhouse, complete with glass windows and a wide sitting porch that curved around the exterior. She wondered if he'd built the place for his marriage to Anna Mae or after.

He came around to help her out of the sleigh, then led her up the walk. "Go on in. I want to put the horse back in the barn."

Lydia started to protest; she didn't want to be so presumptuous as to enter alone, but he'd already turned away, so there was nothing left but to go on inside.

The interior was warm. She looked around the small foyer and saw that there were three rooms evenly spaced around its circumference. One room had a door that was closed. The two remaining entrances were without doors but were framed by tied-back deep crimson draping

trimmed with braided gold fringe, a common way of decorating in the Midwest.

Her attention was then caught by a beautiful copper-
framed mirror hanging on the foyer wall and the startling
sight of the bleached-out skull of some type of animal with
long curving horns hanging on the wall above it. She peered
at the head this way and that and supposed it could be a
cow, but she wasn't certain. She was certain that she'd
never seen anything quite as exotic displayed in a home
before. Did all Texans decorate their homes this way? Since
she had no way of answering that, either, she turned away
from the skull and walked over to peek into the other
rooms. One was a sparsely furnished parlor. Inside, the
turned-down wicks of the lamps barely illuminated the two
upholstered chairs and the settee, but the roaring fireplace
burned brightly with a beckoning light of its own.

The other room was the dining room, where stood a
table set for two, complete with snow-white tablecloth, polished tableware, matching china, and gleaming crystal gob-
lets. The sight took her breath away. Centering the table
were two ivory candlesticks standing tall in crystal holders.
Lydia thought the display simply beautiful. When she heard
Gray enter behind her, she turned and said to him, "The
table's very lovely, Gray."

"But not half as lovely as you, my lady," he wanted to
say. Instead, he replied, "I'll relay your compliments to
Marie, my housekeeper. She's the one responsible. Let me
have your cape."

Lydia undid the frogs at the collar, then slid the garment
from her shoulders. Gray took the cape from her hand and
his eyes lingered on the cameo hanging against her skin. It
was as beautiful as she, and Gray found the sight of her so
arousing, he had to force himself not to move closer, because in reality he wished to slowly brush his lips against
her throat and inhale the scent of her perfume. The carved
ivory keepsake had been his gift to her for her fifteenth
birthday. That she still had it and wore it tonight made it
even harder for him to remain where he was. Reminding

himself once again of tonight's innocent purpose, he took her wrap over to the hooks by the door and hung it there.

Lydia could feel the desire stirring the air as well. One of the other reasons Burton Shaw had broken off their engagement was because she hadn't been moved by his kisses. He'd called her an iceberg. She certainly didn't feel cold with Gray.

When Gray removed his coat, Lydia saw his black-vested suit for the first time. It fit his tall frame well and she knew there wasn't a woman alive who wouldn't be moved by such a glorious man. As if he'd sensed her thoughts, he turned, and their eyes met. Both stilled as thoughts mingled and memories surfaced, bringing back stolen kisses, humid touches, and the newly awakened senses of adolescent love.

Gray surveyed this grown-up Lydia and thought she'd come back home as polished as a jewel. He wondered how far she would throw him if he suggested making love. "Marie left us warm cider in the kitchen. Would you like some?"

"I would. Thank you."

"Go on into the parlor; it's probably warmest in there. Let me stoke up the fire in here and then I'll bring your cider."

Lydia walked slowly into the small parlor. The blazing fire in the grate drew her to walk over and warm her hands against its heat. She tried not to think about where this evening might lead, but even a spinster of thirty-one could feel the currents rising. She moved her mind away from that and took a seat on the large overstuffed sofa that was angled before the fire. Lydia's virginal urges wouldn't let her rest, however. What would it be like to be kissed by him again? Would they be different now that she and Gray were grown? Her last chance at marriage was gone now that Burton had backed out of her life. Lydia was neither young nor able to bear children, qualities most men placed great value upon. That in mind, she stood very little chance of ever feeling the loving sweep of a man's hand or learning the mysteries of the marriage bed. She would go to her grave never having heard a man whisper to her in the dark or whisper to him in return. Lydia was sure society would be scandalized by the directions her thoughts were taking— headmistresses weren't supposed to dwell upon such matters—but this homecoming was making her look at many things hiding deep in her soul.

Gray returned a few moments later carrying two mugs of cider. She took one. He kept the other, asking, "Are you comfortable?"

She sipped delicately and nodded. The cider was warm and good. "Yes, I am."

She tried not to acknowledge how nervous she'd suddenly become and chalked it up to her scandalous musing of a few moments ago, but Gray's presence certainly wasn't helping. He was seated in a chair opposite her, and his dark eyes seemed to blaze as vividly as the coals. What she read in them made her senses flare all the more. "This is a very nice house," she said in an effort to move her thoughts to calmer ground.

"Thank you." He let her take another sip before asking, "Remember the creek where we used to fish?"

"Yes," she said with a smile.

"That's where this house is."

She met his eyes. "Really? I guess it's been so long since I've been home and with it being dark, I didn't realize where we were." She hadn't thought about the creek in years. They'd had some wonderful times there. "Remember that old boot I caught?"

He chuckled. "I do. Took us three-quarters of an hour to land the thing."

"It was pulling on the fishing line so hard, I knew it had to be a whale."

They laughed, the first one they'd shared in a very long time. They seemed to realize that, and a silence descended upon the room.

A now-serious Gray looked her way, still unable to believe she was truly, physically here. "Do you remember the first time we met?"

Feeling her barriers melting fast, she replied, "I do. I was beating the tar out of Hamilton Green for stuffing my brand-new mittens into Mr. Tart's inkwell at school. You called yourself coming to my rescue."

Gray remembered the incident, too, because he'd fallen in love with her the moment he saw her. "Good thing I did. Otherwise, Ham might not have lived to grow up to become my best friend."

The memory filled her heart. "How is Ham?"

"Doing fine. He and Bert live up in Muskegon. Five kids, last count."

"My goodness. So many?"

"Well, remember, Bertrice has seven brothers and sisters. She's accustomed to a house full of younguns."

Bertrice Sullivan had been Lydia's best friend. Hamilton Green had been Gray's. Having to leave Bert behind when Lydia left town had hurt Lydia as much as it had to leave Gray.

Gray sensed her change in mood. "Didn't mean to make you sad."

She told him truthfully, "I'm not sad. Sometimes your mind takes you places you can't control, that's all."

They both sipped cider in the silence; then Gray asked, "Are you ready to eat?"

"Yes, I believe so."

Gray stood and gestured her to walk ahead of him. They entered the now-cozy dining room and he helped her with her chair. Standing behind her, Gray had to fight off the urge to place a soft kiss on the back of her bare neck. Taking a deep calming breath, he stepped away and took his seat across the table from her.

"I forgot something," he said, and withdrew from his pocket a box of matches. After he lit the tall candles, the soft glow added even more intimacy to the room. "How's that?" he asked as he sat down again.

She gazed at him through the shimmering points of the

twin flames. "Very nice." And it was; everything was nice: from the setting, to the company, to how she felt inside.

He raised his cider to her in toast. "To old friends."

Lydia followed his lead and saluted him in response. "To old friends."

After taking another sip, she set her drink down very aware that he was watching her every move.

Gray's past knowledge of Lydia's moods and mannerisms made him say softly, "There's nothing to be nervous about, you know."

"I know. It's just that we're not adolescents anymore, Gray."

He ran his eyes over the way she looked in that gorgeous dress, then said to her, "No, we aren't, so how about we let the evening bring what it brings, OK? I won't make any demands; I promise. Lord knows I'd like to, but that isn't why we're here."

She met his eyes and wondered if he felt the heat rising in the room, too.

He did.

"OK," she said in reply.

"How about passing me your plate and we'll start on Marie's feast."

They ate the meal languidly, enjoying the plump roasted pheasant and its well-seasoned stuffing, along with the squash, cranberry relish, and bread. They talked of old times, old friends, and the events that had taken place in their lives while they'd been apart.

"What made you want to teach?"

"I have to start from the beginning."

"OK."

"Well, when I went to Chicago to stay with my aunt, she was working as the school's cook at the time, and she got me a job in the kitchen there as well. One day I came across one of the younger girls crying in the hallway. When I asked what was wrong, she told me that she couldn't do some of the sums she'd been assigned in preparation for an upcoming examination, and none of the older girls would help her. So, I did."

"Good for you." He toasted her with his water goblet. Gray had decided not to have wine this evening because her presence was the only intoxicant he needed.

"Thank you. Well, word got around, and soon, the other girls were seeking me out for help, and when Mrs. Isaacs, the headmistress, found out what I'd been doing, she took me out of the kitchen and placed me in the classroom. A few months later, she sponsored me at Oberlin, and when I finished the Women's Program, I came back to teach full-time at her school."

"Is Mrs. Isaacs still teaching as well?"

"No, she died a few years after my return from Oberlin. She had no other kin, so she willed her school to me."

"Is the place doing well?"

"It is. I have thirty students. Some live on the property, but most are local children."

"Girls and boys?"

"No, only girls."

He studied her. "Why no boys?"

"Because boys can receive an education anywhere. Many young ladies can't."

"I see. Do your girls know what a hellion you were growing up?"

She grinned. "No, and I forbid you to tell them."

"Forbid? That's a pretty strong word for a girl who put tadpoles in old lady Webb's lemonade."

Lydia exploded with laughter. "Oh my. I'd forgotten about that prank." Old lady Webb taught Sunday school at the church. "I was so tired of her telling me I was going to hell."

He smiled. "Back then, all hellions went to hell."

"Well, it was embarrassing to hear her declare to the whole class every Sunday that I wasn't going to heaven. She hurt my feelings, and that picnic gave me the perfect opportunity to pay her back."

He remembered. "I remember you couldn't sit for a

week after your mother learned what you'd done." Then he added, "Come to think about it, you were in trouble a lot back then."

She cut him a look of mock warning. "That's not the point."

"Well, I still think someone should warn the parents of your students that you weren't as pristine then as you seem now."

"Do I seem pristine to you?"

"Very."

Lydia wondered if he found her cold, too. "Pristine and cold—as, say, an iceberg might be?"

Gray puzzled that over for a moment, then asked her quietly, "What are we talking about here, Lydia?"

She waved him off. "Nothing. I'm sorry."

He peered at her through the candles. "Lydia?"

"It's nothing, Gray. Really."

"Talk to me, Lydie."

He'd spoken her nickname so softly, so familiarly, her walls tumbled. She took a moment to frame what she wanted to say, then began, "All right. I was engaged to a man named Burton Shaw, but this past summer he broke things off."

So, there had been a man in her life. Gray admitted not liking knowing that. "Go on."

Lydia sensed his displeasure, but rather than ask what right he had to be upset by her confession and start a row, she carried on with her story. "Burton decided he couldn't marry me for a number of reasons, one being I can't have children." She looked up into his eyes and let him see the pain of that.

Gray's heart broke. He wanted to pull her into his arms, hold her tight, and tell her it didn't matter. "I'm so sorry."

She nodded, appreciating his caring and concern. She smiled a bit. "My students make up for it in many ways, but I did want children of my own."

"I know."

In their adolescent world of love, Lydia and Gray, like

many other young couples, had often fantasized about the
gender of the children they would have, how many there
would be, and what these mythical children might be
named, but sometimes reality mows down fantasy like a
fast-moving train, and that's what the news from the doctors had done to Lydia.

Gray was admittedly upset that Lydia had been treated
so shabbily by her intended, mainly because it called to
mind his own mistreatment of her. "You shouldn't let his
crying off sour you on getting married in the future.
Granted, some men want heirs, but not all."

When Lydia and Gray were young, no matter how many
scrapes, fights, or other dramatic escapades she found herself embroiled in, he had always been at her side, her champion, her warrior, her love. "It wasn't his only reason."

"What was the other?" Gray asked. Apparently, Shaw
had no clue as to how precious Lydia Cooper was; once,
fifteen years ago, Gray had been just as ignorant.

"He called me cold—an iceberg. When you described
me as being 'pristine,' that made me think back on Burton."

"Why did he call you that?"

Lydia raised her chin. "Because I never warmed to his
kisses."

Gray cheered inside but was careful not to show it on
his face. "Did you love him?"

Again she told the truth: "No. I said yes to his suit because we had common interests and I thought he was a
decent, upstanding man." Only later did she learn that he
was both arrogant and overbearing. In truth, she had been
relieved when he called the whole thing off.

Chapter 6

After listening to her story, Gray decided that it was time for the man he had become to bare his soul and offer her the apology she was due. "I never apologized to you."

Emotions wafted through Lydia: sadness, loss, anger. She sensed her barriers going up again. "This isn't necessary, Gray."

"Yes, is it. I did you a great wrong."

Lydia remembered the pledge she'd made to her mother about listening to what he might have to say. Lydia also took into account the softening of her own feelings toward him. "Then go ahead," she said to him.

He reached across the table and placed his large hands on top of hers. The warmth seemed to penetrate to her bones. He looked over into her eyes. "If there was a way for me to go back and undo what I did, I would. I hurt you very badly, and the guilt has been eating at me since the day you left. I wanted to cut out my heart when you left town."

She whispered plainly, "And I wanted to cut out mine when I heard you were marrying Anna Mae." Anger was laced with that truth, an anger Lydia now wanted to lay to rest. "My mother's letters said you weren't married very long, though."

He drew away. "No, we weren't."

Lydia's hands felt cold.

"I didn't love her," Gray confessed. "Anna Mae had it in her mind that once we became man and wife I would, but of course, I never did." Gray knew that the reason he'd had no room in his heart for Anna Mae was because he'd already given it to Lydia. "The whole affair was a sham from beginning to end."

"It must have hurt to know she lost the babe, though."

His eyes went cold. "There was never any proof that she was carrying."

Lydia cocked her head. "Surely she would not have lied about something so serious."

He spoke bitterly: "I learned early on that Anna Mae and her relatives would lie about their names if they thought it would pay. Yes, Anna was thrown from her horse—there were witnesses—but the rest?" He shrugged. "She was taken to her mother's house immediately after her spill, and the doctor was supposedly brought in. I wasn't informed until hours later, and when I arrived, her mother told me Anna had miscarried."

"I'm sorry."

His mood darkening, he replied, "Don't be. It's my fault, all of it."

Lydia couldn't dispute that. His youthful lust had resulted in ramifications still echoing today, but her mother was right: he had suffered. Lydia could see it in his eyes. She could hear it in his voice, and she knew then that the breach between them had to be healed so they could meet on level ground once more. "Gray—"

He waved his hand dismissively. "I don't know what I was thinking inviting you to dinner. After the mess I made of everyone's life, why am I even subjecting you to my company?"

He got up from the table and went and stood in front of one of the room's windows. He stared out at the darkness with his back to her.

She replied quietly, "Oh, I don't know. I'm having a fairly good time."

He went still, then turned. He searched her face.

Lydia asked with amused eyes, "Did Marie make us any dessert?"

He still hadn't moved. "Dessert?" he asked as if he'd just heard her request.

"Yes. I'm the one with the sweet tooth, remember?"

He shook himself, then said, "I thought you wanted to talk."

"You wanted to talk. I want dessert."

He stared.

She said earnestly, "Gray, my mother said something to me today that I've decided to take to heart. It was about living in the past and how it can keep you from relishing the blessings that might await you in the present. I hated your very name for many years. I hated Anna Mae. I hated myself in a way, because when a woman is young and has her heart broken, she ofttimes believes the fault was her own."

"It wasn't your fault."

"I know, Gray, but at some point one has to go on, and I've decided to do just that."

"Then you forgive me."

"No," she chuckled.

"No?!"

"No. I will never forgive you for giving Anna Mae what was supposed to be mine." It was the most daring declaration she'd ever made in her life, but the words were true.

A surprised, amused, and, yes, shocked Gray stared at her with disbelief. "Lydia?"

She replied with more confidence than she felt, "Women these days are being encouraged to speak their minds. I'm speaking mine."

"I see." He wasn't sure what he was seeing, though. "So, what are you telling me, Lydia Cooper?"

She raised her chin and said with a sly smile, "That I want my dessert, Grayson Dane."

His eyes sparkled. "Oh, really?"

"Yes, really."

Gray wondered if she'd intended to sound so provocative. "Then that is what you shall have. . . ."

Dessert was chocolate cake. It was her favorite, and when he brought the three-layer beauty out to the table, the sight touched her feelings. "You remembered."

Gray said softly, "Of course." He set the cake onto the table, cut her a wedge, and placed it on a plate.

She took the plate from his hand and beamed. "Thank you."

"You're welcome."

Lydia forked up a small piece and as it melted into her mouth, she groaned pleasurably, "Oh my . . ."

Gray's manhood stirred at the sensuous sound. "That good?"

"Oh, this is heaven."

Gray thought her heavenly, too, and found himself becoming more and more aroused. He thought back to what she'd said a moment ago about never forgiving him for giving Anna Mae what should have been her own. Her frankness made him smile. It also made the male in him wonder what it might be like to make love to her now. Here. "Were you really going to marry that Shaw character without being in love with him?"

"Yes. There are very few love match opportunities for a thirty-one-year-old spinster."

"Is that how you see yourself?"

"Yes." Then she added, "I am who I am, and according to my former fiancé, I should add cold fish to my list of qualities as well."

Gray told her, "There's nothing wrong with you. You were just with the wrong man. . . ."

Lydia studied him. "How so?"

"Any man worth his salt should have no trouble heating up his woman."

The bluntly voiced statement made Lydia's heart flutter.

"Shall I show you . . ."

Lydia was already warm and he hadn't even come near her.

He slowly set his napkin aside, then rose to his feet. He walked around the table to her chair. When he reached her, he looked down and extended his hand. A shaking Lydia put down her fork and rose to join him. They stood no more than a breath apart.

He stroked her cheek and said to her softly, "As beautiful as you are . . . you shouldn't have to settle for anyone or anything."

While she reacted to that, he slowly traced a finger over her mouth, then leaned down and gently pressed his lips to hers. "Let me show you. . . ."

He gave her a series of sweet short kisses that teased and beckoned, kisses that drew her closer to him, kisses that tempted her to join him and made her lips part so that he could dart his tongue languidly over the sensitive corners. The initial feel of his tongue thrilled her as she kissed him back, learning, following. Soon, the short sweet kisses ceased to be enough. Passion rose. Intensity flared and they both caught fire.

Her arms circled him as the kiss deepened. Groaning with emotion, he tightened an arm across her back, pulled her closer, and let all the feelings he'd been forced to bury for fifteen years pour forth like a flood.

Lydia returned the kiss joyously, welcoming him, inviting him, wanting to make up for lost time as well. Tears in her eyes, she savored holding him and being held in return. She'd dreamed of this moment and now knew that sometimes dreams do come true.

Easing his lips from hers, Gray wrapped both arms around her and held her as if he would never let her go. "Lord, I missed you," he said huskily as he rocked her against his chest.

Ignoring the tears sliding down her cheeks, Lydia clung to him as if life depended upon it. "I missed you, too. So very much . . ."

Gray was so overcome by emotion, his eyes were misty,

too. "When no one would tell me where you'd gone . . ." The days following her disappearance had been terrible ones for Gray. Granted, Miriam had assured him repeatedly that Lydia was alive and well, but he hadn't wanted words; he'd wanted to see her with his own eyes, even though he no longer had that right.

Lydia could hear his heart beating beneath his soft wool vest. She, too, remembered how awful it had been being separated. "I cried every night for weeks after I left."

In response to her whispered confession, Gray tipped up her chin so he could study her face. He brushed away the tears staining her cheeks. "I joined the cavalry hoping I'd forget you, but it never happened."

She laid her palm lovingly against his strong jaw and confessed, "I never forgot you, either."

Gray turned her palm to his lips and planted a tender kiss in the center. He knew then that no matter where this reunion led, he would continue to love her until the day he died.

Lydia could feel the woman inside herself calling for more kisses. "Will you do something for me, Gray?"

He pressed his lips to hers and whispered, "Anything."

"Make love to me."

He drew away slowly. The four words were the most beautiful ones he'd ever heard, but he wasn't sure she meant it. "That's a mighty powerful invitation, school-marm."

"And not one I toss out lightly, soldier man."

Gray hardened instantly. "You're serious."

Lydia said boldly, softly, "Yes, I am."

He searched her face for any doubts. "What about after?"

Lydia shrugged. "I can't become pregnant, so there will be no reason for an after."

Gray wasn't talking about babies but decided they could discuss the future later. He traced her lips, then kissed her softly. "You're supposed to be an iceberg."

Lydia could feel her body pulsing with newly awakened

sensations brought on by his kisses. "But I'm not, am I?"

Gray grinned. This was the sassy, outrageous Lydia he once knew and loved. "No, you aren't." The idea that such a woman lay hidden beneath the prim and proper exterior made all kinds of carnal desires fill his head.

Lydia leaned into him and asked coyly, "So, will you do this for me?"

He grinned and declared softly, "Oh, yes, ma'am." Aroused by the scents and reality of her, Gray slowly lowered his head and kissed her again, like a lover this time, deeply, possessively. Leaving her breathless, he kissed her jaw, her throat. He brushed his mouth over the skin above her breasts, and Lydia melted into her shoes. His lips were hot, and that same heat burned a slow path back up to her jaw. His mouth claimed hers again. He slipped his tongue into the sweetness he found there, and his tongue mated hungrily with hers. His hands slowly mapped the lines of her back and waist; then his fingers skimmed over the skin around the cameo.

Gray wanted to undress her and have her for dessert. Now. He wanted to raise her skirts, lovingly spread her angel's wings, and show her the way to paradise, but he tasted an innocence in her fiery kisses, the innocent fire of a virgin, so he needed to let her set the pace.

Lydia could hear her breathing mingling with the silence and the crackle of the fire. His kisses now descending to explore her throat had left her mouth parted and swollen. She was afire, her heart was beating in time, and she wanted this night to never end.

Gray moved a dark finger over the heart-shaped décolletage and when her head fell back in response he kissed her open mouth deeply. "Lord, you're sweet . . . sweeter than I ever imagined."

Lydia thrilled to the words, then lost touch with everything but him when his hands possessively cupped the weight of her breasts and he brazenly circled his tongue around the edges of the ivory cameo. He eased down one side of her dress, freeing a brown nipple from her chemise to his boldy dallying fingers. As he pleasured her, Lydia died and went to heaven. He kissed her mouth, making heat pulse in her blood and the bud between his fingers harden like an exotic jewel.

Gray was not the adolescent boy Lydia had left behind; the man fueling her senses this night was experienced in the gifting of pleasure. His touches were both potent and dazzling. As the virgin headmistress of a school for young women, she had no business encouraging such scandalous behavior, but she didn't want him to stop.

Gray's eyes glowed malely at the sight of her body crooning to the tune he was so boldly coaxing from her nipple. "Shall I stop?"

Lydia's body pulsed with a warmth that was centered between her thighs.

When she didn't answer, he promised in a hot, thick voice, "If you don't tell me to stop, Lydie . . . I'm going to touch you, and kiss you in places that are going to make you scream with pleasure. . . ."

Fitting actions to words, he lowered his head and took her well-prepared nipple into his mouth. She dissolved. A strangled growl rose out of her throat. He rolled the bud around his tongue, then bit her gently.

Next, he lowered the other side of her dress and helped himself to that passion-tightened bud as well. She could hardly stand. Her legs had all the strength of gravy, and her world reeled from his hotly worded promise.

Gray's manhood was hard as a railroad tie. The reality of enjoying her this way made him even harder. Still feasting on the jewel-hard points of her breasts, Gray moved his hands up and down her back, then over the yielding flesh of her hips. The gown slid smoothly, letting him savor the curve of her behind while his palms burned over her underskirts and then beneath them to the thin fabric of her drawers.

Lydia trembled, but this was Gray, her Gray, and she might never be given this gift again. She whispered against his mouth in reply, "Teach me. . . ."

Gray was rock-hard. He couldn't stop touching her. He slipped his hand into the opening of her drawers and found her swollen, ripe, and responsive.

That first intimate touch sent Lydia spiraling. "Oh, Gray . . ." She'd never had a man touch her so intimately before. She felt him toying, lingering; a storm was building, and its passion and heat made her widen her stance to better feel the thunder.

Gray gazed down at her rucked-down bodice, and the sight of her nipples drew his lips, even as his fingers continued to explore and tease the flowing treasure between her thighs. He could feel her hips moving with the age-old rhythm of desire, could feel her trembling on the edge of completion. "Let's bring you to pleasure. . . ."

Lydia had no idea what that meant and was too buffeted by the storm to care, but when Gray fitted actions to words by easing a long lusty finger into the passage to her soul, the erotic claiming made the orgasm explode, buckling her, arching her body until she cried out in the silence just as he'd promised she would.

His manhood roaring, Gray guided her with his touch and watched her ride out her pleasure.

Lydia came back to herself on shaky legs and pulsing everywhere. Her harsh breathing finally slowed and she focused on Gray's watching face.

He gave her that crooked smile that made him look seventeen again and said, "Well?"

She grinned. "Well, what?"

"Guess you really aren't an iceberg."

Still feeling the echoes of her orgasm, she said, "Guess not."

He echoed, "Guess not."

Lydia was immediately embarrassed and happy, and she dropped her head to hide her pleased smile. She never knew that a man's touch could shatter her so. Her eyes lifted to his and she said teasingly, "It's a good thing we never did this when we were young; otherwise my mother would have been the person standing over you with a shotgun instead of Anna Mae's daddy."

He grinned and toyed a finger over her bare breast. "And I would have gone down the aisle willingly, knowing I could do this . . ." He ran a finger over her bare breast and watched her eyes lid shut in response. ". . . and this. . . ." He lowered his mouth to the hard, damp bud and sucked at it luxuriously until her head fell back and her lips parted. He asked hotly, "Would you have liked that? . . ."

Lydia moaned with quiet pleasure.

His voice was thick with desire, his blood pulsing. "You have to answer me, Lydie; otherwise, I can't tell you what else I could have done. . . ."

He raised his head and gazed into her passion-lidded eyes. His fingers played with her yearning nipple. "Do you want me to go on?"

Entranced by him and all the heady sensations whipping at her from all sides, she whispered, "Yes. . . ."

He gave her two soft kisses to reward her for responding. "Had I married you . . . we wouldn't have had to wait years for me to lift your skirt like this . . ." He slowly raised her dress and petticoats to her thighs to expose her stockings, garters, and drawers. The shimmering Lydia braced herself against the sturdy edge of the dining table.

". . . so I could touch you here. . . ."

His words and touch set her afire, and she widened her thighs shamelessly, willingly, so he could play.

Gray had no idea Lydia would be this passionate or uninhibited. Each touch made him want to touch her that much more. Unable to resist, he slid to his knees and kissed the inside of each silken thigh. He ran his fingers up to the citadel of his pleasure and slid them over her until she widened the way even more. Only then did he gently tug down her drawers and assist her steps out of them.

"Hold your dress aside for me, darlin'."

Lydia did as he asked. Nothing in life had ever prepared her for such an event, but this was what she wanted and she'd wanted it to be done by Gray. That in mind, she let him kiss the insides of her thighs, let his fingers touch and explore her in ways that made her mind weak and her senses soar.

He whispered then, "Had I married you . . . I could've brought you home and kissed you this way. . . ."

When she felt his finger open her and his lips give her the most sensual kiss imaginable, the shocked Lydia's first impulse was to jump away, but it was too late; she was already in the throes of his expertise and so could do nothing but hold onto her dress, hope her legs would continue to support her, and ride the waves of his brazen, brazen magic. And it was that; she'd never known lovemaking could be so scandalous and yet so blissfully delicious. He lingered and teased, nibbled and seduced. He gave her a hot and glorious lesson in a subject she never knew existed, and the tutoring didn't end until she screamed.

In the silence that followed, the eyes-closed Lydia couldn't believe the joy washing over her body. She thought him absolutely scandalous. Before she could fully recover he swept her up into his arms and began to walk her from the room. "Where are we going?" she asked, finally managing to find the words.

"Upstairs to my bed. I want you here and now, but your first time shouldn't be on my dining room table."

The words thrilled her. "What about the second time?"

Shocked but pleased, Gray laughed. "You need a keeper, do you know that?"

Lydia, still pulsing from his lessons, said, "I think you just got the job."

He grinned and said, "Just you wait, schoolmarm. The night has just begun."

Chapter 7

The short journey up to his bedroom could have been accomplished sooner had Gray not stopped every few steps to steal more kisses. Lydia didn't mind; she fervently returned all he had to give. By the time he carried her over the threshold, her passions were ignited again and she was eager to be schooled further. He didn't disappoint. He began with the slow removal of her dress. The small buttons that ran the length of her back were tackled first, and he took his own sweet time. Standing behind her, he saluted each new inch of bared skin with a kiss that sent pleasure-filled shivers up her spine. When the gown had opened enough, he slipped his hands into the gaps on each side and cupped her breasts held up for his delight by her lace-edged stays. As he leaned over to kiss her raised mouth, his fingers dazzled her pebble-hard nipples until she arched back against him sensually. He continued to ply her and kiss her until she moaned softly. Only then did he draw the gown down and off.

Gray gently turned her to face him. Against the backdrop of the fire in the grate and the wavering shadows, she made a lusty sight in her disheveled stays, stockings, and shoes. He looked at the dark vee of hair tempting him from the tops of her thighs and whispered, "You seem to have lost your drawers, ma'am." And he touched her there, making her eyes slide shut and her thighs tremble.

"A soldier took them," she whispered just as hotly.

Gray didn't know how much more of this play he could take, but he wanted her ready when the time came, not afraid or unable to enjoy his size. "You shouldn't let pony soldiers take your drawers."

Lydia didn't know what was heating her more—his words or the ripening enchantment his fingers were stoking between her thighs. "He rewarded me, though."

Delighted by her, Gray slipped a finger into her now-flowing core and felt her flesh tighten around it in erotic response.

Lydia mewled lustfully.

Gray watched her and asked in a passion-thickened voice, "Would you like another?"

Lydia couldn't respond. Her virgin's body had no stamina. When he slowly and deliberately removed his finger, then circled it wantonly over the swollen, throbbing treasure, she climaxed again, shaking and crying out hoarsely. She was still incoherent when he picked her up and carried her to the bed.

He removed the rest of her clothing with a sureness that made her sensitive body continue to sing. Leaving her nothing to wear but the ribbon and the cameo, he kissed her from her lips to her navel, including all the parts in between. While he withdrew for a moment to remove his own clothes, Lydia preened atop the soft flannel sheet.

Lydia had never seen a naked man before. Gray was a glorious sight to behold. His dark muscular frame gleamed in the firelight. The part of his anatomy that would make her a woman drew her eyes especially. She looked from that up to his mustached face. She raised herself to her knees and rested her weight back on her heels. In a voice as quiet as the room, she asked, "May I touch you?"

He was standing beside the bed. "Be my guest."

Emboldened, Lydia closed her hand around him and was pleasantly surprised by how warm and alive he felt. "I've never touched a man before."

"I'm glad your first time was with me."

She looked up and smiled shyly. "So am I." He felt like velvet-covered iron in her hand. "Tell me what to do."

Gray obliged, but her hot little hands were so good and so brazen, he quickly found himself on the verge of what the French called *la petite morte,* or the little death, so he growled and backed away.

Lydia was concerned. "Did I do something wrong?"

His mustache twitched with amusement. "No, but if I let you continue I'll have nothing left for the main event." He crawled onto the bed, then kissed her mouth. "Are you ready?"

"Yes."

As it turned out, they were both more than ready. After a few silent moments of arousing kisses, thrilling touches, and caresses that made each of them arch and strain for more, Gray entered her slowly. The pace was not easy to maintain. He was on fire for her and wanted nothing more than to surge home and stroke her until sunrise, but she was a virgin and Gray was no brute. "This may hurt, darlin'."

Lydia knew that, but for the moment her body was more than willing to accept his claiming. He filled her little by little, easing in and out, keeping her body hot and her core flowing. Then, just when she thought it couldn't get any better, he breached her barrier and suddenly—pain. She tensed and he offered soft kisses and even softer apologies. "I'm sorry, sweetheart. . . . This will be the only time it will hurt."

Lydia found herself not wanting to do this anymore. "Gray . . ."

He sensed her distress and whispered, "Give your body a few moments to adjust. If you want to stop, we will." Lord knew he didn't want that, but it would be her choice.

"Is there a pony soldier remedy?"

He grinned. Was it any wonder he loved her? "It may take a few moments to work, but I think I know what might help."

"Then fix me, please."

So he began to stroke her gently, gingerly, teaching her yet another rhythm in hopes of showing her just how powerful lovemaking can be.

For the first few moments Lydia felt only a fiery invasion, but as he began to work her slowly, the pleasure returned. "Oh, better," she murmured in pleased tones. "Much better. . . ."

It was music to Gray's ears. She was now rising and falling in tandem with him, meeting him stroke for slow stroke, running her hands up and down his arms, even as she purred lustily. He was doing his best to hold back, but she was too tight, too responsive. All the sensual play leading up to this moment, coupled with the joy of being with her again, was more than any man was expected to carry, and it fueled him to increase his pace. He wanted her to know how much he loved her; wanted her to feel how much.

Lydia had no more pain. Bliss had overridden it. His hands on her nipples were bliss. The deep, soul-thrilling strokes were bliss. When he increased the pace, she went with him willingly, rising and falling under his lusty direction. The powerful strokes were compelling, breathtaking, and so overwhelmingly wonderful that a few splendid moments later her entire being exploded and she was flung into a thousand brilliant pieces.

Gray felt the sensual contractions of her climaxing flesh and he couldn't hold out any longer. His release rose. Throwing back his head, he surrendered with a roar that echoed loudly around the room.

In the quiet aftermath, Gray and Lydia lay cuddled together. The crackling of the fire was the only sound until Lydia said softly, "Thank you, Gray."

He kissed the top of her mussed hair. "No. Thank you."

She asked playfully, "Was it worth a fifteen-year wait?"

He ran a slow finger around one of her nipples. "Most definitely, but I don't want to wait another fifteen to do it again. Marry me."

Lydia stilled.

He turned over so he could see her face in the dark. "Marry me and we can love until we're both old and gray."

Parts of Lydia were jumping with glee at the prospect, but she set them aside. "That isn't why I wanted this night, Gray."

"I'm aware of that."

She searched his face in the shadows. "You know I'm going to say no."

"I'd considered that." He hadn't really, because the idea to propose had just come to him.

"But—" she said.

Gray had forgotten how well she once knew him. "But I've decided I'm not taking no for an answer."

She chuckled softly. "Arrogant as ever."

"And you're stubborn as ever. Give me one good reason why you can't marry me."

Lydia chose not to voice her main reason because it was too painful to admit. Instead she offered, "How about my school and the students who will expect me to return after the holidays?"

"I'm not asking you to give up your school."

"Then you are willing to move to Chicago? Running a school is a twenty-four-hour-a-day undertaking."

Admittedly Gray had no intentions of moving to Chicago. "There are trains, you know."

Lydia remained silent.

"Give me another."

"You said one," she reminded him in an amused voice.

"That one wasn't good enough."

She smiled and shook her head. "How about, I don't need a man to take care of me?"

"Economically, you are correct, but physically, that's another story." He kissed her to prove his point, leaving her breathless and dazed as she asked, "Are all men so conceited?"

"Just us transplanted Texans."

As much as Lydia wanted a repeat of his loving, she sat

up instead, saying quietly, "I should be getting home. Mama's probably worrying."

"What are you running from, Lydia?"

She'd forgotten how well he once knew her. "From you, Gray."

Her truthfulness had always been one of her stronger traits. "Why?"

"So that I won't say yes to your proposal."

He stroked the satin skin of her back. "I want to marry you, Lydia."

"I know, but it isn't a good idea."

As much as it pained her to do so, Lydia slipped from the bed. "Is there someplace I . . . can wash?"

"Yes, through that door."

She supposed she should be embarrassed by her nudity, but she wasn't. If anything, the intensity of his gaze filled her with a newborn sense of feminine power. "I had a good time, Gray."

He nodded, wanting her to stay, but she disappeared into the bathing room.

It was a bit past midnight by the time they started out. Lydia sat beside him on the seat of the sleigh. She was huddled beneath the buffalo hide trying to convince herself that turning down Gray's proposal continued to be a sound decision. Nothing more had been said about her refusal, but she knew Gray well enough to realize that the discussion would probably be revisited; she just had to keep saying no—even if she didn't want to.

Gray was determined to change her mind. It was plain she hadn't offered up the real reason behind her refusal, and it irked him that with the holidays looming he didn't have much time to ferret out the truth. Now that he'd found her again and had made love to her, he didn't want to lose her again. He wanted her by his side as his wife, companion, and lover for the rest of their lives. He sensed that she wanted the same, but something haunting her was holding her back.

When he pulled the horses to a halt in front of her mother's cottage, Lydia sighed. The night was over. In the morning, she would wake up and life would go on as before. She'd been changed, though. The knowledge of Eve was now her own, and no matter how much she wanted to return to the paradise she and Gray had created, Lydia knew she was destined to walk the rest of her life's journey alone. Leaning over, she kissed him softly, then whispered, "Thank you. I must go."

And though Gray wanted to prevent her flight, he did not. With emotionless eyes, he watched her hurry up the walk and go inside.

The next morning was Sunday, and Lydia and Miriam went to church. Lydia knew a house of worship was not the place to be dwelling on Gray's lovemaking talents, but remnants of the glow remained, making it hard for her to concentrate on the reverend's fiery sermon. It didn't help to know that Gray had come to church this morning as well and was seated at his mother's side. He'd met Lydia's eyes upon entering, making every caress he'd given to her last night float back with vivid detail. The only saving grace was that he was seated across the aisle, though the distance did little to dampen her senses to the powerful call of his presence.

After church, Lydia was greeted warmly by the folks she'd grown up with, the church ladies, parents of her old friends, and Mrs. Dane. Elizabeth gave her a strong, loving hug. "Oh, Lydia. It is such a joy to see you again."

Lydia returned the embrace just as strongly. "Hello, Mrs. Dane. It's good to see you as well."

Gray was standing beside his mother, but Lydia ignored him for the moment—or at least attempted to.

Mrs. Dane stepped back and said, "Gray says you're leaving again after the New Year?"

"Yes, ma'am."

"And that you're a teacher?"

"I am."

"That's wonderful. I'll bet your students love you."

Lydia chuckled, "It depends on how much work I've assigned."

Mrs. Dane smiled. "You've grown into such a beauty. Hasn't she, Gray?"

Gray didn't lie. "Yes, she has."

Lydia's eyes moved to his. The heat she saw reflected in them made her hastily look away.

Mrs. Dane said, "I must be going, but if you find the time, please stop by so we can visit. I'd love to hear more."

"I will if I can."

Mrs. Dane gave her another strong hug. "Welcome home, Lydia."

"Thank you," Lydia replied genuinely.

Then Mrs. Dane and her son departed.

Just as Miriam promised, Dr. Watson Miller came to dinner that evening. He'd missed church this morning because of one of the neighbors had suddenly taken ill. Miriam was obviously glad to see him. She presented him to her daughter: "Lydia. You remember Dr. Miller?"

Lydia did. The love in his eyes when he looked upon her mother's face told Lydia all she needed to know about the depth of his feelings. "I do. Hello, Dr. Miller."

"Hello, Lydia. Look at you. You're all grown up."

Lydia acknowledged him almost shyly. "Yes, I am. How are you, sir?"

"Just fine. You?"

"I'm well. I hear you want to marry my mother."

"I do. Very much."

"Then let me be the first to offer my congratulations."

He smiled beneath his thin graying mustache. "Thanks. Took me a long time to get her to say yes, but when she did, she made me the happiest man in the world." He slipped his arm around her mother's trim waist and eased her in against his side.

Miriam beamed. "How about we eat?"

Dr. Miller helped her mother with her chair at the table and in the process of doing so whispered something in Miriam's ear that made her giggle like a schoolgirl. Lydia couldn't hear what transpired, of course, but the sight of her mother's happiness touched Lydia's heart and made her smile. It also made Gray's face rise in her mind and what the two of them might have had together, had life turned out differently.

Gray sat across the table from his mother. The food on his plate lay untouched because he wasn't hungry.

His mother noticed the still-full plate. "Gray dear, are you ill?"

Her voice broke through his brooding. "No. Well, not in the real sense. I asked Lydia to marry me last night, but she turned me down."

"Then I take it matters between you have been smoothed out."

He thought of how passionate Lydia had been in his bed last night. "To a point, yes."

"Did she give you a reason why she said no?"

"She did. She talked about not wanting to leave her school and such. I sense there is something else at play, but she refuses to tell me what it is."

Mrs. Dane said then, "The fact that you two have reconciled is heartening. I loved Lydia very much."

"I know, Mother. I did as well."

"But is wanting to marry her truly in your heart, Gray, or are you simply trying to make up for the past?"

"Both. I still love her. Marrying her and showing her just how much I do will make up for the past."

Mrs. Dane studied her only son. "Well, you know I wish you luck. I would love to have Lydia as the mother of my grandchildren, even now."

"She's barren, Mother."

Mrs. Dane studied him.

"She took ill while in Chicago, so there will be no grandchildren if we marry. I'm sorry. Had she not left town to escape the scandal she would not have gotten ill. That, too, is my doing."

His mother placed a sympathetic hand atop his. "You don't know that for truth, Gray. Please don't fault yourself."

"She wanted children. *We* wanted children. Now—"

"Now, there will be none, but I love her no less."

He placed his hand atop his mother's. "You have always stood by me, no matter the price."

"You are my only child. My son. I will stand with you until my last breath."

He squeezed her hand emotionally. "Thank you." He then asked, "Am I wrong in continuing to pursue Lydia?"

"What does your heart say?"

He smiled. "To find out her real reason for turning me down."

"Then that's what you should do."

"If I marry her, there will be no one to inherit all you and Father worked to build when I am gone."

"Does that matter to you?" his mother asked.

"No. I want Lydia for herself. Not for her childbearing potential."

"Have you told her this?"

"The discussion never progressed that far."

"It could be that that is what is plaguing her."

Gray thought on that for a moment. "Surely she knows that wouldn't matter to me. It can't be something so simple."

"Not being able to bear children for the man you love is not a *simple* matter, Gray."

He was instantly contrite. "I didn't mean to sound so flippant, but I don't care whether she can bear children or not. I want her for my wife."

"Well, if the love you two had is still there, I'm sure you will find a way to resolve whatever the issue may be."

Gray sincerely hoped she was right.

Chapter 8

Christmas Day was fast approaching. The church choir had been rehearsing since last week for the Christmas Day service, and the residents of Sumpter were putting the last touches on gift making, holiday baking, and planning for the arrival of family and friends. Lydia and Miriam's holidays had traditionally been quiet ones, even when Lydia was young. This year her mother would be getting married and Lydia couldn't think of a better way to honor the birth of the Lord.

Gray's marriage proposal continued to plague Lydia, however, following her, tempting her, making her remember his lovemaking and her own brazen responses. Would she ever be able to forget his volatile kisses or the way she'd shamelessly held aside her dress so he could feast upon her lustily? Now that her body had experienced the passionate sweep of a man's hand, she wanted to again. He'd whispered to her in the dark and she wanted that again also, yet it could not be. Gray had many business interests. His father had worked hard to accumulate all that Gray had inherited. When the time came, Gray would pass that legacy on to his own son, but to do so Gray would have to have a son, and Lydia could not bear him one. Her barrenness made marrying him impossible. In her mind, the novelty of her homecoming would fade for him once she returned to Chicago, enabling him to set his sights and heart on someone else. Lydia had lost him once to Anna Mae and no, she didn't want to lose him again, but the race needed men like Gray and it needed their sons. Since she could not contribute, it would be better if she stepped aside.

Gray's desire for Lydia had him so hog-tied, he couldn't work, sleep, or eat. He saw her face everywhere he looked. Since the night they'd made love he'd been craving her kisses, her smile, and the weight of her soft breasts in his hands. He dreamed about her every night, dreams that left him hard and pulsing when he awakened each morning. If he didn't find out why she wouldn't marry him, and find out soon, he thought he might explode from his pent-up emotions. He looked down at the ledger he'd been working on and realized he'd added the column of numbers wrong again. He swore softly, then shoved the offending ledger aside. This was all Lydia's fault. Were he not so madly in love with her, he would have no problem accepting her refusal, but he did love her, desire her, and want her in every way. The time had come to root out whatever cards she was holding, because dammit, he wanted her to be his wife and he wouldn't let her say no again without telling him the real reason why.

His decision made, Gray left the office, retrieved his wagon, and headed toward Miriam Cooper's cabin.

Miriam answered his knock on the door and, upon seeing him, smiled. "Well, hello, Gray. Come on in."

"Thank you. Brought you the wagon wheel you ordered. Do you want me to put it on?"

"How about we wait until after the holiday? I won't be needing the wagon for a while, and it's terribly cold out there."

It was an awful day. A storm was moving in from the west, bringing with it frigid winds and gray clouds fat with snow. "That will be fine. Is Lydia here?"

Lydia came out of the bedroom. "Yes, I am. Afternoon, Gray."

Even in the simple day dress, she was a beautiful sight to behold. "I'd like to talk with you, if I may?"

He then turned to Mrs. Cooper and said, "Did she tell you I asked her to marry me?"

Miriam's eyes widened slightly with surprise. She looked over at her daughter. "No, she did not."

Lydia felt the guilt and wanted to clobber Gray for spilling the beans. "I didn't tell you because you've enough on your mind with the wedding and all."

Miriam didn't reply to that but asked instead, "And how did you respond?"

"I said no."

"I see." Miriam looked from her daughter to Gray. "Then I shall leave you two to sort things out."

Gray confessed, "I was hoping Lydia would join me for dinner?"

Lydia's eyes met his. If she had dinner with him, who knew where the evening might lead? A part of herself greeted the idea with sensual anticipation, but the thinking part of herself wanted to decline. Restating her refusal to marry him and making him believe it once and for all seemed necessary, however, so she said, "Dinner would be fine."

Gray had expected an argument from her and was pleased by her positive reply. "I'm on my way home now. Would you like to come along? I don't know if the storm is going to allow much traveling later on."

"Let me get my cape and I'll be ready." Lydia still felt bad about not informing her mother of Gray's proposal and so vowed to sit down with her and bare her soul when she returned. Right now there was only time to give Miriam a departing kiss on the cheek. "I'll be back later. We'll talk then."

Her mother squeezed Lydia's shoulder affectionately. "I'll be here, but if the storm comes, you two stay put. Don't want you trying to travel back in a blizzard."

Lydia and Gray nodded their understanding, and a few moments later Gray escorted Lydia out into the cold.

By the time the wagon reached his farmhouse, it had begun to snow in earnest. The thick swirling flakes made it difficult to see, and the speed with which the flakes were covering the ground was a sure indication that the storm would be a major one.

The interior of the house was cold due to its having been unoccupied all day. Gray hastily built a fire in the parlor, and while it struggled to life he went to the grates in the other rooms and built fires. In the meantime, Lydia shivered before the fire in the parlor and tried to warm her ice-cold hands.

Gray soon joined her and had her exchange her snow-damp cape for a thick plaid flannel shirt that had come from his room upstairs. She drew it on quickly and found its large size and heavy warmth more than an ample substitute. "If it keeps snowing like this, you may not be able to get back home."

"I know." Lydia didn't want to think about where being alone with him on a stormy night might lead because she already knew. His eyes told her that he did, too. "Did you really invite me here to talk?"

He didn't lie. "Yes, and no. In reality, I just wanted to see you again."

Her heart missed a beat. "I'm not marrying you, Gray." Her words came out soft, not firm like she'd intended.

"I heard you the first time, Lydia. I just don't believe you."

The heat in his eyes touched her and she hastily looked away, but he gave her no quarter. He came and stood beside her. "Do you know why I don't believe you?"

She raised her chin, determined to remain in control. "No, why?"

"Because I've tasted your kiss, Lydie . . . made love to you. You feel as deeply for me as I do for you."

The words made her shimmer inside, and all the control she'd wanted to maintain began to evaporate. "I can't deny what I feel for you."

Gray was pleased by her response.

"But I can't marry you."

He reached out and traced his finger over the soft, ripe

flesh of her bottom lip. "You keep saying that," he murmured. "Are you trying to convince me, or yourself?" He kissed her then, slowly, deeply. He nibbled her bottom lip and teased his tongue against the corners of her mouth. Lydia knew this wasn't in her best interest, knew she shouldn't allow this, but deep inside she didn't want him to stop. In truth, she relished the feel of his lips upon hers, savored the way his tongue tempted hers, and so kissed him back as potently as she knew how. Even if he married another, Lydia wanted him to remember her as more than just his adolescent love.

While the wind and snow continued to howl outside, inside Gray's parlor the temperature was beginning to rise. The kisses became deeper, the caresses more intense. When he began to undo the buttons on the front of her green day dress, she didn't protest; she simply stood there with passion-closed eyes and kiss-swollen lips and let him. As he'd done the last time, he greeted each newly bared swath of skin with kisses that stole her breath. He breathed huskily against the scented skin of her throat, "Tell me why you won't marry me, Lydia. . . ."

His expert fingers were slowly untying the ribbons on the front of her stays. When the task was done he parted the two halves and ran his warm palms over the already-pleading nipples of her breasts. "I need to know, darlin'." Giving her no time to answer, he bent and sucked both dark buds gently. She responded with a strangled cry of joy. "Talk to me, please. . . ."

Lydia couldn't speak. All of her abilities were muddled by his bold seduction. Desire licked at her insides like kindling. This novel inquisition had turned her body and senses into willing conspirators in her downfall. Both wanted nothing more than for him to continue. As a result, her hold on herself was almost gone. "I can't marry you," she whispered, breathed.

The kiss he gave her then was so overwhelming, it made her resonate like the peal of a church bell. His hand wandered beneath her skirts. A possessive palm moved over her hips encased in the wool trousers she'd donned to keep her legs warm during the ride here, and she groaned excitedly. The buttons were freed, and soon the pants were pooled at her feet. His ardent hands mapped the soft bare skin that remained, warming her legs and thighs more vividly than any trousers could.

"Now," he whispered thickly, and slipped a potent hand into her drawers. The first touch found her already ripe and swollen. "Lydia?"

Lydia's eyes were closed. The wickedly delicious manipulations made her widen her trembling legs. "No fair . . ." she breathed.

He smiled around his soaring desire and continued his slow play. "Fair . . ." he countered. Her nipples were hard as jewels. He bent and flicked his tongue over each. Her growl of response made his manhood harden more acutely. "Tell me, darlin', or I'll stop. . . ."

Climbing the peak toward orgasm, Lydia heard the velvet threat. "Don't you dare. . . ."

His quiet chuckle floated on the silence. Gray was bluffing; he was so hot for her, nothing on earth could make him turn her loose, but she didn't know that. He slid a finger into the soft, wet vent, and Lydia sucked in a grateful breath. Watching the reactions on her beautiful face, Gray eased his finger out, then back in, repeating the movements with a languid erotic rhythm until her hips began to move in aroused response. "I'm still waiting, Lydia. . . ."

"Oh, Gray . . ." she ground out. The last time he'd touched her this way, she'd been a novice, but now she knew where the rising sensations would lead.

"What?" he inquired thickly, not breaking the sultry cadence. He could tell she was almost ready, so to help her along, he lowered himself to his knees. "Lift your dress . . ." he commanded gently.

Shuddering, Lydia followed orders and stood with panting anticipation for the glory to come.

Gray gifted her with a kiss on the inside of each brown thigh, then asked, "Are you going to tell me . . . ?"

In the silence he drew down her drawers, and Lydia swore her legs would melt. His fingers touched her first, preparing her; teasing her, making her croon. With the tenderness of a lover he opened her, then demanded hotly, "Tell me. . . ."

His tongue found her, and Lydia groaned aloud in reaction to his carnal kiss. "Oh, Lord. . . ."

"Tell me. . . ."

Lydia widened her legs shamelessly, greedily.

"Tell me. . . ." He increased the pace of his conquering, leaving no part of her unloved.

The orgasm exploded with a world-shattering force that buckled her, but he didn't stop. He continued to ply her, love her, drive her, until she could take no more. "Because I'm barren!" she confessed hoarsely as wave after wave of pleasure buffeted her. "I can't marry you . . . because I'm barren. . . ."

When she came back to herself, she was still holding her skirts aside, her undone dress and chemise framed her damp, hard breasts, and the pulsing between her legs was as strong as her pounding heart. Gray thought her the most fetching schoolmarm to ever command a classroom.

He rose to his feet and leaned down to give her a soft, soft kiss. "You're such a silly goose, Lydia Cooper."

She kissed him back. "Why?"

He drew away and looked down at her with serious eyes. "Do you honestly believe you being barren matters to me?"

Lydia turned away. "Yes."

He turned her chin back and explained with love-laced tones, "No. It doesn't. I told you before, it matters to *some* men, not all."

"You say that now, but—"

"I'll say the same thing a hundred years from now. I love you, Lydia. *You.*"

She didn't dare hope that he might be speaking the truth. "Your parents worked hard for years. Surely you want it all to stay in the family."

"It doesn't matter. My foreman has five sons. I'll leave

the business to him. All I care about is spending the years we have left . . . together. Just the two of us."

Lydia searched his handsome familiar face, and she began to cry.

He was so surprised, he pulled her close and wrapped her up in his arms. "Why in the hell are you crying?"

"I was so worried over all this."

"Well, you can stop now, so how about we go upstairs and make this merger official?"

Lydia's eyes sparkled. "You are so scandalous."

"Me? You're the one without any drawers."

She grinned and punched him playfully on the shoulder. He grimaced dramatically, then hoisted her into his arms and carried her upstairs to his bed.

On Christmas Day, Miriam Cooper and Dr. Watson Miller stood next to Lydia Cooper and Grayson Dane in the Coopers' small parlor. Miriam's pastor, Reverend Leonard Keel, opened his Bible and read the words. Mrs. Dane, the only other person in attendance, cried more than either of the brides.

That evening as Lydia and Gray journeyed by sleigh back to their home, she said to him, "Do you know how much I love you?"

He grinned over at her. "Nope, how much?"

She leaned into him lovingly. "Enough to have waited fifteen years for this moment."

He gave thanks for her and for himself. "I love you, too."

Epilogue

Lydia closed down her school in Chicago and opened a new one in her hometown. On August 28, 1884, she gave birth to a six-pound baby boy. She and Gray named him Gabriel Cooper Dane. The doctors were wrong.

The Way
Back Home

BY MONICA JACKSON

Chapter 1

Anne Donald hunched her shoulders against the evening cold as she hurried across the campus. Reflections from the Christmas lights flickered on freshly fallen snow and turned the grounds into something resembling charcoal velvet sprinkled with rare, sparkling jewels.

Anne heard laughter echo behind her and her steps slowed. Turning her head, she saw Danitha Lewis and two of her friends coming toward her from the direction of the black student union. As they passed, Danitha gave a tiny nod of recognition but didn't break stride. The other women didn't bother to acknowledge Anne. Why should they? She wasn't really one of them. She seemed to be doomed to be on the outside, looking in. It was her first year of graduate school and things still hadn't changed.

Anne ducked her head down and hurried behind them. Their destination was the same. Danitha and her friends were also going to hear Dr. Trey Fraser speak on how to empower the African-American community. He was a young professor from Morehouse University—only twenty-seven—yet his controversial book had garnered much critical attention, most of it positive.

He'd written about the failure of integration and opined that the future of black America rested in its economic strength and the regeneration of the black family. Anne was entranced by the power and cadence of his words when she read them. Although her father had been African-American, she'd never known or been a part of the community that Dr. Fraser wrote about so passionately. *What would it be like to be among people who acknowledged you as one of their own?* she wondered.

When she'd heard that he was coming to speak at her campus, her finger had longingly traced his handsome dark brown features on the back jacket of the book cover. She was finally going to see in the flesh the man who filled her daytime fantasies and nighttime dreams.

Applause swept through the auditorium, accompanied by the scraping of chair legs as the audience stood to acknowledge him. Trey's gaze swept the crowd, and his smile felt as if it were a mask. He still felt a combination of embarrassment and gratitude at the adulation. He waited out the enthusiastic applause until he could incline his head and move to the back of the auditorium to sign his books.

An hour later, another book slid into his line of vision. He automatically flipped it open to the title page. "What would you like me to sign?" he asked.

"It's for me. My name is Anne Donald."

"How do you spell that?"

"With an *e*."

He looked up, and pale gray eyes set in a face with skin the tone of light buttered honey captured his gaze. She wasn't beautiful in the traditional sense. Freckles sprinkled her tan skin, and her reddish brown hair was pulled tightly back into a bun. Despite her fair coloring, Africa was stamped in her features. Her nose was a tiny bit wider than what would be considered ideal. Her pink, moist lips were so full and sensual that at that moment he wanted nothing more than to taste them. Had her ghost eyes cast an enchantment over him?

A cough sounded from behind her and the spell shattered. He realized that they'd been staring at each other. He signed the book and slid it across the table to her. He watched her with a sense akin to loss as she picked the book up and moved away.

"Dr. Fraser?" the next person asked, pushing another book in front of him.

He forced his attention to the matters at hand. "Whom should I sign this to?" he asked, glancing at the rapidly decreasing pile of books to his left.

A little more time and he could retreat to the solitude of his hotel room. Speaking engagements, publicity tours, and pressing the flesh were necessary and, in many ways, a blessing, but they were something he had to force himself to do. He was happiest alone with his ideas, his fingers spinning words on the page.

Finally, the moment arrived when he could pull on his coat and walk out the door to his rental car. A memory of ghost-colored eyes returned, and he wished that there had been some way to get her phone number.

Then the Boston cold hit him with a physical blow and he shuddered against it. Maybe it was for the best that the woman had simply walked out of his life. Not only was she not his type, she also lived too far away from him. He couldn't wait to return to the gentle Southern winters he was used to.

"Dr. Fraser?"

He glanced up and looked into the ice-colored eyes he remembered. Was she a witch? How long had the woman waited out here in the frigid cold for him? Witch or no, there was something about her that felt like magic. He smiled at her.

"I wondered if you'd like a cup of coffee?" she asked. "I know you must be tired, but . . ." She bit her lip. "I'd really appreciate it," she ended.

He couldn't believe his luck. "That sounds wonderful," he said.

She looked surprised at his sudden assent but fell in step beside him. She barely reached his shoulder. There was something familiar about her, like she was somebody he once knew well and had forgotten.

He wasn't able to discern the lines of her body under the big, thick, and shapeless down-filled coat she was wearing, but from the softness of her chin he guessed she was overweight. He couldn't understand why she interested him so. He'd always been attracted to lean, elegant model types—well-dressed women who wouldn't be caught dead in the khaki-colored Michelin man–shaped coat she was wearing.

He reached his car and almost dropped his keys in his eagerness to get out of the arctic cold. He opened the door for her, and she climbed into the passenger seat.

As he started the motor, she removed her gloves and rubbed her hands together. He pulled out into the street, the tires crunching the snow. The silence between them had seemed fitting. It was too cold for words to flow easily, but it felt odd not to know her name.

"What's your name?" he asked.

"Anne Donald. You signed my book." She patted her bulky shoulder bag.

Anne with an *e,* he remembered.

"Take the first turn to your right to the coffee shop," she said. "It's about a block down on your left."

He felt a tinge of uneasiness. His ready acceptance of her invitation was out of character for him. Right now he should be resting in his hotel room with a good book and a cup of decaf rather than driving around in the Boston snow with a woman he didn't know.

What if she wasn't stable? He sensed a sort of sadness and vulnerability, but his inner intuition told him there was something solid and strong about her. Intelligence and warmth shone from her eyes despite their glacial color. He wondered how her face changed when she smiled.

Inside the brightly lit coffee shop, she ordered hot chocolate, rich with cream. He ordered regular coffee, strong and black. Once he sat down, he realized how badly he needed the caffeine.

The drinks arrived quickly. She took a sip, and a soft sigh emanated from her. "It's so good," she murmured. The hint of a smile hovered about her lips and he eagerly waited for it to break.

"Did you want talk to me about something?" he asked. His voice was too abrupt. He felt remorse as the shadow of her smile disappeared.

"It's hard to put into words," she said. "You write about the black community and the responsibilities of blackness so well. What I wanted to know is . . ." Her voice trailed away.

Trey sipped his coffee as he waited for her to finish her sentence. The coffee was good, hot and rich. He almost felt the caffeine rushing to his brain, erasing traces of his fatigue.

"I want to know how to do it," she said.

Baffled, he asked, "Do what?"

"Be black."

A chuckle emerged from his throat. "Lady, you don't need lessons. When you look like you do, it's something you just are."

"Not necessarily. My parents were killed in an automobile accident when I was a baby. I survived and my white grandparents raised me." Her voice had fallen to a whisper and Trey had to strain to hear the words. "They've spent the entire twenty-two years of my life trying to keep me and anyone else from realizing what I am."

Trey raised an eyebrow. "Which one of your parents was black?" he asked.

"My father."

"Your mother's folks resented him?"

"Terribly. They blamed him for her death."

"That's tough."

"I look somewhat like my mother. They've always been wonderful to me except for this one thing—if I deal with anything black they think they'll lose me just like they did her."

"What about your father's people?"

"I don't know who they are."

"Why not?"

"My grandparents took great pains to keep that knowledge from me."

"But you're grown now. How can they continue to keep this from you?"

"True, I'm well over eighteen, but no matter how hard I try, I can't make any black friends. I've never dated a black man. What will make that change once I meet my black relatives? What if they—" She stopped and took a deep breath. "When I try to connect, it's as if everyone seems to know I don't belong."

Trey felt a rush of sympathy for her. It was a certainty that, looking as she did, she didn't feel as if she fully belonged with her white relatives, either. Her dilemma puzzled him. "America doesn't let folks escape the fact of their blackness if they look even slightly black," he said. "I can hardly believe you've been rejected by everyone you've approached."

"Not rejected; it's more like a feeling of not fitting in, not belonging. Maybe I'm not doing something right," she said.

"I don't see how you could do anything wrong if you use the usual social graces. Have you been to a black church?"

"A couple times, but it didn't work." She studied her hands. "I realize that it's not them; it must be me, too."

Trey caught that one word. "Them?" he asked.

"Yes, them. Everybody is *them*—whites, blacks, Asians, Hispanics. Believe me, Dr. Fraser, I haven't escaped my race. I just can't figure out how to experience it." Her eyes looked like frost melting, and defeat laced her voice.

He was unsure of what to say. For some reason, he had the impossible urge to fix everything for her. "What do you know about your father's family?" he asked.

"I know they are from Atlanta. His last name was Smith. Evan Smith."

"Maybe that's where you should start. Finding them could be a first step."

She looked away. "But *how* do I start?" she murmured, as if to herself.

"Start with your grandparents. Maybe it's time to confront them with who you are." He could almost feel her withdraw from his words. "No. Maybe I'm wrong," he continued. "I think you need to start with yourself. It's going to take courage and determination. Never give up on what you want. And most important, never give up on who you are."

She stared into the swirling brown depths of her hot chocolate.

Trey couldn't stifle a yawn. Concern crossed her face. "You must be exhausted," she said. "I can't tell you how much it means to me that you've given me your time and attention." She touched his hand and electricity rushed through his body.

"No problem." He wanted to invite her to his hotel room, but resisted the crass impulse. As much as he regretted it, he was going to have to let her walk out of his life. He took out his wallet and removed his card, his personal one with his address and private home phone number.

"Nobody can keep you from who you are but yourself, Anne. When you make it to Atlanta, please let me know how you're doing."

She took his card and stared at it. Then she glanced up at him through her long lashes. He had the feeling that she didn't want their time together to end, either. If she was the one to make the suggestion, it didn't have to. His heartbeat accelerated at the thought of how it would feel to kiss those soft, full lips, to make love to her.

But all she said was, "Thank you."

Disappointment filled him. But maybe she'd come to Atlanta soon. He'd like to see her again on his home turf.

Chapter 2

Not only was Trey Fraser gorgeous, but he was a nice guy, too, Anne decided as she walked away from his black Toyota 4Runner and got into her small pickup truck. Suddenly aftershocks of excitement and giddiness felt like an anxiety attack. She leaned her burning forehead against the cool plastic of the steering wheel.

She could hardly believe that she actually had talked to the man of her dreams, much less spilled all her business like a babbling fool. How had she found the nerve to approach Trey Fraser in the first place? Certainly asking him out and blabbing her private pain indicated that she'd finally lost the few marbles she had left. Jeez! How to be black—had she really asked him that? No wonder he'd laughed. But he'd listened and treated her with respect.

Anne shook her head as she started the motor and put her truck into gear. A few minutes later, she pulled into the driveway of the split-level home she shared with her grandparents, a nice home in a nice neighborhood where the lawns were cared for and property values mattered.

As she tramped across the snow to the house, her head overflowed with thoughts of Trey. His smile, his voice, his easy stride, and his strength—he reminded her of a black panther on the hunt, lean and sleek muscles seemingly relaxed but coiled and ready to spring. When his long, sensitive fingers circled the rim of his cup as he talked, she couldn't help but imagine how they'd feel against her skin. Even the scent he wore, reminiscent of fresh air and Georgia pine trees, enticed and thrilled her.

The blare of the television interrupted her thoughts as she entered the house. Anne was hanging up her coat in the hall closet when her grandmother appeared, a heavy woman with a ruddy pink face that showed evidence of years of hard work.

"Have you eaten?" Grammy asked. "I made meat loaf."

"Sounds good," Anne said.

Her grandmother followed her into the kitchen and watched while she filled her plate with meat loaf, mashed potatoes, green beans, and rolls.

Anne settled down across from Grammy and picked up her fork. Her grandmother liked to talk to Anne in the evening before she left for her night-shift job as a licensed practical nurse. Anne doubted that Grammy talked much to Papa anymore. She'd worked nights for as long as Anne could remember while he worked days fixing air conditioners in the summer and furnaces in the winter. Her grandparents lived separate lives.

"How was the meeting?"

"I went to a lecture. It was good," Anne replied.

"Betsy's going to be able to come up for Christmas after all. She's bringing Todd and the baby, too."

"That's great. Been a long time."

Grammy nodded. "Too long."

Anne shifted in her chair. Now was as good a time as any to bring up her father. "That lecture I went to on campus brought up the importance of knowing your roots. I wondered . . ." Her voice trailed away as she watched the expression on Grammy's face change to guarded anxiety and resentment.

"What made this come up all of a sudden?" Grammy asked, her eyes narrowed.

Anne shrugged. "It seems strange that I don't know anything about my father's family."

"I don't see anything strange about it. We've raised you;

we've housed and clothed you. I'm dragging myself into work every night so you can get an education. We are your family."

Anne stared at her plate, her appetite gone. "I know that and I'm grateful, but . . . but I thought it would be good to know something about my heritage—"

"Your heritage! Your heritage is people who care about you, who work hard to give you everything you need. We are your heritage, honey."

Anne flushed with frustration. "Was my father all that terrible?"

"If it weren't for him, my daughter, your mother, would be alive today." Grammy shook her head. "I can't bear to talk about it. Anne, your father is dead and buried, and I suggest you leave him in the past where he belongs." With those words, she got up out of the chair and left the kitchen.

Anne scraped her plate and rinsed it. She had no intention of leaving the topic of her father and his family alone. She'd been obediently silent for her twenty-two years about the fact of her blackness. It was time she found out what she wanted to know. Also, in a few weeks her relatives would arrive for Christmas. They'd have some idea about the man her mother had married. Most of them resented Anne anyway. She doubted that the uproar that was sure to follow over the closet skeletons she rattled would upset them overmuch.

Anne went upstairs and ran her bath. Staring at the steaming hot water filling the tub, she wondered what her father had looked like. She closed her eyes and tried to picture him. But the image of Trey's face was the only thing she saw.

Three weeks later, Anne got off the plane at the Atlanta airport Christmas evening. This Christmas could go down in history as one of the worst in her life. When Anne had rattled the skeleton in the family closet of her mother and the black man she had married, it was as if the bones fell to pieces and the family along with them.

But amid all the accusations, the screaming, crying, and yelling, a calm came over Anne. She walked upstairs and packed her suitcase. The family looked stunned as she announced her intention to go to Atlanta and seek out her paternal relatives.

But by now her initial bravado had fizzled and the airport seemed as lonely and deserted as she felt. Its once-festive Christmas atmosphere had grown tattered and old before the day was even over.

Anne retrieved her one bag and made her way to the taxi stand. "Merry Christmas," she said to the turbaned driver.

He looked at her and shrugged. "Where are you going, lady?"

She hesitated. She'd planned to get a hotel room near the airport. That would make sense. But it wasn't sense that made her flee her family and her grandparents' split-level house on Christmas Day. It had been anger and pain, frustration and need. She'd been sensible all her life, and look where it had gotten her—alone and without a place to go on Christmas Day.

Anne pulled out the business card she'd kept in her pocket for the past three weeks and stared at it. Trey Fraser had told her to come and see him when she arrived in Atlanta. His concern and interest had been the catalyst that had caused her to finally break free from the inertia that had gripped her for so long and find out who she truly was. It was crazy, but right now there was nothing she wanted more than to see him again. If she followed her heart, where would it lead her?

When she walked out of her grandparents' house, suitcase in hand, it was as if a new chapter of her life had started. For once, she wasn't going to play it safe and do what was expected of her. She was going to take a risk, a wild gamble of the heart. What did she have to lose?

She read Trey Fraser's address to the driver.

*   *   *

Trey was happy to get home. He loved his family, but a heavy dosage of them was exhausting. He was the only male in a family of three women. His mother and sisters had had a fit when he showed up without his ex-girlfriend Renee. They'd questioned him to death about the demise of the relationship. That's what he got for breaking up with Renee before the holidays.

The first thing that greeted him when he walked into his house was the red light flashing on his answering machine. He hung up his coat in the hall closet and pushed the button.

"Hi, honey. Merry Christmas. Detroit is cold as Hades frozen over. Wish I were in Atlanta with you. I'll be in town tomorrow. Maybe we can get together. Love you."

Trey sighed. So Renee was going to pretend as if nothing had happened between them even though he'd sat her down and had the talk. With Renee, he should have guessed that a subtle, albeit direct, approach wouldn't work. Sometimes it took the verbal equivalent of a sledgehammer to drive in something that Renee didn't want to hear. It was over between them and she was going to have to realize it.

The relationship wasn't fair to her and that was why it had to end. She'd grown to be nothing but a habit to him, an available escort and convenient sex. He had no desire to marry her. He prayed Renee would find the right man for her. Every woman deserved someone who could truly love her.

He simply wasn't the man for Renee, and she couldn't understand why. She argued with him every time he tried to end it. They were compatible and got along, she'd say. He'd given up and given in to her until he finally decided to stand his ground and end it.

"Why *not* me?" she'd asked.

The answer was a simple one. What stood in the way was Trey's dream that one day he'd fall in love. He'd been waiting all his life for that special feeling to finally hit him.

Renee had called him a fool to believe that he had a soul mate out there somewhere. Maybe she was right—he should settle down with her or some other suitable woman and start the family he'd always wanted. But something inside him whispered that he needed to wait, that he needed to be free and available. Something told him that his soul mate was out there somewhere. He knew in his bones that the reason he'd never fallen in love was because when it happened to him, it would be a once-in-a-lifetime, forever-after sort of thing.

He could imagine her. He'd always liked long, lean women with braids or dreads and satiny deep chocolate skin. He'd bet his soul mate looked like that. She'd be classy and confident, with a ready laugh and a sharp tongue like his mother and sisters. White teeth gleaming—

The ring of a doorbell disturbed his reverie. Trey's eyebrows rose. Who'd be out visiting on Christmas Day? Carolers, maybe?

He pulled open the door and blinked at the light-skinned short and plump woman standing there, wrapped in a down-stuffed parka large enough for her to winter in Antarctica. She had a suitcase by her side, and the expression on her face was anything but confident.

"You don't remember me," she said, her voice quavering.

It was the ethnically confused woman from Boston. He'd never forget her inexplicable appeal. "Anne with an *e*," he said.

Profound relief crossed her face.

He glanced at the large suitcase. Did she expect to stay? Generally, he didn't like unexpected visits, and uninvited houseguests were anathema. But for some reason, letting this particular woman and her suitcase into his home didn't bother him at all. "Why don't you come on in?" he asked.

Her icy eyes seemed to melt away. "Th-thank you. Th-thank you so m-much," she stammered, pushing her suitcase through the door in front of her. "I don't mean to impose. It's so kind of you. . . . Oh, the cab is waiting. . . ."

Trey motioned for the cab to go and picked up her suitcase. When he closed the door behind her, there was something significant and final about the sound of the door shutting, a line in time that marked something new. He felt as if he should know this woman well. She wafted on the edges just past his memory. There was a connection that he couldn't understand, along with an unbidden urge to care for her. "Please, make yourself at home," he said.

She smiled at him, and it was as if the sun broke through the clouds. It had to be a sign.

Chapter 3

Anne struggled out of her coat. Trey took it from her and tried to hang it in the hall closet. It was too bulky for the hanger and promptly fell off. When the coat hit the floor the third time, he gave up and handed it back to her. "Why don't you lay this on that chair over there?"

She cleared her throat. "OK," she said.

He settled on the couch and watched her as she tried to hang the monster over the back of the armchair, gave up, put it on the seat, and sat on it. Her face, while plain, was pleasant, soft and gentle, as were the rounded curves of her body clad casually in a light blue sweatshirt and jeans. "I can't tell you how grateful I am to be here," she said.

The memory of their conversation weeks ago returned to him. "So what brings you to Atlanta on Christmas Day? Are you visiting your father's family?"

"I've just flown in." She shifted, not meeting his eyes. "I'm sorry to barge in on you like this. I was on my way to a hotel and it was an impulse."

"It's all right." And to his surprise he realized that it was. Her presence was like her, soft and easy. "Would you like something to drink?" he asked.

"Tea would be great, herb or decaf if you have it."

He nodded and went into the kitchen.

He returned shortly with two steaming mugs and handed one to her. "Herb tea, a cinnamon spice blend."

"Good for the season," she said, and smiled at him.

Again her smile made his breath catch. It transformed her face from the ordinary to extraordinary. Her beauty wasn't like a gaudy sunset, spectacular and immediately arresting. It was like a subtle sunrise, pastel-tinted, special, and rarely observed.

"How have your holidays been so far?" he asked. He wondered why she was traveling on Christmas.

"Not too good. Remember when you said I should start with asking my family about my father's people? Well, I did."

"And? Did they tell you?"

"Eventually. My grandparents were upset that I brought the subject up, as expected. But I finally took the initiative and did my research. Much about my father and his family was easy to find. I don't know why I didn't do it sooner."

"Maybe you didn't want to rock the boat?"

Anne nodded. "My grandparents worked hard to make things easy for me all my life. That's the reason why the others in my family resented me. In return for the care my grandparents lavished on me, the unspoken deal was that I avoid that one taboo subject."

"Your race," Trey said.

"Exactly. The part of me that is my father and any mention of him. So when I brought up what I'd discovered about my father and my desire to know about my African-American heritage in front of the entire family, the boat not only rocked, it capsized." She set the mug carefully on the coaster. "It was a pretty bad scene. Basically, I was given an ultimatum—maintain the status quo or get the hell out. I got out."

"I'm sorry."

"Thanks. But I guess it was time to go."

"It sounds like it."

In a comfortable silence, Anne sipped her tea and Trey got up to light the logs in the fireplace. They stared into the crackling flames and Trey wished she'd sat on the couch. He wanted to put his arm around her and snuggle into her warmth while they watched the fire.

But not only would it be tacky to let this woman into his house and make a move on her; also, he couldn't understand his attraction to her. She was too different from any woman he'd wanted before.

"Where do your father's people live?" he asked, breaking the silence.

"Not far from here. My grandparents had three children, two girls and my father. I have two aunts, both with children."

"What happened between your mother and father?" Trey asked.

Anne set her cup down on the coffee table and leaned toward him. "My father was a new teacher in a community college, just out of school—he was only twenty-three—when he met my mother. He taught math. She was a nineteen-year-old secretary who worked for the college. They fell in love and she got pregnant.

"My grandparents furiously opposed a marriage. My mother had me but apparently kept a secret relationship with my father. In the meantime he'd gotten a job here in Atlanta and made a down payment on a house. She'd asked my grandmother to keep me and told her that she was going on a weekend vacation with her girlfriends. She and my father drove to Las Vegas intending to marry. They never made it."

Trey absorbed this. "Have you called your father's family yet?" he asked.

She looked away, biting her lip. "Not yet," she said, her voice so soft that he had to strain to hear.

"It's just past nine. Your call could be the best Christmas present they receive."

"Or it could be nothing more than a nuisance."

"What are you afraid of, Anne?"

She sighed and rubbed her eyes. "What if I'm not like them? What if they can't accept me?"

"If so, you've lost nothing that you had before. But I doubt that will happen. They are your blood. They are a part of you and your culture as much as anything else."

"I barely know anything about being black. No more than the average suburban white woman knows from television and other media. I've never been white, but I've never been black, either. . . ." Anne's voice trailed away and she looked dejected.

The art of being black was only one of the enjoyable lessons that Trey wanted to teach her. "This is a good time for learning about your heritage," he said.

"The holidays?" she asked, puzzled.

"Yes. Tomorrow is the first day of Kwanzaa. I'm one of the organizers of the community festivities. Do you know about Kwanzaa?"

"Not much. I know it's some sort of holiday."

"The name of the festival is *matunda ya Kwanzaa*. It means 'first fruits.' It was established in the sixties and is held in the tradition of African harvest festivals. The purpose of the festival is to bring together people of the African diaspora in our own celebration of solidarity, community, and family. Seven principles are the basis of Kwanzaa."

"Principles?" Anne asked, seeming fascinated.

"Yes, principles—one for each day of Kwanzaa: unity, self-determination, collective work and responsibility, cooperative economics, purpose, creativity, and faith. The point is to emphasize values. Come over here and look at this." He stood, took her hand, and led her to the dining room. "These are the symbols of Kwanzaa I've set out."

Anne circled the small table where he'd set out the *kinara*, the candlestick holder with its seven candles, three red, three green, and one black candle in the middle, the unity cup, and the basket of fruit on a straw mat.

"What are these for?" she asked, picking up dried grains of corn he'd scattered on the mat.

Heat flushed his face. She'd gone to the one symbol that had personal meaning for him. He cleared his throat. "Families usually put out ears of corn, one for each child in the house. I put out the grains because they symbolize the hope of the children I plan to have one day."

She carefully replaced the corn on the tabletop and her gaze rose to the flag he'd put on the wall over the Kwanzaa table. "Which country's flag is that?" she asked.

"It's the flag for black people, the African peoples scattered in the diaspora. The red in the flag is for the blood we shed, the green for Africa, the land we came from, and the black for the color of our skin."

Trey took a deep breath, surprised at the intensity of his emotions. He wanted to show her all this and more. He wanted to teach her all the positive aspects of her heritage that he would bet she hadn't learned in the environment in which she'd been raised. But what came out of his mouth next surprised him. "I want you to celebrate Kwanzaa with me."

The moment he waited for her reply seemed to stretch out to minutes.

"I'd love to celebrate Kwanzaa with you," she answered, a glimpse of that glorious smile hovering.

He exhaled, relieved. He hadn't realized he'd been holding his breath. His nose was widening for this barely black, dumpy, not-his-type woman, and he didn't know what to make of it. "Good. One more thing." He reached over to the end table and picked up the phone. He pressed it into her hand. "Like I said before, what has kept you from the rest of your family all these years was fear. It's time that you broke the cycle."

Anne's hand tightened on the phone. She stared at it a moment and pushed the numbers that she must have memorized by heart.

"May I speak to Helen Smith?" Anne asked the man who answered the phone.

"Who may I tell her is calling?" he asked. He was an older man by the sound of his voice, possibly her grandfather?

"My name is Anne Donald." Her sweaty palm tightened on the phone receiver.

"One moment."

"Hello?" a woman's voice answered.

"Is this Helen Smith?"

"Yes. How may I help you?"

Anne closed her eyes. This was as difficult as she had imagined it would be. "I'm calling about your son, Evan Smith."

"Yes." The woman's heightened tension was evident in that one syllable.

"Ummm. Did he tell you about his girlfriend, Lydia Donald?"

"My son has been gone for many years; please get to the point." The woman's tone shifted from buttery cream to vinegary sharpness.

"Lydia Donald had a daughter by Evan Smith. He's my father."

Silence. Then a moan, more like a whimper.

"William!" Anne heard the woman call. "William, come here!"

A moment later the man who had answered the phone demanded, "What's this all about? You've upset my wife so that she can hardly speak. What's this you're saying about our son?"

"I'm his daughter . . . his daughter by Lydia Donald. I grew up in Boston with her parents—"

"Evan told us about Lydia, but he never told us she was pregnant. Why should we believe what you say is true?"

"I have evidence," Anne whispered.

"Where are you?" the man asked abruptly.

"What?"

"Where are you now?"

"I'm staying with a friend."

"Where?"

Anne gave him Trey's address.

"We'll be there within a half hour." And the man, her grandfather, hung up the phone.

*   *   *

Trey opened the door and blinked at the people huddled on the front steps. An older couple was surrounded by a group of younger people who ranged from middle-aged to a baby in arms. "Come in," Trey said. The older man took his wife's hand and led her through the door. The others followed like an incoming flood.

Anne stood behind the sofa, her birth certificate clutched in her hands.

Trey looked between her and the people who'd streamed through the door. She'd have no need of the proof she held in her hand. Her kinship to those people was etched in her features. She was a young honey-and-vanilla version of the older caramel-colored woman.

"Merry Christmas," Anne said.

Trey saw traces of anxiety in her eyes as she surveyed her family, but she held her chin high and her shoulders resolute. He was proud of her for facing her fear. He knew how much she wanted these people to accept her.

"I'm Anne Donald," she said.

The older woman had put her hand to her mouth, her eyes filling with tears. She embraced Anne in her arms. "My baby's daughter. My Evan's child," she whispered, rocking Anne back and forth.

Trey watched as Anne was hugged and fussed over by one person after another. She glowed from their acceptance and affection as if she were a star. The room overflowed with warmth and cheer, as satisfying to Trey as his favorite warm eggnog topped with nutmeg and whipped cream.

He supposed he'd never witnessed a better ending to any Christmas Day.

Chapter 4

"Come back home with us," Anne's grandmother urged.

"Anne's staying with me to celebrate Kwanzaa," Trey said in a matter-of-fact tone, just as if he were a longtime boyfriend instead of a man she barely knew.

But it felt right. She crossed the room to Trey's side, and the warm feeling inside her grew to encompass him. "I promised I'd stay here during Kwanzaa," she said. "I'm looking forward to the holiday. I've never celebrated it before."

"We always celebrate Kwanzaa. We'll be at the community center on the first and last day of the holiday, but we like to kick it off with a family celebration. Why don't you two join us tomorrow?" her grandfather asked.

Anne looked at Trey and he reached for her hand. "That sounds great," he said. "We'll be there."

Anne smiled and nodded, but she couldn't quite get past the feel of Trey's fingers entwined with hers. Warm and strong, the feel of them made her breath quicken, a buzz tingle through every part of her body, and her thoughts scatter like seeds in the wind.

Trey was saying something, but his words didn't make it through the tumult within her that his touch was causing. "What did you say?" she asked.

"I said that I'd see you in the morning. I'm beat and I'm

going to bed. To her family he said, "I'm looking forward to seeing you again."

She watched him walk away.

"That's quite a man you've got there," her Aunt Jewel said.

"Yes, he is quite a man," Anne said. The hand that had been tangled with his fingers was still warm and tingling.

"I've always admired Trey Fraser," her grandmother added.

Anne nodded in agreement, then frowned as she realized that she had no idea where she was going to sleep or the location of anything in this house.

The next morning, the mixed aromas of brewing coffee, baking bread, and sizzling sausage permeated the air. Anne opened her eyes and immediately felt disoriented.

Then she remembered and smiled to herself as she threw the covers back. Her newfound family hadn't left until almost two in the morning. She'd found a room that was obviously a guest bedroom with an adjoining bath, brushed her teeth, and crawled under the covers and must have been asleep before her head settled all the way down on the pillow.

For the first time in a very long time she was eager to get up and face the day. Standing in the shower as the water sluiced over her body, she marveled over how her life had changed in a single day.

Her family seemed to want to hear all twenty-two years of her history in one night. Her grandmother sat beside her and would occasionally reach over and touch her hand, as if making sure she was real. The faint echoes of herself within the features of the people gathered around her had seemed surreal. They were all she had hoped for—loving and steeped with intelligence, tradition, and strength. It was as if an angel were looking over her. A Kwanzaa angel, guiding her to her roots, bringing her back home.

Anne quickly pulled on a pair of jeans, one of her favorite pairs, overwashed and frayed to the perfect degree of softness. Anticipation fluttered through her as she ventured toward the kitchen looking for Trey.

His back was to her as he pulled a pan of golden biscuits from the oven. She eyed his wide, strong shoulders. The muscles of his back were visible through a tight T-shirt. His lean waist tapered down to a rounded and tight rear and eased on down to long, lean legs, slightly bowed. Heavens, the man looked good.

She cleared her throat. He turned, his gaze assessing. Then he smiled lazily, and excitement and embarrassment raced through her body.

"Habari gani?" he said.

"What does that mean?" she asked, walking toward the coffeepot to hide her confusion.

"It means 'what's the word?' in Swahili. It's a customary greeting during Kwanzaa. The answer is the principle of the day. Today is the first day of Kwanzaa and the principle is *Umoja,* which means unity of our families and community. It seems especially fitting since the celebration tonight will mark a reunion with your father's family."

Anne sipped her coffee. "I can hardly believe my luck."

"Did you have any doubt that you had good genes?" he said, grinning at her, looking so handsome that her heart skipped a beat.

"Sometimes I've wondered."

"It's great that your family is in touch with cultural traditions. I think family celebrations are the heart of Kwanzaa."

The warm glow filled her again, at the memory of her father's family, her family. "They were so happy about my father having a child. Helen, my grandmother, said it was as if a little of my dad lived on."

"Your anxieties seem to be allayed."

"Mostly. After you went to bed, I told them a little about what happened between my mother and her family. They were very understanding. They'd known about my mother and apparently my father had mentioned he had a big surprise for them when he came back home. They never dreamed that it would be a child."

He set a full plate in front of her—scrambled eggs rich with melted cheese, link sausages, biscuits, and some white substance with melted butter.

"What's this?" she asked, pointing.

He looked at her in disbelief. "Grits. Don't tell me that you've never had grits."

"I grew up in Boston with white folks, remember? My favorite is hash-browned potatoes."

"That's because you haven't had grits yet," Trey said. He sat across from her with his own plate. "This evening the Kwanzaa community program will start. We gather at the community center on the first and last days of Kwanzaa. There are smaller functions and the family celebrations the other days."

"So what happens?" Anne asked, mumbling around a mouthful of grits and eggs.

"Every community and family shape Kwanzaa to best suit them. What's important is that we highlight the principles of community and family unity and the spirit of Kwanzaa. At the community center, we decided to have a program with speakers, performers, and singers on the first evening of Kwanzaa and a big party, the *karamu,* on the seventh and last day. Most families also celebrate individually and exchange gifts."

"I can't wait to see how my family celebrates Kwanzaa."

"Me, too," Trey said softly, looking into her eyes.

Something passed between them and Anne felt flooded with a feeling of belonging that she'd never experienced before. It was as if she belonged in this man's home, in his life. So instant and complete, it seemed as if they were a couple—two parts of a whole.

A rush of heat covered her face and she turned her attention to her food.

"How are the grits?" Trey asked.

Anne scooped up the last forkful of the delicious white stuff. "You're right. I love them," she said. It was mere wishful thinking, a figment of her fevered imagination, to believe that a man like Trey Fraser could actually want a woman like her, much less that they were a couple.

Maybe he believed she'd only come down to Atlanta because of his suggestion. She wondered if his insistence that she stay with him was laced with obligation. This was so good that it had to be a dream she'd wake from in one fashion or another.

The ring of the doorbell shattered Anne's reverie. A tiny frown appeared on Trey's brow as he left the room to answer the door.

Anne heard a coy and seductive feminine voice from the other room. She strained to hear the words between them. She couldn't make out what they were saying, but the tones of the woman's voice grew strained, then louder and challenging.

"What do you mean you have someone staying here?" Anne heard the woman say as the staccato tap of heels on Trey's hardwood floors moved closer to the kitchen.

A woman strode in with an air of possession and stood staring at Anne with her hands on her hips. She was dark-skinned and wore an elegant black pantsuit that fitted her slender form perfectly. Her braids were pulled back in a loose knot at her neck. Anne got the impression of energy and motion suppressed within the woman like a tightened spring.

Anne's first emotion was alarm. She'd never been much for confrontation, and this fiery-seeming woman looked like she could cut her to shreds with her tongue. Anne's second emotion was envy. What she wouldn't give for a body like that.

"Who the hell are you?" the woman demanded.

Anne raised an eyebrow.

"Hold up, Renee. You don't talk like that to a guest in my home."

The woman rounded on Trey. "Our bed was still warm from when I left it before you put this fat yellow heifer in—"

"That's enough. Get out." Trey's voice carried authority and command. This was not a man to fool with. Apparently Renee realized it, because she backed down.

"Damn no-good dog," she muttered, and stalked out. A second later the slam of a door reverberated throughout the house.

Chapter 5

Trey wanted to strangle Renee. It wasn't so much that her visit had discomfited him and that she had insulted Anne, but she'd wiped the satisfied, happy smile off Anne's face and replaced it with an anxious, guarded expression.

"Forgive Renee," he said. "She has a hair-trigger temper and was speaking out of her hurt. We just broke up."

"Uh, sorry," Anne said.

"Yeah, so am I."

"That you broke up?"

"No. I'm sorry she upset you."

"I'm all right."

But the easy camaraderie they'd shared had evaporated. She looked at her watch. "I should call my folks in Boston. I'm sure they're worried sick."

"I thought you said that there was no love lost when you left."

"I was angry; they were hurt and upset. But they're the only parents I've ever known. That's a fact I can't run away from."

"You love them."

Anne nodded. "They've been good to me, in the best way they knew. I have to accept their limitations, but I'm not going to allow them to limit me anymore, much less define me."

"What are you going to do?" Trey asked.

"I don't know yet, except that things are going to have to change."

Trey reached out and touched her hand, an intended gesture of comfort. He was stunned by the current that passed between them, the rush of sexual energy, unbidden and unwanted. Why was he attracted to a woman who for all intents and purposes shouldn't attract him? He liked slim women, he liked culturally aware women, and he liked *black* women. But he wanted to lean over and pull this plump, light, and bright woman to him. He wanted to kiss her and feel her rosy lips under his.

He didn't need the complications in his life. He liked things simple and straightforward. He was a logical man, and things he didn't fully understand . . . well, they scared him. She scared him—this woman with the witchy cloud-colored eyes who seemed to hold some spell over him.

Anne pulled her fingers away from his and stood, clearing her throat in the manner that he recognized signaled her anxiety. He also stood, and headed for the coffeepot to cover his own confusion. When he looked her way again, she'd gone, silent as a ghost.

"I don't understand how you could have just up and left us Christmas Day without letting us know where you were all night. We were worried sick," Grammy said.

Anne took a deep breath. "I should have called sooner."

"Where are you anyway? I've called your friends, everybody who I could think—"

"I'm in Atlanta."

"Are you staying with *his* people?" Grammy asked after a too-long pause.

"Would I be welcome back in your house if I were?"

"If it weren't for him, you'd still have your mother. . . . I'd still have my Lydia."

"It was an accident, a tragic accident. They loved each other."

Silence.

"You didn't answer my question," Anne said in a soft voice.

"Why are you doing this to us after all this time? Why now? Didn't we do enough for you?"

"I'm not doing anything to you. I'm simply trying to find a part of myself. I should have done it sooner. I suppose you've answered my question. I won't darken your door again." Anne gave a bitter laugh. "Pardon the pun."

"This is your home and it always will be. You're my grandchild and I raised you as my own. Nothing can ever change that. This has nothing to do with race."

"Are you kidding?" Anne said. "This has everything to do with race. You can't stand the fact that I'm finally acknowledging what everybody else has known from the get-go: I'm a black woman."

"You are not a black woman."

"No, Grammy. I am a black woman and there's nothing bad or shameful about it. There's a whole side of myself that I tried not to see because you never wanted me to. But you know what? It changed nothing. I am black and I've always been black. I can see it in the faces of my white friends and my white relatives. I'm not one of you. I'm treated like someone fundamentally flawed, as if I were born with some sort of birth defect."

"It's not true," Grammy whispered.

"You know that it's true. As a child I believed that I was treated differently because I was ugly. It's time I faced the fact that I'm not extraordinarily ugly; I'm treated differently because I'm black."

"You're Lydia's child; you're as much white as—"

"Black. My God, you can't even say the word," Anne said. Her hand tightened on the phone as she heard the sound of her grammy's soft sobs.

"Please come home," her grammy said, pain crinkling her voice. "We can work this out. We love you. I love you. Just . . . please come home."

She felt more at home with Trey than she'd ever felt in

her life. But she couldn't say that to her grammy. "Later. I have to do this first."

"Have you met them yet?"

Anne drew in a breath. "I have. They are nice people. You'd like them."

"When will you be back?"

"I'm not sure. Possibly after Kwanzaa."

"After what?"

"Kwanzaa. It's an African-American holiday over the next seven days. I'm celebrating it with them."

"Will you at least let me know where you are?"

There was a pleading tone in her grammy's voice. Anne wished she could hug the woman who'd raised her. She did believe that her grandparents had done the best they could. They were old Boston Irish, a product of a prejudiced and more insular generation. Maybe asking them to change was too much. But if they wanted her to continue to be a part of their lives, they'd have to change. She wasn't turning her back on who she was any longer.

"Do you have something to write with?" Anne asked.

She waited as her grammy wrote down Trey's address and phone number.

Tears filled Grammy's voice as she said good-bye. "I love you, Anne. Please don't forget that," she said.

"I love you, too, Grammy."

Anne wasn't sure what she should wear on this special evening, the first day of Kwanzaa and the first day visiting her paternal grandparents' home. She still basked in the warm glow of their acceptance, but she couldn't deny her fears. Would she fit in? Would she be good enough?

Anne had had a lifetime of not fitting in. It would be almost too painful to bear if she felt that too-familiar polite distancing, that unspoken communication that she wasn't one of them. This had to be where she belonged and where she was accepted. Her grandmother Helen had welcomed her home.

She prayed that it was true as she reached for the simple

black dress hanging in the closet. It would have to do; it was all she had. She'd always believed in traveling light. She took special care with her makeup. When she was finished, Anne stared at herself in the mirror and frowned. She didn't like the way she looked. Tonight she wanted to look special.

She reached back and uncoiled her hair from her customary knot. She shook her hair loose. It cascaded around her face and over her shoulders like an auburn cloud.

Her hair was wild and bushy, with a woolly texture. Unacceptable. Which was why she always wore it tightly pulled back. When she was a child, Grammy would drag her to white beauty salons and beg the hairdressers to straighten it. Anne couldn't deal with the hair breakage that seemed to inevitably ensue and refused to go as she became older.

Despite the grief her family and friends gave her over her hair, she had always secretly loved it. She touched it now. Her hair was strong and healthy, long and natural. She had never wanted straight and silky locks.

Anne picked up a brush and ran it over her hair. Even with its tight woolly curl, it reached to her mid-back; straightened, it would easily be waist-length. While she had inherited her hair's length and color from her mother, its texture branded her as a black woman. Tonight she'd proudly wear it loose in public for the first time in her life.

She walked into the living room to meet Trey and drew in a quick breath at the sight of him in African garb. His orange, blue, and brown–striped hat matched his flowing tunic and accentuated the handsome masculinity of his features.

He was staring at her like she was an apparition who had materialized suddenly in front of him.

"What?" she asked.

"Your hair . . ."

She touched it, suddenly feeling self-conscious and defensive. "I wanted to wear it down. I generally never do."

"It's beautiful. More than beautiful—glorious."

Anne felt her face warming. "Thanks," she muttered.

He reached out to touch it. "I love it natural. You should never straighten it."

"I won't. It breaks it off."

Her words were a cover for the pounding of her heart. She felt the heat radiating from his body, generating an answering heat from her own. She could almost swear that her hair had grown nerve endings from where his hand lingered.

It felt natural to tilt her head upward as her tongue slipped out and moistened her lips. She wanted this man to kiss her more than anything in the world. She needed it. Needed to feel his body next to hers.

She stared into Trey's half-lidded eyes, at the unmistakable sexual challenge within them, and reached out a hand. Moving close to him, she touched the tight, wiry curls at the nape of his neck.

He exhaled and her eyes closed; his arms circled her body and drew her close. He lowered his head and his lips covered hers, warm and firm, wholly masculine.

The room spun. When his tongue gently touched hers, she felt a shudder of passion explode through them both. He drew her closer against his hard body and the once-gentle kiss became hungry, needing. The hard ridge of male flesh drove all thought from her mind. Her body wanted it, wanted him. She couldn't help moving her aroused, swollen flesh against the hard heat of him. He groaned and the sound of it reverberated through her body, sending a rush of dampness. Their kiss turned ravenous and they slid rhythmically against each other. She gasped as desire rippled through her, coiling tight in her belly, ready to explode.

"Let's go to the bedroom," Trey whispered in her ear, his voice husky and hoarse. His hands were reaching under her dress, his lips traveling down her throat to her breasts—

Anne turned to ice inside. His bedroom meant clothes shed, penetration, and *exposure*. She drew away, trying to steady her breathing, and clenched her hands to gain control of her aroused body. It needed the one thing her mind also desired but feared.

"What's wrong?" Trey said.

"My family is expecting me. We just can't not show up."

"We can be a little late," he said, reaching for her.

"Trey . . ."

He grinned down at her. "OK, I know how important this is to you." He kissed the tip of her nose. "Tonight," he whispered.

Chapter 6

"*Habari gani?*" Anne's grandfather asked.

"*Umoja*," her family chorused in unison. Many were dressed in African clothing.

Kwanzaa felt new again to Trey as he watched Anne's happy and excited face as her grandfather lit the middle black candle in the *kinara*, the traditional Kwanzaa candle-holder with its seven candles.

"Is he going to light them all every night?" Anne whispered.

"No. A candle is lit each successive day of Kwanzaa, starting with the black candle in the middle—that candle symbolizes the unity of the African peoples," Trey answered.

He saw Anne touch a lock of her hair. "My people," she whispered.

Her statement didn't call for an answer. He smiled down at her, feeling her wonder at belonging to a rich heritage she was newly discovering. Sharing and observing Anne's interest and pride in Kwanzaa made it more meaningful than ever to him.

Finally, the family stood gathered around the long dining room table, loaded with food. They joined hands and bowed their heads. As Trey held Anne's small warm hand in his, emotion filled him that he couldn't quite place. An ache in his heart, a sort of longing?

The heat between them, although surprising to him in its intensity and with this particular woman, was something he could understand. He knew about sex and passion, and the responses of his body were predictable. But what this woman was doing to his emotions and mind was something else. There was a deep uneasiness within him at the un-expectedness and newness of it all. But for now, he decided to simply accept the rightness of her by his side, her hand in his. He would deal with how he felt later.

"On this first day of Kwanzaa our guiding principle is unity," Anne's grandfather said. "We thank you, Lord, for the unity, strength, and love we share within this family. We thank you for the special blessing and privilege of knowing Evan's child. His spirit and blood live on in her. We praise you, Father, for bringing her home to us."

Trey watched Anne's eyes fill. He couldn't imagine how she must have felt growing up—somehow alienated from the world that her family insisted she stay in, different and set apart and not fully able to grasp the reasons why. He'd wanted to protect her and was more than grateful that there was no need. These people were loving and caring and they showed no hesitation in enfolding Anne within their family.

The warmth and spirit that he sensed within Anne echoed throughout this family. Her grandparents' home had a feeling of refuge and sanctuary. He would bet that their daughters still spent a lot of time here and that grandchildren were always in and out of the house.

After the meal, Trey leaned back, groaned, and probably wasn't the only one who had to surreptitiously let his belt out a notch.

He started to rise to help Anne and her aunts clear the table. "Those dishes aren't going anywhere," Helen said. "Jewel and Eve will have their girls wash up after the Kwanzaa celebration at the community center. We don't want to be late."

Trey held the door open for Anne as they headed toward

his car and the community center. "So what do you think?" he asked.

"I'm overwhelmed. I haven't even gotten their names all straight yet, but I feel like one of them already."

"You look like them," he said. He studied her features. How could he ever have thought of her as ordinary or plain? She was beautiful, a honeyed Botticelli Venus surrounded by a cloud of glorious hair.

The atmosphere within the car grew heavy and thick with tension, longing, and, yes, desire. He smelled her scent, a smoky blend of woods and spices. Was that what she was really like? Smoky and complex, exotic, earthy, and sweet?

He wordlessly ran a finger down her cheekbone, letting his touch speak for him. He lowered his head and touched his lips to hers. Her soft lips, the warmth of her skin, and the scent of her surrounded and intoxicated him. He needed to know her, wanted to touch her, to sink inside her. He hated the confines of his car; he needed to feel her against him. He wanted to feel her against him. All of her.

Suddenly he heard a tapping on the window. "Y'all are steaming up the windows!" one of Anne's young cousins called, giggling.

"Come on here, girl, and leave them alone."

The voices receded and Trey pulled away from Anne and grasped the steering wheel, breathing hard. He hadn't been aroused so quickly for a long time. He turned his head and saw that Anne's lips were moist and swollen and her hair spilled over his leather seat. Her coat had fallen open. Her breath was coming rapidly between her parted lips, and he could see the outlines of her nipples through her black dress.

Trey inwardly groaned. He wanted to forget about the celebration at the community center and make love to her all through the night. Patience. Tonight she'd finally be his. He tore his gaze away from her and turned the key in the ignition.

*   *   *

"This is my mother, Rachel," Trey said. "And my sisters, Tess and Tina," he added.

Anne's smile faded at the sight of his mother's and sisters' assessing gazes. "Nice to meet you," she said.

"Trey said you're from Boston. You're visiting family?" his mother asked.

"Uh, yes," Anne said. She felt uncomfortable with this woman's unsmiling stare and staccato question.

"I imagine you've known each other for quite a while for you to be staying with him instead of your family." Trey's mother's words had the certainty of fact combined with the force of a question.

"Well . . ." Anne said.

"We've known each other long enough, Mom," Trey said, his voice dry and clipped.

"Dr. Fraser, there you are." A small woman clad in striped *kente* cloth hurried up to him. "The speakers have been waiting for you to read over their intros before they go on," she said.

"I'm sorry, but I need to get backstage," Trey said to Anne. "I'm MC for the first part of the celebration. Save me a seat and I'll join you when the speakers are finished."

Anne nodded and watched Trey leave with what she hoped was an imperceptible sigh. She turned back to his mother.

"It's nice you're staying with my son." Her words were polite, but Trey's mother's facial expression looked like she'd just bitten into an orange and discovered it was a lemon. "How long do you think you'll be in Atlanta?"

"I plan to stay through the Kwanzaa holiday."

"You're spending the whole seven days with Trey?" one of his sisters asked.

"Yes. Maybe longer."

Silence.

"Hmmm. I'll call you," his mother said. "Oh, look, Tina; there's Renee over there."

Anne felt a leaden weight settle in the pit of her belly.

"Oooh, look what she has on. She sure looks good,"

Trey's sister said with a grin, darting a glance to Anne and nudging her sister in the ribs.

"She sure does." His sister's gaze traveled slowly down Anne's body from head to toe.

Anne turned her head to look at the woman who'd referred to her as a fat yellow heifer earlier that day, garbed in African golden metallic robes and a matching gold head wrap. Trey's mother was making her way through the crowd toward Renee. The leaden weight in Anne's stomach turned red-hot when she saw Trey's mother greet and embrace Trey's ex-girlfriend.

Trey's sisters subtly turned away from Anne, excluding her from their circle. The line had been drawn. She'd been measured, judged, and found wanting compared to who must be their great, good friend, Renee. All Anne wanted to do was escape these women with their hard eyes and even harder attitudes.

Renee and Trey's mother, Rachel, were coming toward them. Anne cast around for her family members. She spied her Aunt Jewel, a large woman in white robes. "Excuse me," she said to Trey's sisters. "It was nice to meet you, but my aunt is expecting me."

"Hi, honey," Jewel said as Anne scurried over to her side. "We were looking for you. Eve saved some seats near the middle." As Anne followed her aunt, she looked back at Trey's mother and sister. They'd crowded around Trey's ex-girlfriend. Anne didn't miss the scornful and dismissive look Renee cast in her direction.

Anne wanted to cry, but she lifted her chin and went on about her business. She always made sure that nobody ever knew how much they'd hurt her, way down deep.

After his talk, Trey returned to the seat in the audience beside Anne. She smiled at him, but anxiety and an inner numbness had replaced her wonder and excitement and the passion of their kisses. The people whom Trey cared about most in the world, his closest family, had let her clearly know they didn't want her in his life. Such a familiar feeling—one she'd hoped that she could leave behind with the discovery of a place where she truly belonged.

It seemed as if her father's family had accepted her. But what if their acceptance of her was only because they were enormously loving and tolerant people? Was the true reality that she didn't belong in either the white or the black world—that she'd remain living on the edges always, merely tolerated, never belonging? Did Trey's family treat her with kid gloves because she was so different from them?

The icy fear started deep in her gut and sent tendrils through her body to her heart, shattering the dreams and hopes that had been starting to grow. Her family was a part of it, but Trey was all of it. Belonging by Trey's side was the fantasy she'd dared not allow to take shape, lest it disappear like the frail hope it was. How could she even dream of belonging to a man whose family brought her worst fears and freshest pains to the surface?

She'd had a taste of what it felt like to truly belong to a family, and she couldn't, she wouldn't, let it go.

Chapter 7

Trey knew a lot of women who'd let him know they were available for lovemaking whenever he desired, but he only wanted Anne. The memory of her soft lips and softer body made his pulse quicken. The Kwanzaa celebration at the community center seemed to last forever as he anticipated what he would do with her when he got her home.

The time had finally arrived. He opened the door and let her walk ahead of him. He laid his coat over a chair and watched her struggle to hang up her monster coat in the closet.

Her body wouldn't have appealed to him before he met her. He imagined what she'd look like nude. Short, around five feet, two inches tall, she probably weighed at least 160 pounds, maybe more. Her breasts were small and pert, emphasizing her hippy, pearlike shape. He couldn't imagine a body more desirable. The thinner women he'd preferred previously now seemed boyish, hard and angular, lacking in form and femininity.

He wanted to know every single inch of Anne. She was the essence of femininity to him and the new standard by which he'd now forever judge other women. How could his tastes change so suddenly and radically?

Maybe they hadn't changed. Maybe he'd gone for the women who'd flirted with him—who'd made themselves easily available. Was it as simple as his being attracted to women who radiated confidence because they were bathed in cultural acceptance and approval for their thin body types? Or maybe he'd tended to choose women whose figures were similar to the tall and thin shapes of his mother and sisters.

For whatever reasons, he'd never taken the opportunity to know a heavier woman in a romantic or sexual way. He'd never been particularly repelled by heavy women— some of the thicker sisters he knew carried themselves like queens—he'd simply never considered them sexually. There was always some thin woman in his face or on his arm or in his bed.

Trey moved toward Anne and encircled her waist from behind, instantly aroused from the softness of her pressing into him. He bent to kiss her neck and was shocked at her stiffness—so different from the yielding passion they'd shared before.

"What's wrong?" he asked.

"Nothing," she said. "I'm tired."

He let her go, and she moved away from him.

"Do you want to talk?"

"Talk about what?" she said, irritation edging her voice.

Trey's eyes narrowed. "Talk about us."

"What's there to talk about?"

"Don't play games with me, Anne."

She took a deep, shuddery breath. "I'm not playing games. I need some time. Everything's been so overwhelming."

Trey was not the sort to press a woman, but he couldn't remember when he had wanted a woman so badly. He ached for her.

"How much time do you need?" he asked huskily, reaching for her again. He couldn't help pulling her against him and letting her feel the full length of his arousal.

"I'll let you know." She pulled away.

Trey watched her walk away, feeling confused, frustrated, and bereft. Damn, it was going to be a long night.

*   *   *

Anne stared sleeplessly into the darkness of the guest bedroom. She'd walked away from the man of her dreams and the undoubtedly sizable erection that was the direct result of physical and mental stimulation from yours truly. Surely she'd lost her mind.

Anne sighed. She'd never imagined in a million years that her fantasies would come true. She'd never imagined that the actual opportunity to get naked with Trey Fraser would come her way. Faced with that opportunity, she choked.

She ran her hands under the covers over the fleshiness of her belly and the thickness of her thighs. How could he want her? Was it just because she was available? But Trey surely had his choice of women. She remembered the angry possessiveness of the slender and attractive Renee. He could have been with her if he wanted.

Maybe she should have held her breath and jumped in Trey's arms. Maybe the water would have been just fine, but the fact remained that she'd never swum before. She was willing and ready to take her first strokes, but her first attempt would probably be somewhat awkward. Someone like Trey was likely used to highly experienced master swimmers. What would he do when he discovered that she'd never even dipped her toe in the pool?

She'd never been penetrated, never had anything more from a man than heated kisses and fumbling fingers. What would Trey do when he had to deal with her sexual ineptness on top of everything else?

Finally, that encounter with his family had done her in. The funky attitudes of his mother and sisters shredded the tatters of the self-confidence she had tried to garner to find the nerve to get naked in front of Trey Fraser.

She remembered his hot passion and hit her fist against the mattress. She should've rushed out and rented some X-rated videos for pointers. She could have turned out all the lights and made sure they were in a pitch-black room. She would have dived for the covers as soon as . . .

Anne sighed again. Shoulda, coulda, woulda wasn't going to get her anywhere. One thing was certain: she wasn't lying when she told him that she needed time.

Oh, well. Tomorrow was another day, and another chance to get it right.

"I really should go and stay with my family," Anne said the next morning as she pulled a box of cereal from the cabinet.

Trey's head jerked up from the cup of coffee he was nursing. "You said you'd stay here at least through the week of Kwanzaa. I don't see any reason for that to change. Why do you?"

Because of the way he talked, the way he moved, the way he smiled, the way he smelled, and, most of all, how badly she wanted him, Anne thought. The man was going to give her a heart attack if she didn't jump his bones, but she might have a stroke if she did. He was a walking, talking catch-22. But there was no way she could say that to him.

"They want me to stay with them," she answered, avoiding his eyes.

"Yesterday you said you were overwhelmed. Moving in with your new family would only increase your stress."

Anne had no answer. She went to the refrigerator and got out the milk.

"I think we need to talk about what happened in the car yesterday. Did I offend you?" His voice was soft and sexy. She shivered in reaction to it. How was she going to deny this man anything?

Anne busied herself pouring the flakes of cereal into her bowl. "You know you didn't offend me."

"I didn't think so, but the way you were last night says otherwise," Trey said, a touch of frustration in his voice.

Anne paused in the act of starting to pour the milk on her cereal, feeling anxious and edgy. She'd thought that she'd be able to dodge talking about the issue. But it seemed that her silence on the matter wasn't going to make it go away. "Let me get this straight," she said. "You think a kiss or two entitles you to instant sex? Is that it?"

Trey leaned back in his chair and stared at her through narrowed eyes. "No, I don't suppose that is it," he drawled.

"Well then," Anne said, picking up her bowl and dumping the cereal in the garbage disposal. The sight of food suddenly made her feel nauseous.

The doorbell rang and Trey got to his feet with a barely stifled curse. Anne heard women's voices, and the state of her stomach didn't improve. What if it was—?

Anne's fears were realized when Trey's mother and sister sailed into the kitchen.

"You're still here?" his sister asked, looking like she smelled something bad.

"Obviously," Anne said, making an effort not to sound snappish.

"What was your name again?" Trey's mother asked.

"Anne."

"I'm Rachel, Trey's mother, and this is his older sister, Tina," she said, just as if they hadn't met the night before.

"I remember you," Anne answered. She glanced at Trey and noticed him watching the chilly interchange with interest.

"We were going out to catch the white sales and thought we'd drop by and see if there was anything you needed?" Rachel said to Trey.

"Nope, we're fine," Trey said.

Anne saw Rachel's lips tighten at the usage of the word *we*.

"Maybe Anne would like to go with you," he added.

"We're picking up Renee," Rachel said. "Anne, I'm sure you understand that might be a little awkward."

"It might be a touch," Anne said, her voice so dry, it could pass for the Sahara.

"Trey, Renee wants us to tell you that she wants her velvet bedspread back."

"That's fine. Hold on; I'll give it to you now."

"Oh no. We don't want to lug that heavy thing around. She'll be around later today to pick it up."

"I don't want her coming by. If she wants the bedspread I'll drop it off by your place later, or you need to go ahead and take it to her," Trey said.

"I have no idea why you're being so unreasonable," Rachel said. "You had a wonderful relationship with a wonderful woman and you tossed it away." She looked pointedly at Anne. "For no decent reason," she added.

Anne had had enough. "Excuse me," she said, and left the kitchen.

"Your taste in women has certainly deteriorated," she heard his mother say. Anne shut her bedroom door behind her and didn't wait to hear Trey's answer.

She needed some fresh air. She grabbed her coat and left Trey's house before his mother and sister emerged from the kitchen. She walked down the street toward her grandparents' house. She'd planned to go and see them today anyway, and right now a walk would do her good.

"There I was thinking about you and here you are. C'mon in. Have you had breakfast?" Helen asked.

Anne's hunger returned full force at the delicious smells coming from her grandmother's kitchen. "No, not yet."

"You're just in time. I made fresh biscuits."

Anne followed her grandmother's small and plump figure to her warm kitchen. It was decorated in hues of yellow and gold, with copper pots hanging from the ceiling. Her Aunt Jewel was sitting at the table digging into a heaped plate.

"It's good to see you, honey. Fill yourself up a plate and come and join us."

Anne was happy to comply. Soon she and her grandmother and aunt were all seated at the kitchen table digging in.

"Where's . . ." Anne didn't really know how to refer to her grandfather. *Grandfather* seemed too familiar. Referring to him by his first name seemed disrespectful, and his last name far too formal and distant.

"Are you asking about William? Call him Papa. Everybody else does."

"That's what everybody calls my other grandfather, too," Anne said.

She stared at her plate. She hadn't thought about her grandparents since she had talked to Grammy. But they were her family, a part of her, and she knew without a doubt that they loved her despite their flaws. She missed them.

"You miss them," said Helen, reading her mind.

"They definitely have issues, especially over my father and race—but yes, I miss them."

"And that's the way it should be," Jewel said with a gentle smile. "They raised you, and from the looks of you, they didn't do a bad job. They obviously valued you, and it shows. You got a pride about yourself despite what you told us about being raised a black girl in a white world."

"They love me," Anne said without hesitation. Of that there was no doubt.

"And that young man you've got. Oooo-eeee, girl. He's so fine, and a professor, too. That's one good catch you reeled in."

"I haven't reeled him in. And he definitely isn't my catch. I really don't know him that well."

Jewel's eyebrows shot up and Anne's grandmother looked surprised. "Then why are you staying with him?" Helen asked. "That is, if you don't mind talking about it," she added.

Anne's mood dropped several notches as she thought about the scene with Trey and the subsequent visit by his mother and sister. "I met Trey a few weeks ago at a book signing at my university. I told him that I wanted to find my father's people and he gave me his card. When I arrived at Atlanta and showed up on his doorstep, he let me in."

"He just let you in?" Jewel asked, a look of disbelief on her face.

"Yes. On hindsight, it seems strange, but at the time it seemed right." Anne chewed her food slowly, musing. "It's as if we've known each other for ages. I couldn't imagine staying with a stranger, but Trey has never, ever seemed like a stranger."

"How romantic," Jewel said.

"Romantic?"

"I see how he looks at you. And he had a fit when we wanted to bring you home with us after we first met you," Jewel said.

"Maybe he feels obligated."

"I doubt that," Helen said. "He doesn't seem a man to do anything out of mere obligation. I bet he's crazy about you."

"He just broke up with his girlfriend—a serious relationship by the looks of it. His mother and sisters are good friends with her."

"Those are the people I saw you talking with at the community center?" Jewel asked.

"Yes. Trey's old girlfriend was there. They let me know I was a poor second compared to her."

"But you're staying with him and she's not," Helen said firmly. "Men don't let women stay in their homes out of obligation, especially on a brief meeting like you told me you had. Like I said, there's something more there."

Anne felt miserable. What was happening between her and Trey certainly wasn't romantic hearts and flowers. Right now it felt more along the lines of steamy lust. "He's a man," she said.

"Yes, he is." Helen raised her cup to her lips. "And smart women don't let men like that go easily."

"His old girlfriend sure isn't."

"I was talking about you," Helen said.

Trey planned to celebrate Kwanzaa quietly at home with Anne that evening. While she was out visiting her folks, he cooked fried chicken and mashed potatoes along with green beans boiled with ham shanks so long they were begging for mercy.

He heard the key he'd given her turn in the door, and

anticipation leaped inside him. He couldn't wait to be with her again. A few minutes later she came into the kitchen, looking tired.

"Busy day?"

"I was out shopping with my cousins. It seemed like they wanted to drag me to every mall in Atlanta." She sniffed. "The food smells great. I'll set the table."

She seemed too quiet and subdued, Trey thought. He was worried but was determined not to press her. As much as he wanted her, if it was meant to be, it would be. He probably had rushed her too fast last night. From now on, slow-and-easy would be his middle name.

Anne's eyes closed as she bit into a chicken leg. "I was so hungry. This is delicious."

"So you like soul food?"

"This isn't soul food," Anne said.

"Yes, it is. Fried chicken is classic soul food."

"We have it all the time in Boston, and believe me, my grandparents don't have a drop of soul."

"With mashed potatoes and green beans with ham?"

"Yes, just like this. Well, maybe the green beans are cooked differently."

"How differently?"

"With margarine and chicken broth."

"Chicken broth has no soul."

"You don't think so? It's low in fat and tasty."

"It has no body, no grease, thus no soul."

"What about margarine?"

"Artificial color added. Case closed."

"That's your verdict?"

"Yes."

They stared at each other and simultaneously laughed.

"Hold on. I have the ultimate in soulful desserts," Trey said.

"What's that?"

"Yellow pound cake."

He went into the kitchen and brought out the pound cake carefully placed on a serving platter. He put a slice on a dessert plate with a flourish and handed it to her.

Anne took a bite and slowly chewed.

"Well, what do you think?"

"Frankly, Sara Lee doesn't have much soul, either."

"Awwwwww," Trey said.

"Impostor. You tried to pass this off as your cooking."

He threw up his hands. "Hey, guilty as charged," he said with a grin.

After dinner, they continued their gentle teasing and banter as they cleaned up the kitchen together.

Then Trey took Anne's hand to lead her to the Kwanzaa table. He lit the first, then the second candle. "Today the second principle is *Kujichagulia,* or self-determination. I thought about you when I was thinking about what to say about this principle."

"Why?"

"It seems that you've been the essence of self-determination lately. You've taken control of your life. You're defining yourself. And you are defining your future. It can be anything you want it to be."

She smiled at him. "You're right. Thank you. That makes me feel good about the choices I've made." She paused. "At least most of them."

He couldn't keep himself from reaching out and touching her hair, which glinted and echoed the crackling fire with its own fiery lights.

Her smile faded.

Anne's moist lips parted and he felt the heat radiate from her. Then he did what he had promised to himself that he wouldn't do. He wrapped her hair around his hand and pulled her to him.

Touching his lips to hers, he felt a tiny sigh of surrender. He kissed her lazily, savoring the recesses of her mouth and tasting her honeyed sweetness fully. Their tongues intertwined and danced around each other. He wanted to feel all of her against him, and from her quickened breaths and soft sighs he knew she wanted it also.

But he only nuzzled her neck and pressed a kiss below her ear. *Slowly*, he reminded himself.

"Why me?" she whispered.

He paused. "I don't know," he answered truthfully.

It must not have been the right answer. He almost swore as she pulled away.

"It's not that I don't want it just as much as you do," she said. "But what will be a quick—"

"Quick?" He grinned and reached for her again. "I'm never quick." She turned her face away from him.

"What's wrong?"

"You just want to dip into some available—"

"You think I want to have sex with you just because you're here?" Trey asked incredulously.

"Maybe."

"It's not true. If that were the case, I could be having no-strings sex with a number of women."

"Maybe that's what you should do," she said.

Disbelief and anger mixed with his arousal. He could hardly stand it. He stood and started to pace. "Tell you what," he said, his words low and clipped. "I'm too old to play games. When you grow up, maybe we can take this up where we left off. But until then—" He turned to her.

He was talking to the air. She'd already gone.

Chapter 8

Trey opened one eye and looked at the clock. It was already nine in the morning, a couple hours past the usual time he got up. Thoughts of the woman who should have been sharing his bed made his rest uneasy.

He rolled out of bed and headed to the bathroom. He showered and shaved in record time, eager to see Anne. They had to talk. He wanted a relationship with her, a sexual one, and he needed to understand her skittish reluctance. But when he opened the door of his bedroom and headed toward the kitchen, he knew something was wrong. The atmosphere of his home was different. It was quiet, too quiet.

He stuck his head into the kitchen and glanced around his family room before he headed to her bedroom. What if she'd left him? He'd noticed that she tended to flee the issue rather than facing it head-on. It wasn't his style. Anne was going to have to face him and deal with him along with whatever was bothering her. His eyes narrowed when he saw the empty guest room. He opened the closet. Her suitcase was still there, but she was gone.

He picked up his keys. He was going to find and confront her. He'd almost reached the door when the phone rang.

"Trey, do you have a moment?" his mother asked.

"I was on my way out."

"Are you alone?"

"Yes."

"I won't be long. I really want to talk to you about that girl you have staying with you. You can't possibly be serious about her?"

"What do you mean?" He knew he sounded exasperated, but he really didn't need to hear this now.

"You had a long-term relationship with Renee. I know you might be hurting from whatever went on between you, but that's no reason to lower your standards so drastically."

"What do you mean?" Trey repeated, his voice softly dangerous.

His mother hesitated. "She's not all that pretty and she's fat. Definitely not your type."

"Maybe my type is changing. Being with Anne is *not* lowering my standards from Renee," he said emphatically.

"What was wrong with Renee?"

"Nothing. I just don't love her."

"And you love that fat, light-skinned woman?"

"Let me tell you something. I thought you knew it, but I'll spell it out. Who I choose to be with is not your business. It's not your place to concern yourself with—much less judge—the woman of my choice. Am I making myself clear?"

"But—"

"There are no buts. That's the way it is. I'm hanging up now."

"Trey—"

Click. He grabbed the keys and walked out the door.

He had to drive around the block twice before he cooled down. His mother rarely pissed him off this badly. Where did she get off judging Anne? Calling her fat and saying he'd lowered his standards to choose her! *What the hell?*

He pulled into a drive-through to get a breakfast sandwich and some coffee before he went to see Anne.

Maybe that was the problem, he thought as he munched his ham-and-cheese biscuit. Maybe she'd picked up the negative vibes from his mother and sister and couldn't deal with it. She seemed like too self-possessed a woman to let some negativity from some women she didn't know rattle her, but who knew?

How could he talk to her about this, though? In case she hadn't picked up on his mother's attitude, he certainly didn't want to enlighten her. He swallowed and washed the last bit of biscuit down with a Coke. He'd have to think on it.

Trey pulled in front of Anne's grandparents' house and rang the bell. He waited and rang it again, then again. Then he looked at his watch and groaned. The volunteer day at the community center! They were probably there already and he was late. He rushed to his car.

"I'm glad you're staying with us," Jewel said. "What happened? That fine man of yours was pretty adamant about your spending the entire Kwanzaa holiday with him."

"He's not my man."

"It seemed like he was. Need to talk?" Jewel sat heavily on the bed beside her and stroked her back. Anne wanted to collapse in this woman's arms and pour out her heart.

"He wants to make love to me," she said through stiff lips.

Jewel chuckled. "I can't see that as a problem, honey."

"I can't see how he could want me."

Jewel raised an eyebrow. "Why not?"

"Look at me."

Jewel looked. "And?"

"No disrespect intended, but Aunt Jewel, I'm fat."

Jewel laughed. "You're a little thick, dearie, but that just makes you easier to hold on to."

"All my life I've been slapped in the face with the fact that men don't like fat women."

"Who told you that? You've been hanging around too many white boys. Baby, real men like all sorts of women. We come in all sizes and shapes and no one shape is going to make a woman any less of one."

"You're right about the guys I've known not liking big

women, or women with frizzy hair, or black women." Anne rubbed her eyes. "A confession: I've never had a boyfriend."

"What! That's a crying shame! You mean you've never . . . done it?"

"Technically not. I've known guys who'd take me out secretly and want to roll around in their cars. Some have wanted sex. But I've never known a guy who wanted me publicly as his girlfriend."

Jewel shook her head. "Those white folks who raised you might have loved you, but they did you a disservice not letting you know any black people. It would have been different. You're an attractive young woman. I have two daughters and bigness runs in our family and they don't lack for boyfriends. I don't think black men put as much stock in skinny women as do white men. I know my husband doesn't."

Anne didn't know what to think. She'd always tried to hold her head up high, but she carried the image of herself as unattractive to men. This had been her experience from her first spin-the-bottle game in the seventh grade, when the boys considered it a loss if they had to kiss her, to her first crush on a boy whom she knew would never look at her twice.

It came from the parties she wasn't invited to and the dates she never went on. From the dances and prom she never attended. Always an outsider, different. Never up to par. In her heart, she knew it went beyond her being heavy. She'd known a few white girls as big as or bigger than her who had boyfriends. But she'd been the only big *black* girl. Her color had been the biggest issue, no matter how much her classmates, friends, and family would deny it.

"Maybe it's time you got over it," her aunt was saying.

"Get over it? How?"

"You said this man wants you. A man like that isn't going to go after someone he doesn't really want. Don't lose him over your own insecurities. You said you've never had a man. You have a chance at a good one now. Running away isn't the answer. You care about him?"

Anne nodded. "I'm crazy about him."

"Then that's that. You know we're thrilled to have you here, but you go back on over to that man's house. And see yourself as the beautiful woman you are. Look at yourself through his eyes. You'll see."

"Are you two going to come eat?" Jewel's daughter called. "We're starving."

The family was gathered around the big table in the dining room. With school out and most of the family taking vacation time from work, everybody naturally gravitated over to Anne's grandparents' home.

Anne sat down with them and joined the ebb and flow of eating and conversation, feeling totally at home.

"We're supposed to meet at the community center at ten," her cousin said.

"For what?"

"For Kwanzaa. Today the principle is Ujima, collective work and responsibility. We're going out into the community to volunteer on several community projects."

Anne wondered if Trey and his family would be there. Probably. Probably Renee, too. She shrugged. Her aunt was right. It was past time she got over herself.

Trey rushed to his station. He was one of the leaders of the neighborhood cleanup team. He soothed his co-leader, Betty, and got her to cover him for a little while longer as he went off to look for Anne.

He saw her over by the boxes of food waiting to be distributed. He'd almost reached her when Renee rushed up to him. He tried to quell his irritation and almost succeeded.

"Trey, I've been needing to talk to you."

"I'm kind of in a hurry."

The contemptuous look that Renee cast in Anne's direction irritated him more. He waved at Anne and his heart lifted at the smile that lit up her face when she saw him. He moved toward her.

"Don't you dare go over to that cow when I have something to say to you. You'd better stay right here!" Renee's voice was tight and shrill.

"Renee, I never wanted to hurt you."

Her smile was full of triumph. "Then don't," she said seductively. She reached out to him and he stepped away, evading her touch.

"I didn't want to have to spell it out," Trey said. "But this is getting ridiculous and I guess I'm going to have to."

"What?" Renee asked, her smile fading.

"Please get lost. It's over. We're through. There is nothing you can do to make me want to be with you again. Understand? Do you finally get it now?"

He walked away, leaving her cursing and sputtering.

He reached Anne and any thought of Renee faded away. Their gazes met and he had to fold his arms to keep from touching her. "Why did you leave without talking to me this morning?" he asked.

"I—I needed some time alone."

"I think we need to talk."

Anne chewed on her lower lip. "You're right. My excuse is that it's hard enough for me to deal with what I'm feeling, but it's harder still for me to imagine talking to you about it."

He nodded. Trey knew how difficult it was to express feelings sometimes, especially if they were attached to a relationship as tenuous as theirs was.

"Maybe we can sit down and talk when we get home?" Anne asked, looking nervous and uncertain.

"Yes, we'll talk when we get home," Trey replied, liking the sound of the word *home*. It seemed to go well with Anne in particular and the entire concept of "we."

Chapter 9

"I planned to go back to the community shelter and serve and eat dinner there, but now I seem to lack the ambition," Trey said.

Anne put her feet up on the coffee table next to his as they both sat on the sofa staring into the fire. "I know what you mean."

He reached out and took her hand and their fingers intertwined. Anne squeezed his hand and in a quick movement she'd sat on his lap facing him. Her knees straddled his thighs and her breasts pressed into his chest. Trey tried to quell his instant arousal and keep his arms at his side. He knew if he touched her, it would be a repeat of their previous encounters. He wanted to clear this up between them, not continue replaying the same scenario over and over.

She softly kissed him on the lips and he responded gently, carefully restraining himself. "I take it that now you're ready to talk," he said when she lifted her head.

"I'm ready to do more than talk," she purred.

"I'm not. We've got to work out whatever is going on between us before we move on. That is, if we want to have a relationship."

She almost fell over. He steadied her.

"You want to have a relationship with me?" she asked.

"That's the point, yes."

"What sort of relationship?"

"This isn't the most comfortable position to converse in. I'm having some difficulty concentrating." That was an understatement with her soft bottom pressing into the most sensitive and responsive part of his anatomy.

"Oh. Sorry." She scrambled off his lap and not a moment too soon, before he'd have to give into the irresistible urge to grab her and kiss her senseless.

The phone rang and they groaned simultaneously. "I think I'm going to get rid of that thing," he said.

"We do seem to get interrupted at the most interesting moments," Anne murmured.

"My mother drops by occasionally, but not too often." Trey decided that this was as good a time as any to get the unpleasant subject of his mother's reaction to Anne out in the open.

"That's not a bad thing. Your mother and sisters don't seem to be too enthused about my staying here."

"I'm sorry. My sister Tina is a good friend of Renee's."

"That's not all of it. They seem to have some sort of issue with me."

"They don't know you. I think it's because you are so different from anybody that I've ever dated. And since this has been so sudden—it's been a shock to them. I've never let anyone stay with me before."

He heard Anne release a soft sigh.

"Don't worry; I'm not going to let them keep treating you badly," he said.

"They will keep on in one way or another if they don't respect me. They need to know I'm not going to put up with disrespect."

Trey nodded. She was right.

"One other thing bothers me about the situation," Anne said.

"What's that?"

"Why does Renee seem so desperate to reconcile with you? Does she love you so much? Did you love her once and don't love her anymore?"

"No. I don't think Renee loves me and I've never said any such thing to her. I believe Renee's problem with our breakup is her pride. The fact that I broke up with her when she didn't expect it is eating at her. She's mainly worried about other people knowing. When I was with Renee, I felt more like her trophy than her man."

"How long were you together?"

"About a year and a half. It was habit. She made a passable escort and I got sick of dating different women. I broke up with her because she started pressing me for marriage and commitment and I knew she wasn't the one. I thought it would be fairer to her to let her go. Maybe she'll find the right man for her. I've told her this again and again, but she doesn't seem to hear it."

"I suppose any breakup hurts."

"Especially if your ego is the size of Texas," he replied.

"Renee doesn't want people to see that you left her for a fat woman," Anne said, looking away.

"You're not fat. You're plump in all the right places."

"Like my hips and thighs?" Anne asked, her smile returning and growing into a grin.

"There's nothing better than a big-legged woman."

"That I am." Anne's smile faded and her gaze dropped to her feet. "Trey, that's another thing I need to talk to you about."

"Your big legs?"

"Sort of. But more like my whole body."

"Oh. But I can think of better things to do than talk about it."

"Seriously. I got grouchy with you because I was afraid . . ." Her voice trailed off and she looked away.

He waited.

"Afraid to take off my clothes in front of you."

Trey supposed this problem was a woman thing, because he sure didn't understand it. "Didn't I make it more than abundantly clear that I want your clothes off? That I find you desirable, I mean?"

"I guess so, but Renee is so thin and your mother is so

scandalized that you're interested in a woman my size. Exposing my body to you will be difficult to do."

"No, it won't," he said gently. "Maybe worrying about it beforehand is difficult, but I don't think when we actually—" He considered suggesting a trial run but decided this wasn't the time.

"There's something else," she interrupted him. "I'm a virgin, Trey."

That was a bombshell he didn't expect.

"A virgin?" He was dismayed that his words sounded so high-pitched and squeaky. He tried again. "You're a virgin?"

She nodded and waited expectantly for him to say something else. Trey was speechless. This was one thing that he'd never encountered in all of his twenty-seven years on earth.

"I guess most women get over it OK," he finally said. From the look on her face, that wasn't the best choice of words. He gave it another try. "Um, I heard that it only hurts for a little while." He studied her frown. "Is it that you want to *stay* a virgin?" he asked, his eyes widening with alarm.

"Of course not," she snapped.

"Oh."

"Have you ever devirginized someone before?" she asked.

Trey studied his hands, trying to review his sexual experience, which he felt was adequate, if not extensive. Nope, his experiences had never included a virgin. "No. I can't say that I've ever devirginized anybody," he answered.

Heavy silence fell.

"Well, it's a barrier that everybody has to get through, I guess," Trey said hesitantly.

"See, I knew this would be awful," Anne said with a sob in her voice. "I should have kept my mouth shut." She fled the room.

Oh Lord, what did he say wrong? Trey wondered as he

followed her. She threw herself facedown on her bed. He sat down beside her.

"Baby, calm down." He stroked her back. "I love your body. I want to know every single inch of it. Ever since I met you, it's been driving me crazy trying to figure out whatever attracted me to a woman like Renee. You make me nuts, girl." He paused. "In a good way," he added. "As far as you being a virgin, well, if you're willing, we'll manage to plow through this together."

That didn't sound right, he thought. "It's a job that somebody has to do and I'll give it my best shot." That was a little better, he decided.

What sounded like a snort came from the vicinity of her face. "Jeez, Trey, stop it. You're gonna kill me," she said, her voice muffled.

Although it sounded as if she was laughing, he hoped she wasn't referring to the obstacle at hand. Trey patted her back in what he hoped was a reassuring manner. "It won't be that bad," he said.

Her shoulders were shaking and she was probably overcome with sobs. He'd ride this out with her. He wanted to always be there for her. Rubbing his eyes, he felt drained. It had been a long day and an emotional one. He wanted to make love to her, but the time wasn't right. But he knew it soon would be. Fate had finally contrived to bring him his soul mate. This initial getting to know each other with all its hurdles seemed an unnecessary bother. He'd never come close to feeling this way about any other woman and knew with cutting clarity that Anne was the love of his life.

Now all he had to do was convince her.

He settled down next to Anne, his arm around her waist, and closed his eyes.

Chapter 10

Anne woke feeling Trey's heavy leg across her and his warm breath against her cheek. He'd been so awkward and funny last night with his consternation over her virginal state that she thought she'd crack something trying to hold back her howls of laughter. He'd fallen asleep next to her on the guest-room bed and she'd soon joined him in slumber.

Now the pink early-morning light cast stripes on the wall as it fell through the slats in the window. She didn't want to stir; she wanted to imprint this moment with Trey at her side in her mind and heart.

But unfortunately, she had to go to the bathroom. Brushing her teeth wouldn't be a bad idea, either.

Anne extricated herself, trying not to wake Trey, and dashed to the bathroom. Afterward, she peeked into the guest room, praying he was still asleep and debating whether to curl up beside him again.

He was sitting up in the bed, his dark eyes fastened on her. "Good morning, darlin'," he said as if the endearment were as natural to him as breathing.

She stepped into the room, more excited than frightened, and nestled into the crook of the arm that he'd held out for her.

"Good morning," she answered.

He brought his mouth down on hers and kissed her,

slowly and deeply, a drugged kiss that made her body go limp and liquid. She twined her arms around his neck and they slid down on the bed, the hard length of his body imprinted against hers. Desire flamed within her, not to be denied.

"All right," she said. "Let's do it."

Trey laughed. "All right, we will," he said.

One by one he unbuttoned the shirt she was wearing and let it fall open. He traced circles over her skin and she shivered with longing, need, and a touch of fear.

"You have to realize how beautiful I think you are," he whispered in her ear. She felt his uneven breathing on her cheek as he held her close. She relaxed, sinking into the feel of his arms around her, his body next to hers.

He twisted his fingers through her hair and kissed her again, his tongue sensuously moving in her mouth, causing a tidal wave of longing to build within her. She moved against him restlessly, seeking, wanting . . . Her hands moved lower and traced the throbbing length of him through his jeans. "Let's do it right now," she said.

He drew in a quick breath. "Lady, we've only just begun," he said.

He trailed kisses down her neck as his fingers worked to unhook her bra and slide her shirt off her shoulders. He kissed the hollow of her collarbone and shoulders. Her nipples rubbed against the soft material of his T-shirt and she felt impatient to feel his skin against hers. She tried to pull his shirt up. He obliged, with a smooth motion pulling the shirt over his head, exposing his lightly haired, muscular chest. Her heart pounded painfully as her body yearned to have this man inside.

He began a languid exploration of her breasts with his lips and tongue. Circling her pink nipple with his warm, wet tongue, he moved from one breast to another, licking, sucking, and flicking her sensitive nipples with his tongue.

"Ohhhhh, that feels so good," she whispered.

He unzipped her jeans and started to ease them and her

panties over her hips. Pausing, he asked, "You're sure you want this now?" his voice hoarse.

"Please."

She reached for the buttons of his jeans and ran her fingers over the hard thickness of his rod. She thrilled in her power over him as she felt a tremor go through his body.

"You set me on fire, girl," he said, pulling her jeans and panties down over her hips. His eyes seemed to memorize her body. She opened to him, surprised that she didn't feel shy or shamed.

"How could you not believe you're beautiful?" he murmured as he proceeded to languidly explore every inch of her body with his lips and tongue.

He worked his way over the swell of her belly and entwined his fingers in her triangle of curls; his mouth and lips worked lower and lower, his hands grasping her knees.

Anne sensed where he was going with his mouth and closed her legs, but he slipped his hand between them and gently pried her knees open.

"I need to taste you." His head dipped and she felt his tongue in the most private part of her. She echoed his moan as tremors of pleasure and shock raced through her body and he fastened his mouth on that tiny bead of pleasure and sucked gently, rhythmically.

She writhed under him. "Yes, yes, yes," she moaned as waves of unbelievable pleasure raced through her body, more intense than she'd thought possible.

Her hands tangled in his hair and she went wild against his mouth, her hips involuntarily bucking. Her sighs and moans intensified to sharp gasps. The world drew into a pinpoint of tense need on the edge of release. Then the tidal wave broke, causing her to quake at the intensity of pleasure battering her. Slowly she came back to herself so spent, she didn't feel she could move again.

A girl could get used to this, Anne decided.

And he didn't stop.

"Enjoying yourself?" he asked, kissing the insides of her

thighs and working down to the backs of her knees. Incredibly, an ember started to flame within her again. Was she building to another climax? She didn't know if her body could take it.

She'd never guessed that the backs of her knees were an erogenous zone.

He rolled off the bed and left the room. She hardly had time to feel bereft before he returned, dropping his jeans and briefs to the floor. His heavy erection jutted out as she ran her eyes over his perfect male form—his narrow waist, long, muscular legs—and raised up and fitted her naked body against him. She wanted to feel him, to taste him, to take him inside her.

He knelt at the side of the bed and pulled himself to her. She fit perfectly, her yin to his yang, light and dark, woman to man. She saw her beauty reflected in his eyes and she no longer felt a shred of self-consciousness. She encircled him with her small hand and felt a shudder go through his body. She felt moisture at the tip of his engorged erection and circled her thumb around the head, flush with pleasure at the power of making him burn and moan for her.

He thrust a condom in her hand. She tore open the foil package and worked it over his swollen shaft with trembling fingers.

And then he was on top of her, his hardness jutting against her engorged folds. "Now," she whispered. "I want you inside me now," she whispered, reaching for him.

He pinned her arms over her head. "Slowly," he said.

She wriggled under him until the tip of his shaft grazed her damp entrance. He kissed her, his tongue thrusting rhythmically into her mouth. She bucked against him, needing what she'd never had before, for him to fill her.

"Slowly. I'm only human, woman," he said, barely banked desire burning in his eyes.

"Please," she begged.

She felt his swollen head at her entrance and tried to engulf it with her body. He slipped it in a fraction of an inch and she paused at the pain she felt.

"Hurts?" he asked.

She nodded.

"Do you need me to stop?"

She shook her head frantically. "Now, now," she gasped, her hips grinding against him.

He moved inside of her another fraction of an inch, his eyes never leaving hers. He tested her depth and width and her tolerance for his thrust. He controlled her and played her like an instrument, stilling her hips that wanted to take him in, moving against him frantically.

"Hold on," he said, easing himself in slowly, so very slowly.

The seconds spread out to minutes. She couldn't stand it any longer. She had to have all of him inside her. "It doesn't hurt anymore," she said.

"Are you sure?"

"Please, Trey, please give it to me now."

She thrust her hips, bucked, and clawed his back until he surged forward, filling her entirely, filling her with a pleasure so intense, she couldn't tell the ending of the pain and the beginning of pleasure.

He gasped against her mouth and she rocked with him, meeting him thrust for thrust and urging him with her body and her moans of pleasure. Their bodies collided again and again, her sensitive bud beating against his hard male form. She was climbing, climbing, climbing, the pinnacle so close, and then she was there, spinning off, falling into ecstasy and calling his name. She heard his hoarse cry and he surged into her wildly, exploding inside her. Her fingers clutched his shoulders.

She knew with certainty that for her, it would be Trey, only Trey, always and forever.

Chapter 11

By the time evening fell, Anne was sore but tingling with happiness. Her body felt more alive than it ever had before. For the first time in her life she felt beautiful. She took Trey's appreciation for every curve on her body, his delight in every secret slippery bundle of nerve endings, his enjoyment in the taste and scent of her, and made it her own. She saw her body in a new light—feminine, powerful, healthy, and capable of bringing her and her man incredible pleasure.

Neither one of them bothered to dress or leave the bed for more than a few minutes the entire day. They leaned against the headboard while Trey examined the contents of the box that Helen had presented to Anne to look over, full of scrapbooks, pictures, and memorabilia of the father she had never known.

"You look like him," Trey said, looking at a picture of her father.

"It's funny how my grandparents always said I looked like my mother."

"You probably look like her, too. I'm a blend of my mother and father also. Different features favoring each parent."

"What happened with your father, Trey? If you don't mind me asking."

"He left when I was around thirteen."

"Sorry. That must have been tough."

"Not really. It was a good thing, actually. He was pretty rough on my mother."

"Was he abusive?"

"Not directly. He wasn't much of a man. He didn't work and drank too much. Laid around the house. He was a drain on my mother, like having another kid around rather than a partner. I don't know why she put up with him for so many years."

"Maybe he was depressed."

"Maybe."

"My papa is the opposite. He works all the time and is never home. He refuses to retire. I think Grammy goes days on end without seeing him."

"Have you talked to them lately?" he asked.

She shifted uneasily. "No, I haven't. Do you realize that we haven't eaten today?" she said, trying to change the subject. She wasn't quite ready to leave the warm, dreamy reality of this bed for the other issues in her life.

Trey's hand went to his stomach. "I'm starving. I can't believe I'm only realizing it now." He looked at his watch. "Damn!"

"What's wrong?"

"I nearly forgot that I have a talk on black economic empowerment tonight at the community center. I need to shower." He jumped out of bed.

"I'll make a sandwich for you to take with you."

Fifteen minutes later, she handed Trey a bag with two sandwiches, some chips, and fruit.

"Bye, baby," he said, dropping a kiss on her forehead. "I'll see you there, shortly?" he asked.

"I'll be in the audience as soon as I dress."

It was after Trey left that Anne realized she was standing in his kitchen as naked as a jaybird without an iota of self-consciousness. Life had certainly taken a turn. It was definitely an improvement, she decided as she headed for the shower, munching on the last bit of her sandwich.

*   *   *

An hour later, Anne listened to her lover speak, filled with admiration for his words, his energy, and his intelligence. The fact that he was hers, at least for the next few days of Kwanzaa, was almost beyond belief.

At the reception afterward, Trey and Anne were nibbling on hors d'oeuvres and discussing how long they should stay before a polite exit could be accomplished when Rachel appeared, flanked by her two daughters.

"You did a marvelous job, dear, as usual," Rachel said, kissing the air near Trey's cheek.

"Hi, Mom."

"What are your plans for this evening? I'd love for you to come with us to dinner for Kwanzaa tonight. I know this African-American-owned restaurant—"

"Mom," Trey interrupted with a frown.

"What?"

"It's impolite to ignore Anne," he said firmly.

Rachel's gaze landed on Anne and flickered away. She gave a shrug.

"That's all right," Anne said sweetly. "Since this is one of the rudest women I've ever met, I suppose that's all we can expect."

Rachel gasped. "Are you calling me rude?" she demanded.

"The description seems to fit you quite well," Anne answered.

Trey looked down at Anne in surprise, but his arm curled around her waist and pulled her close in support.

"Are you going to stand here and let this woman insult your mother?" Rachel asked Trey.

Trey studied his mother a moment before answering, his face carefully bland. "Since you've done a good job of insulting her so far, I'd call it tit for tat," he said.

Anne figured that a person pretty much decided how other people treated her by what she put up with. She'd had about enough of putting up with Rachel, and it was time to nip it in the bud. "I don't appreciate you calling me fat," Anne continued. "Don't do it again or I'll be calling attention to some of your own physical flaws."

"Trey!" Rachel cried.

He took Anne's hand. Anne felt his support and caring through the strength of his fingers intertwined with hers. "I'm not going to rescue you, Mom," he said. "As far as I'm concerned, this is between you and Anne."

Rachel took a deep breath.

"It's all about respect. Treat me with it and it'll be returned in kind," Anne said.

A newfound regard mixed with caution shone from Trey's sisters' eyes as they studied Anne.

Rachel turned on her heel and walked rapidly away.

"She'll be OK," his sister Tess said. "She's been upset over a promotion she lost at work and she's been having problems with her boyfriend, Ralph. I think your breakup with Renee brought it home. Ralph called it quits with her."

Trey frowned. "I don't think Ralph is any great loss."

"Me neither, but you know how Mom is. She has to have some man in tow, even if it's just a piece of one."

His other sister nodded. "Give her some time," she added.

"We'd better be going," Tess said.

"I'll see you two later," Trey said.

Tess nodded at Anne and Tina's gaze touched hers. "Good-bye," they chorused.

For the first time Anne felt acknowledged, along with the beginnings of a glimmer of respect between them. She realized that she didn't really care anymore if Trey's family liked or accepted her. Trey was who mattered. She couldn't go on basing her self-esteem on other people's actions, especially when they so often had problems and agendas of their own.

She laced her fingers through Trey's. "Let's go get something to eat," she said.

Three days later, Anne was in the kitchen making a sumptuous brunch. Trey had left for the community center to help prepare for the last day of Kwanzaa celebration, the *karamu* party. She couldn't wait to wear the African costume that Trey had helped her pick out, a beautiful robe and matching head wrap made of brightly colored *kente* cloth.

She'd just slid the muffins into the oven when the phone rang.

"Hello?" she said.

"Is that you, Anne?"

"Papa? Yes, it's me."

"We need you home right away," he said.

Fear iced through her veins. "What is it?"

"Grammy's had a heart attack."

Anne's eyes closed and an involuntary moan came from her throat. "Is—is she . . ."

"She's alive. But she's not doing well and she's been asking for you."

"I'll be on the next plane out," Anne said.

She replaced the phone on the cradle, picked it up, and punched in the number to the community center.

"May I speak to Trey Fraser?"

"He's not here."

"Where is he?" Anne asked, feeling panicky. She needed him.

"He went to buy some items that we need. He just left and he'll probably be gone for a couple of hours. May I take a message?"

"This is Anne. Tell him—tell him that I have to go back home to Boston. I'll call him later."

She replaced the phone on the receiver, her hands shaking, and then raced to the bedroom to throw her clothes in her suitcase. Her fault, her fault, her fault. The words echoed through her mind. Why hadn't she called Grammy? Why had she run away instead of working it out like Grammy had asked her? If Grammy died, she . . . she didn't think she could bear it.

Chapter 12

Grammy looked way too small in the ICU bed with all that machinery blinking, whirring, and beeping around her. Silent tears poured down Anne's face as she watched her. She approached the bed and took Grammy's hand.

Her eyes opened and her gaze focused on Anne's face. "My baby," she said, her voice full of love. Anne's throat felt as if it would close with grief and guilt.

"Grammy, I'm so sorry," she said.

"You don't have anything to be sorry about. I've been doing a lot of thinking. I wanted to talk to you before—" Grammy coughed, a cough so feeble that it sent tendrils of fear through Anne.

"Don't talk. Please, please just concentrate on getting well. Save your strength."

"Listen to me, child. Papa and I did you wrong and we realize that. We wanted to make amends. We bought a ticket to Atlanta for that Kwanzaa cow-a-moo party and we were going to leave today and surprise you. Unfortunately, this happened." Grammy sighed. "You should have seen the African outfit I bought."

"You bought an African outfit?" Anne asked, surprise replacing some of her grief.

"Yep. Head wrap, too."

"Oh, Grammy." A smile glinted through her tears at the

thought of Grammy in African garb. "I can't wait for you to get well so I can see you in it."

Grammy squeezed Anne's hand. "You're going to have to be strong," she said.

"No, no." Anne shook her head, unwilling to hear.

"You're a strong girl. We made a lot of mistakes raising you, Papa and I. If I had it to do over, I'd do it differently. I needed to let you know that and this, too. Despite everything, we must have done something right, because I'm proud of you. Always have been."

Anne leaned over and laid her head in her favorite place on Grammy's stomach, right below her ample breasts. Since she was a toddler, it was the place where she'd run when she needed comfort.

She lifted her head and looked in Grammy's eyes. "You're going to get well. I'm back for good. I promise not to leave you again. Just get well soon and come back home."

Grammy smiled at her, a sad smile. "Don't promise not to leave me. We all have to leave sometime. It's a part of life. When it's time to go, we have to move on."

Anne buried her head again, smelling her grandmother's familiar sweet scent, and her tears started afresh.

"We're a part of each other, child," Grammy said. "That's one thing that can never change."

"What do you mean, she said she's gone back to Boston? Is that all she said?" Trey asked Betty. People bustled around them, busily preparing for the *karamu* celebration tonight, the last day of Kwanzaa.

"She said she'd call you."

Uneasiness filled him.

"I'm going home," he said to Betty.

"But—"

"If Anne shows up after all, let her know that I'm home waiting for her."

When he walked into his home, the first thing he did was head for the guest bedroom. He stared into the empty

closet. She was gone. Back to Boston, she'd said. He didn't
know how to reach her in Boston.

They'd gone so fast, he'd forgotten for how short a time
they'd known each other. There were so many gaps, gaps
he thought he'd have all the time in the world to fill in.
But all Anne had promised him was Kwanzaa. Maybe he
should have taken her at her word.

It was one of those particularly bleak days in Boston that
varnished everything gray, even people's faces. A day to
match the state of her heart, Anne thought. A fitting day to
bury Grammy.

Ever since Grammy died, it was as if Anne had turned
into a shadow, a mere wraith drifting through the hours
and days. Losing Grammy was losing the only mother
she'd ever known. It was the hardest thing in her life that
she'd ever had to endure. She expected to see Grammy at
every turn, to hear the sound of her voice.

Anne stared at the image of Grammy in the casket, waxy
and cold, like a statue, covered with lilies, her favorite
flower. She couldn't hear a word the minister said. Was it
grief that seemed to have numbed and deafened her or the
tumult of guilt and remorse rushing through her? *Was it
her fault that Grammy was gone?*

She'd left with barely a word and when Grammy asked
her to come back, she'd shut her out. She'd met her father's
family, but it was Trey who had consumed her and turned
her thoughts away from what she'd left behind.

Her grief consumed her, and guilt prevented her from
reaching out to the man she loved and craved with every
cell of her body. Maybe soon the emptiness would fill and
she could go to him. But this time she had to give wholly
to Grammy. She at least owed her that.

After the funeral, Anne moved through the house, saying
the right things to the mourners, adding platters of food to
the overloaded dining room table. As she carried another
casserole she thought she heard a voice.

"Anne."

She turned toward the familiar voice, her eyes focusing on the tall black man who stood there. Trey.

"I just found out about your grandmother," he said. "I'm so sorry."

The sight of him sent a flood of emotions through her, slicing through the numbness that had descended since Grammy died—grief, not empty and gray and numb, but sharp and cutting with ice-cold pain, guilt, overwhelming and suffocating, regret, and longing washing over her, drowning her.

The casserole crashed to the floor and she ran.

Instead of running away, she ran into the warmth of Trey's open arms. He cradled her, and the comfort of his embrace crept through the shroud of grief and guilt that cloaked her.

"I was going to call, Trey, but I had to take care of Grammy first. I had to take care of Grammy."

"I know, baby. Her death wasn't your fault. You have to realize that."

Suddenly she heard her Grammy's voice as clear as her memory: *"Don't promise not to leave me. We all have to leave sometime. It's a part of life. When it's time to go, we have to move on. We're a part of each other, child. That's one thing that can never change."*

Her past was a part of her, and despite everything, it had made her strong. But her future held her in his arms. It was time to move on.

"My entire life, I wondered what was missing," Trey said. "Then I met you. I can't ever let you go, girl."

Looking for her heritage, she had discovered herself. She also found what her parents had found—something that had no color, no race, and no boundaries. She'd found love. She looked into Trey's eyes. Without words, the love shimmered between them with an almost palpable magic. That was all that really mattered.

Anne touched his cheek. "Take me back home, Trey."

Epilogue

A year later
The tables were laden with African-inspired dishes. Laughter filled the community center, and children ran and played. People dressed in bright colors chattered and mingled while African drums played in the background. *Kinaras* filled with seven green, red, and black candles burning brightly were scattered throughout, lending a glow to the festive decorations. It was New Year's Day and the Kwanzaa *karamu* celebration.

Anne stood at one of the tables with a plate in her hand, trying to decide whether to get the fried chicken drenched in country-style gravy or the tomato-based African chicken and rice dish. She decided on a little of both. Suddenly an arm circled her waist from behind and a hand sneakily grabbed a country-fried chicken wing off her plate.

"Trey! Quit it. You've eaten enough food to feed an army."

Trey moved to her side but didn't let her or the chicken wing go. He grinned down at her. "It's impossible to get enough of those chicken wings. Mmm-mmm good."

"This plate is for Papa. Keep your paws off."

Trey cast a glance over to Anne's grandfather, who was flanked by three women but had his attention fixed on an overflowing plate of food.

"My father-in-law seems occupied. I'd say the last thing he needs is another plate."

Anne looked over at him. "He wanted more chicken. I guess he got it for himself while I was helping Helen rehearse her song for the Kwanzaa show later."

"He's quite the man with the ladies," Trey said, eying the older women surrounding her grandfather.

Anne nodded. Papa had grown quite popular with the ladies and he seemed to thoroughly enjoy being chased. She wondered what Grammy would think of the black church-going lady Papa was seeing back in Boston. Who'd have thought it?

If she were granted one wish, it would be to see Grammy again. It wasn't fair that Grammy would never know how Anne had bridged the gap between two totally different families who'd suffered the bitter losses of their children, her parents. Grammy would never see how they'd all grown to know and respect one another. She'd never witness the miracle that was the love that Anne and her husband shared and the new family they were creating.

Life had given her more than she'd ever dreamed, and if she could see Grammy one more time, her happiness would be complete. She missed her so much.

Trey read the sadness on her face. "Your grandmother wanted the ones she loved to be happy. Even Papa and his new girlfriend."

Anne opened her mouth to reply, but the sounds in the room seemed to fade away. She caught a glimpse of a woman out of the corner of her eye and turned toward her. A plump older woman with brightly colored African robes smiled at Anne. Her blue eyes were full of otherworldly light, radiating wisdom and love mixed with a sort of perfect acceptance and affection. It was Grammy.

"Anne, what's wrong?" she heard Trey's voice, sounding as if it came from a great distance away.

Anne's gaze flickered to Trey's face. "Look," she whispered, her voice hoarse with wonder.

When she looked back at the spot where Grammy had stood, no one was there.

But where sadness lingered, joy now filled, as she was sure her grandmother had intended. Grammy was finally celebrating Kwanzaa.

"We're a part of each other, child. That's one thing that can never change."

Anne's fingers intertwined with Trey's, and she tilted her head upward, looking into his eyes. The love she found there reached down to her heart and held it firmly.

Grammy had come to remind her that while the past no longer existed, love could never die. A smile touched Trey's lips and it was if their future had rushed up to meet them, shining bright with love and promise.

The Seventh
Principal

BY GERI GUILLAUME

Chapter 1

"I'm not telling you how to run your school, Mr. B. After all, you are the boss man, the big cheese, the head honcho, the—"

"Something you want to tell me, Norah?"

Wednesday morning Norah Gilbert stopped me in the hall and passed me a stack of messages from the school attendance assistant. As far as I was concerned, it was *waaaay* too early in the morning for my assistant principal to be looking so glum. The students hadn't even begun to arrive yet. And she had called me Mr. B. Norah only did that when she wanted to warn me that Big, with a capital *B*, trouble was brewing. Any other time she addressed me, it was just Paul.

For a moment, I felt just like the guy from that television show *Boston Public*—besieged by his intense but well-intentioned AP. Only difference was, I had a sinking feeling that the problem Norah was bringing to me this morning wasn't going to be solved as quickly as that television show's running time.

"I think you need to see these."

"What are these?" I asked, taking the pink stack from her and flipping through them as I continued down the hall.

"What do they look like?" she returned.

Norah had a habit of answering a question with a question. She fell into step beside me. The *clompity-clomp* of her sensibly heeled shoes echoed loudly in the nearly empty corridor as her slight, five-foot-two frame somehow managed to keep up with me, over a foot taller than she was, moving a little more quietly in high-topped cross-trainers.

Still in my workout clothes, I was on the way to the boys' shower room after my morning run when she stopped me. Every morning, rain or shine, I wake up before the sun and try to make at least six miles around the school's jogging track if I don't walk the twelve miles from my house to here. Gets me to school early, tired and sweaty—but the health benefits are worth it. Being compared to that larger-than-life actor/principal on that television show wouldn't have been flattering.

"All of these kids can't be sick," I muttered, noting the hastily scrawled messages that were supposedly from the parents of the afflicted students. "The school nurse would have told me if we had some kind of epidemic on our hands."

"Ms. Campitelli is very efficient—on top of every sniffle, every sneeze, that goes on around here. She can smell a fever from two floors up and is usually on the phone to the parents before the digital thermometer finishes ticking off the degrees. Some of these messages were on the answering service. That means that some came in last night. And this is only a few of the messages that came in. I've got another stack sitting on my desk."

"So what's really going on here?" I asked, looking at her.

"You're in the wrong place to be playing dumb, Mr. Barrett. You *know* what's going on around here," Norah said, her tone insistent.

"No. . . . Come on."

She raised her eyebrows at me in answer.

"You've got to be kidding me." I stopped in midstride, folding my arms in front of me and glowering down at her.

Norah didn't even flinch. "Do I look like I'm laughing, Mr. Barrett?"

She had a game face that could put a champion poker

player to shame. Whenever she looked at you from over the rim of those cat-eye glasses and pressed her crimson lips together into that tight line, there was no mistaking that she meant business. It was one of the reasons that I valued her so much. She handled the students so well, so expediently, that only the most delicate situations ever crossed my desk—which was why, I knew, she was coming to me now. As capable as Norah was, this situation was stickier than usual, involving students who were more intense than usual.

"Was it wishful thinking to hope that we'd solved this problem three days ago?" I asked, handing the stack of phone notices back to her.

"We suspended those boys for fighting three days ago. We didn't solve the problem of what set them to fighting in the first place."

"So, some of the students are still going through with the threatened sick-in to protest the suspension." It wasn't a question, but a statement of fact.

I'd been forewarned by several of my staff members that some of the students were going to try it—to stay out of school for the next few days to coincide with the return of Zane Donovan, Brian Chalmers, and Rayford Vaughn. Three seniors who'd been suspended for fighting. An automatic three-day suspension was in line with the high school's zero tolerance policy.

If I had my choice, I would have let them off with a warning. Made them perform some service to the school to set the example. I'd even told them as much. But like it or not, my hands were tied. Violence in schools was a hot button lately, getting more media attention than usual. And zero tolerance meant just that. None. Zippo. Zero. Zilch. Fighting, no matter what the cause, could not be tolerated in the schools. Trouble was, these were popular boys. Not necessarily model students, but the rest of the student body seemed to rally behind them.

Here it was two days into the suspension. The boys were scheduled to be back tomorrow and I was still getting calls

from upset students. This was wasn't good. Not like senior
skip day, when everyone expected students to go AWOL.
Besides, it was too early in the season to go on the hunt
for the students, assured of their graduation status, wanting
to ditch school for one last fling to jump-start the summer
before separating for their respective colleges and trade
schools. This was something entirely different. A malady
that had spread across all four grades.

"All of this drama over what could very well have been
an attack of hay fever."

"Wasn't that Zane Donovan's story?" Norah didn't
sound convinced.

"That's the story he's sticking to." I shrugged. Since it
had been so early in the morning, there weren't very many
students to witness what had started the ruckus—just how
it ended. I only had the word of three boys on what happened.

"According to Rayford Vaughn and Brian Chalmers,
Zane deliberately spit on them while they were out raising
the school flags."

"I don't know, Norah. I have a hard time believing that."

"Why? Because Zane is so 'popular'?" She held up two
fingers of each hand, putting quotes around the last word.

New to Calhoun County, our pastoral little Mississippi
town, Zane's family had transferred from California just a
few short weeks ago. His American literature teacher had
submitted his name to participate in the school flag-raising
ritual to help him adjust and to foster a sense of belonging.
An average student, Zane didn't say much. Kept mostly to
himself. I guess he was still too much in culture shock.

But it didn't escape my notice that most of the dissen-
sion surrounding Zane's suspension came from the young
ladies in the school—all mesmerized by Zane's sun-
streaked, spiky-gelled, ultrablond hair and wide, guileless,
blue-eyed California surfer boy looks. He looked like he'd
just stepped off the cover of some teen heartthrob music
magazine.

On the other hand, I was also getting pressure from the athletes who supported Brian and Rayford. The two boys were star players on our football team. A suspension from school could also get them an additional suspension from the team. With an important game coming up, how could I be so cruel? So uncaring? So totally absent of school spirit? Their words . . . not mine.

"Popular? No, that's not it," I said slowly. "Because Rayford and Brian are both the size of small planets, defensive backs for our football team, they've made an early career of learning how to hurt people. I can't imagine Zane picking a fight with them. They would pound the kid to an unrecognizable pulp if he even looked at them cross-eyed."

"Sneeze or no sneeze, the boys thought that Zane was disrespecting them. What's the phrase they used? Oh yes . . . not giving them their 'props.' " Norah rolled her eyes.

"This whole situation would have been a lot simpler if this was just a case of school jocks hazing the new kid," I said, handing the stack of notices back to her.

"And you know how sensitive folks are around here about those flags, Mr. B. When the fight started, all of them wound up on the ground. All of them. The Stars and Stripes. Our school flag. *And* . . ." Her voice trailed off dramatically.

I held up a hand to stop her. "Please don't say it." I knew where this was leading.

"Whether you want to face it or not, the students of this school respect our state flag. That's how they were raised."

"Oh, yeah," I said sarcastically. "Let's not disrespect the state flag, the good ol' homage to the Confederate flag. Because everyone knows that the South will rise again. Tell me now, how long has it been since the Civil War ended?"

"That's not the point," Norah said, shaking her head. "There's a lot of proud Southern heritage and tradition surrounding the Mississippi flag."

"You mean that time-honored tradition of institutionalized slavery and oppression?" I retorted.

Norah blinked slowly, her calm expression taking a lot

of the heat out of me as she replied, "You sound just like Mr. Spann."

You would have to know Mr. Spann for her retort to make any sense. That was her way of telling me that I was arguing for the sake of arguing. J. T. Spann, the boys' athletic director, was notorious among the staff for doing just that. He would argue even when he didn't wholeheartedly support the proposition he was defending. Mr. Spann was a grad student, working on his master's. He took every opportunity to use the staff as test subjects, ironing out the kinks in his dissertation regarding the effects of manufactured aggression and its impact on modern-day athletes. J.T. got more than he bargained for when he helped me bust up that fight between Brian and Rayford and Zane.

"And furthermore," Norah continued with a sniff, "the Civil War was just as much about states' rights. A lot of good Southern folks who fought and died in that war didn't even own slaves."

I should have known better than to go head-to-head with a former history teacher. Being an English major myself, I would have been on better footing if I'd argued the points of whether William Shakespeare or Francis Bacon had penned most of the classic required-reading plays and sonnets.

"Don't sound so surprised that feelings are still running high. You grew up here in Calhoun County. Your daddy was born and raised here. And your daddy's daddy. You of all people should know what the people are like."

It was on the tip of my tongue to thank Norah with the utmost sarcasm for the lesson in genealogy. But I didn't. I held back. I'd been taking some on-line courses lately. Working on developing my people skills.

When I started this job four years ago, I wasn't necessarily the warmest person. But I was working on that and I think it was finally paying off. At least now I wasn't getting blank stares whenever I cracked a joke.

"Seems to me that the students would find something more meaningful to protest. Violation of human rights around the world, global warming, the mystery meat that we're still serving in the cafeteria . . ."

"One crusade at a time, Mr. B." Norah held up her hands, backing away. The upper right corner of her lip twitched. That was as close Norah came to an all-out, gut-busting belly laugh during school hours. Not that she didn't have a sense of humor. You couldn't be a teacher for over two decades and then accept a position as the school vice principal if you didn't have one.

"What? Did I say something funny?" My expression was deadpan, making the other side of her mouth curl up. I was on a roll now.

"So what do you want to do about the students who called in sick?" Norah asked.

All kidding aside now, I answered without missing a beat. "First, figure out which ones really are ill. Let's pull the attendance files of all of these students. Check their absences. Then have the attendance assistant call the parents back and let them know that we can't accept phone calls as excuses for their absences. We have to have written and *signed* notification. If any of those kids have more than three unexcused absences, make sure you let the parents know that's automatic grounds for failure of the six-week term."

"Are you serious, Mr. Barrett?"

"As a heart attack."

"We can't fail them. Some of the kids in this stack are A students. They really could be out sick. It's fall. Flu season. Mono. Maybe some of the parents are taking an early Thanksgiving break. It could be anything."

"It's two weeks before the Thanksgiving break, Norah. I doubt if parents will be taking vacation that early. But we'll find out for certain once we start making those calls, won't we?"

"But do you think that's wise, Mr. B? I'm not telling you how to run your school, but I don't think that's what the school counselor would suggest is the best way to handle this."

"I *am* running this school, Norah," I said evenly. Though she had gotten under my skin with that last crack. It's not that I can't have my judgment questioned. Every person in a position of authority does. I relied on my staff as sounding boards to help me make the right decisions. "Ms. Kayin's not here now, is she? And even if she was, the decision would still be left up to me."

Norah blinked again. "Ms. Kayin?" She stepped close and said softly, "Paul, Kirby's not the school guidance counselor here anymore. It's Mrs. Adair now."

I had to catch myself. Old habits were hard to break. I wish I could say the same for old hearts. "Oh. Yeah. Right. I knew that," I said, bobbing my head. "It was just a slip of the tongue. But neither one is here. So, I guess we'll just have to muddle through this on our own. OK?"

Norah sighed heavily. "It's your call, Mr. B."

"Actually," I said, grinning at her, "it's the attendance assistant's call. Let me know when she's reached all of the parents. I'm heading for the showers. Be back in a bit."

Chapter 2

The calls to the parents to get the students back to school should have been enough to squash the sick-in. And to the credit of the parents, a few students did come trickling back that afternoon. I called some of them to my office to discuss why they felt the need to protest, but I wasn't getting much out of them. I guess they were still ticked off that I'd interrupted their early vacation.

The ones who really had a knack at getting the students to open up were out of pocket. The current school counselor, Shirla Mencken Adair, was on her honeymoon. As much as I wished her and her new husband well, I wished more that she were here giving me as much guidance as she did the students.

Since she started at the beginning of this school year, she'd managed to gain the trust of me, the staff, and the majority of the students. I was proud that she'd accomplished so much in such a short span of time. She'd had a hard act to follow from the previous school counselor.

The other person I'd thought of to help me get a handle on school unrest . . . well . . . let's just say that she wasn't available, either. The former school counselor was Kirby Kayin. Also very well liked by the students. Almost revered. It was hard losing her. Not because of the effect that she had on the students but the effect she had on me. No wonder her name had slipped so easily off my tongue.

She'd been on my mind lately. On my mind and in my heart.

We'd started out together at this school together . . . in more ways than one. Friends through high school, lovers through college, and, though she didn't know when she made the decision to leave Calhoun County, she was on the verge of receiving a marriage proposal from me.

I had it all set up, planned out. I would propose to her during homecoming. Pretty clever on my part, since we were the senior homecoming king and queen back in the day.

But when I came to pick her up for the game and the school dance afterward, the excitement on her face, the shine in her eyes, had nothing to do with the homecoming chrysanthemum, complete with glitter and ribbons of the school colors, that I'd brought her. Something bigger than me had captured her heart and it wasn't easy to hear. Still, I couldn't fault her. She'd been given the opportunity of a lifetime. To travel, to work with disadvantaged kids, to be a counselor in a new concept school in South America where the need for educators was desperate. Helping others was in her blood. Her parents had been missionaries. Had traveled the world for humanitarian interest. Even though they were killed in a plane crash when Kirby was thirteen, they still had an enormous impact on how she saw the world.

When the opportunity presented itself to continue the work her parents had begun, how could she say no to that? And I wouldn't give her the chance to say no to me. To force her to make a choice. I supported her decision as best I could. Put my plans on hold until she let me know that she wanted them to become her plans as well.

The long-distance relationship is hard on us—taking a greater toll on me than I want to admit. We try to keep in touch. But phone calls are expensive and E-mail is kinda impersonal. The things I want to say to her I don't want to put out there into cyberspace.

She tries to make it back to the States on major holidays, but her time isn't her own. Her days are rushed and jam-packed with to-dos she has to accomplish before going back. I can't help but feel that she's slipping further and further away from me. A sense of loss I can't shake. When anyone calls to my attention the fact that she isn't here, isn't close to me, I'm shaken. And it takes a while to get my equilibrium back. The only remedy I've found is exercise—which is good for my health. And work—good for my career. By focusing on the students, I've managed to gain a rapport with them. But I don't think I'll ever have anything as close, as connected, as Kirby had with them. That's just the kind of woman she was.

Listen to me. Talking in the past tense as if I've already lost her. It was so effortless with her. With me, I've got to work harder at it. Which was why I was determined to get to the bottom of this sick-in. Find out who initiated it. If I could convince the leaders that it wasn't a good idea, I could get them to convince the die-hard, committed students to come back. As long as the hint of rebellion was out there, it was going to disrupt the school.

I'd just have to find another way to get the information that I needed. It was a well-known fact that when you needed to know, you needed Mayron. Mayron had been the school's custodian since it opened. He was as much a fixture as the brick and mortar that held the school together. He'd been the eyes and ears for each principal. Mayron was a trusted source of unbiased, unfiltered information. I should know. I'd relied on him more times than I cared to count—when I was a student here many, many moons ago, and now as an administrator.

Some of the kids called Mayron "Narc" or "Snitch." He wore that badge proudly. Mayron knew that when the kids wanted the staff to know something but didn't feel comfortable going themselves, they spoke openly and pointedly in front of Mayron. Better than Western Union for getting a message through.

Was I a little jealous of the trust the students granted to Mayron? Maybe, sometimes. I was also jealous of Kirby's ability. Still, I could use it to my advantage. As the students trusted them and they demonstrated trust in me, the students began to see me as much as an ally as an administrator. I hoped to be thought of as the type of principal who was fair in all his dealings, showed an honest interest in their development, kept their environment safe, and encouraged them to want something more for themselves than what could be found within the twenty-mile radius that was Calhoun County, Mississippi.

I went to the boys' gym to shower and change. It might be early enough to find Mayron there. He could be restocking the towels. But he'd already been there and gone. I could tell that by the fresh stack of chlorine-smelling, sandpaperlike towels neatly folded on the cart. After asking around, I found Mayron behind the cafeteria, dumping cardboard boxes into the recycling bin.

I walked up beside him, making sure to come up on the side with his good eye—on the left. Mayron's right eye was a glass one. How he'd lost it no one was quite sure. But he liked to tell the students that he'd lost it when a student ran through the hall, improperly holding scissors by the handle instead of the blade, and tripped. And to save another student from certain impalement, Mayron contends that he gallantly stepped into the path. Made a good tale. But the one circulating around the school about Mayron throwing himself in front of an unsuspecting student to save her from the exploding cafeteria mystery meat was the best tale yet.

" 'Morning, Mr. Barrett. What brings you out here on a frosty November morning?"

"Come on, Mayron. Don't snow me. I think you know," I replied, grabbing a stack of flattened cardboard boxes and tossing them into the recycling bin as well. The wind caught the box and lifted it into the air, before dropping it back into the bin again.

"Mr. Barrett, you shouldn't be out here," Mayron said solicitously. "You might get something on that nice suit."

"You let me worry about that, Mayron."

"Something tells me that ain't all that you're worried about, eh, Mr. Barrett?"

"That's very perceptive of you."

"Perceptive," Mayron repeated the word experimentally. "Is that anything like smart, Mr. Barrett? As long as I've been workin' here, I keep hopin' that some of that book knowledge will work its way into this thick skull of mine. Did you know that I only made it to sixth grade?"

"No, I didn't know," I replied. "And you're right, Mayron. *Perceptive* means smart. Very smart. So smart that it's got us folks who did manage somehow to get past the sixth grade to come to you for answers."

Mayron grinned at me—a wide, crooked, yellow smile. "I reckon you're here about them rumors."

"If I said, 'What rumors?' that would be a dead giveaway that I didn't know what was going on around here, wouldn't it?"

"Dead giveaway," Mayron echoed. He threw his head back suddenly, sniffing deeply. His thin, purple-veined nostrils flared. "Smell that, Mr. Barrett?"

"Kind of hard not to," I said, frowning. With each gust of wind, the smell of garbage from the bins wafted back. I'd thought that by now Mayron would be immune to it. As he had spent the years mixing cleaning chemicals to keep the school spotless, I often wondered what that did to his senses.

"It ain't the garbage stink that I'm talkin' 'bout, Mr. Barrett." He stepped up to me, folded his arms across his chest, and leaned forward at the waist. That was his usual stance for when he was about to let me in on a juicy bit of gossip. He was about to let me in on a secret. Only trouble was that it wasn't such a big secret. Half the school was in on it.

"Then what is it, Mayron?" I prompted, needing him to get to the point. The area behind the school, in between the garbage bins, wasn't sheltered; it seemed more like a wind tunnel. I gritted my teeth to keep them from chattering.

"Rumors mostly. You know how fast word travels around here."

"Rumors about what?"

"Why . . . the race riot, of course," he said calmly. Too calmly. I wasn't sure I heard him correctly, so I asked him to repeat it.

"A race riot?" I said tightly. "Mayron, what are you talking about?"

"Not me, Mr. Barrett. I'm not the one doin' the talkin'. No siree. It's them kids. As soon as them boys you suspended get back from that three-day suspension, it's supposed to be on. Them that don't wanna take sides is staying on neutral territory. That is, they're staying at home."

"Big surprise. All the kids calling in sick," I muttered.

"Yupper." Mayron reached into his overalls, pulled out a crumpled sheet of paper, and held it out to me. I scanned it quickly, not believing my eyes.

"Where did this come from?" I asked, shaking the paper at him.

"Heaven only knows, Mr. Barrett."

"Heaven's got nothing to do with this."

A single sheet announced an off-campus rally. I'd seen similar flyers floating around the school advertising a party at someone's house or a pep rally before a big game. Generally harmless. The flyers usually had a contact name, an E-mail address, or a phone number where you could get particulars. Circumventing problems at those types of events was easy. A few calls to the parents of the student having the party and the parents of friends were usually enough to alert anyone who needed to know to keep on the watch.

But this . . . this was something different. There was no contact person. It was an organization. Some group calling itself the Association of Southern Students called for any interested person to show up at an appointed place, at an appointed time, with enough conviction to protect the honor and sanctity of their Southern heritage. What that meant exactly, I couldn't say for certain. But I didn't like the tone.

"A flyer from the A.S.S. Looks like some of the students from Calhoun High want to make asses out of themselves," Mayron said, then cackled at his own wit.

"You think this is funny?" I snapped.

He quickly recomposed his face. But I could tell he would be giggling at his own pun for a while yet. "No, sir. I don't."

"This is serious. I'm not going to let this happen."

"Why not?"

"What do you mean, why not? You think I'm going to let a bunch of knot-heads who can't seem to get it through their thick skulls that the South lost to come up in here and disrupt my school?"

"Says nothing about disrupting the school, Mr. Barrett," Mayron pointed out.

"They've already disrupted my school if I have a sudden absentee rate of fifteen percent."

"I hate to be the one to tell you, Mr. Barrett, but there's really nothin' you can do about the rally, sir."

"Watch me."

"It's away from the school grounds, not during school hours. You gonna take away the students' right to assemble?"

I looked oddly at Mayron. He sounded very learned for a man with supposedly only a sixth-grade education.

"Can't do it," he continued. "You try and the next time some of your students want to meet to hold a vigil for your Martin Luther King holiday, you'll have just as many parents a squawkin' at you. Claimin' that you're playing favorites. Do you want that stink on you?"

"That's different, and you know it. This is hate mongering—pure and simple."

"Can't tell by reading the flyer. I only got a sixth-grade education. But I can read them words. And they don't tell me to hate."

"Come armed with your conviction?" I read aloud. "Sounds like a call to arms to me."

"You're readin' between the lines," he insisted. "Some

folks might say that you're readin' more into it than what's actually there."

"You're telling me that I should stand by and do nothing while this filth gets circulated around my school?"

"No, sir. That's not what I'm sayin' at all. I'm just sayin' be careful about how you handle it. Or folks will think that you're prejudiced."

I snorted at that. We all had our notions and misconceptions. But if folks wanted to say that I was prejudiced against stupidity, then color me prejudiced. I took a deep, calming breath. "OK, maybe the flyer doesn't come right out and say it, Mayron. But something has got these kids worked up."

Mayron leaned close again, pulling out another sheet of paper. "As long as you're bustin' up folks' natural right to get together, better make it fifty-fifty."

He passed another flyer to me. I read it and rolled my eyes. "Lord have mercy. Don't these kids know anything?"

Another flyer, supposedly circulated by the Warriors for the Motherland, called for open opposition to the Association of Southern Students. There was no mistaking the tone of this flyer. It called for students who were willing to advance the civil rights of African-Americans by any means necessary.

"Any idea what students circulated these?" I asked. "I never heard of any of these supremacist groups before."

"Yupper," he said, but pressed his lips tightly together.

"Well?"

"I ain't gonna tell you that, Mr. Barrett."

"Why not, Mayron?"

"You already know the answer to that. The kids trust me to bring their troubles to you; but if they thought that I was giving up their names, they'd dry up. And there goes your information pipeline. You're principal now, so you had to ask me to give up the names. But I remember a time when you begged me to keep my mouth shut."

I shook my head, grinning at him. "I'd almost forgotten about that."

"Not me, Mr. Barrett. Old Mayron don't forget so easy. 'Cept when it's convenient for me to do so."

Over twenty years ago, I blessed Mayron for his convenient memory lapses. If he'd not so conveniently remembered catching me skipping classes with Kirby, hiding under the bleachers to make out our senior year, I would have been in a heap of doo-doo.

"Tell me something, Mr. Barrett, if you would?"

"If I can."

"Whatever happened to you and Ms. Kayin?"

"Oh, she's still around," I said to Mayron.

"That's not what I meant. How come she quit? How come she's not around *you* anymore?"

I didn't mind answering the personal question. He was just as responsible for getting Kirby and me together as anyone. He made it possible for Kirby and me to spend some quality time together.

"In fact, she's supposed to be back home at the end of the week to spend the holidays."

Mayron snorted. And I could read a world of contempt in that. He took it very hard when she left. As hard as the students. And the few times that she'd been back, she'd made it a point to see him before heading back. Good for him, but I was fiercely jealous of anyone who took time away from the scant time that she and I had.

"She shoulda never left."

"Believe it or not, Mayron, there's a world outside of Calhoun County. I guess Kirby wanted to see a bit of it."

"Guess she's never seen *The Wizard of Oz*," Mayron muttered, turned up his collar against the wind, and turned his back on me.

Chapter 3

I didn't need the help of the alarm clock's waking me up on Friday morning. I was up long before that annoying *beep-beep-beep*. Long before the sun, too. I can't say for certain that I even slept. But I must have. Dreams plagued me, kept me tossing and turning. I couldn't remember anything specific about them. I guess I was just anxious about seeing Kirby again. I needed to see her. To hold her. I'd offered to pick her up at the airport, but she'd already arranged for some colleagues who were flying in with her to take her home.

Colleagues? I didn't even like the sound of that. A little insecurity made me wonder how many of those colleagues of hers were men. Did they sit with her on the long flight home? Keep her company? Keep her mind off of me?

It was the kind of anxiety that gnaws at you, keeps you staring at the clock into the wee hours of the morning, even when every bone in your body is dead-dog tired and you're praying for blissful sleep.

More than once, I got up during the night, crossed the floor to the bathroom for a sip of water, then crawled back under the covers shivering for a few minutes until I warmed up again.

The weather was starting to turn colder. I could tell by the feel of the wind working its way underneath the crack between the windowsill and the ledge—a constant low whistling that gently rattled the miniblinds and my nerves.

One of these days, I was going to fix that window. Add some more weather stripping, maybe. But I wasn't going to do it that night. That night, I just listened to the wind blow and wondered what I would say to Kirby when I saw her again. Three months didn't seem like a long time. But when you love someone, it could seem like a lifetime. You'd think that in all of that time, with all of the reunion scenarios I'd concocted in my head, I would have thought of something witty, funny, or poignant to say by now. But I couldn't think of a thing. Not a single, solitary thing. Maybe that was part of my nightmare—that I'd stand there, with my hands in my pockets and my mouth gaping wide open, staring speechless at her like an idiot.

That night, I'd closed my eyes, even breathed deeply. But that couldn't be called sleeping. By no stretch of the imagination. When I got tired of pretending that I was resting, I got up, showered, and dressed for work.

No workout clothes for me today. I wasn't going to risk being late or showing up at the school all sweaty. I wanted to give a kick-ass impression. So I took extra care in selecting my clothes. Didn't even try to fool myself into thinking that I was doing so because I was naturally fastidious. I was doing it for her. I wanted Kirby to take one look at me and have her mouth drop open. Secretly I hoped that she'd open her eyes, see what she was really missing, and make the decision to come back.

I chose neutral, conservative colors. The ultimate professional. Still, before I walked out the door, I couldn't help but add a certain item to catch her attention. A tie. Dark but with tiny diamond-shaped flecks of periwinkle. It was Kirby's favorite color. That is, it had been her favorite color back in the day.

By the time I got to the school, it was only six-forty. The student flag detail wouldn't show up for a while yet. There were only a few cars in the parking lot that early in the morning. I recognized Mayron's '72 Impala. Beside him was Mr. Spann's black Dodge Durango. Mr. Enoch, the substitute, was back today, too, in his yellow VW Beetle.

As I pulled into a parking spot near the school's side entrance, I also noted an unfamiliar vehicle. A huge Ford Excursion. The windows, tinted as dark as the law allows, were rolled up so that I couldn't see inside. But I really didn't need to see. Not with my eyes. Instinct told me what my eyes couldn't. I knew who it was and grinned. I tried to imagine Kirby, my little Kirby, behind the wheel of that great big truck.

I parked a couple of spaces away. I figured the walk, even if only a few paces, would give me a chance to compose myself. As I came around the side of my truck, my heart must have pounded loud enough to wake the dead.

Sweat collected on the underside of my collar and trickled down my neck. God, I felt as foolish as I did as a seventeen-year-old kid the day I went to pick up Kirby for the homecoming dance. I stepped toward her SUV. If it weren't all so nerve-wracking, it would be funny. This was the woman I'd considered my soul mate, and yet I was acting as if she were an auditor for the Internal Revenue Service. In fact, somewhere midway between our two vehicles my apprehension struck me as funny. Hilarious, even.

It started as a tiny quirk at the corners of my lips. The quirk tugged into a smile. And by the time I'd reached her door, I was leaning on it for support. Laughter rolled up from my stomach. As I leaned onto Kirby's Ford Excursion, gasping for air, I banged on the roof to get her attention. As if my laughter weren't attention enough! I don't remember ever having laughed so long or so loud.

Slowly, cautiously, the window rolled down. Out of the corner of my eye, I caught a glimpse of cinnamon-colored spiral curls—as bright and as unruly as I'd remembered them. Kirby leaned her head out of the window, peering at me from behind rose-tinted silver-rimmed sunglasses. She was shaking her head, but I could see the beginnings of a smile twitching at her lips.

"You know, that doesn't look very dignified, Mr. Barrett." Her voice was richer, huskier. And I think she was starting to pick up a hint of that distinct South African accent.

"I . . . I . . . I know. B-but I c-c-can't help it!" I sputtered. Resting my hands on my knees, I leaned forward and took deep, slow breaths to regain my composure.

"I'm not crazy," I denied, shaking my head. *Except about you,* I added mentally. Always was and suspect that I always would be, no matter what happened over the next few months. As long as she kept coming back to me, I would keep waiting for her. Keep loving her.

She opened the door and stepped out. Long legs, clad in sheer, silky hose, gave way to a skirt most folks around here would have considered too short. But I liked it just fine. Her royal purple hip-hugging skirt complemented a matching jacket buttoned almost up to her neck with shiny gold buttons. A periwinkle scarf with streaks of yellow, gold, and green was tied around her neck. Her hair was pulled away from her face and twisted up into a French knot, but even the constriction of bobby pins and holding spray couldn't tame the wild corkscrew ringlets that I wanted so badly to touch.

"It's good to see you, Kirby. You're looking . . ." I couldn't even finish the sentence but let the expression on my face, the eager sweep of my eyes over her, convey what words couldn't. "Damn." It was all I could get out. Not the most eloquent compliment. But I think she understood me.

"And you . . . look at you." She gestured at me with a slender hand, neatly manicured with a pale gloss brushed over the nails. "You're wearing a suit!"

She knew about my exercise routine, had seen me often in workout clothes this early in the morning. I knew she wouldn't be expecting me to be this dressed up. And now I knew she liked what she saw and it made my chest swell.

"Looks good on you, Pooh Bear." Her eyes swept over me, openly appraising.

I tried to frown and found that I couldn't. She was still

calling me by the nickname my Aunt Callie had given me
when I was six months old. Something about seeing my
belly poking out from under a red T-shirt that was a couple
of sizes too small for me—even though the tag on the back
read: THREE TO SIX MONTHS. What was it my folks used to
say about me? That I was a healthy baby? As I grew older,
I wasn't fat. Just big-boned. Call me picky, but a thirty-
seven-year-old man should not be called *Pooh Bear*. And
I'd worked hard to shed the pounds, as much as the image.
Now, I was just a big man. Just Bear to most of my friends.
Kirby and I were more than friends. That was the only
reason that I let her get away with calling me Pooh Bear.

"Rule number one is no calling me Pooh Bear on school
grounds," I said firmly.

"So, are you going to stand there like a statue or are you
going to come over here and hug me?" She encouraged me
by throwing open her arms. Not that I needed that much
encouragement. I was just waiting for her, letting her give
the clues, set the pace, so I knew where I stood.

Kirby caught me in a hug so tight that my ribs squeaked.
I wrapped my arms around her waist, holding her and making a vow to myself. I didn't care what it took, what I had
to do or say, I wouldn't let her out of my life again. I'd
take her on whatever grounds, whatever rules she'd set. She
felt so good, so soft in all the right places.

"I'm glad you're here, Kirby," I whispered. Sounded
lame, even to my own ears. There was so much more I
wanted to say. "God, I missed you."

"Me, too, Bear." She settled her head against my shoulder. "Me, too. I couldn't wait until after school to see you.
It's one of the reasons why I came out this morning."

I'm not sure how long we stood there in the parking lot,
holding, hugging. We rocked from side to side, without
being truly aware of why. If I had to say, I think it was a
silent way of telling each other how well we fit together,
how our hearts and bodies were in total synchronization,
even after all the time and distance between us.

My eyes were closed. I didn't want to note the passing

of time. I didn't want to see other cars pulling into the parking lot. As far as I was concerned, there was only Kirby and me.

Later I'd ask all the appropriate questions. *"How have you been?" "What have you been up to?" "How is your project going?" "How many students do you have?" "How long are you staying?" "Are you seeing anyone else?" "Do you still love me?"*

Not now. I didn't want to know. Didn't want to think. Just feel.

I raised my hand to the back of her head, caressing her hair. For a moment, I thought that I'd heard her sigh. It couldn't have been the wind. There was a good, brisk one blowing up, so I adjusted my body, trying to shield her from the brunt of it.

I felt Kirby's body meld into mine. She lifted her face, brushed her lips at the base of my throat. My entire body thrummed to life. It had been so long. So long!

It was the wrong place. The wrong time. But the sentiments were right. What had started out as a simple, welcoming hug between us escalated out of control. I didn't remember maneuvering her against the car, pressing against her. Kirby moaned my name, her stance widening even farther. It was an invitation—bold, passionate, but forbidden at this moment in time.

"Damn it, Kirby!" I tried to inject a note of sanity back into this situation. "It wasn't supposed to happen like this." I made a half-hearted attempt to pull back, but Kirby clung tightly to me.

"Come on, Bear," she soothed, stroking the back of my neck. "It's all right." She peeked around my shoulder. "It's still early. Nobody's around."

"No, it isn't all right," I said, gritting my teeth. "I want to make love to you, Kirby, not screw you. That's what we'll be doing if we don't get our heads back on straight."

"You know, there was a time when you were doing all the coaxing," she reminded me.

"We're not kids anymore, Kirby. And this is where I work."

She might not have seen anyone, but I had a feeling. Mayron was never too far from sight. He knew everything that went on, inside and outside the school. How else was he going to maintain his coveted status as school confidant?

Kirby opened the door to the SUV.

"Get in," she said with a nod of her head.

I shook my head. "Nuh-uh. I know what's going to happen if I climb in there, behind those tinted windows."

"I'll be good. I promise." She grinned at me.

"That's what I'm afraid of." My tone was wry, but it made her laugh. It was good to hear her laugh again. Laugh in person, not marred by the static of poor phone connections.

"Just get in, Bear. I just want to talk for a few minutes. To have you to myself before you have to go inside to your students."

I understood exactly what she meant. I walked around to the passenger's side and climbed in. She'd said "your students." A clue that she had put a lot of emotional detachment between herself and the kids she used to know.

Kirby climbed in on the driver's side, slammed the door, and settled herself comfortably in the seat. Even though she'd said she wanted to talk, she didn't speak for a few moments. It was so quiet inside, I could hear nothing but the sound of our breathing. The silence grew uncomfortable for her. I could tell. She started to fidget, rummage in her purse. She pulled out her compact. A small brush, a light dusting of powder over the shine of her forehead and nose, was about all Kirby needed to restore her polished look.

"You're staring at me," she said softly.

"Does it bother you?" I asked, smoothing a strand of her hair back into place.

"No. Not really. I was just wondering what you were thinking."

"You used to know what I was thinking, Kirby. Used to be able to complete my sentences for me," I reminded her.

"Not too hard since you were just a big jock anyway," she teased. When she turned to face me, her eyes were troubled. "Paul—"

"Sh—" I interrupted. "I know."

"No, I don't think you do. We need to talk, but . . ."

"We will. When the time's right. I've got a lot to say to you, Kirby." The engagement ring that I meant to offer to her was practically burning a hole in my pocket.

"All right," she said. "But first things first. Come on, Bear; help me with some of my things."

"What things?"

Kirby then indicated several boxes in the trunk. "Help me out with those, would you?"

She climbed out on one side and I climbed out on the other. So much for our heart-to-heart talk. Kirby opened the trunk and I reached for a box.

"What have you got in here?" I asked, dragging the heavy box across the carpeted bed. "What are these for?"

"A few learning aids," she said. "When we get inside, I'll show you. We can talk more about what's been going on in your school."

I shot her a surprised look. I hadn't told her much. Made light of what had happened. She knew about the fight and the suspension, but I'd said nothing about the flyers. I kept silent for a number of reasons. One: I figured I could handle the situation on my own. Two: I didn't want to spend our limited time together talking about work.

"What do you know about what's going on here?"

"Enough to let me know that you've got some real issues working."

"Tell me something I don't know."

"That Jolene McHenry was the one who spilled it. I could tell by our last conversation that something was bothering you."

Jolene was president of the school's parent-teacher organization. She was also a close friend of Kirby. "So you ran to Jolene and she blabbed?"

"She didn't blab. She was just a little more open than

you were about what was bothering you. And I can see why you're concerned, Bear. The bad news is, your school isn't the only one that's going through this kind of crisis. It's happening all over the U.S."

"But why?"

Kirby shrugged. "It's hard to say. Analysts are all over the map. You know as well as I do that bigotry and hatred aren't new. And it isn't just among Southern schools. It seems as though after September eleventh, there's been a surge in national pride that's been taken to the extreme. Everyone wants to wave the American flag, but no one wants to remember that the American flag is supposed to represent tolerance and diversity."

"Hell, half the folks around here who are waving that flag can't even spell *tolerance* and *diversity*," I retorted.

"That's not funny," she chastised me.

"I didn't mean it to be. I'm an educator, Kirby. I know the types that I'm talking about. I've seen it. It's a lot easier to pick up a gun or a knife or a baseball bat than to reason your way out of confrontation."

Kirby stopped, squared her shoulders. "Well, that's what I'm here for. While I'm here, while I can, I want to help your students work out their differences. I've asked Jolene to meet us here today so we can talk about a strategy. We want to have a plan in place for your PTO meeting next week."

"Just like the old times," I said softly. For however long it lasts.

"The three of us back in high school again. Now there's a scary thought." Kirby grinned at me. "I'm sure Ms. Gilbert is already polishing up her glasses, so she can peer over them in disapproval at us."

"But the students will be glad to see you back, Kirby."

I leaned on the front door with my shoulder, holding it open for her as she passed inside.

Chapter 4

We'd all met up in my office. Jolene McHenry sat thoughtfully twirling her coffee with a plastic stirrer while Kirby outlined her strategy for approaching the student unrest. Jolene was open, receptive—which translated to me as desperate. At this stage, she was willing to grasp at anything that would get the students' minds back on track instead of worrying about watching their backs.

". . . And in this case, Jolie, I used a combination of one-on-one private counseling sessions to help students deal with a student suicide. Here, take a look at this. This is a report that I submitted for the administrators' review. It notes the increase in attendance, the raised test scores, even an informal poll of the students asking them to rate the safety of their school—all indirect indicators that the students had regained their confidence by the time I'd completed my program."

"I'm not sure that I see how that applies here. No one here has died," Jolene said.

"No, but your students are dealing with the anxiety and fears associated with the threat of violence. I believe that I can apply some of the same principles and techniques here that I did for this other school. The trick is to get the students and the faculty talking to me again, to express their fears."

"Everybody's already talking," I said.

"I'm not talking about the fearful rumor-mongering that I'm sure is running rampant through your halls right now," Kirby said. "I'm talking about focused, directed discussions by trained individuals. Namely me. No offense to you and your teaching staff, Bear."

"None taken," I said, knowing that she would forgive me for that little stretch of the truth. I was *very* protective of my staff.

"How are you going to get them to open up to you again, Kirby? As much as the kids may like you and miss you, how are you going to deal with the fact that some of the kids think that you abandoned them? You chose some students in some faraway country over them."

Kirby heaved a sigh. "I didn't abandon them." She looked directly at me, as if assuring me as she would the students. "I just thought that those other students needed me more. I think I can address their feelings and manage to get through to them."

"And the fact that you don't work here anymore?" Jolene pressed.

"That's just a formality, a question of paperwork. We can hire her on as an interim counselor until Mrs. Adair returns. That is, if you're committed to stay for that long, Kirby." It was my turn to pass on the unspoken message. How committed to me was she? Yes, those other students needed her. But so did I. And they could never love her as much as I could.

"That's where you come in, Bear. When you introduce me during the assemblies, you have to stress that I'm not an outsider. I'm not a stranger. You have to make them understand that I've come back home expressly for the reason of helping out my own."

"We could always drag out your high-school yearbook picture," Jolene suggested, grinning mischievously at Kirby.

"Oh, good heavens, no!" Kirby cried out. "If the students ever got ahold of that, seeing me in my big teased hair and Apollonia wannabe wardrobe, they'd lose all respect for me."

"Yeah, it took a while for me to get my respect back for you, too. Everybody knows that Vanity was way finer than Apollonia," I interjected.

"Both of y'all are crazy. The woman to be was Cyndi Lauper."

"You mean the woman that *you* wanted to be," Kirby retorted. "How long did it take you to grow back your hair to its natural color when you died it cotton candy pink?"

"Too long." Jolene shuddered.

All of us fell silent for a moment. The mental image of Jolene in her black spandex biker shorts, orange ballerina-style tutus, combat boots, and bright pink hair had us speechless.

"So—" I cleared my throat, getting us back on track. "After you've talked all you can talk, Kirby, what do you plan to do next?"

"To get your students and staff focusing their energy on something positive, we'll need some kind of event or exercise. Something that will bring them all together."

"Any ideas?" Jolene prompted.

"A few, but none that I'm entirely satisfied with. An idea will come together after I've had some time to talk to the kids, find out where their heads are. I need to know what motivates them. I already know what scares them spitless."

"You won't have a lot of time to get them to talk to you, Kirby. As soon as you start any kind of momentum, it'll be time for Thanksgiving break," Jolene reminded her.

"I know. And that's fine. In fact, it's probably better this way. I'll need these few days of assemblies to meet and greet everyone. Then everyone can spend the holiday thinking about that. Nothing too heavy. In the meantime, they'll have other, hopefully more positive things to think about— food, family, friends. By the time we get back, my office will be all set up with the rest of my counseling aids."

She flipped through a few sheets of paper, glanced at the contents of some files. "One thing I want to be sure to do, however, is to make certain that I speak with Chalmers, Donovan, and Vaughn."

"Why especially them? If you single them out, won't it look like you're picking on them? I mean, they've already completed their suspension," Jolene objected.

"I'm not picking on them, Jolie," Kirby denied. "Those three, whether willing or not, were the catalysts for the events transpiring at your school. I want to try to get those three as allies for my efforts. If I can't win them over, I can forget the rest of the students."

"Sounds like a solid plan," Jolene agreed.

"It's going to take time, but I think I can help get good ol' Calhoun High back to some degree of normality."

"Normal?" I snorted. "Normal is the last thing I want to come back here." I didn't feel there was anything normal about continuing to worship a long-dead symbol of war.

"What you want won't happen overnight, Bear," Jolene cautioned me. "You can't change generations of sentiment in one fell swoop. You try to introduce too many changes and you'll get an entire community against you. Right now, you've got their support. But if you push them . . . push us . . ."

Her voice trailed off, but I understand exactly what she meant.

"Still griping about that school mascot?" Kirby said, with a wry twist of her lips.

"Don't you know it."

"I can't slay that dragon for you. You'll have to go after that one yourself. Let me worry about stemming the race riot. You worry about that school mascot."

"You two still don't get it. The two are intricately connected. One feeds into the other. The mentality, this Southern culture, somehow it's all so . . . backward."

"You make it sound like we're battling against a legion of devils. It's not that bad around here. We've made some progress. I should know. I grew up here, too. And I didn't turn out so bad, huh?" Jolene said.

"You were always different," Kirby mused. "You were one of the few white kids that hung out with us."

"We were *all* different," Jolene insisted. "And you didn't do nearly as much hanging out with the black kids as you think that you remember that you do . . . and don't ask me to repeat that because I'm not sure what in the world I just said."

"But I know what you meant. I didn't hang out with any group, really, except for the two of you." Kirby's smile was nostalgic.

"What a trio we made." I laughed reluctantly. "The blimp, the trailer trash, and the Oreo."

"Bear!" Jolene and Kirby exclaimed in unison.

"I never liked that word *Oreo*. When some of the girls called me that in school, made me mad," Kirby said.

"They were just jealous because you were naturally gorgeous, made good grades, had all the guys panting after you . . . Wait a minute; I think that was me that was jealous!" Jolene laughed. "Isn't the politically correct term *bi-racial*?"

"Nobody was worried about being PC back then. That's what they called us. Don't deny it. You know that they did. We hung out together because we had nowhere else to go." Whatever the reason, despite the anguish, the three of us had grown up practically as close as family.

"I had the cheerleading squad," Jolene spoke up.

"Oh yeah, like that was a step up." Kirby rose from her seat, clapped her hands in a mock spirit chant. "We've got spirit; yes, we do! We've got spirit! How 'bout you!" She pointed at Jolene.

"Cow," Jolene grumbled.

I snickered, ducking when Jolene threw a punch at me.

"At least you guys got your revenge. Homecoming king and queen. Ruled the school."

"Speaking of ruling the school, are we ready for tonight?" I asked, turning the focus back to work.

Jolene shrugged, but Kirby gave a definitive nod of her head.

"All right then. Let's do this," I said, and then called for an office assistant to pull the necessary paperwork for me.

Chapter 5

The PTO meeting was supposed to start at six. But by five o'clock the parking lot was full. Too full for just my teaching and administrative staff. I took a look at the previous agenda and started to crumple it up. We had planned to discuss how to raise funds for the senior trip, whether to initiate a girls' football team, and whether it was time to update the school's image by changing the mascot. I had a feeling that we wouldn't get to those topics tonight. The more students I talked to through the day, the more I realized that the fight and the resulting flyers had gotten out of hand.

I stood at the window of my office, peering through the blinds and thoughtfully munching on an apple. Some of the vehicles I recognized as belonging to my students. Tran Le's little souped-up Honda, with exhaust system tweaked to sound like those speed freaks from that movie *The Fast and the Furious*. Caitlyn Mahoney's '84 two-toned short-bed GMC with mounted twin American flags whipping from the bed of her truck. Lakeshia Moore's Jeep Cherokee with the soft removable top. Still driving it with pride even though thieves had sliced the top several times to get the equalizer and radio.

I don't know how long I stood there watching the parade of headlights of vehicles vying for limited parking space. Students, parents, and anyone who'd also gotten wind of what was happening filled the staff and student parking, lined the edge of the drive and the bus loading zone. When I thought I saw the old clunker that Amity Stinson of the *Calhoun County Herald* drove, I knew that I was in for a tough time tonight. When Amity covered an event, she didn't say much. She was not the most aggressive of reporters. Then again, she didn't have to be. She always faded into the background but never failed to note every detail. Nothing would escape her prolific pen.

Forget my previous discussion points. I only had two items on the agenda tonight. One: to calm the fears of the parents so that they would feel confident to allow their children to return to school. Two: to find the source of that poison killing the peace of mind of these children and draw it out with a vengeance.

A light tap at my door. "Mr. B?"

"Come on in, Norah."

Norah Gilbert poked her head in the door. "I think everyone who's going to show is here, Mr. B."

"I'm ready."

"I don't see how," she commiserated. "I don't think anyone saw this coming. Who could believe it? I mean the holidays are coming up, for Pete's sake. Peace, love, good tidings toward all. Isn't that the way it's supposed to be?"

I flashed her a *get real* look. If things were all so peachykeen in the state of Mississippi, we wouldn't be arguing at a state level on whether we should continue to fly the Confederate flag—a flag that evoked as much passion as it did pain.

Breathing deeply to steady myself, I reminded myself that we were not here tonight to espouse political views. We were here to discuss the implied threat to our children.

"We'd better go on in." Norah gestured toward the door.

"Right behind you."

The corridor was still packed with meeting crashers as we made our way to the gymnasium. When Mayron had seen the number of cars heading for the school, he'd quickly arranged for the bleachers to be extended.

Sitting at the table were Iain Wilson, a representative of the board of education, and Jolene. Jolene smiled at me, but she was busy talking into a cell phone, giving instructions to her kids. Her finger was jammed in the other ear to drown out the multiple conversations echoing in the gym around us.

She looked at me apologetically, put her hand over the receiver, and said, "This'll only take a minute, Bear."

"Like I'm really in a hurry to start this," I retorted. Sitting down in a chair beside her, I clipped to my tie the wireless microphone that had been conveniently provided. The folding table sat in the center of the gym floor. Right in the middle of the painted school mascot—the Johnny Reb soldier.

The irony didn't escape me. This was the very center of our problem—or rather, my problem. I had issues with the image the mascot projected. And since I was the head of the school, my problem was everyone's problem. One that I planned to resolve very quickly. If not at this meeting, then at the next. One way or another, I was going to personally lead the initiative to get the mascot changed. Not like I hadn't tried. I'd been trying since I became principal here. Met with resistance every step of the way. Change didn't come easily to Calhoun County. It had its traditions, yes. But sometimes, *tradition* was just another word for laziness. It was much easier to let things stay the way they were than face the discomfort of change. But I wasn't going to give up.

I took not a small amount of pleasure in knowing that though I was the seventh principal in the school's history, I was the first African-American principal at Gilbert Aubrey Calhoun High School.

Built in 1952, the school had a long history but few administrators. Once you were hired to hold that job, you didn't leave it. Not unlike being appointed as a judge of the Supreme Court. Principals who came here stayed here. Made the state's educational policy into their binding law. A few had retired from the job. And more than one principal of the school had died while still principal. I guess that'll be me someday, too. Because they're going to have to pry the reins of this school away from my cold, stiff, six-feet-under fingers.

But up until now, all of the principals had been Caucasian. And for the most part male. Lonnetta Paine, the principal before me, and my mentor, had broken the cycle. She'd taken the job in 1983. Almost twenty years later she was ready to retire. But she wasn't ready to let be undone all of the changes she'd implemented since she'd taken the job. Updating the curriculum, bringing in a guidance counselor who'd steer capable young women into the science and technology fields, making certain that theater arts got as much attention as athletics—this was the legacy that Lonnetta left me. The least I could do was leave a legacy of my own. Tearing down some of the traditional images that supported the school would be that legacy.

I wondered if Mayron had been responsible for setting the table exactly in this position. Knowing how I felt about the school mascot, it would be like him to exercise his unique, rather twisted sense of humor. Would the Association of Southern Students appreciate the humor of my black butt positioned in the face of their beloved mascot?

Jolene looked at me oddly when I laughed without an apparent reason. She exchanged glances with Norah and then turned back to her conversation.

Moments later, Jolene folded the phone, set the ringer to vibrate only, and dropped it onto the table.

"Whew!" She blew back a curly red lock that had fallen into her face, then clipped a microphone to the lapel of her blouse. "What a night!"

"It's just started," Iain Wilson remarked, reaching for a pitcher and a cup. He looked underneath bushy white eyebrows at the crowd gathering before him. "Almost make you wish that there was something stronger than water in this carafe."

"You don't need a drink, Iain. By the time you work up a good buzz, we'll be out of here. Short and sweet, folks,"

I reminded them. "You know the drill. Don't let them get a chance to get up a good head of steam."

My mentor had taught me that. To keep control of a meeting, you let the parents have their say, but you should always have the last word—if only just to say good night. Yours should be the last voice they heard to close the meeting. The final voice of authority.

"Then let's get this circus on the road," Iain said.

Jolene leaned over and whispered to me, "Where's Kirby?"

"I'm not sure," I said, scanning the crowd for her face.

"We need her. The kids need to see her. To feel assured that everything's going to be all right."

"Don't worry, Jolie. She said that she'd be here."

Iain turned on his microphone, stood, then held up his hands for silence. "Ladies and gentlemen, if you'll take your seats . . . That's right; come on in. Plenty of room."

The meeting started as usual, with an obligatory welcoming speech and introductions. As quick as Iain was to get through the introductions, I could sense the crowd's restlessness—a low muttering that felt a little like thunder, a threat of an impending storm.

Iain could feel it, too. He hurried through his introductions, then quickly handed the floor over to Jolene.

"I guess we all know why we're here," she said without preamble, and held up a copy of the flyer. "My Shelly had one of these in her backpack. Normally, I wouldn't go through her things—"

That brought a round of reluctant laughter from the parents and some boos and hisses of disapproval from the students.

"OK, don't let me lie," she corrected. "Normally, I wouldn't be *caught* going through her personal belongings. But this . . . this is something different. Something serious. You all believe that; otherwise you wouldn't be here tonight."

She had the crowd's attention now. I knew that by the hush that fell over the room. Good ol' Jolene. She always did know how to work a crowd. I guess that's why she was head cheerleader for Calhoun High three years straight.

Jolene read aloud a few lines from each of the flyers that she had in her possession.

" 'Protecting the purity of our superior race . . .' "

She flipped to another flyer. " 'Sending the inferiors back where they belong.' "

Jolene then shuffled to another page. " 'Casting out the white devils . . .' "

Seemed as though there were several different flyers circulating around the school. Different organizations, with similar goals, all relayed the same messages. No matter how they phrased it, it all spelled hate. Even though I'd seen it with my own eyes, it still amazed me how quickly and efficiently the hate groups mobilized.

I wasn't naive. I knew that they existed. But I'd always thought of them as fringe groups—unable to really affect the normal, rational human beings. I won't make that mistake again. Just seeing how quickly they infiltrated my school was my wake-up call.

"These pieces of filth are making their way into the hands of our children. Our children!" Jolene's voice boomed for emphasis, sending a whine of feedback through the speakers. The crowd winced, as much from her vehemence as the squeal from the speakers.

"Now, I'm not going to stand up here and tell y'all who to like and who not to like. Who you want for your neighbors is your own business. But when crap like this infiltrates our school, interferes with the business of educating our children, setting them at each other's throats, that's something that we can't tolerate. And it doesn't matter the color of our skin."

"All learnin' don't come from books, Jolene!" someone from the bleachers yelled out. "Some of us need to get smart and wake up to the fact that this school ain't what it used to be."

"Is that you, Eddie Lee Pickard?" She tilted her head to get a better look.

"Yes'm, it is." A tall, blunt-jawed man in a dark blue Dickey's work shirt, oil-stained denim jeans, and thick-soled work boots stood up to respond. He stared directly at me, contempt clearly written on his face.

I tapped Jolene on the arm, asking for the floor. "Let me handle this, Jolie," I asked.

She sat down in her seat again. "It's all yours."

"You'd think that in over fifty years you'd want the school to change, Mr. Pickard," I suggested. He was as brusque, as bullying, as he was back when we both attended Calhoun High together. He hadn't changed a bit and was as resistant to change now as he was then.

"Not all change is for the better, Mr. Barrett," he returned. "I don't like the way things have changed around here. I was gonna pull my daughter out even before I heard about this race riot."

"Your daughter is Angela Pickard, isn't she?" I asked, searching the bleachers immediately around him for Angela's face. She was a sweet girl, an average student but always trying hard to please. She was a member of the drill team. Co-captain, if I wasn't mistaken. It had taken Angela until her senior year to gain the confidence and the popularity to try out for the high-profile position.

"That's her," he said cautiously, wondering where I was going with this conversation. Angela was his baby girl. The last child after five sons. He wasn't about to see her held up to ridicule and I knew that. Not that I ever would hold up a student as an example of bad parenting. But in Eddie Lee's case, I thought I could make an exception. I didn't like him and he knew it.

"Seems a shame to pull her out of school, after she'd worked so hard for her achievement, don't you agree?"

"What good are them achievements if she's lying face-down dead, Mr. Barrett? Huh? I'm not going to see my baby girl shot up like them Columbine kids."

Oh, Lord! What did he have to mention that unfortunate incident for?! The resulting cry of dismay and agreement that rose up drowned out any call for calm or quiet we three at the table could make. I had to get control back or I wouldn't be able to reason with the parents as long as emotions clouded their judgment.

"Nobody is going to shoot up my school." Stepping out from behind the table, I spoke each word with conviction, charisma. A year of Toastmasters had finally paid off. I held up my hands until the crowd had settled down again and I had their undivided attention. "Besides, that's not what the flyers say."

"It's what they don't say that worries me," another parent called out. "We all know how these things escalate."

"You're all reading between the lines," I said, with a nod toward Mayron.

"If you think that these things don't pose a threat, then you're not reading the writing on the wall, Mr. Barrett. My Darius was so scared that he threw up his Pop-Tarts this morning."

"Man, Mama!" Darius Leary, a sophomore, sat beside his mother and looked as if he wished he could sink beneath the bleachers. "What you have to go and say that for?"

Some of Darius's boys hooted at him, called him a mama's boy.

"Abandoning the school is not the answer," I insisted.

"I'm not going to let a bunch of trigger-happy rednecks go gunning for my Darius. He hasn't done anything to anybody."

"And I keep telling you that isn't going to happen," I said with all of the conviction I could muster.

"Can you say that with absolute certainty? Can you look me in the eye and tell me that I shouldn't be worried?" Eddie Lee challenged.

"No," I said truthfully.

"That's what I thought. You can't guarantee that. That settles it for me, then. We're out of here." Eddie Lee Pickard nodded to his sons, grabbed Angela by the hand, and started for the exit. For a moment the crowd milled, uncertain of what to do; then a few more started to climb from the bleachers. Then a few more.

"Wait a minute! Please!" A voice rang out from the crowd. Kirby's! "Don't you think the welfare of your children is worth a few more minutes of your time?"

She moved from the back of room, making an entrance. It had the desired effect. On seeing her, several students cried out in surprise, then pleasure. I heard her name ripple through the crowd, some voices as soft as a whisper. Other times, students stood up to wave to her.

The increasing flow of traffic for the exits slowed to a trickle. Some of the parents didn't bother to stop but went through the doors anyway. Others paused by the exits, curious to know who that woman was.

But I was pleased to see that more than those two groups combined resumed their seats. I let the impromptu reunion go on for a few minutes more before drawing attention back to me.

"This is my school," I said. "Every child in here belongs to me. Can I tell you that there is no cause for concern? No. I won't insult your intelligence by doing that. But I can tell you this. No one is going to hurt my students. No one. Not while I have breath in my body. That includes all of you. You parents. Make no mistake. Pulling them out and adding to their anxiety hurts them even more than these flyers. From you comes the poison, from the most trusted source. Poison they can't crumple up and throw away."

I balled up one of the sheets of paper for emphasis and dropped it to the gym floor. By that time, it was so quiet in the gym that the sound of the paper hitting the floor resonated as loudly as a gunshot to me.

Out of the corner of my eye, I thought I saw Mayron shaking his head. I'd probably hear it from him later—a custodian's view of littering. But for now, I had the parents back where I wanted them. Listening. Not walking.

"I'm not pointing fingers," I continued. "I don't know if some of you out there helped to make these things or helped to organize these meetings. Can you look me in the face and tell me that you haven't participated? If only just to spread the rumor, fan the flames of hate and dissent?

Can you? Or you? Or you?" My gaze swept the entire room. I made mental note of who met my eyes and who shifted uncomfortably.

"Get to the point," someone interrupted.

"The point is," I said tightly, "to stop all of this bickering and let us get back to the business of providing a proper education for your children. I know some of you are worried, scared. You think that it's not safe to come to school. I want you to know that we've heard you and we're doing everything we can to make this a safe place. If you're still not sure, want to talk to us about it . . . well, that's what I'm here for. And that's what Ms. Kayin is here for."

I held out my hand, gesturing for her to step forward, to come to the center of the school floor. "Some of you already know Ms. Kayin. She was the school counselor here for four years. Those of you who don't, I encourage you to stop by after the meeting to introduce yourselves."

Iain Wilson then stood up. "Take some time. Come by the school. Chat with Ms. Kayin or take advantage of the teachers' conference periods. If you aren't satisfied with how we plan to resolve this, then you can start pointing fingers and laying blame." He fielded a few questions from the crowd, talking off the top of his head about what could be done to ensure the safety of the students. But all eyes were on Kirby.

Chapter 6

For the next couple of hours, students, parents, and administrators surrounded Kirby—each with a million questions for her. I could hardly get close to her. So I didn't try. Just hung back. Watched. Waited for my turn. A couple of times, her gaze caught mine above the heads of the crowd. She smiled at me, flush with the success of her return.

When the crowd thinned, I moved forward, one hand resting lightly, possessively, on her elbow. The other hand was tucked deep into my pocket, fingering the engagement ring.

Tonight. I would ask her tonight. I was taking a big chance. I knew she had commitments back in South Africa. I knew that she'd only planned to be here until after the New Year. But if I had anything to say about it, I would make her stay a permanent one. I would make her *want* to make her stay here a permanent one. Here was where she belonged. With me.

"Walk you to your car, Ms. Kayin?" I offered.

"Sure. Just let me grab my coat from your office."

"See you later, you two." Jolene waved, winking at me. "Don't do anything I wouldn't do."

"You already have," Kirby teased back. "That's why you have four kids."

"Hey, hey, enough of that kind of talk," I said. "There

are still impressionable young minds within listening distance."

"Where do you think I got the information from about preventing a fifth kid?" Jolene raised an eyebrow at me.

Kirby and I swung by my office to pick up her coat. She was talking, a steady stream of plans for the next couple of weeks for the students. I listened intently—as pleased as I was at the sound of her voice as I was by the fact that it sounded like she intended to stay.

But by the time we made it out to her car, something was bothering me. She was talking *too* much. That wasn't like Kirby. I have a student who talks incessantly when she wants to avoid saying what's really on her mind. Something was bothering Kirby, too. And she didn't want to say it.

We stopped beside her car, her hands nervously fumbling with her keys.

"Something you want to tell me, Kirby?" I asked, trying to keep my tone as light, as conversational, as hers had been.

"No. . . ." She quickly shook her head. Then, "Yes. Yes, I do. We need to talk."

"We have been talking. Correction. You've been talking."

"But I haven't been saying what I need to say."

My hand clenched around the engagement ring. *Do it! Do it now!* The voice in my head yelled at me to plunge ahead. But I didn't. I couldn't. Something serious was on her mind. Maybe something I didn't want to hear. I wasn't going to make it harder on her.

"What do you want to tell me, Kirby?" I asked softly.

"I've . . . uh . . . been doing . . . I've been doing a lot of thinking, Bear," she said haltingly. Chewing on her lower lip, Kirby was barely able to meet my gaze.

"Intellectuals are known to do that," I agreed. A weak attempt at a joke. I could imagine that didn't even rate on Norah Gilbert's mouth quirk meter.

"We've both been very busy with our careers." Her

voice was flat, mechanical, as if she were half-heartedly reciting a speech that she'd prepared.

"Some busier than others," I replied. "You should be very proud of yourself." I placed my index finger under her chin, lifted her face.

"I am proud," she said, a glimmer of the former life in her tone. She folded her arms across her chest. Warding off a chill or body language to push me away? "But I'm also very ashamed. Ashamed of what I've done to you."

"To me? What . . . what have you done?"

"I haven't been fair to you, Bear. I've been true to you, so if it's infidelity that you're worried about, you don't have to."

"Never crossed my mind," I said quickly.

"Sweet. But you're a terrible liar. I'm ashamed because I've kept you here, hanging on a string while I went off to pursue my parents' dream. They were educators, too. Missionaries. I didn't understand at the time how they could have left me so many times. Now, I think I do. As hard as it is to leave you each time, it's my dream now, Bear. It's what I want to do. I didn't realize how much I wanted to go until I was out there. I always thought that I would grow up, raise a passel of kids, and die here in Calhoun County."

"But that's not what you want?"

"Please don't misunderstand me, Paul Barrett. I love you. Have always loved you, even when we were kids. But something's calling me. I have to answer to that higher calling."

I took a deep breath, leaned against her car, regarding her for a few minutes before continuing. "So, why did you come back? Why are you here now?"

"Because you needed me." She shrugged. I wasn't convinced.

"To say good-bye one last time." This time, I let the bitterness slip into my voice.

"Maybe. I don't know."

"So when are you leaving?" My voice was growing

harder by the moment. I had to. I had to prepare myself that this time it could be for good.

"I told you. After the New Year. I hope that we can squash this problem in your school by then. If not, won't your regular counselor be back?"

I nodded. The lump in my throat competed with the knot of pain in my heart—throbbed and grew to an unbearable size. She placed her hand against my cheek. I steeled myself against its softness, the emotions she thought she was soothing. Instead, she sent them into turmoil. Kirby rose on her tiptoes, planted a kiss on my cheek.

I silently pleaded, *Please don't say we could always be friends*. After all we'd been to each other, I didn't want to go back to just being friends.

"See you early Monday morning."

I'd known her for about twenty-eight years. Ever since the third grade. You'd think that in all that time a person would change—even only just a little bit. Not Kirby. She'd remained exactly the same. I should know. I tried my hardest to find something about her that time had altered. I stared long and hard into her face. I didn't want to. Couldn't help staring. I couldn't help reaching out to touch her, either. My tentative fingertips traced the curve of her full lips and the sweep of her finely arched eyebrows and over thick sandy-colored lashes. My thumbs slid down the bridge of her nose.

As always, she slipped out of my grasp. I couldn't hold on to her. Not the way I wanted to. The elusiveness of her image reminded me why she hadn't changed. She hadn't changed because that's how I'd capture her forever in my memory. If I couldn't have her in the flesh, at least I could hold on to her in photographs.

As I sat in the middle of my floor on a Saturday night, with scattered memorabilia all around me, I held a photo of Kirby loosely in my hands. I held the picture carefully— half-expecting the twenty-year-old photo to crumble like my resolve not to feel the pain of time's passing.

I dragged a shoe box closer to me and dumped out its contents. A periwinkle hair ribbon, some ticket stubs from a homecoming game, and a near-empty bottle of Jack Daniel's whiskey. There was barely a swallow left in the dusty bottle. Jolene, Kirby, and I had guzzled most of it down. Too young to be drinking. Seventeen. Eighteen. We'd suffer for our foolishness the next day. But we weren't thinking about that then. We'd all drunk from the same bottle to celebrate. Celebrate what exactly I'm not quite sure of. A football win? A birthday? The fact that soon we would be graduating and leaving this Podunk town behind?

It didn't really matter what we were celebrating. We were all together, at the height of our youth and glory. And that was cause for celebration enough. I'd kept the bottle—vowing as only a starry-eyed seventeen-year-old could that I'd hang on to the last drops. In essence, hanging on to my youth.

If I wasn't mistaken, Kirby was the last one to drink from it.

"Welcome home, darlin'," I murmured, then unscrewed the cap and polished off the last of the Jack Daniel's. The resulting slow-acting burn as it washed over my tongue and slid down my throat wasn't nearly as bad as I'd remembered. But then again, I couldn't trust my feelings. Couldn't trust my memories.

"If your papa catches you with that, he's going to beat you until you can't grow anymore." I thought I'd heard Kirby's voice clear as day warning me as she did back then.

Papa. She was the only one who ever said "papa." We all said "daddy" or "dad" or "pops." She always was different. I knew that from the moment I first laid eyes on her when she walked into my class in the third grade. My third-grade teacher, Mrs. Mulholland, had guided Kirby to the front of the room and made her tell about herself. But even before she started talking about herself, I knew that there was something about her.

She was different—from her mop of cinnamon-colored ringlets ineffectively held back by a black velvet headband down to her orange patent-leather Mary Janes. She had to be different. It wasn't an affectation. It wasn't forced. It was just the way she was.

"Hell, he can't hurt me. I'm a grown man," I bragged. Seventeen years old, six-foot-three, and 250 pounds of solid swagger. That was me. Fresh off of a football win, I was riding high on my glory that night. For the look Kirby gave me, so full of sweet sentimentality, I would have faced an entire legion of angry fathers.

"That ain't nuthin' but pure booze talkin'," Jolene insisted, deflating my ego. "You'd better get rid of that bottle before Mr. Barrett shows up here with his leather strap."

Jolene made a thwacking sound, the sound of leather against bare skin, and a mock cry of pain afterward. "Toby! Kunta Kinte! Toby! Kunta Kinte!"

The name that I called her in response was just as ugly as the idea of a whipping.

Kirby collapsed beside the driver's-side tire, holding her sides and giggling so hard that she could hardly catch her breath. Her caramel-colored skin pinked. The light spray of freckles across her nose stood out boldly. I couldn't take my eyes off of her face. I must have counted every freckle.

Kirby hardly ever laughed out loud. Not since her parents were killed in a plane crash while on a missionary trip just before her eleventh birthday. She was so serious all of the time after that. When she did laugh, her entire face lit up. And that night, tears squeezed from her eyes as if they leaped at the chance to be free after being trapped for so long behind her facade of bravado.

"Want the last hit?" I asked, shaking the bottle at Kirby, making the amber liquid glint under the stadium lights.

"Where's . . . where's my cup, Bear?" Kirby fumbled for her paper cup.

At first, she wouldn't drink from the bottle. Always so prim and proper. If she was going to sneak a drink, she was going to do it with class. She tried to make Jolene and me drink from that cup, too—telling us that drinking from the same cup was ritualistic, symbolic of our unity.

I wouldn't do it. Not the way they left lipstick stains all over the cup. At first, I wouldn't drink from the cup. But that didn't mean that I wasn't fascinated by what Kirby was doing with it.

"*Kikomba cha umoja.*" Kirby had held the cup out in front of her in both hands and whispered the words softly, solemnly.

"What in the world does that mean?" Jolene asked, scrunching up her face.

"Never mind her, Jolie. The preacher's kid is just speaking in tongues," I taunted Kirby.

"You don't know what that means, either, do you?" She looked at me with one eyebrow raised. Maddeningly superior. "Your education is sadly lacking, Paul Barrett." She sounded like her grandfather just then. But Kirby couldn't help it. Old people had raised her. Made her old before her time.

"You go to the same high school as I do," I reminded her. "If I'm dumb as a post, then you're the next post over."

"It's derived from Swahili," Kirby told me. "One of the tongues of our motherland. One of these days, I'm going to go back there."

"What motherland?" Jolene demanded. "You come from the good old US of A just like we do." She pointed at the ground, stomping on the green football turf.

"But your folks are Irish," Kirby continued, tugging at Jolene's red hair. "Don't you celebrate Saint Patty's Day?"

"I wear green. But I wouldn't call that celebrating."

"Anyway," Kirby said with a long-suffering sigh. "It means something like unity. I was trying to show you two how much I appreciate your friendship. You've been like family to me." She pinned us both with a teary-eyed stare. "I never had brothers or sisters. Barely know the cousins I have. And I don't think I could have made it through this insane asylum called high school without you. So, I was offering to make you a literal part of my family. All you have to do is drink from the unity cup."

"It makes more sense than pouring out perfectly good liquor on the ground," Jolene had insisted.

When I'd first uncapped the bottle and offered my libation to the players' field, Jolene looked at me as if I'd lost my mind. She'd reached out, grasped my wrist, and pulled it back.

"Have you gone like totally insane, Bear? What do you think you're doing wasting perfectly good liquor like that?" She knew what flaming hoops we'd had to jump through to get that bottle. Kirby had kept my mom occupied with some sort of debate about whether Paul or John the Baptist was the better biblical figure after Jesus. Jolene had asked my pops to show her his work-in-progress truck kit while I ransacked the liquor cabinet. With all of that carefully coordinated effort, it didn't make sense to spill a single precious drop of it. But I had. Poured a considerable amount on the ground.

Kirby and I looked at each other and said in unison, "This is for the brothers who ain't here."

"Don't tell me." Jolene put her hands on her hips, jutted to one side, "It's a black *thang*."

She absolutely hated it when Kirby and I knew things that she didn't. And we tried our best not to exclude her. I didn't know why she was so jealous anyway. She and Kirby had a connection, a bond, that I could not share. Even to this day.

"It's a Cooley High thing," Kirby corrected.

"We all go to Calhoun High School," Jolene insisted. "Girl, you must be drunk. You don't even know where you are."

"Not as drunk as you are. I'm talking about a movie, Jolie. Sit down before you fall down." Kirby reached up and yanked on Jolene's pleated red-and-white cheerleader's skirt. Down she went, facedown in the grass in the opposing team's end zone. That's where I'd parked my truck long after the game had ended and the last of the spectators had emptied the stands.

Originally, I'd planned to back my truck over the goalpost, to knock it down to show the other side that they couldn't come on our home turf and mess with us. But Kirby talked me out of it. This close to graduation, we didn't want to do anything to screw up our chances of walking with the rest of our class. Nothing would make my pops prouder. He'd only gotten an eighth-grade education himself. So we wound up parked in the end zone instead, looking for other ways to let off steam.

"I dunno where that cup is." I looked around, too, then pointed to a small white piece of paper sticking out from under Kirby's left thigh. "There it is."

I'd reached for it, but she'd slapped my hands away.

"Don't you try to sneak a feel on me, Bear Barrett!" she chastised.

"In your dreams!" The words flew out of my mouth, but if I'd been more honest, I would have told her that touching her was the desire of *my* dreams—and of the dreams of every boy in Calhoun County.

Kirby and I were friends. Just good friends. I guess that's why she felt comfortable enough to be there that night. She knew that I wouldn't try anything to take advantage of her. But sometimes I hated the sound of those words "just friends." There was nothing *just* about the relationship. Nothing fair about it all. She had all of the advantage. Kirby had known all of the ways to get to me, to get under my skin to make me squirm.

I unscrewed the cap and wiped my sleeve across it. "Good enough for you?"

"No. It certainly is not good enough." She'd looked down her nose at the bottle. "What about your backwash?"

"What backwash? There's no backwash." I was sure that I meant to sound offended. Indignant. But it might not have come out that way. My words were probably as slow and slurred as my memory of that night. I had drunk too much. And so had Jolene.

What were we thinking back then? I was the only one who could drive my truck. No one else could handle the standard shift behemoth we affectionately called the Tank.

When the curiosity of the stadium after hours faded, what were we expecting to do? How were we going to get home? Hindsight is twenty-twenty.

"Let me see that." She'd held out her hand, so I laid the bottle in her palm. Kirby held the bottle up to the light, inspecting it carefully, turning it this way and that.

"What do you expect to see in there? Your future?" I sneered.

"Pepperoni," she said, and then giggled as if the sound of her own voice tickled her. "Isn't that what you scarfed down after the game, Bear? About six slices? Or was that six pizzas?"

"You're so full of it, Kirby. You've had enough. Give me that bottle back." Normally, I could stand Kirby's teasing. I usually retaliated by teasing her about being a show-off, know-it-all, holier-than-thou preacher's kid. But not that night.

"Nuh-uh. You gave it to me. No fair asking for it back."

She jumped up and started to walk backward, holding the bottle behind her. "You want it? Come and get it."

I must have chased her ten yards and back, only half-heartedly lunging at her. I could have caught her at any time. Any time. But the near misses, my swipes at thin air, were just like Kirby and me. So close and yet so far. Always running after something we knew that we wanted, but never quite bringing ourselves to take the extra effort.

There was something elusive about Kirby. As if she didn't want anyone getting too close. Even if I had managed to catch her while she darted away from me, I still don't believe I would have held the true Kirby. That part of herself that I couldn't fathom she held in secret. Kirby was full of secrets. Always had been. Maybe that's what drew me to her. I was naturally curious. Knowing that she was a puzzle that I couldn't figure out made me want to try more.

"You go on and take the last of it," I said as if I were in control of the situation. I was really just tired of running.

Huffing, I sank down next to the truck. The passenger-side door supported my back.

Kirby adjusted her denim skirt as she sat next to me. She swirled the contents one last time, making the silver and imitation ivory bracelets on her wrist jangle as she tilted the bottle to her lips. She could only stand a sip or two before the liquor got to her.

"Whooo!" Kirby blew out a long breath. Fanning her face, she stuck out her tongue to cool the burn, then touched her tongue to the corner of her mouth to swipe away a few remaining drops.

"It burns going down," she'd whispered, tracing the hollow of her throat with her index finger. "I can feel it all the way here. And here. And here."

Mesmerized, my eyes were glued to her slender finger as she drew a line from her throat and then down the front of her spandex tank top, ending at her navel. Her hand splayed across her stomach, massing in slow, hypnotic circles just under the hem of her shirt.

"Does it hurt?" I asked.

"Would you kiss it if it did, Bear? Make it all better?"

Somewhere, in the back of my mind, I thought that maybe she was teasing me again. But her eyes were all seriousness. Kirby had never teased me like this before. Her taunts had always been about *my* body. Not hers. I wasn't sure how to take that. My head swam—from the liquor and from the delirium of my own desire. My thick-lipped response was unintelligible, but she seemed to understand.

Kirby laughed again. Not the girlish giggle of a seventeen-year-old. Her laughter carried with it the wisdom of ages and the power of generations of women who knew when they had total control of a man. In that laugh, I caught a glimpse of the woman-child she was. She'd leaned back on one elbow, lifting the hem of her shirt.

"Kiss me right here, Bear. Make it feel better."

I crawled to her, afraid that if I tried to walk like a man I would wind up stumbling toward her like a weak-kneed baby. My lips touched her stomach. The barest hint of a kiss. But the heat of her flesh seared me and sealed me to her for what seemed like an eternity. She smelled so good. Her skin was so soft. Her breath quickened; I could tell by the rapid rise and fall of her chest.

I kissed her a couple times. "Better now?"

"A little," she whispered. "Try here." She raised her shirt a little farther, so I obliged by kissing her ribs.

Kirby's arms had wrapped around my head; her palms cupped my ears and pulled me higher. I lifted her shirt and revealed the lace-clad curve of her tender breasts. The heat in my body had nothing do with the whisky after that revelation. It wasn't alcohol but pure adulation.

She trembled, whether from the autumn air or from my exploratory touch I was never sure. She was scared, as scared as I was. But she was determined to continue. No teasing now. Kirby was committed to this course and would not turn back. The look in her eyes mirrored the type of woman she was—all softness and shadows, sugar to my steel. I covered my body with hers, holding her, settling her nerves, soothing her fears.

My bulk never seemed to bother her. Seventeen. Serious. And naturally sensuous. She knew how to encourage, incite, even soothe when I pushed into her—too fast, too fresh. Certain of my desire but inexperienced in technique, I instinctively knew that it couldn't have been as pleasant for her as it was for me.

I tried, though. I tried my very best to make her happy. Not the most ideal of circumstances lying out there on the cold, wet ground. Jolene snoring loudly and the bright lights of the stadium both added to my apprehension.

But Kirby was there with me. That made everything all right. And that night I made her my own. I gave her all I had. My heart poured out, teenage longing spilling over her even as I spilled into her.

The memory of her constricting around me, sending waves of pleasure shooting through me, made my hand constrict. The near-empty bottle clattered to the hardwood floor, spinning around and dribbling the last precious drops of fluid. I caught up the bottle, clutched it to my chest as a drunk clings with desperation to his last swallow.

"*Kikomba cha umoja*," I whispered aloud. The irony hit me hard. No unity here. Not now. We hadn't been together in over three months. Yet the very thought of her was as vivid as if we'd joined yesterday. The way my body reacted—the unbidden hardening of hidden flesh—played the cruelest of tricks on me. It should have been just yesterday we made love. It could have been that way if I'd never let her out of my life, if I hadn't been so noble. Maybe I should have been more selfish.

But that was just my issue with Kirby. I didn't let her walk out on us. I'd had no say in what happened. Kirby had decided. One minute we were inseparable. In fact, we were voted the couple most likely to marry right out of high school. But we didn't. We put our education first. And after our education came our careers. Now that we had both, knowledge and career status, what did we have left?

Chapter 7

This close to Thanksgiving break, the students' minds weren't on talking to teachers. Everyone, including the staff, was waiting for the final bell to ring so they could all gallop out of here in a thunderous rush.

I have to admit, I wasn't thinking much about those stupid flyers, either. My mind was on Kirby and how I was going to maintain that everything was all right when it wasn't. I wasn't thinking very friendly thoughts each time she sashayed past me in that burgundy-and-black two-piece jacket-and-skirt combination. The skirt was long, with a slit up the back that revealed the long line of her black leather boots. I would be surprised, even grateful, if I managed to get through the day without asking her to reconsider.

The students did surprise me, however. I had really misjudged them. I thought they would have jumped at the chance to get out of class. Kirby's offer provided the perfect opportunity to kill some time. They didn't take advantage of it.

Simply knowing that Kirby was once just like them wasn't enough to gain their confidence or their trust. They say that the kids of today are smarter, more savvy and sophisticated. I translate that as being more suspicious.

By the end of class day on Tuesday, several students had come to see Kirby, but they only wanted to talk about what she was doing now. Not about the fight between Zane

and Brian and Rayford or their apprehensions. Only two
students had come by to see Kirby to discuss the events
that had brought her counseling skills back to the school.
One was the journalism class photographer, and the other
was the editor of the school newspaper. They made it very
clear that they had only shown up to interview her for an
article. Nothing more. She wound up doing most of the
talking.

Kirby had answered their questions and made sure that
she was not misquoted when she stressed how she was there
to help.

"Two students," Kirby told me as we walked out to our
cars together on Tuesday afternoon. "Only two students
touched on the subject with any depth."

"Not exactly the mad rush we were hoping for, huh,
Kirby?"

"O ye of little faith." She laughed at me. And I wondered how she could sound so light-hearted after crushing
the life out of me on Friday.

"Those same two students will be able to reach more of
the other students faster than I will. Once my story gets
circulated in an article put into their own words, you'll see.
The students will be beating down my door to talk."

"I hope that you're right. I haven't seen any more of
those flyers. But that doesn't mean they don't exist. Hate
doesn't give up so easily."

"And neither does love," Kirby said, laying a hand gently on my cheek for a second. Just as quickly, she dropped
her hand away. She must have known how her touch was
affecting me. Realized her mistake. Her voice sounded
oddly shaken as she said, "So, what kind of plans do you
have for Turkey Day?"

"Oh, the usual. Try really hard to stick to my diet while
Mama loads the table with enough food to collapse it."

"I meant to tell you, Bear. You're looking good. That
was the first thing I noticed when you got out to meet me."

"Well, you know, a brother does have to try," I said,
sucking in my stomach and flexing my biceps.

Kirby laughed appreciatively and pinched my arms.

"And what about you?"

"My grandparents are holding a dinner at the church. It's open to everyone. You ought to stop on by. They'd love to see you, Bear."

"Thanks for the invite. I'll try to make it." Had to keep it light, casual. After all, we were just friends. Who was I kidding? A pack of rapid dogs wouldn't keep me away from her this weekend. Even if I had to drive a thousand miles, braving holiday traffic, to get to her. I'd wallowed in self-pity at her unintentional rejection all day Saturday.

Sunday, after church, I had a fresh perspective. How could I expect the Lord to move mountains for me if I couldn't even pick up a rock? I'd been carrying that ring around with me for too long. It was time to move it or move on. Since I was still here in Calhoun County, made my home here, I figured I wasn't going to be moving on anytime soon. Somehow, I had to make her see that she was just as needed here.

"Dinner starts at eleven after the special service and runs to about six. I hope you can make it," Kirby said as she climbed into her SUV.

"Do I need to bring anything?"

"Nope. Just your appetite."

Kirby's eyes lowered automatically, taking me in from head to foot and pausing somewhere in the middle. My body responded as heatedly to her direct stare as it did to her unintentional implication. Her reaction gave me reason to hope. She never said that she didn't love me, didn't want me.

"What about tomorrow?" I blurted out, leaning on the door, almost climbing into the car window.

"What do you mean?" Kirby asked.

"What are you doing tomorrow? Any special plans?"

She shrugged. "Helping Granny do some last-minute shopping. But that's about it. Why? Did you have something in mind?"

"Want to do something?"

"Something like what?" she said cautiously.

"I dunno. Nothing too stressful. Just hang out."

"We're not in high school anymore, Bear. Aren't we a little too old to be just hanging out?"

"Nope. Never too old." I shook my head. "We're just two old friends, enjoying each other's company. And my folks have been asking about you. Mama's hurt that you haven't come by to see her. Why don't you come by the house tomorrow?"

"OK. It would be nice to see them again. What time should I swing by?"

I was the very model of friendly nonchalance. "Whenever. I should be home."

"And will your folks be there all day?"

It was a strange question for her to ask, but I think I knew what she meant. If Kirby was trying to distance herself from me, it wouldn't help matters if we were left alone for too long. But that was exactly what I was counting on. If she had any doubts, I was going to erase them. Make it clear once and for all how I felt about her.

After Tuesday afternoon, Kirby and I became virtually inseparable. Whenever you saw one, you saw the other. It was almost like being in high school. Sometimes Jolene hung out with us, but she cut the evenings short. She had the little ones to get back to. Not so with Kirby or me, which in and of itself was a mixed blessing. I was grateful for the time we had together, but I lamented the time that we'd lost.

From Wednesday to Sunday we had five days. I wasn't going to waste a minute of it. I called her at six o'clock in the morning on Wednesday just to let her know that I was going out for my morning walk and to ask her could she meet me at my parents' house. I didn't think she could, but it was the thought that I wanted to convey—the idea that I wanted her with me every step of the way.

By the time I got back from my walk, she was already there. I found her in the kitchen with Mama, rattling pots and pans, preparing for tomorrow's feast.

Normally, on a day like that, I wouldn't be caught dead anywhere near the kitchen. All of that tempting cooking and experimental tasting, not to mention the cleaning up afterward—a man didn't stand a chance. But I had to go in. Kirby was there, helping to rinse, mince, slice, or stir as needed. And wherever Kirby was, that's where I was going to be.

"Don't go in there," my pops warned me as he dragged a trash can from the rear kitchen door to the roadside. He wiped his nose with the back of his green plaid sleeve, sniffed disdainfully.

"Why? What's wrong?" I paused, using the opportunity to stretch my muscles.

He simply pursed his lips and shook his head. "Don't say that I didn't warn you, Bear."

I stepped up onto the back porch reaching for the screen door handle. I was quiet, I know I was, barely making a sound. Listening at the door, I tried to catch a hint of why Pops was warning me away. They couldn't have heard me. I know they couldn't have. But as soon as I placed my hand on the screen door and grasped the wooden handle, the peals of laughter that had been ringing as far as the backyard stopped abruptly.

When I opened the door, I heard Mama shush Kirby. She stifled a giggle, then looked up at me with wide, innocent eyes.

"Hey," I said in greeting, warily watching them as I headed for the refrigerator.

"Hey, yourself," Kirby responded. She bent her head, her hair hiding her face as she leaned over a bowl of fresh snap beans that she was helping Mama to prepare. Kirby reached for another bean, snapped off the ends, and dropped the vegetable into a huge bowl. Her shoulders were shaking with suppressed laughter.

"Have a good walk, Pooh Bear?" Mama asked, standing at the stove. "You're back quicker'n I thought you'd be."

"I cut my walk short."

"Why?" Kirby asked innocently.

"Maybe because I don't trust you two alone together," I said, pointing the water bottle at each of them.

"Who, us?" Mama's eyebrows climbed. "Why would you have reason to mistrust us, Pooh Bear?"

"Mama, *please* don't call me that in front of company," I insisted.

"Oh, hush now. Kirby isn't company. She's family. Isn't that right, honey?"

"As good as, Mrs. B," Kirby agreed.

"So, what have you ladies been talking about while I was out?" I pulled up a chair, turned it backward, and straddled it. When I reached for a raw snap bean, Kirby slapped my hand away. "Cut that out. You'll ruin your appetite for lunch."

"The way *Paul*"—Mama made sure to stress my name— "has been dieting, Kirby, that little scrap of a bean *is* his lunch." She frowned at me. "Look at him. He's wasting away to skin and bones."

"I doubt that, Mama."

"He looks fine to me," Kirby smirked. While Mama's back was turned, Kirby reached out and laid her hand on my thigh. It was my turn to smack her hand away—as much as it pained me to do it.

You cut that out, I mouthed to her.

"Make me," she whispered loudly. She grabbed a handful of the vegetable ends she'd set aside for the trash and tossed them at me. I flung a few back at her and then threatened to splash water on her.

Kirby jumped up from the table, nearly overturning the bowl of green beans.

"Behave, you two!" Mama clapped her hands as if she were demanding order from a classroom of unruly kindergarteners.

"She started it," I insisted.

"Paul, why don't you make yourself useful? I've got some things stored out in your garage. There's a big yellow box marked for the dining room. Can you bring that out to me?"

"Yes'm," I said, rising from my chair, too. As I turned my back, I felt one last parting shot—a green bean thumping against the back of my head.

"Mama, did you see that? Kirby . . . she . . . that is . . ."

"Paul Robeson Barrett." Mama used the mean voice on me, pointing toward the back door.

Muttering to myself, I started outside. Pops was already ahead of me, striding toward the relative peace and quiet of the drafty garage.

"Pops," I greeted him.

"Told you," was all he said. My father never was much for words. Always said that my mother did enough talking for the both of them.

He worked on an unlit cigar in the corner of his mouth as he searched through gray metal shelves. He finally found what he was looking for—a socket wrench to loosen the near-rusted spark plugs on his '69 Chevy truck. As he strained and grunted under the hood, I spent a few minutes walking around him, the truck, and the confusing maze of boxes, bags, and covered furniture from my parents' house.

"Need some help?" I offered when I heard him let loose a stream of curses after grazing his knuckles.

"Nope." He shook his head. I was actually relieved. It was a little too cold to be out here anyway. My breath hung in the air, even inside the garage. The droplight that he used under the hood barely cast a pale, cool glow over the area. "You'd better get back to your mother. What'd she send you out here for anyhow?"

I grinned at my father. I knew exactly what he was thinking. As long as I was there to run and fetch for Mama, my pops didn't have to do it. I was running interference for him. "Some kind of box. It's got dining room stuff in it, or something."

He jerked his thumb, indicated a far corner of the garage. "Over there."

"Thanks," I replied, looking at the collection around me. There were more of my parents' things in here than my own. "I would've never found it in here."

"Life's funny that way," Pops went on, his voice muffled as he banged on the engine block.

"What do you mean?"

"We spend half our time searching for something that was under your nose the whole time."

I turned to face my father. Homespun wisdom from the man of few words. "You mean Kirby, don't you, Pops? You're talking about her?"

"Who, me? I'm just talkin' 'bout you and a big yella box. Nobody said a word about the girl."

I started for the door, but Pops spoke up again. He wasn't mumbling. He wasn't cursing. His question was clear, direct. "How long is she back for this time?"

I shrugged. "Dunno. She didn't say."

"I suppose it doesn't matter." Pops turned back to his truck. "Big yella box, big yella gal. I'll bet you won't waste any more time looking for either, will you, Bear?"

"No, sir," I agreed. "I suppose I won't."

School was out, but that didn't mean the learning had to stop. My pops had the damnedest way of cutting to the heart of the truth.

When Kirby had first broken up with me, I'd gone to my mama for advice about how to get her back. She was a woman after all, with a woman's heart. If anyone could, she could tell me what I could do to win Kirby back.

But when Kirby had moved away, cutting my wooing efforts off at the knees, I had gone to my pops for consolation. He was a man who understood the pain of loss and disappointment. A black man born and raised in Mississippi. If anyone knew about disappointments and lost dreams, he would. He had a unique perspective all his own. He'd gone through ups and downs, along with his beloved home state, and had come out a better man for it.

It was Pops who told me how to pick myself up, to carry on, and to get on with my life no matter what obstacles were thrown ahead of me. Yes, she'd hurt me. But as my folks are fond of saying, *what doesn't kill you makes you stronger.*

She'd also loved me. What could I learn from that? What had she taught me? That I was capable of a deep, abiding love that could withstand the test of time. Not the obsessive, self-destructive love that drives a person to insane acts such as stalking or suicide. But the kind of time-tested commitment and connection that wouldn't let me settle for anything less than what Kirby offered.

Yes, we were young. And maybe we didn't understand at the time what was happening to us or what we were doing. But God takes care of fools and angels. Me being the former. Just because he'd given Kirby and me at an early age what most folks spend a lifetime searching for didn't make our feelings any less valid.

I'd been given a second chance. I didn't have time to waste. While she was here, for however long that was, I would seize the moment and make it my own. More than that, somehow, I had to make her mine.

When I got back to the kitchen, Mama and Kirby were both sitting at the table, their expressions now serious. Their conversation must have taken a heavy turn.

"Just set the box over there, son." Mama waved her hand toward the utility room. "There's a tablecloth in there. A big bright red one in a protective plastic bag. Throw that in the washing machine."

I dug through the box, looking for the tablecloth. She had thrown all kinds of seasonal dining room decorations in there, too—from floral wreaths with teeny-weeny Easter bunnies hiding among the foliage to table runners decorated with holly wreaths and berries.

"Careful with that, Paul!" Mama said distractedly as I clattered and banged my way through the box's contents. She turned back to Kirby. "Go on, honey. Now what were you saying?"

"I was just telling your mother about some of the crises that I've counseled, Paul," Kirby included me in the conversation.

"And I just think it's a cryin' shame that we even need crisis counselors in the school. I can understand guidance counselors, someone to help students get into the right colleges or find a suitable trade. But helping them find their sense of security after one of their classmates has committed some unspeakable, horrible act . . . it's unthinkable."

"It's not like when you were in school, Mama, when you could be sent to the principal's office for chewing a pack of gum. Every day I worry that some kid won't be sent to me for packing a gun."

"Times may be different, but kids are all the same. They all need love and understanding, a firm hand of discipline. That much hasn't changed."

"For whatever reason, they're not getting that," Kirby lamented.

"Or they're rejecting it when it's being offered," I spoke up. Kirby understood what I meant. It bothered me that no one had come to her.

"They're just afraid of being singled out, ridiculed by their classmates." Kirby rose and joined me at the utility room. She touched her warm, smooth hand to my cheek. "Give them time. They'll come around."

She reached into the box and pulled out a tablecloth made from *kente* cloth.

"For your Kwanzaa display, Mrs. B?" she asked, holding the material up to her and wrapping it around her like a skirt.

Mama nodded, smiling. "Your father gave me that, Kirby. It came from one of his missionary trips. You were only nine years old then."

"Oh, my God. I'd almost forgotten about that. If I recall, I was a real brat that day."

"How you cried when he gave it to me. You wanted to keep it for yourself."

"It was so pretty . . . yellow and red and green. I wanted to make doll clothes out of it."

"I remember that," I spoke up. "That was the day you, me, and Jolene wound up cutting the arms and legs off of all of your dolls and burying them in the backyard."

"Why in the world would you do that?" Mama exclaimed.

"I guess that was my way of acting out my anger."

"Well, good for you. I was always concerned about you, Kirby. I worried that you'd turn out to be one messed up kid the way you kept your feelings bottled up all inside of you. You were such a lonely little girl."

"She wasn't alone, Mama. Jolie and I were with her," I said. "You want to know what happened to that Tonka truck that I got for Christmas the year before? I buried my Tonka truck right along with Kirby's dolls. And Jolene buried her collection of Nancy Drew mysteries."

"If I'd known all of that was going on, I would have kept a closer eye on the three of you," Mama said with a sniff. "Would have marched all three of you to the nearest psychiatrist."

I laughed out loud. "We turned out all right, Mama. We were our own self-help therapy sessions."

"The dolls were no big loss. My mother didn't like me playing with dolls anyway," Kirby remembered. "Not the blond-haired, blue-eyed ones that I kept getting for presents from her side of the family anyway. She said that was only part of who I was. I guess when I buried all of them, it made me have to rethink who I was and who I wanted to be."

Mama stood up, presumably to take that box away from me before I ruined her decorations. She tenderly ran her fingers over the cloth.

"Sounds like Dr. Marenga's concept of *Kujichagulia* to me," Mama mused.

"That's exactly what it was. Only, back then, I was too young to really understand what it meant."

"Nine is a little young," Mama agreed. "But . . ." Her voice trailed off for a moment. An odd, pensive look crossed her face. "Fifteen isn't. Or sixteen."

"What do you mean, Mrs. B?"

"I think the students at Calhoun high could benefit from a little lesson in the *Nguzo Saba*. Especially *Kujichagulia*.

If more students had a clearer understanding of who they were and what they were about, then fewer of them would be looking to outside hate groups to help define themselves."

Kirby and I exchanged glances. Mama may have retired, but she was still an educator. Through me, she was still tied to the school where she'd attended and taught.

"After Thanksgiving, everyone will be swapping out their seasonal bulletin boards and displays," Mama said.

"Instead of snowmen and reindeer and—" I continued her train of thought.

"And fat old white men in gaudy red suits," Kirby spoke up.

"Not instead of," Mama warned. "Your fundamentalists get a little crazy when you start messing with their traditional nonreligious symbols of Christmas."

"In addition to," Kirby amended. "It's a little early, but we could put up a Kwanzaa display in the school. It's a nonreligious observance, so there shouldn't be any flak about separation of church and state. I'll put up a display near the world cultures and history classes."

"That's only half the battle. Kwanzaa is a uniquely African-American observance," I reminded Kirby. "Calhoun High School has an almost fifty-fifty split between blacks and Caucasians. What are you going to do when some of my melanin-challenged students start to feel excluded?"

"But some of Kwanzaa's tenets are universal. Unity of the community seems to be one we all need a refresher course in."

"You know that I'll support you in whatever you decide to do, Kirby."

"Thanks, Bear. I appreciate that."

"And I'd appreciate it if I got the rest of my beans prepared," Mama broke the mood by returning to more immediate concerns.

"And I have to be going." Kirby sighed reluctantly. "I told my grandmother that I'd be back by this afternoon to help her finish her grocery shopping. It was nice seeing you again, Mrs. B." Kirby kissed Mama on the cheek. "And thanks for worrying about me," she whispered loudly so that I'd hear her.

I thought that I did a good job of not showing my disappointment. No Academy Award for me. I didn't want her to leave.

But as she started to collect her things, I remembered Pops's words. I didn't have time to waste. So forget about putting up a false front. She wasn't going to leave. Not just yet.

I grasped Kirby's hand. "Do you have to go?"

"I've got a long drive back."

"Tell me about it." I grimaced. "Six hours."

"Closer to seven. Traffic is getting bad out there. Lots of crazies on the road."

"Then don't go. Stay here tonight. I can take you out to your grandmother's in the morning. We can finish her shopping then."

"Now you're being silly," she began. "But sweet."

I don't remember when Mama left us. I heard her saying something about getting my Pops to run her to the store. Or maybe I just imagined that I heard her say something. I wished she was gone.

When I heard the back door slam shut, it was all of the opening that I needed.

Chapter 8

By the time I vaguely heard Mama's car crank up, I was kissing Kirby so intensely that I didn't give her time to think that maybe she should have walked out with Mama.

"Bear, wait!" she said breathlessly. "Wait a minute."

"That's about all the time we'll have before they come back," I muttered, nipping at her lower lip. "You sure you want to waste a minute of it arguing?"

"B-but I thought we talked about this! We're . . . f-f-friends, r-r-remember?" Kirby stammered.

"Being rejected is not something a man forgets, Kirby."

"I didn't reject you." Her voice was strained, nearly cracked with unshed tears.

"Like hell you didn't." My own voice was hoarse as I clung to her. My hands splayed against her back, drawing her even closer to me. I could feel her heart pounding, even through the layers of our clothing.

"Paul—" Kirby began.

I didn't let her finish the protest. "I could understand if you didn't care for me anymore, Kirby, or if we'd grown apart. But we haven't. We've just moved apart. If you still love me, then you could teach on the moon and it still wouldn't make a difference. So I have to know. Do you still love me?"

She didn't hesitate, answered almost immediately. But in my mind, even the almost was enough to make me doubt.

"I do love you, Paul."

I did what any man, desperate and wanting her bad enough to beg, would have in my situation. I improvised.

Reaching into the big yellow box, I pulled out the wreath of Easter bunnies and spring flowers. Mama's table centerpiece. I held it up in front of Kirby and then placed the wreath on top of her head like a crown. "My queen," I intoned.

Kirby shook her head. She was laughing as she said, "You are so cheesy, Paul Barrett."

"The word is *horny*," I said bluntly. "And it's all your fault."

"My fault?" She pointed to herself. "How do you figure that?"

"You shouldn't have come in here looking delicious enough to eat." I emphasized my point by leaning forward and nuzzling her neck.

"I don't get roses?" she teased.

"Next time," I promised.

"And what about a romantic candlelight dinner?" Kirby prompted.

"Man, you're a tough woman to please," I said as I turned back to the box. I pulled out Mama's *kente* cloth and spread it over the dining room table. Then I grabbed her *kinara* and stuck a few candles into the holder. The final touch—I reached into the fridge and pulled out a bowl of green salad that I had intended for my lunch this afternoon.

"Good enough for you?" I asked.

"You know, you're really not being true to the spirit of Kwanzaa," she chastised me. "You're just trying to get into my panties."

"Can you think of a more symbolic way to demonstrate unity?" I asked, raising my eyebrows at her.

"You don't even have all the candles in the right order." She rearranged the candles. "It's black in the middle, the three reds on the left and three greens on the right. And you're not supposed to light them all at once."

I wrapped my arms around her waist and drew her to me. "As crowded as it is around here, Kirby, I think I could stand one more."

"Or even several more if we do this right," she murmured, moving her hips in a way that was driving me crazy.

"Do you want to go upstairs?" I whispered huskily. "To my old room?"

"Have you cleaned it since the last time I was there?" she teased me.

"The bed's made," I assured her.

"It's a start. Do you have condoms up there?"

"I might."

"Then I might," she said amiably.

Up the stairs, down the hall, and into my room—it was all a hazy blur. As we fell across my bed, Kirby tugged on the drawstring of my sweatpants. From there, she had no difficulty freeing me as I worked on her sweater and skirt.

The smell of desire filled the room, made my head swim with its intensity. I don't think I could have stopped, even if I'd wanted to. As she stroked the length of me, the warmth of her palm moistened my skin. I felt an inevitable surge building, threatening to spill forth. A moan, low and throaty, signaled my imminent release.

"You'd better do somethin', Bear," Kirby said in warning. "Or it's about to get very messy down there."

I reached out, fumbled for the nightstand drawer. My hand closed around the foil packet even as Kirby's hand closed around me and squeezed from me a precious drop of fluid. My hands trembled as I rolled onto my back, opened the packet, and unfurled the condom.

"Let me help you," Kirby offered. Her fingers were sure, steady, as she drew the condom downward.

"Kirby, please. I can't hold back anymore." My patience, my resolve, had been tested to its limits. Both were going up in flames.

Kirby pressed the heels of her hands to my shoulders as she threw her leg over mine to straddle me. I placed my hands on her hips and eased her slowly, lovingly, onto me.

I felt sweet, torturous pulsing as her body adjusted to accommodate me.

"Ummmm," Kirby hummed deliciously. "You've grown."

"It's all the veggies," I panted.

Kirby lifted her hands to begin unbuttoning her blouse.

"No, don't move!" My voice was hoarse. Raw. I didn't want her to move a muscle. Each time she shifted, waves of intense pleasure shot through me. I had no illusions about what I was feeling at that moment. Some call it love. Some call it passion. I knew it to be pure, unadulterated desire. Nothing else could have driven me to this point of mindless, instinctual coupling. After a fashion, I knew that I could come to her with some degree of self-control. I would whisper tender words. Words worthy of a song or a sonnet. But not now. Not yet.

Kirby leaned forward, offering me a tantalizing taste of her flesh. Each time she closed with me, my tongue lathed her full breasts. Greedily I suckled her. Her hips moved in perfect rhythm to my thrusts. Her hands cradled my head, keeping me fused to her.

I don't know how many times our bodies collided. Twenty? Twenty times twenty? I rose to meet her, marking the years—the wasted passage of time—with each thrust. I came to her seeking retribution for all of the time lost and the unanswered questions. I came to her seeking absolution for the young pain that I'd caused her the first time we joined.

Kirby's nails raked over my shoulders, down my forearms. I winced, my face twisting. Was she punishing me, too? For what, I could only imagine. As her breath quickened, her movements more pronounced, I couldn't help wondering was she taunting me, telling me with her body of what I could have had all along? Maybe I should have fought harder to get her to stay. She had a calling, but I was the one who knew her—better than anyone else.

She was here now and I was unwilling to let her go. Not yet. Not until she fully understood how much I needed her.

I arched my back, straining toward her. A sigh bubbled from my lips as molten liquid shot from my groin.

"Paul!" Kirby sobbed my name, and shuddered as her body constricted around me. Spasms of pleasure wracked her body. She fell forward—heaving, sobbing, gasping for air.

I stroked her back, feeling her heart thud against my chest. Her tongue reached out and dabbed moisture across her lips.

"OK, so I didn't need roses," she panted.

I grinned at her. "Roses are overrated anyway."

When I started to pull away, Kirby cried out in dismay, "Where are you going?"

"I'll be back," I promised.

She sat up on one elbow, watching me as I reached into the pocket of the jeans I'd planned to wear after my workout.

I clasped the ring in my hand, warming it to the touch before bringing it to her.

"I wanted to do this right. . . . What's the word they use around here? With tradition?" I started slowly, my fist still closed. But I could tell from the sudden glistening of her eyes that she knew what was coming up next.

"Candlelight dinner, roses, the works," I continued. "But you never have been conventional, Kirby. So, I'm coming at you like this, my soul bared to you and all the world."

One by one, I unfurled my fingers. The ring I'd carried for so long, a simple diamond solitaire in a white gold setting, rested in my palm.

"Oh . . . oh, my God." Kirby's chest heaved. Her hands flew to her mouth. "Paul!"

"Take it, Kirby," I urged her. "Take me."

She closed her eyes, letting tears flow freely.

"You can't tell me that you didn't know how I felt about you, Kirby. I've known since grade school that we belonged together. I love you and I want you for my wife. Whatever I have to do to make it happen, I will. Want me to quit my job, move to South Africa, I will. Want me to wait until whatever's calling you to grow hoarse, I'll do that. Just say that you'll marry me."

"You really mean that, don't you? You'd wait for me? Follow me?" She sounded incredulous, pleased, scared all at the same time.

"In a heartbeat. As long as you know that your heart's mine."

Slowly, hardly noticeable at first, Kirby's hand reached out to mine. She clasped her hand over mine. Palm to palm, the warmth of her hand fused with mine. When she took her hand away, I almost moaned in despair.

Until I realized that my palm really was empty. She'd taken the ring. Then, with all the deliberateness and confidence I'd known Kirby to have, she slid the ring on her finger.

"Yes," she said, her voice clear and strong. "I'll marry you, Paul Barrett."

Chapter 9

By the time students made their way grudgingly to first period, Kirby had already placed several colorful displays around the school. Each display focused on a single Kwanzaa symbol or principle. But a full-blown display was set up at the front entrance of the school. She'd talked me out of letting a student raise a *bendara* along with our other school flags. Instead, she tacked the red, black, and green flag against the wall as a backdrop to the table with all of the other symbols.

Mr. Percy, who ran the local Farmers' Market fruit and vegetable stand, always willing to help, donated the *vibunzi* and *mazao* samples. If I could have, I would have placed an ear of corn for every student in the school. In some way, I felt like they were all my kids. Again, Kirby said that was going overboard.

"What do you want to do, start a riot?" she'd challenged me. "I thought that's what we were trying to avoid. You put this much food out for the students to snack on, especially those overgrown football players on your team, and that's exactly what you'll have on your hands."

Mama gave us the three red candles, three green, and one black for the *kinara*—but threatened bodily harm if I let anything happen to her candleholder. And, as a special gesture, she also gave back to Kirby the *kente* cloth that she'd once cried buckets over in place of the *mkeka* when

I suggested that Kirby could use one of the red mats from the girl's gym instead of the traditional straw one.

"One more," Kirby threatened me. "You have just one more flaky idea and then I'm going to deck you!"

I leaned close and whispered, "OK. You can knock me out, but this time, you're on top."

I ducked, but not fast enough. The book that Mrs. Melanie had loaned us from the library on the history of Kwanzaa clipped me on the ear when Kirby launched it at my head.

"Hey, be careful with that!" I exclaimed. "That's very valuable merchandise."

"Oh, stop your whining, Bear. I barely nicked you."

"I'm not talking about my head, Kirby. That's hard as a rock."

I was referring to that book. I had it on an extended loan from Ms. Melanie. That book *had* to get back to her in mint condition. I didn't want her coming after me twenty years later, or after my kids, trying to collect book fines.

That morning, Kirby and I walked the halls together, herding the students on to class. At the same time, we noted their reaction to our displays. I watched their expressions. Some of them twisted in confusion. Others lit up with delight. While others still had expressions that bordered on disgust. I just knew that I could expect a phone call or two from their parents. Let them call. We were finally getting a reaction from them. Something to start the dialogue going again.

On Monday, a few students did trickle into Kirby's office. On Tuesday, a few more. By Wednesday, Kirby had a steady stream. She'd started accepting early-morning and after-school sessions as well.

Thursday afternoon, I walked Kirby back from lunch. She went on and on about some of the ideas the students had suggested themselves about how to increase the atmosphere of cultural tolerance and diversity.

"They are the living embodiment of *Kuumba*," Kirby

said proudly. "Creativity is flowing out of their mouths where curses used to be."

"Uh-huh. Curses," I echoed.

"You know that sweet little Angie Pickard? She suggested that the students paint a mural on the cafeteria wall. Peace leaders, past and present. Each year, the students will suggest an addition to the mural and have a vote."

"Cafeteria," I responded. "Vote."

"And then she suggested that Ms. Gilbert dance naked in the music hall. Tap dancing and reciting the lyrics to 'Dixie,' " Kirby continued.

"Uh-huh. Naked tap dancing."

"You're not even listening to me!" Kirby exclaimed, pinching me on the arm.

I have to admit that I had only been half-listening to her. My attention was split between listening to Kirby and keeping an eye on Mara Jackson, a freshman, and Phillip Xavier, a senior. The rumor mill had it that those two had been cutting third-period class, sneaking off campus. It wouldn't surprise me if the rumors were true. Phillip was wearing his hormones on his sleeves. And Mara, eager to prove that she was just as popular as her senior junior sister Lara, was more than willing to give Phillip a hand—literally.

"Hold that thought," I interrupted Kirby. I stopped in the middle of the corridor, made an abrupt turn, and followed them to the row of junior lockers.

I found them there, locked in a kiss so intense that the other students around them had started hooting and hollering in encouragement. I stopped in midstride, memories of my weekend with Kirby flooding back. And, I hate to admit it, a foolish grin came over my face. I had to catch myself. These were not two consenting adults. Whether their feelings for each other were as intense as Kirby's and mine at that age, I couldn't say. But since I'd stumbled up on them, I couldn't let them get away without a token chastisement.

"All right! All right!" I tapped Phillip on the back of the head. He never even heard me coming. "Break it up. For